Advance Praise for ***Jabbok***

Kee Sloan really captures the tone and feel of boys in the rural South in the 1950s–60s, with their language rendered just right. He depicts the mindless and hurtful racism of the period, yet also shows how some were able to break through it. *Jabbok* is a good read.

—**John Boles**
Professor of Southern History, Rice University

At once uplifting and poignant, *Jabbok* is replete with life lessons told in an authentic Mississippi voice that rings true across regions and cultures. Buddy and Jake are the central characters in this well-told story, but many others will remain with readers also. A book to keep and learn from.

—**Lynda Lasswell Crist**
Editor, *The Papers of Jefferson Davis*

Kee Sloan's *Jabbok* is beautifully written, and the author is a fine storyteller. Having been reared in the South, I was embarrassed at being reminded of the rampant racism I grew up with. I was also genuinely touched by the depth of love that grew between the young white boy Buddy and the old black preacher Jake. The book invites us to experience genuine spirituality in every dimension of life and of death. *Jabbok* is a book well worth the read.

—**John K. Graham**, MD, DMin
President and CEO, Institute for Spirituality and Health at the Texas Medical Center
Houston, Texas

Peake Road Press
6316 Peake Road
Macon, Georgia 31210-3960
1-800-747-3016

Library of Congress Cataloging-in-Publication Data

Sloan, John McKee, 1955-
Jabbok / By John McKee Sloan.
pages cm.
ISBN 978-0-9915744-0-7 (pbk. : alk. paper)
I. Title.
PS3619.L6274J33 2014

2014001227

Kee Sloan

JABBOK

for Miss Tina

who shows me how and why

Acknowledgments

So much of my own story is woven in and out of this story that I've begun to think of it as a sort of fictional autobiography. No character in this book is based on any one person; all of the characters except maybe Buddy are some combination of people I've bumped into at some point. Buddy is mostly me, more how I wish I might have been than how I actually am or was. The great thing about fiction is that you have the chance to portray everybody as either better or worse than they actually were, as fits the story.

Jake started out as a blend of two men I loved: the first is my grandfather, Spencer Bayer, a great teller of stories; the other was a man that I worked with at summer camp named Jimmie Lee Washington.

My favorite story Grandpa used to tell his grandchildren was the story of the Bull and the Hog. Grandpa played football for the University of Tennessee from 1911 to 1914, back when the players played both offense and defense. One year when they played the University of Alabama, he lined up across from Hargrove Van de Graaf, who was called "Hog." Grandpa was called "Bull" Bayer; the Bull and the Hog had been at it all day long. Toward the end of the game, the story was told, Hog Van de Graff stood up holding his ear in his hand, blood streaming down his neck. He pointed to my grandfather and accused him of biting off his ear! At that point in telling the story Grandpa would pause dramatically until one of his grandchildren would ask the inevitable question: "Grandpa, is that really true?" And he would deliver the punch line: "Well, it makes a good story." I also remember

Grandpa saying that any story worth repeating was worth improving a little bit.

Grandpa was a devout man who wrote two books: *On Moonlight Lake* and *Old Mose Tells His Grandchildren about the Bible.* Grandpa taught me that a regular person could write a book and that truth can't always be reduced to facts.

Jimmie Lee Washington had no more than a third-grade education. I met him when he was in his sixties and working as a maintenance man at the Episcopal church camp in Mississippi. He took a special interest in me for some reason and taught me a lot about life and God while we were fishing for bream in the camp lake. When I went off to seminary, I wondered what Jimmie Lee would have thought about some of the lectures, and I began to think about what it would be like for him to be there as a student, and then, more startlingly, as a lecturer. That thought became a story, which served as a way for me to translate some of the lofty thoughts and words of academia into plainer language so I could understand them. Somewhere along the way, writing a story for myself became writing a book for others.

I have been privileged to work at summer camps for nearly forty years, and I have been particularly fortunate to have been involved in camp sessions for people with disabilities. These campers have taught me a lot, especially about respecting the dignity that all people have as children of God. I am indebted to many, many campers for sharing their joys and pains with me. Much of the plain wisdom I've put in Jake's words has come from them. I especially want to thank Mr. Neal Rosenblatt, the camper who took care of me when I was his counselor in summer 1971, and who later became a member of the adult staff of sessions I directed in Mississippi.

Dr. Sprague is not based on any professor I had, and Eddie is not anyone I ever met; they both represent the worst in all of us and our institutions.

It turns out that it takes a lot of people to write a book. I especially thank my wife, Tina, who is more patient with me than she will admit, and our children, McKee and Mary Nell, for their love and encouragement. I thank my parents, Crofton and Mary Sloan, my brother, Crofton, and my sisters, Becki and Fran, for their love and for a wonderful childhood. I thank the Episcopal Church for giving me a place to belong and for putting me to work, and the members of all the congregations I've served who've touched me and taught me or just put up with me. I am indebted and grateful to friends who read the story as it developed and gave helpful suggestions.

I want to thank my determined agent, Kathleen Davis Niendorff, for all of her work to get this published, and I thank her especially for not giving up on me or this project. I want to thank Phyllis Tickle for her wisdom and encouragement and for introducing me to Kathleen. I want to thank Leslie Andres, my insightful editor, and Keith Gammons, my publisher, who was willing to take a chance, and the folks at Peake Road Press.

Contents

Prelude 1

1 An Odd Mix of Peace and Death 3

2 Blood, Mud, and Worms 9

3 Lonely Notes Deep Down Inside 23

4 Not Near Long Enough 39

5 Now You Got to Decide 51

6 When It's Dreadful Dark 59

7 Mourning the Death of a Chipmunk 73

8 More Than Our Mamas 91

9 Inherited Wisdom 109

10 Folks You Don't Much Fit in With 125

11 A Rose Blooming in the Swamp 139

12 The Kind of Drivel They Teach 151

13 The Great Parade of Pagans 163

14 We Is All Sinners Most of the Time 175

15 You Got to Be Careful Who You Is Naked With 185

16 Deuces and One-eyed Jacks 193

17 Laissez les Bon Temps Rouler 205

18 All Them High and Lofty Professors 225

19 The Problem of Evil 239

20 Odd Sacraments 255

21 Heights, Depths, Heights 269

22 Somethin' to Lean On 281

23 Words Are Powerful Things 293

24 The Acting Dean 305

25 A Come-as-You-Are Celebration 313

26 Flyin' Over the Water 325

27 Just Mutts 337

28 The Resting Place 345

29 Depart, O Christian Soul 359

30 Have a Little Faith, Preacher 365

31 Let Me Go, for the Day Is Breaking 381

32 And When from Death I'm Free 389

Postlude 395

Prelude

He asked me to preach his funeral. It's the highest honor ever to afflict me, the heaviest burden I've ever had to carry. And even though we both figured nobody would be at the graveyard but me, we also knew it was important. After he died, when I started to think about what I would say at his grave, I realized that I had too much to say, and that even if I said it all it wouldn't be enough. I've always been better at writing than talking, so I started to write down our story, about Jake and me. After a while, my reflections at his graveside became a penance of sorts, and, some years after that, they grew into this book. That's my reason for writing; I suppose you'll have your own reasons for reading.

One of the things Jake taught me about stories is that it's hard to find where they start: each story presupposes the listener knows something that involves a previous story. Jake told me once that I ought to start every story I ever tell with "I was born on a Sunday" and go from there. And of course stories never truly end. Still, when you're writing one down, there has to be a first page, and that's where we are.

A couple of times I remember Jake asking, "Shall we continue in sin, that grace may abound?" I never knew what to make of it, and he never gave me the answer. I was surprised to learn in seminary that it came from the sixth chapter of Romans, written by the Apostle Paul, who followed the question with his emphatic answer: "God forbid." I suppose most of the time I've probably put more weight on continuing in sin than on grace abounding, but I'm counting on grace as I write this story. I need to write what I have to say before I listen to that little voice in the back of my mind that tells me, "You don't know what you're doing; you've never written a book before." God forbid.

But it's important to me that I write this. Even if it's never published, even if you never read a word of it, it's important to me to write it, just to set my thoughts in order. And it's important for me at least to pretend you'll read it, so I'll have to put it all down in some sort of understandable order. Whether this comes across as sinful or silly, I need to do it as if I know what I'm doing. I'll trust for you and for me that God's grace will abound.

1

An Odd Mix of Peace and Death

Every time I learn this, the truer it gets: we can only live our lives looking ahead, and we can only understand them looking back. And so I couldn't have known at the age of eight, in the simmering humid heat of a Mississippi afternoon, as I co-mingled with the mud and water and various creatures of Tadpole Creek, that I was about to meet one of the most amazing people I've ever known, a man who would change and shape my life from that day to this.

It would not be long, in the grand sweep of things, before I had to keep my promise and preach by his graveside, but on that day, there was another death to attend to. And I couldn't understand it, either.

Like most of the other boys in the neighborhood, I was taking refuge from sisters and parents and the relentless sun down in the woods behind our houses. I grew up south of Vicksburg, Mississippi, outside a little town called Beaumont, just a couple of miles from the Mississippi River. I was alone, playing with a few little boats I'd made with cane and my trusty pocketknife. The boats were all different: some had outriggers, two had sails made of cottonwood leaves, and I imagined one looked something like a catamaran I'd admired while looking for pictures of naked ladies in a *National Geographic* magazine at school.

I was all mud and sweat and knees and elbows, crouched down by the side of a creek that only flowed when it rained. My feet, liberated from shoes and socks in the summer, were deeply buried in the creek's muddy bank. I probably would have made a good picture in *National Geographic* myself; I believed that the more mud I could get on me, the more difficult it would be for the mosquitoes to get to me. So I had scooped out handfuls of the brownish-gray clay and smeared it from my hairline to my toes.

It was my favorite section of the creek because it had water in it all the time. It had formerly been a sort of muddy pool, but earlier that spring I'd stolen twenty-eight heavy red bricks from Mr. Haskins, who lived across the gully from our house. I had hauled them down the hill and made an eight-inch-high Hoover-looking dam chinked with clay from the creek, so that part of the creek was now at least five feet wide, and nearly two feet deep in the middle. There was plenty of water for my boats. It was my favorite place in the world: I would sit there for hours, watching the crawfish chasing the tadpoles, and the little bream coming up to eat the squiggling mosquito larvae.

The morning I met Jake, I was oblivious to everything else, bent over my little pool and putting every bit of concentration into pushing my little boats into their mud ports and stick piers with a long section of cane. So I didn't hear the deer until she was almost on me.

I'd seen deer before, but never up close, and usually in the fall, during hunting season. Now all at once she was there, not twenty feet from me, crashing through a section of blackberry sticker bushes all the kids in the neighborhood had learned from painful experience to avoid. I saw her, but as still as I was, and camouflaged with mud from ears to toes, she didn't see me. I remember thinking a deer was supposed to be pretty and how lucky I was to be this close to one, but I could tell right away that something was terribly wrong.

She was breathing funny; she wasn't holding her head right. She stood still for what seemed like a long time, looking back over her shoulder and flank. I held my breath. She wobbled a little, tried to take a step, and collapsed into a bed of ferns.

The ferns surrounded her so thoroughly that in a few moments it was as if she'd never been there at all. I got up from kneeling at the creek bank, half hoping that I'd just imagined her in a daydream, but I hadn't: she was lying in the ferns, breathing hard with a great effort, her tongue lolling out to the dark damp earth beneath her. When I walked slowly toward her, she lifted her head feebly, saw me coming, and let it fall back. In her huge soft eyes I saw panic and fear, as if she was desperate to run, and at the same time it seemed that she was beseeching me to help her. Then I saw the blood on her side, matted in her fur.

My first thought was that she had scratched herself in the stickers. But the blood was oozing out steadily, too much for stickers. I wanted to help but couldn't imagine what I might be able to do. We were still as stumps for what seemed like a long time, both of us fixed in the other's stare, both of us helpless, both of us growing more desperate by the second.

Off to my right, I heard something crunching through the underbrush, not nearly as loudly as the doe had. This time I heard the noise before I saw what was causing it, and I had time to scare myself. I remember seeing the knife before I saw anything else: a long, sharp-looking blade gleaming cruelly even in the shadows. It was held by an old man. His long ragged pants and T-shirt were two shades of gray, although you could tell they had started off different colors that the gray had overcome with age and dirt. The hair under his gray hat was gray, or it would have been without all the dust and dirt. Everything about him was gray and dirty except his stabbing light brown eyes and the cold shine of his knife.

The Gray Man glanced at me and dismissed me quickly: his focus was on the wounded deer. He was talking to her softly. I couldn't hear what he was saying, but it sounded like a mother talking to a hurt child. I hoped he would be able to help her.

It wasn't until I tried to say something that I realized I'd been crying. "Mister, what are you gonna do?"

He looked at me again, but glanced back at the doe before he spoke. "You need to go on, boy, get on home. You don't want to see what I got to do here." Then, more quietly as if to himself or maybe the doe, he said, "You need to go on, get on home."

At the time, I think I told myself I had to stay to protect the deer; probably the truth was that I was too scared to move. Either way, I didn't leave. Quicker than it takes to write it down, he took the doe by the ear and slit her throat with his pitiless knife, one quick, strong stroke. She gave out a sickening gasping cough as the blood gushed out on the man's gray boots and into the mud, and then she was dead.

Now, more than forty years later, I remember the moment as if it were earlier this morning. My whole body was shaking, and my mouth seemed full of ashes. I watched the Gray Man tie a rope to her back legs and hoist her up over the low limb of a little oak tree to drain her blood. I worried that her blood would flow into my little creek.

I wanted to leap up and save the doe, or maybe avenge her death. With all the rage an eight-year-old can muster, I stood up, my muddy legs all wobbly, to perform some heroic though yet unspecified act. But in fact, all I managed to do was to throw up.

When I finished, I realized the man was holding me in his lap, talking to me as he had to the deer. He had a filthy rag wet with water from the creek and was wiping my forehead. His touch was gentle.

But I was being held by the enemy, the deer-killer.

It was too much. I struggled to my feet, angry and upset. "Why?" I sobbed. "Why did you have to kill her? Why couldn't you make her well?"

"She been shot, boy. She was fixin' to die." He wiped again at my forehead with the rag, more gently than I would have thought possible. Then, he said even more softly, "Go on, boy. Get on home to your mama."

I remember thinking he was trying to get rid of me, figuring I had caught him in the act. He must have been the one who shot the deer! I picked up the long, thin stick that had been pushing the boats and waved it like a baseball bat. "You killed her!"

Some part of me thought I would hit him, but most of me assumed he'd do something to stop me before I did. He looked at me as I came toward him, looked deep into me, but made no movement. When I saw that the resistance I expected wasn't there, I stopped myself and wondered what to do next.

He sat there, an odd mix of peace and death, and looked at me with his penetrating eyes. They were the kind of eyes that always smiled, but they held a deep sadness, too. "I didn't shoot her, boy," he murmured. "Some other fool done that. Now he done lost her, let her go off to die by herself. We all got to die, all of us. I was just helpin' her pass more easy, just helpin' her pass."

I was crying again, for the deer, for my helplessness, because we all have to die. I didn't know what to say, and I stood transfixed, looking at him with tears cutting through the mud on my face. Again he told me, "Go on, boy, get on home." I turned and ran up the hill until I was out of his sight, and then I lay down in the leaves and cried until I couldn't cry anymore. After a while, having recovered whatever dignity I had left, I walked home.

All the way back to our house, I thought how I'd tell the story to my family. But when I got there, Mama fussed at me for being so muddy (usually I washed the mosquito protection off in the creek), Daddy fussed at me for being late for supper, and my brother Lee teased me about crying. He could always tell by my eyes when I'd been crying, and he always made a big deal over it. I had wanted to tell somebody about the deer and the Gray Man, but I figured Lee would make fun of me for letting it upset me, for getting sick and crying, so I kept it to myself. It was usually easier to get along if I avoided attention.

So it became an experience I kept inside. It became my story, something special to me, not to be shared with anyone. At first, as I relived the events in my mind, I tried to make the Gray Man into the villain. But as I rehearsed the story, I had to admit that he was the one who helped the deer while I sat helpless in the mud. I wanted to think he was mean and cruel, but I couldn't help remembering how gently he held me, how kindly and softly he had talked to us, the deer and me.

You might think that not much happens to an eight-year-old in Beaumont, Mississippi, and you'd be correct about that; nothing happens of real consequence, anyway. Now that this had happened, though, my mind returned to it again and again, savoring it, reliving it. The story got better every time I told it to myself. As I remembered and re-remembered the death of the deer, the Gray Man increasingly played his role as the hero. I gradually improved on the facts a little, and where memory meets fantasy, I continued the story so that the

Gray Man and I helped the deer together, and then he and I hunted down the hunter and chased him through the sticker bushes until he begged us for mercy. And we let him run off after he promised he'd never come back into our woods again.

2

Blood, Mud, and Worms

On an early fall Saturday morning a few months later, I set off into the woods to go exploring with my brother and the other boys in the neighborhood. The woods ran for miles behind our houses, well past the parts we knew; there was always "the unexplored frontier." We didn't live in a neighborhood, exactly, all strung out on Ridge Road as we were. The guys usually gathered at our house, since it was somewhere near the middle, with an easy, well-worn path down into the gully that led to the woods.

I was the youngest of the boys, three years younger than my brother Lee, who was, by mostly mutual consent, the leader of the group. He came about as close as any of us to being liked by most of us most of the time. I never liked him much, of course, but that was to be expected since I was his little brother.

The main challenge to Lee's authority came from Purvis Calhoun. He was smaller than Lee, but scrappier. He was the best spitter in the group and the most proficient cusser, always ready for a fight, never one to miss an opportunity to prove how tough he was. Hardly a week went by that we didn't hear about some fight he'd been in, most of which we knew he'd started himself. Eager to take offense, Purvis was determined not to take anything off anybody and never forgot a grudge.

I don't remember his mother, but I remember well that we didn't like his father. Mr. Calhoun had coached Lee in Little League baseball one summer, and Lee was scared of him. And I was automatically scared of anything Lee was scared of. Mama never liked for us to play with Purvis or his younger brother, Durant.

Durant was a little chubby, always in hand-me-downs that didn't quite fit, a kid with perpetually dirty hands who laughed a lot and cried easily. He was affable for the most part, but he invariably went along with his brother in an argument or a fight. Lee and I liked Durant a lot better when Purvis wasn't around.

Last, and usually least, was Lewis. He was short for his age and terribly thin. His mother was always trying to get him to eat ice cream and doughnuts and stuff that the rest of us wished somebody would make us eat. Lewis's primary handicap was not so much that he was exceptionally smart but that his mother knew it. He wore new clothes all the time, and he couldn't play with us the next day if he got them too muddy. Three afternoons a week, his mother would call him in at four o'clock to practice the piano. He lived less than half a mile down the road; we used to sneak up to the window of their living room while he was practicing, hiding in the azalea bushes and trying to make him giggle so his mother would come fuss at him. He didn't like football; he wasn't athletic; his mother put a Band-Aid in his pants pocket every day in case he got hurt. We all called him a sissy, even though we knew it wasn't really his fault. He was three years older than I—Lee's age—but I was a little taller and outweighed him by at least ten pounds.

These were the boys of my childhood. None of us particularly liked any of the others, but we were the only kids any of us knew in any depth. Actually, Lewis and I generally enjoyed being together, but neither wanted the others to know, both of us figuring our stock would go down within the group if the information got out.

Our favorite activities were aggressive and combative. We especially enjoyed playing football, or dodge ball, or Wiffle ball. And we had wars: dirt-clod wars, acorn wars, sweet-gum-ball wars—anything that was competitive, involved throwing things at each other, and had the potential to produce pain. Lewis and I were often one team or army or side, and everybody else was the other. Lewis and I figured we were lucky to be included, so we just played along as best we could, tried not to get hurt, and tried not to cry when we did.

When we got tired of hurting each other, or when Lewis and I were no longer a sufficient challenge, sometimes we would all go exploring. These were some of my favorite times as a kid, when we were all working together, cooperating rather than competing.

This particular Saturday morning, Lee declared that we should follow the creek behind our house until it came to the Mississippi River. We had explored far enough to know that our little creek, almost always dry, continued until it met a bigger creek, which we called the Bayou. The Bayou was wide but not deep except in a few well-loved spots, and it flowed slowly, almost imperceptibly. Going to the Bayou was an all-day affair that we had agreed to hide from our parents, to save them from the burden of having to worry about us down there.

The Bayou was greatly mysterious, twisting and turning so much it was hard to tell if it was ever going anywhere at all. But Lee and Purvis figured it had to be heading in the general direction of the river, on which we could hear the whistles of the great diesel towboats as they negotiated the Vicksburg Bridge, struggling to push their huge tows slowly upriver, trying to maintain control as they careened downstream.

We went to our homes to gather supplies and reconvened in our backyard. We put our army surplus canteens on our belts and packed sandwiches and apples in paper sacks that Lee made Lewis and me carry. Lee had his hatchet, Purvis his pocketknife, and Durant and I carried long straight sticks that we imagined were like staffs in the story of Robin Hood and Little John. Lewis had a length of cane that he'd gotten Purvis to whittle a point on; he called it his spear. We wore no shoes and no shirts, just cutoffs. Actually, Lewis had to wear his shoes and shirt until we had walked well away from his mother's eyes. Then he took his shirt off and carefully folded it and laid it over the limb of a hickory sapling, then removed his shoes and socks, rolling the socks up and putting them into one shoe.

Lee led the way, with the rest of us following in the usual order: Purvis, then Durant, then me, and Lewis bringing up the rear. We ran when Lee ran, our bare feet slapping the dirt of the well-worn path; we listened when Lee listened, hearing birds and an occasional squirrel; we rested when Lee rested, stopping to catch our breath until the mosquitoes caught up with us, and then it was time to push on, with Lee ever and always in the lead. We followed our creek until it came into the Bayou, exotic and alive with the potential for danger and mystery. We sloshed along calf-deep in mud and muddy water until we came to the first of the deep places we'd found on previous expeditions. There we sat in the cool water and mud, ate our sandwiches. We put the apples in one of the sacks for the way home, slinging the bag up over the limb of a tree so a bear wouldn't get them. The fact that there were bears in our woods was not something we questioned, not because we'd ever had any evidence of their existence, but because we all understood that the idea of bears made the woods that much more dangerous and exciting. It also kept our sisters up the hill and out of our woods.

After a little splashing and playing, but before it turned into an all-out mud war, we set out again. We didn't go far before we realized we were at the limits of our knowledge. From that point, it was all new territory. Durant, never one to shy away from the drama of a moment, suggested that "no man has ever walked where we are now." Lee told us to watch for snakes, "especially moccasins," and Lewis suggested that he ought to go before me, figuring that a snake would likely get either the first of our group or the last of us, and that he should not be either. I suppose he just didn't want to trouble his mother with a snakebite. There are some things a Band-Aid won't help.

After an hour or so of slogging through the muddy water, we saw that another creek joined the Bayou, and together they formed a fairly large stream. If you're picturing a brook burbling over rocks, your mind is visiting someplace else; this was more like a long, thin lake than a swiftly flowing stream.

Lee thought it would be best if we stopped walking in the water, since we couldn't always see the bottom. The Bayou was eight to ten feet wide there, and some places looked deep enough to be over our heads. The creek had burrowed itself into the mud so that the surface of the water was six or eight feet below the floor of the woods. We walked on the banks of the Bayou, down in the ravine it had cut steep and muddy along the floor of the gully. It would have been cooler up out of the ravine, but the creek bank was mostly clear of the undergrowth of vines and stickers that made walking so hard, especially barefooted as we were. We walked beside the creek, watching for water moccasins, talking in quiet whispers.

Something slid into the water ahead of us, making a small ripple, but large enough for each of the intrepid explorers to see. Durant and Lewis started trying to climb up the bank to get away, but Lee and Purvis rushed ahead to see what it was. I followed them hesitantly, balancing curiosity with fear. Sure enough, it was a snake.

In truth, it wasn't all that big, not nearly as big as it became in the stories we told about it later, probably a little more than three feet long. I don't actually know what kind of snake it was; it became a water moccasin in the telling. And it was definitely not "after us," but trying with some urgency to get away from us, sensing with some snaky intuition that its doom had drawn nigh. We were explorers, and we had met the enemy, that which our parents had warned us against and threatened us with: we would vanquish it or be shamed.

Quickly recognizing that hatchets and pocketknives were not called for in snake killing, Lee called for me and Durant to come forward with our staffs. By this time, the snake was out of the water, trying to slither up the steep bank to freedom. I was more than willing to let the older boys use my stick, but Durant insisted that since they were our staffs, we ought to be the ones to kill the snake. While they argued about it, it looked like the snake was about to get away, so Lee gave in. "Okay, fine. But you better kill it."

And we did. Durant and I jabbed the poor thing to death with our sticks as it tried hopelessly to get away. Long before it died, we all knew it didn't have a chance. I felt sorry for it, even though it was a snake. There was nothing quick or merciful about this death, and the trophy we had when it was all over could hardly be identified as a snake, it was so mauled and ground into the mud. It took a while for it to stop moving, even after it was surely dead, so we kept on killing it until it finally lay still.

But still, a triumph is a triumph, and we celebrated with long drinks from our canteens and various retellings of the story from each of our points of view, each showing the others where he had stood and what he had done, even though we'd all been there to see it for ourselves. We all felt manlier after that, even Lewis, who'd waited until the snake was clearly not going anywhere to jab at it with his spear. We'd taken the worst the woods had to threaten us with, and we'd overcome it. We were hunters, conquerors, explorers; let the woods beware!

We walked on for what seemed like hours, until one bend in the Bayou looked pretty much like the one before, and I was fairly sure that the next would be the same as well. Lewis and Durant were hinting and suggesting that it was time to turn around and go home. I knew we weren't going to turn around until Lee said so, and that my suggesting we go back home would only delay his deciding it, so I stayed quiet. We came around a bend to a place where the Bayou widened to twenty or thirty feet from bank to bank, and we couldn't tell how deep it might be. And off to our left, sitting on the trunk of a fallen oak, was a man fishing.

I realized with considerable agitation that it was the Gray Man, the hero of my private story, the man who'd killed the deer. Now that I had time to look at him a little more clearly, I saw that he wasn't actually gray, just dusty. He had three cane poles, all held up by forked sticks stuck in the mud, and he was intently watching three porcupine quill floats. He was still gray, but he wore a straw hat and was smoking a pipe. He seemed unaware of us, though we had certainly been making at least ten boys' worth of noise.

Lewis whined again that he thought it was time to go home. Purvis told him nobody was keeping him there, knowing Lewis wouldn't go home by himself. Lee suggested that we ought to go talk to the man. I let the other boys go ahead of me and stayed back, where I hoped the Gray Man wouldn't notice me.

Lee called out the standard fisherman greeting, "Caught anything?"

The man didn't look up but replied, "A few."

Lewis had never been fishing so didn't know the etiquette involved. The rest of us, more sophisticated in this area, knew that the next thing we were supposed to say was, "Any size to 'em?" to which the response was either something like, "Not much," in which case the fisherman doesn't want to show you because he's not doing so well, or, "One or two of 'em's all right," and then he'd hold up the stringer for admiration. But Lewis was inexperienced and overeager. "Let us see!" he called.

The man smiled patiently at the breach of protocol and held up a stringer with a few catfish, a couple of bream, and two or three large fish we didn't recognize. I relaxed a little, glad that the Gray Man seemed friendly and agreeable. I looked at the others; everybody seemed at ease except for Purvis, who was looking at the Gray Man with such apparent hatred that I wondered if they'd met.

Durant didn't know whether he was supposed to be polite or not, confused by Lee's affable question and Purvis's glare. He asked, "What's them?"

The Gray Man answered quietly, "Fish."

This seemed to anger Purvis. "What kind of fish is that right there?"

"Buffalo."

Lee said to the rest of us, "I never seen a buffalo fish before."

But Purvis had. "My daddy caught one once, up in Thompson Lake. He threw it back, though, said only niggers ate 'em."

I want to take a moment to explain the word "nigger" here. I've written this story several times and substituted "darkie" or "Negro," which I'm sure would be easier for some to take. But the truth is that "nigger" was then and still is a mean and hateful word, and using a euphemism only takes the teeth out of what Purvis meant to be a vicious bite. It was intended to be malicious.

It was a word we heard a lot in Mississippi in the early 1960s, though never around polite adults and never in the presence of an African-American person. Actually, the only African-American person any of us had ever known was Ethel Lee, who worked for Lewis's family and ours once a week. Mama said Ethel Lee was "colored." She was also our babysitter on the rare occasion that Mama talked Daddy into going out. She was a dear, sweet woman, tough as nails when she needed to be, whom Lee and Lewis and I loved wholeheartedly.

One time Daddy had to take Ethel Lee to her sister's house, and I asked him if I could ride with them. He said I could, but he warned me that we were going down into the Bottom, where a lot of "colored people" lived. I was excited that I would see colored people, imagining them to be different colors, like M&M's. And I remember how disappointed I was that they were all just brown, the same color as Ethel Lee.

I also remember my father coming out to break up a shoving match in our front yard. We'd been playing kickball, and a dispute had broken out over the interpretation of the rules or whether the ball was kicked fair or foul, and it was on its way to escalating into a fight between Lee and Purvis. It had passed the name-calling stage, in which the N-word was used to great effect, and was just beginning the shoving stage when Daddy slammed the screen door open, anger obvious on his face.

It took just a second for us all to understand that he didn't care about kickball, or whether the ball was in or out, or who would win a fight between Lee and Purvis, for that matter. He called all of us together, gathering us around him on our little front porch stoop, and told us that the next time he heard any of us say "that word," he would whip that boy, whether it was his son or not. He said the times were changing, that we didn't use that word anymore, and carefully explained that we were to say "nigrah" instead, or "nigress" for a woman.

So we were careful that no grownups heard us use the word, but after that it had even more power. For boys like us back then, the word didn't have as much to do with race or color as the fact that it was the ultimate insult, the thing our parents didn't want us to call each other. I guess most of us used it as a weapon, all the more injurious since it was a word forbidden to us. Still, we all knew it was talking about colored people in a mean way, and I was both surprised and alarmed to hear Purvis say it right there in front of a nigrah. He spoke it with venom, like an accusation.

It also had the effect of expanding my idea of the Gray Man, who until that moment had not been assigned an ethnicity in my mind: he was the Gray Man.

Purvis needled, "You eat buffalo fish, mister?"

"I have. They ain't much good. I'd ruther have a bream."

Durant seemed amazed that anybody could eat these fish, even though he'd never heard of them until a few minutes before. "You gonna eat these?"

"I'll eat the bream, sell the rest. You boys best go on and go where you're goin'. You messin' up my fishin' with all your noise and whatnot."

But Durant sensed his brother's approval, a rare and valuable commodity, and persisted, "Who you gonna sell 'em to?"

Before the man could speak, Purvis answered for him. "Other niggers, 'course. They's the only ones that eat them buffalo fish."

The Gray Man looked down at the ground, and said with a low, cold voice, "You need to be careful how you talk, boy. They's some folks would take offense at that word, they sure would."

Durant, never one to let not knowing what he was talking about keep him from talking, goaded the old man, "What word?"

Again Purvis had the answer. "Nigger!" He spat out the cruelest word with furious vehemence. "He don't like to be called a nigger, but that's all he is. He's just an old nigger."

The man kept looking down at the ground, as if he saw something interesting there. Lee tried to regain control of the situation. "Hey, c'mon, y'all, let's go." Lee started to walk up the bank of the creek, and Lewis and I went with him. But Purvis wouldn't let it go, or couldn't, and Durant stayed with his brother.

Purvis was yelling now, even though we hadn't gotten far at all. "Wait! It ain't our fault he's a nigger! Y'all come on back; he ain't gonna hurt you! Hey Lee—you ain't *ascared*, are you?"

"Ascared" was a carefully chosen word. I think it originally came from Lewis's little sister Lucille, who was trying to encourage her big brother, whom she called Bubba, of all things, to swing out on a vine behind their house. She'd pleaded, "Don't be ascared, Bubba." It was sort of a cross between afraid and scared. We had teased Lewis about that for years, and now, using it on Lee, Purvis was calling his manhood into question. When you're only eleven, you're serious about your manhood, which is always precarious, sometimes dubious. We all recognized it for what it was: Purvis was challenging Lee's leadership.

The predictability of Lee's response made it no less sad for me. As he clambered back down the muddy bank, he announced with a great show of manliness, "Hell, no, I ain't afraid of this ol' nigger. I just got more important things to do, that's all."

Lewis and I stayed up on the top of the creek bank. Nobody was questioning our manhood: Lewis was a sissy and I was just a kid. The Gray Man looked right at me, and I knew he knew who I was, but he didn't say anything. I was grateful to him—the secret we shared was safe.

Purvis's resolve was strengthened by Lee's support, and he took up his cause anew. "Well, nigger, what have you got to say?"

The man stood up. "You boys best move on now, I mean it."

Purvis was enjoying the mess he'd stirred up, and he couldn't back down in any case. "Or what? What you gonna do, nigger?"

The word stabbed at the man, and at me. He quietly started to pick up his fishing poles, gather his fishing tackle. I remembered his eyes looking at me as I was coming toward him to hit him the day he killed the deer. He wouldn't have stopped me, and now he wasn't going to stop Purvis. The difference was that Purvis wasn't going to stop himself either.

"I said, what you gonna do, nigger?"

I should have said or done something, shown some courage, but I didn't know what to say. Lewis beseeched him, "Leave him alone, Purvis. Let's go." I was proud of Lewis, even while it added to my shame for saying nothing.

Purvis turned around to look up at us, took a step toward us. "What's the matter, Lewis? Ascared? He ain't gonna hurt us. He's just an ol' nigger. Buddy ain't ascared, are you, Buddy?"

Everybody's called me Buddy for most of my life. The family story is that I argued with my grandmother, who called me by my real name, insisting that my name was Buddy because that's what Lee called me, but I don't remember it.

When Purvis turned the attention to me, I was paralyzed. I knew Purvis wouldn't be done with it until I declared myself one way or the other. And I knew I wasn't going to win either way. I looked at Lee for some help, but he was studying his feet. Purvis and I stared at each other for a long moment. The Gray Man was watching, too, with a focused concern to see which way I was going to go. I swaggered, "I ain't afraid of him, and I ain't afraid of you, either." Purvis was furious, but I saw the man smile a little to himself, and my heart leaped into my throat.

The Gray Man continued to collect his gear. But when Purvis turned around and moved toward Lee, his foot got tangled in the line of one of the man's fishing poles, and a hook found its way into the calloused pad of Purvis's bare big toe.

Purvis screamed in impotent rage, "Goddamn it! Goddamn nigger!" We all gathered to see it, as we always did when somebody got hurt. The hook still had a worm squirming on it, and as Lee extracted the barbed point from Purvis's foot, I remember seeing with some satisfaction a little of Purvis's blood mixing with whatever makes up the inside of a worm. It seemed an appropriate combination.

The Gray Man watched. When Purvis stood up, he asked, "You all right, boy?"

Purvis was almost hysterical. "Hell no, I ain't all right! I been hooked in the foot by a goddamned nigger!"

The man said simply, "I am sorry you got yourself hooked."

Purvis grabbed Durant's staff and waved it menacingly. "Sorry? You're gonna be sorry!" I thought he was going to hit the man. The Gray Man just stood and looked at him, not daring him, but not resisting, either. Lewis took off running, until he remembered he wouldn't be able to get home by himself. He stopped behind the thick trunk of an oak and started to cry.

The man looked sad and tired. "If you is goin' to hit me, boy, go on and do it." That took a little of the wind out of Purvis's sails. The man continued with what I thought was a remarkably calming voice. "I been hit before, by bigger and meaner than you. Mostly it's the waitin' and wonderin' that's hard on a man. If you goin' to hit me, go ahead and do it, just go ahead."

Purvis didn't know what to do. Even he couldn't hit a man who was just going to stand there and let him, not even a colored man.

Lee urged, "C'mon, man, let's go home. You need to put some Mercurochrome on that foot. *C'mon*!"

Lee and Durant helped Purvis up the bank. I breathed a sigh of relief. I turned toward home, thinking that we were on our way, when I heard Purvis's voice behind me. "Hey, nigger!" he said in a tone of either defiance or desperation.

I turned to see that he'd picked up a handful of the mud and clay on the creek bank, and I watched as he threw it at the man, hitting him on the left shoulder. The man stood there with an expression of resigned sadness, like he'd done this before. He looked at Purvis and then looked at me. I froze, both physically and emotionally.

Purvis taunted, "Go on, nigger. Ain't you gonna run for it? I'll count to ten 'fore I throw again."

But the old man replied, "I've run before, too. I'm all done runnin'. If you want to throw dirt on me, that's somethin' you got to live with. But I ain't goin' to run. That's something I ain't willin' to live with." And he continued to pick up his fishing gear, in no apparent hurry.

That enraged Purvis, who scooped up another handful of mud and threw again. The mud missile hit the man square in the back as he stooped to pick up his stringer of fish. Now Durant picked up some mud and threw, but he missed. Purvis was delighted. "Now there's a *white* man! C'mon, Lee, you're missing all the fun!"

Lee looked at me, and I tried to send him a message with my face, to tell him that he didn't have to do this. But I guess he didn't get it; he picked up some mud and threw, too. His mud hit the man square in the face as he glanced up at us. He had to put down the things he'd gathered so he could wipe his eyes.

It was more than I could stand. "Stop it! Leave him alone!"

Purvis laughed at me. "What's the matter, Buddy, ascared?" Purvis threw again, and then Durant.

The man watched me, mud all over his face and clothes. As our eyes met, I was sure that he was something different from any other man I'd ever seen. "Stop it!" I screamed, crying, but they ignored me.

At the time, it seemed to last for hours, but I think it probably didn't take the Gray Man more than a couple of minutes to get his tackle together and shamble away. Durant wanted to follow him, but Lee walked away, toward home, and I went with him. When it became clear to Purvis and Durant that we were leaving with or without them, they came, too. Purvis was starting to feel the pain of the noble wound that he now believed he'd suffered for all white people everywhere, and he told us the story of how he had "put that nigger in his place" twice before he remembered me.

"Hey, Durant," mocked Purvis as he rubbed some of the mud off his hands. "You know what I think little Buddy is?"

Durant had years of practice with his part of this tag-team bullying. "No, Purvis, what?"

Purvis sneered the punchline: "I believe ol' Buddy is a nigger-lover."

I'd never heard the term before but I could tell by the way he spoke that being a nigger-lover was almost as bad in his mind as being colored. All the guys were looking at me, waiting for me to defend myself.

"No, I'm not." I wish I'd said something stronger, heroic, enlightened, but the truth is that this was all I could think to say.

Purvis, of course, had a lot to say. "Oh, yeah, I think you are. I didn't see him throwin' no mud on that ol' nigger, did you, Durant?"

"Nope, not a bit."

"What about you, Lee, did you see your nigger-lovin' brother throw any mud on that foot-hookin' nigger?"

Lee, checking out his feet again, muttered, "No."

Purvis continued, "Well then, I believe that makes you a nigger-lover. What do you say to that, Buddy?"

We were going up a steep hill, back in some woods that were familiar to me, and even though it was still a long way from home, I knew I could get there alone. I also knew I was going to have to answer Purvis. "He didn't do you any harm."

Purvis snarled, "You call a hook in my foot no harm? It hurt like hell!"

"That was your own fault, and he said he was sorry."

"Of course he's sorry. He's just a sorry nigger! And you're just a sorry nigger-lover!"

I figured Purvis couldn't run very fast with a sore foot, and that neither Durant nor Lee would chase me, so I took off running. As I got to the top of the hill, I turned back to get the last word: "I am not!"

3

Lonely Notes Deep Down Inside

It was October of the following year before I saw the Gray Man again, just a couple of weeks before I turned ten.

Purvis and Durant had made fun of me for a few weeks about being a nigger-lover, but Lee and Lewis never picked it up, so after a while it ran out of steam.

That next year, when Halloween came, it seemed to me that I was coming into an awkward age: too old to trick-or-treat but young enough to be bothered by missing out. Halloween was on a Friday night that year, and I found out that Lee and the Calhoun boys were planning a campout. Lee told Mama he was going to spend the night at his friend Clayton's house in Vicksburg. When I found out about it, I did what any self-respecting little brother would do: I threatened to tell Mama.

Lee realized his grand plan was in jeopardy and made the supreme sacrifice. He invited me to come camping, too, if I would keep quiet about it. I didn't actually want to go; I just didn't want to be left out. So I told Mama I was going to spend the night with Nelson, a boy I'd met and disliked in Sunday school. He always dressed neatly, was always polite, and his parents had a lot of money. I figured Mama would be pleased, and I was right.

Lewis was not invited to the campout and was not welcome. Lee told me several times not to tell Lewis, because he would tell his mother, who would tell our mother, and we'd all be in trouble. So when Lewis asked me what I was going to dress up as for Halloween, I told him I was too old for all that, and that I wasn't going to go trick-or-treating at all. He looked a little hurt; he and I had always walked the route together. He told me his mother had made him a pirate costume; I told him that stuff was for little kids. But even at that moment, I wished I was going as a pirate, too. I didn't know then how much more I would wish it later.

Friday finally came, cold with a strong possibility of rain. Dad took me to the road that Nelson's house was on, and then he went off to drop Lee at Clayton's on his way to the high school football game up in Rolling Fork. For several years, Dad had picked up a little extra money officiating high school football games, and that night he was running late.

I started to walk down the road as if I was going where Dad thought I was going, but after he was out of sight I turned around and started walking back toward home, to the place where we planned to camp. We had sneaked some blankets and pillows into an old suitcase we'd gotten out of the attic, and I'd put a can of Vienna sausages and an apple in my knapsack. By the time I found the campsite, it was almost dark, and everybody else was already there. They had a fire going, Clayton's Boy Scout tent set up, and a kerosene lamp ready to be lit.

I remember being nervous, excited, and more than a little scared. That Mama didn't know where we were made it seem even more exhilarating. After the lamp was lit, we ate our supper. Clayton had stolen a pack of hot dogs and some buns from a little grocery store in Vicksburg that we all called the Jiffy. I remember being amazed. I was so afraid of the Lebanese man who was always at the Jiffy register. He had the bushiest eyebrows I'd ever seen, and he spoke with an accent.

Clayton, Purvis, Durant, and Lee had it all planned out before I got there, and had already gotten sticks with two prongs to cook their hot dogs. Lee, mad at me for tagging along, explained that they only had eight hot dogs and that the big boys needed two each, so there wouldn't be any left for me. He suggested I might want to go back home if I wanted supper. I watched them cook for a while, watched

Durant lose one of his wieners in the fire and Lee drop one of his in the dirt. So even though it wasn't all that much, it was a small victory of sorts when I pulled out my Vienna sausages and apple, although I was mindful not to be too obvious as I enjoyed them.

After dinner, they decided to tell ghost stories; it was Halloween, so ghost stories were expected. Clayton went first, telling one I'd heard before but tried to forget, about a crazy black man who had escaped from the Parchman Prison Farm by killing the guards with an ax, and who now lived out in these woods and was always trying to kidnap little boys. It wasn't much of a story, although he went to great lengths to describe the gore and blood involved in multiple ax murders, but it set the stage.

Purvis told a story about a man who died during the Civil War in the siege of Vicksburg. He was a Union soldier who got his right hand "blowed off" by a cannonball, and he died after much suffering and indescribable pain. "Now his spirit wanders these woods," Purvis said, in the tone one only uses for telling ghost stories, "searching for his lost hand and exacting vengeance on the Sons of the South for his grief and misery. And when he finds them, and if he finds us, he'll come up from behind us and grab our hands to see if they might be *his.*" Just when Purvis said *his*, as apparently prearranged, my loving brother Lee reached over and grabbed my hand.

I had already decided I wasn't going to be scared. I knew I was on somewhat thin ice with this group anyway, especially since Lewis wasn't there to share their abuse. So I didn't want to let on that I was afraid, no matter what. But when Lee grabbed my hand, I lost my composure and screamed. They all laughed, and that was the end of the stories. I was terribly embarrassed.

After they'd enjoyed my momentary loss of self-control several times, a shrill shriek shattered the night, and we all screamed with it. Nobody had much dignity left at that point, even though we assured each other that it was just a screech owl. They make a huge sound for such small birds, like children screaming out in the night. We all laughed uncomfortably, each of us telling the others how somebody jumped or mocking the face he made. I thanked the unseen owl, whose screech had provided a distraction just when I'd truly needed one.

Clayton, who'd told his mother that he was going to spend the night at Lee's house, asked, "Have you boys ever been to that old graveyard at night?"

Lee, whom I figured was anxious to steer the subject away from any appearance of weakness on his part, perked up. "What graveyard?"

"That ol' graveyard up on the big hill over the wide place in the Bayou, by that big ol' sweet gum tree."

Now he had Durant's interest as well. "No! Is it scary?"

Clayton played it cool. "Hell, no. It might scare you, but it don't scare me." It was a recurring theme of being a boy, one we could never seem to resist: a challenge to our manhood, which continually had to be determined, defined, and defended.

There was little discussion about whether or not we would go; the issue was never in doubt. I don't think any of us actually wanted to, or thought we ought to, but we went to the graveyard just the same. It was Halloween.

It wasn't much of a graveyard, really, about twenty small tombstones on top of an overgrown hill. There was only one tree on that hill, the biggest sweet gum I've ever seen. There was no fence or gate, no flowers on any of the graves; at first glance it looked like nobody had been there in years. I tried to read the inscriptions by the light of the three-quarter moon, but they were either so old or written in such poor stone that I couldn't read much at all.

Two graves stood side by side apart from the others, a little taller than the rest. They were right under the big tree, and it wasn't so overgrown around those two, as if someone had actually been tending them. One of them was covered in rectangular pieces of metal, and the letters and numbers on the front looked to be in different colors. Rather than being carved *into* the stone, these letters were coming *out* from the metal. But before I could figure it out, my attention was drawn to the other guys.

They had predictably started horsing around, and, unable to resist all the fallen sweet gum balls just begging to be thrown, they'd started a war. But this time, instead of me and Lewis against everybody else, it began as a free-for-all, every man for himself. Before long, Lee ran over and huddled behind the metallic tombstone I'd been looking at, and he and I agreed without a word that we were an alliance. Not long after that, Durant found Purvis, and they formed the enemy army. Clayton remained a free agent, enjoying each side's efforts to recruit him.

The moon dodged in and out of the clouds racing across the sky. Most of the time it was bright, and we had plenty of light, but every once in a while a cloud covered the moon, and then it was pitch dark. Each time the moon came out of hiding, I thought, "This isn't so bad," but when it was dark, it was scary.

Purvis sent Durant to find more ammunition while he guarded their fort behind a bush of some sort. Lee took advantage of the cease-fire and sent me out to do the same. Purvis had just hit me with one of his remaining gumballs when Durant tripped over a tombstone, and it cracked into two crumbly pieces.

Lee was horrified. "Oh, man, you broke that tombstone. We're in big trouble now."

But Purvis threw another gumball, just missing my head. "Naw, man. Nobody ever comes up here. All these people musta died a long time ago. Nobody even knows where this place is anymore."

With that, we all started to run around in a perverse game of chase, jumping over tombstones, trying to push each other into a marker. A cloud covered the moon, and we all stood still, unable to see where we were going. When the cloud passed, I saw Durant on all fours behind Lee. It was one of their favorite tricks: Durant would get on his hands and knees behind somebody, and Purvis would push the person over him. I recognized the trick too late, and could only watch as Lee went crashing down into a grave marker in the shape of a cross.

In the moonlight we could see the cross, bent over and broken. Lee was horrified. "Aw, man, look what you made me do! That was a tombstone! And a cross!"

Purvis sneered, "Hell, boy, it's just an ol' nigger grave. You ain't a nigger-lover, too, are you?" The implication was clear; everybody looked at me. Another cloud was racing to cover the moon, a big one that would put us all in the dark for a minute or so.

Clayton had heard the story, of course, and wanted to be a part of it. "Why, I just can't believe ol' Buddy here is a nigger-lover. Hell, I bet he'd just up and kick over one of these tombstones if he wanted to. Wouldn't you, Buddy?"

There was a long pause while I considered my options. I knew that if I told them I would, they wouldn't be satisfied until I did. I knew that I would eventually be pressured into doing it, but that somehow it wouldn't be enough, and they wouldn't let it drop. Again I missed Lewis: without him, I was the group's only target. If I was going to give in, I needed to do it quickly. If, on the other hand, I decided to hold my ground, I knew it would make for a long and difficult night.

I looked at the tombstone nearest me and was surprised to see that I could read the name by the light of the moon. It was a little girl, Annie Washington, who died when she was just six. The faint inscription gave her name and dates and also said, "Jesus Took Our Angel Home." I knew I couldn't kick over all that was left of a child who'd died at age six, so I decided to run for it. I didn't know what I was going to do after getting away from the older boys; I just needed to be somewhere else. I looked up at the cloud, getting closer and closer to the moon. The other boys checked the moon, too, knowing I was going to run, calculating the time left, what paths they would take in the darkness to catch me.

The cloud began to cover the moon. I faked to my left and ran to my right. This almost never worked, but it was almost always my strategy: it at least showed that I was genuinely trying to make a run for it. I ran into something, something not a tombstone and not a tree, softer, but still solid. It gave a little, then pushed back. I remember thinking that whatever it was hadn't been there a few seconds before. I tried to turn and run the other way, but whatever had stopped me now reached over my right shoulder and caught me. It had grabbed my arm and was holding me!

When I screamed, nobody heard me; I didn't even hear myself. What we all heard instead was a sound like the end of the world: BOOM!

I looked up to see a silhouette in the gathering light of the returning moon: a man with a broad-brimmed hat, holding a shotgun still smoking. It was the Gray Man. By the time I took my eyes off of him to look around, all the other guys were long gone.

I started to cry. "Let me go!" He made no response, looking and listening into the woods as if he didn't realize I was there, like he'd forgotten that he was holding me.

"Help! Come back!" I yelled to the boys, "Lee! Durant!"

The man and I both listened for their response, but heard only the wind whistling through the trees, sending the autumn leaves hurtling to the graveyard ground to start another cycle: life, death, regeneration.

"You and me ought to have us a little talk," he murmured.

"No!" I screamed. "Leave me alone!" I made as if I was going to bite him. He didn't move. Remembering what he looked like in the daylight, I decided that I didn't want any part of him in my mouth. I had enough problems without catching an incurable case of Gray Man Cooties.

He looked down at me patiently. "You don't want to be out here all by yourself, boy. You know how to get home?"

I started to cry again.

He talked to me real soft, like I'd heard him talking to the dying deer. I had to stop crying to hear what he was saying.

"You all right, boy," he soothed. "You just need some better friends, that's all is wrong with you."

"What are you gonna do?" I asked, not knowing what the possibilities were but unable to imagine that any of them would be much to my liking.

"What you want me to do?"

"I want you to take me home."

"I can't do that. Neither you nor me know how to get you there, and I ain't 'bout to spend the whole night wanderin' around in the dark tryin' to find out. 'Sides, it's goin' to rain pretty soon, comin' up a storm."

Somewhere in the distance, a dog howled. It sounded lonely and cheerless, outside at night with a storm gathering. But at least it was right outside its own house—I didn't even know which direction my house was.

"Well, just leave me here by myself then. My brother will come back for me and take me home," I bluffed.

"Your brother is Lee, right? The one the little weasel boy shamed into throwin' mud on me down there at the fishin' hole? He ain't comin' back, boy, you know he ain't. He's already makin' up a story to tell your mama how it's your fault you ain't with 'em. Ain't that 'bout right?"

I felt my blood running cold in my arms and legs as I realized the truth in what he was saying. Then, for the first time, I thought about what was likely to happen.

Mama would wait the next morning for me to call to ask her to come get me. She'd wait until just before lunch, when she figured I was about to become an imposition on Nelson's mother. Then she'd call and find out that I'd never been there at all. She would be hurt and angry. When Lee came back, she'd ask him if he knew where I was, and he'd lie: "No, ma'am." And Mama would cry and worry, and Daddy would clench his jaws and wait with steel in his eyes for me to come home.

The Gray Man put his hand on my shoulder and brought me back to the moment. "Tell you what. I'll take you home tomorrow mornin'. Tonight we can stay at my place."

I didn't want to go; I wasn't sure I could trust him.

"That's 'bout the best I can do, boy."

"Why are you here?" I asked him.

"I live down here."

"Down here in the woods?"

"Yep. My daddy and my boy is both buried in that graveyard."

"Oh. Sorry." His father, his son? It hadn't occurred to me that somebody like this would have had a family. We'd been knocking over their tombstones; that's why he had scared the others away. But not me. "Why did you hold me? Why didn't you let me run, too?"

"I was tryin' to scare them other boys, but I didn't want to scare you."

"Why not?"

"Why didn't you throw mud on me that day at the creek?"

"Huh?"

"Why didn't you go on and hit me with that stick that day I had to kill that doe? Why didn't you call me names when the other boys did?"

I eyed him suspiciously, and he eyed me suspiciously back. Confused, I asked him, "Who *are* you?"

He thought for a moment and then seemed to make a decision. "We ought to have us a little talk," he repeated. I had no response, so I just looked at my feet. He continued, "It's goin' to come up a hard rain 'fore long. Look, boy, I'm goin' home. It's just down this hill, at the top of that hill over there."

Without another word, he turned and walked off humming a mournful tune. I didn't want to go with him, but I knew it was pointless to wait for Lee and the guys to come back, and it didn't make sense just to stand in the coming rain.

Away in the night, the dog howled as the moon briefly came out of hiding again, and it harmonized with some lonely notes deep down inside me. I looked in the direction the Gray Man had gone, and wished I was home, too.

I felt a few cold drops of rain then, and a gust of cooler air. I was sad, lost, lonely, and betrayed. And, along with all those other things, I was soon to be either wet or in the home of a man I didn't know.

A few more drops of rain, and my skin decided the issue for me. I started up the hill. It was dark; the moon was through for the night. I scraped my shin on a vine or sapling.

Then it started to rain in earnest. I lost track of which way to go. "Hey, mister!"

"Over here, boy." His voice sounded like he was only a few feet away, off to my left, but I couldn't see him.

"Where are you?"

"Just follow my voice, boy. That's it. Keep on comin'. On over this way."

I still didn't know which way to go, and with the rain and the dark I may have never found him; I couldn't see. So I stood still, with no thought of going anywhere or doing anything, until a huge hand closed over my wrist and pulled me directly at what I thought was a large tree. It looked as if he was going to pull me right into it, but the hand brought me around to the right and behind it. Between the big tree and another smaller tree was an odd, low, dark opening. The hand drew me into it, pulling me past something cold and wet. Then suddenly I was no longer outside; I was inside, in a place like no place I'd ever been.

It was a small room, too low for the man to stand, barely high enough for me. As my eyes adjusted to the light, my mind tried to adjust to where I was.

It's hard to describe the Gray Man's home. Imagine the numbers of a dial on a pear-shaped clock, with the stem on the small end at twelve. Now lay the pear-clock down, with the stem away from you. That was the shape of his home, roughly, defined by trees in the walls at three, four, six, eight, and nine o'clock. It was about twelve feet long, and about six feet wide at its widest. On a line between ten and two were three cedar fence posts, holding up a piece of plywood for a ceiling in the smaller end, which had been dug out of the hill. The wall on the far end, from eleven to about twelve-thirty, was a big green sign with white letters that read "Quaker State." It wasn't large, but was clearly a complete home for the Gray Man.

At about nine-thirty was a small smoldering fire in a little fireplace made of clay and a few bricks. I wondered if they'd belonged to Mr. Haskins, too, like the bricks of my creek dam. To the left of the fireplace, an ax rested on a stack of wood. To the right was a shelf built into the chimney, holding a small stack of lumpy-looking bowls and cups. And on the fire, hanging from an iron hook worked into the fireplace bricks, was a black cast-iron pot with something bubbling and steaming out from under the heavy lid. I realized all at once that whatever was in the pot was making the whole place smell the way it did, that it was aromatic and appetizing, that it had been a while since I'd eaten, and that I hadn't eaten much then.

"You hungry, boy?"

"Uh, nope." Then, remembering my manners, "No sir."

He got two of the lumpy bowls down from the shelf and put them side by side in front of the fireplace. "Got another spoon 'round here somewheres."

As he searched for the stray utensil, I looked around. His home was in two distinct parts. The back seemed to be mostly a place for storage, occupied by two tackle boxes, several wooden boxes holding cans of food, a few pots and pans, and some rumpled clothing. Next to the boxes hung a saw, and behind that was a larger stack of firewood. In the front, beside the fireplace and hearth, there was just room for a plastic bucket of water covered with a towel, and a sleeping bag. On the wall by the sleeping bag hung a shelf he'd made from a wooden Coca-Cola crate, which held an unlit candle, an old black book, and a small framed picture of somebody. I couldn't make out who it might be, just that the person seemed to be wearing a hat.

"You thirsty?" he asked as he searched through a milk crate filled with pots and pans.

"No sir."

I was just about to go over and look at the picture when he found an old stainless steel spoon. He gave me the spoon with some pride, and then got one of the lumpy cups down from the shelf and dipped it into the bucket of water. I truthfully hadn't thought I was thirsty until I saw him drinking. I guess he saw me looking thirsty. He looked at me long and hard and then got another cupful. He drank it slowly, and it made me even thirstier.

He smiled a little then. It was the first time I'd seen him smile, and I remember thinking that it seemed like that's the way his face was supposed to be, but it rarely was. It made me feel glad to give him something to smile about.

"What's your name, boy?"

"Buddy. Buddy Hinton."

"My name's Jake. You don't trust me, do you, Buddy?"

I was startled, not only at the question, but that he was talking to me like I was a grown-up, and that he would even care whether I trusted him or not. I didn't know what to say, so I just stood there, looking at him.

"Look, boy, I ain't goin' to hurt you none. You got no need to be 'fraid of me. Or to lie to me."

"I'm not lying!"

"Sure you are. You hungry, you thirsty; you know it, I know it. The water's fresh, I got it this mornin'. The bucket's clean, so's the cup. The stew'll be tasty, I think. Even if it ain't no good, it's warm, and you're cold and wet."

I started to say something—it seemed like time to say something—but I didn't have anything to say. He was right, and we both knew it.

Jake chuckled. "You goin' to tell me you ain't wet? You ain't cold?" Another fitting smile improved his face, like polishing a dirty old car until it looks like it did on the showroom floor. It also raised my level of trust. "Here, drink some water. I'll get you some stew."

I drank from the lumpy cup he handed me. It wasn't cold, but it was more than satisfying. When he handed me a lumpy bowl, I tasted the stew cautiously, suspiciously, but after the first taste I ate with conviction. It was delicious, and I was hungry. I thought about asking him what it was, partly to make conversation and partly to find out what I was eating, but then I remembered that it was bad manners. Also, I worried that knowing what was in the stew might spoil an otherwise wonderful meal, so I backed away from the thought before it could get too far.

When we were both finished, Jake took the bowls and spoons, put them into another plastic bucket he got from the back, and poured some water into it. He took the pot off the hook and put it outside. He picked several pieces of wood to put on the fire, and poked at it until it was lively. Then he got a pipe and some tobacco from a small wooden box behind the head of the sleeping bag, tampered with it a bit, and lit it with a match. The smoke went up the chimney. Then he settled back on the sleeping bag, leaning against a pine tree. I'd never seen somebody enjoying sitting so thoroughly.

"You got questions, boy. Now would be a fine time to ask 'em."

He was right again. I did have questions, and I asked them, for what seemed like hours. Now, decades later, I don't remember his answers, and certainly not in any semblance of the order he gave them to me. I'm sure I've forgotten some of the questions I asked, and maybe I've put in a few that I asked later. But I believe the following is reasonably close.

"Is this where you live?"

"Yes sir, this is it."

"How long have you lived here?"

"'Bout seven years."

"Why do you live down here in the woods?"

"I want to stay close to my boy."

"How long has he been, uh . . ."

I couldn't say it, so Jake did for me. "Dead? 'Bout twenty-one years."

"Where did you live before?"

"Some things you don't want to know, boy."

I was afraid I'd hurt his feelings then, but there was his fitting, easy smile again, like a dog that had been cooped up running free, encouraging me to keep asking.

"Do you have a car?"

"No sir. Hell, I ain't even got a road!" I was surprised that he said "hell"; I'd heard adults cussing before, but only when they thought all the kids were out of earshot.

"Do you have any money?"

"Not much. But they ain't much I need."

"Why are those cups so, uh, lumpy?"

"I made those cups and bowls and whatnot out of some clay I got in the creek, fired 'em right here in my fireplace. They ain't much, but they hold water or stew pretty good, sure do. You like 'em?"

"Yes sir." There was an uneasy pause while I considered what might be appropriate to ask. "Do you have any friends? Or family?"

"No."

"What's your house made of?"

"It's sort of a circle of trees, with cane-thatch walls. The roof's cane thatch, too, with garbage bags to keep the rain out. Back there," nodding toward the storage part, "is dug into the hill."

"How old are you?"

"Fifty-eight."

"Do you have a job?"

"I catch fish."

"And sell 'em?"

"Right." A longer pause, and as I tried to figure out how to ask what I wanted to know, he told me, as if he were almost asleep: "A long time ago I was a preacher. But I ain't now, not no more." Then it was like he woke up. "Now I catch fish, mostly catfish and buffalo, and sell 'em."

I was relieved to be back on easier ground. "Who do you sell 'em to?"

Obviously remembering Durant's question at the creek, he gave Purvis's answer, but this time with a big grin. "Other niggers, 'course."

I was scared again for a second, but then I saw that wonderful, patient, wise smile, and I realized he was making fun of the Calhoun boys, and I relaxed. Our dislike for Purvis and Durant was something we held in common.

"They's a fish house on the Ridge Road that buys all I can catch. Mr. Howell runs it; he don't give me much, but it's enough. It works out pretty good for both of us."

He puffed on his pipe for a little while then, and I watched the fire. I wanted to ask him about being a preacher, but I didn't want to make him mad. Still, he'd invited me to ask whatever I wanted. I worked up my courage, he drew on his pipe, the fire settled a little. Finally I asked, "You were a preacher?"

He looked at me like I'd reminded him of a great pain, and crawled toward the deerskin doorway. As he crawled out into the night, he said, "Yessir, I sure was."

After a while I crawled out, too. I was afraid maybe he'd left me down in the woods alone. It had stopped raining, but a lot of big heavy drops were still falling from the trees. I heard him before I could see him; he was whistling a melancholy, mournful tune. Even at ten years old, I could hear his soul connecting to the sweet notes he blew. I came to love that tune. I learned to hum it before I could whistle it, and long before I realized that it had words that went with it.

The Gray Man was leaning on a tree, his back to me twenty or thirty feet away from his home, looking up into the night sky. The rain had passed for the moment, and the moon had gone back to dancing in and out of the clouds. It was getting cooler; I could see my breath in the moonlight. I thought about asking him to take me home, but decided against it. So I just stood there listening, not knowing what to do or say. And he just leaned there whistling for what seemed like a long time. I soaked the tune in as surely as the rain had soaked into my clothes, and I decided I wanted to learn how to whistle.

At last he spoke. He didn't turn around to face me; he just spoke aloud words I will always remember, in a voice I could believe had belonged to a preacher. "They ain't many boys know how to be quiet, thank you. Hear me say this now: the mysteries is ever before us."

I couldn't tell if he was talking about the sky or about God; I had no idea what he was saying. I said, "Huh?"

He turned to look at me. "You got a lot of questions, Buddy, and you know how to listen. That's good, that's real good. Now you is startin' to dig around in things you ain't goin' to understand easy."

It was exciting and scary, and not just a little threatening. It was like something that one of the bad guys would say in a comic book. I murmured, "I'm sorry," because it seemed appropriate, but I wasn't sure what I was apologizing for.

He laughed a laugh that filled all the space between us and the limbs of the trees over our heads. "No, boy, you ain't got nothin' to be sorry 'bout. You ain't askin' nothin' I ain't goin' to tell you. I just ain't much used to talkin' anymore, that's all."

He motioned to a fallen sweet gum tree, and then he went and straddled the trunk, leaning against a large branch that was coming out, reaching for the sun. The tree had somehow survived its fall and continued to grow. It was big enough for us both to sit on, and he patted a worn space beside him. I sat down. He tapped all the tobacco out of his pipe, knocking it against his shoe before putting it in his pants pocket. Then he said, “Listen here, boy. It’s late at night, and it may be you want to go ahead on to sleep. But if you ain’t sleepy, I’d be glad to tell you how I wound up here.”

I wasn’t at all sleepy and was completely fascinated by this Gray Man. “Yes sir. Please tell me.”

4

Not Near Long Enough

And he did. He talked a long time that first night, and I'm pretty sure I slept through some of it. It's impossible now to remember when he said what, whether on that first night out on the fallen sweet gum or through the years as I heard this story several more times, but as close as I can remember, this is how he told his story.

"I was born right here in Beaumont, Miss'ippi, on January twenty-third, in Nineteen and Oh-Five. My father used to say I was born on 'one two three oh five.' He was a preacher, my father was, the Reverend Joe Jefferson. He preached up at the Second Baptist Church in Beaumont for a while, but had to leave 'cause of some dispute or whatnot, and that's when he went to tent preachin' instead. But he walked close to the Lord, my Daddy did, walked real close.

"I was seven when I began to preach at my daddy's services, mostly just playin' like I was him. It just caught on, though, sure did, and before long I was a regular part of his travelin' tent preachin.' By the time I was twelve or thirteen, all my daddy did under the tent was to welcome folks there, introduce me, and take up the money and whatnot. I did all the preachin' myself, yessir: 'Come hear Little Jacob Jefferson, the Gospel of the Lord out of the Mouth of a Child.' Then after the peoples left, we'd put that big ol' tent back in the wagon and hitch up the mules to go on to the next town.

"I don't really remember my mama much at all . . . just never there."

I remember interrupting the Gray Man then. "She was never there?" I asked, because I saw that sadness that came over him and almost put out the sparkle in his eyes.

He lamented, "No, *I* was never there.

"For a while me and Daddy was on the road together. They was happy, hard-workin' days, when I knowed we was doin' the work of God. Daddy taught me how to read, so's I could read the Book. I believed all that stuff and whatnot way back then."

"What book?" I asked. "All what stuff?"

"I'm talkin' 'bout the Bible, 'bout God and Jesus, and such as that."

I was amazed. Was he saying he didn't believe it now? I'd heard about people who didn't believe in God, but they were Godless Heathens, people to avoid. And here I was with a real live Godless Heathen; he seemed to be a pleasant and sensible man. And there was a certain reverence in his voice when he talked about the Book, a reverence that had never left him.

If he even noticed my incredulity, he disregarded it and continued. "Now, is we goin' to chat, or is you goin' to listen to what I am sayin'?"

"Oh. Sorry."

"I married Chantille Preston in nineteen and twenty-three, when I was eighteen. She was a beautiful light-skinned woman from up in Greenville, looked like she had money and class, too. She just took me all by storm, yes sir; I'd never had any woman pay me much mind before. Daddy had always told me to stay away from womens we met on the road, said it was easy for them to see you shinin' up there in the pulpit; said you ain't always goin' to shine so bright like that. 'Don't never go with no woman who would go with a preacher,' Daddy said. He never did like Chantille, no sir, never did like her much at all.

"Daddy died that next year, when I was nineteen. I never worked so hard as that to preach a sermon, as hard as I did to find what to say as when I went to preach his funeral. All that religious whatnot is different when it's your own peoples dyin' and gettin' buried and such as that. Still, we did it up right, the way I used to think a funeral ought to be preached: we went into it all sad and cryin', and came out with love and joy and hope. We buried him right up there in that graveyard where you boys was playin'. Had a pretty good crowd, too. They used to be an old church out here somewheres; the church is long gone now, but graveyards last forever, I reckon.

"The next year, in nineteen and twenty-five, my son Joseph was born, a fine, smart, good-lookin' boy. I named him after my daddy. He favored his mother, with her nose and eyes and color. He loved the Lord, too, just like . . . just like my daddy did.

"Pretty soon after that, the Depression hit. Took a while for us to feel it down here, but when it got here, it hit us pretty hard, yes sir, hit us pretty hard. Peoples would still come to the preachin'; they just didn't have much money to put into the collection plate. But that was fine with me. They'd give me a meal and a place in they house to sleep, and the next day I'd get up and go on. I was preachin' hope back then, and hopin' it, too. And the peoples was eatin' it up, too, boy, just eatin' it right on up.

"The church preachers didn't like it, though . . . didn't like a travelin' preacher comin' through, stealin' they thunder. 'Course, times was hard for them, too, and I guess I was takin' money out of they collection plates when they peoples came to listen to me. They'd preach against me, in the beginnin', tell they peoples to stay away. And a lot of 'em did, too. But not all of 'em.

"Those was hard times, but they was happy, too. When I didn't have someplace to take the preachin', I went home to Chantille and Joseph. My mama was gone by then. I didn't never see her again after Daddy's funeral. So Chantille and Joseph was livin' in the old house in Beaumont. 'Course, Chantille didn't like it. She didn't never like much at all, really. She was the contrariest, gripin'est woman I ever did meet. She hated Beaumont, wanted to go to Memphis, said I needed to hit the big time. 'They got some big ol' churches up there,' she would say. 'We could get you one and settle down.' I wrote a couple of letters and sent 'em up that way, but nothin' ever come of it. So she just fussed and complained, and I s'pose I figured that was the way she wanted to be.

"Somewhere along the way, I realized I didn't want to be goin' home at all, except for Joseph. Oh, dear God, I can still see his small face clear as I see your own, his sweet little face, the way his eyes would light all up when he laughed. And when I come home he would run out into the yard to hug my neck and hold me with his little arms, real tight for just a short moment, never long enough, not near long enough. And then it was time for him to show me what he could do. 'I can jump high,' he'd say, or 'I can hit that can with a rock,' or one day I come home and he told me he could whistle now. Near broke my heart; he wanted to whistle 'cause it was like me, but I hadn't been there to teach him.

"Way back then, I thought a lot 'bout sellin' the tent and doin' somethin' else. One time I went to see a man 'bout a job at the sawmill, even agreed with him that I'd take it. Would have been a good job, too, a steady job. Lot of times now I think back on that, and wonder how things might have been, how different my life would have been. But it didn't seem right somehow, didn't seem like what I ought to be doin'. I packed the tent into the truck and set out, just left the sawmill man waitin' for me to come to work.

"Then, in Nineteen and Thirty-Seven, I got a big break, a half-hour preachin' show on the radio. Five radio stations in Miss'ippi and Louisiana all sendin' me preachin' out over the radio waves, mostly late at night, five stations. A white man from Natchez, Mr. Buskins, he heard me preachin' when I was comin' through Woodville and St. Francisville, and I s'pose he was impressed. Mr. Buskins owned these five radio stations, and he told me he wanted to put me on the air, put my preachin' on the radio. Said he'd give me two free months, to build up my base of support. Said I'd need to ask for contributions on the air, to raise money for airtime, as he wouldn't be able to continue to just give it away. Said it was the opportunity of a lifetime. Said the Lord needed a good colored man to preach some sense to the other colored folks. Said it was a callin' from God to put my message out in the big time. Said my ship had come in.

"By Nineteen and Forty I was on thirteen stations, and they wasn't all so late at nights anymore. Chantille's brother Archie had come around to help me with arrangements, drivin' the truck, gettin' local mens to help set up the tent, whatnot such as that. It left me more time to study and think 'bout what all I needed to say, and to record my radio messages. When we came to a town, Archie would go all over and put up some flyers with my picture on it on telephone poles and whatnot, and under the picture it he'd write, 'The Reverend Jacob J. Jefferson, Evangelist, Elder, and Prophet.' Archie handled all the details, and after a while, he took care of the money, too.

"Those was good times, busy times. Seemed like the peoples knowed me wherever I went. When it came my time to talk, them peoples would listen, yes sir, they was listenin' hard. It's a terrible thing to have peoples believe ever'thing you say, you start to thinkin' you're somethin' special, like nothin' you say ain't goin' to be wrong. It's a terrible thing, like somethin' callin' out to you to take yourself more serious than a body ought to.

"After a while Archie was havin' some trouble with the liquor. A couple of times I had to bail him out of jail. Each time he'd beg my forgiveness and tell me he was goin' to repent. I was hopin' he'd find the right woman, somebody to help settle him down. They was several womens, but he never had none of 'em on a regular basis.

"I believe it was in the summer of Forty when a woman came up to the front of the tent where I'd been preachin'. I'd already preached up and down, and was mostly through, 'cept for the offerin' and the call to dedication, when this poor ol' raggedy-lookin' woman was pushed up by a crowd of peoples. We was 'bout to have some special music to be sung by some local woman, and I was sittin' up there fannin' myself and tryin' to look like I was official and important. This woman's peoples brung her up to the front and pointed her toward me with a little push. Then I sees that the woman is blind, looks like she can't see nothin' at all. She comes up all meek and timid like I'm the king of England or somethin', like she was a mouse, afraid to get too close. I asked her what did she want, and she whispered somethin' so quiet I couldn't hear. I asked her to repeat it, but I still couldn't hear. I told her to wait a minute, 'til the music stopped.

"When the music stopped, I bent over to hear what did she want, and she 'bout hollered, loud enough for me and most ever'body else in that tent to hear, 'I want you to *heal* me!' Seems as she had heard me on the radio, talkin' 'bout how Jesus went 'round healin', how all healin' comes from God if we would just have faith to receive that healin'. She claimed she had the faith, that she wanted me to put my hands on her and heal her. Well, hell, I didn't know nothin' 'bout healin' nobody; I didn't know what to do. It didn't occur to me at the time to wonder why she wasn't timid all of a sudden when ever'body could hear her.

"I believed in healin', and in miracles, they's in the Book and whatnot. I just didn't know nothin' 'bout no miracles done by me. I thought I'd been called to preachin', never really thought 'bout healin' nobody. The whole tent was as quiet as a snake in a graveyard, ever'-body watchin' me, waitin' to see what was I goin' to do. Right 'bout then I heard my brother-in-law Archie behind me. He said, 'Just put your hands on her eyes and tell her she been healed by the power of God!' Yep, ol' Archie Preston tellin' me, 'Have a little faith, preacher.'

"I put my hands on her eyes and prayed that God would give her back her sight. It was real awkward that first time; I felt like I was tellin' God what to do. I wasn't really 'spectin' much, but I was wrong. The woman let out a whoop and fell down grabbin' her eyes and all—when she stood up, she hugged me real tight and turnt around to the peoples and hollered, 'I can see!' And sure enough, she could!

"She could sure see, sure could, after that. She read some verses right out of the Book, right there in front of all of us. It occurred to me then and there to see was she really blind to start with. But as I watched her gettin' hugged and 'gratulated, and all them peoples was hollerin' and prayin' and praisin' Jesus, they was believin' things I'd been tryin' to say, seems like most of 'em was either linin' up to be healed or goin' home to get they sick folks. It seemed like unbelief if I was to ask much 'bout it. And I still ain't sure—it may be she *was* healed. Hell, I don't rightly know, I still don't."

Somewhere in the telling of this story, the clouds covered the moon convincingly, and then big fat raindrops found their way through the canopy of oaks and sweet gum trees. Jake stood up and went back into his little house without looking to see if I would follow. I did, and he continued his story inside.

"After that blind woman could see, peoples would come up for healin' almost ever' time we set up the tent, they sure would. Peoples walkin' with limps, peoples with arthritis, deaf peoples, peoples with bad hearts or back pain or various ailments and whatnot, all kinds of peoples with all kinds of problems and whatnot. Some of 'em walked away with the limps and aches they brung, but some . . . I still had my doubts; some of 'em I thought just wanted to be healed so bad they made theyselves believe they was. Others I thought might have been fakin' so they could get up and make a big to-do 'bout theyselfs. But some . . . at least it seemed at the time, some I thought was healed. And it may be they was, it could be, it may be they was. I don't really know.

"Well, 'course the crowds grew then. Now we'd roll into a town and seems like most times they'd be 'spectin' us. Archie got him an assistant, a tall skinny sneaky-lookin' boy named Leon. Leon would go all 'round town puttin' up posters, big ol' posters with a picture of me on it, and under the picture it was wrote, 'The Rev. Jacob J. Jefferson, Called by God Almighty to Prophecy, Preach, and HEAL.'

"We had to get us a bigger tent made, and borrow some chairs from the local churches wherever we went. Now the preachers would come out and help us set up, wanted to introduce me to the crowds, have they pictures taken with me. Now all of a sudden they was on our side, seemed like. My preachin' was on damn near thirty stations then on the radio, near thirty.

"We got us a full-time piano player, a clean little boy named Geoffrey, and he recruited some womens to travel with us for a choir; four great big ol' fat colored womens. Two of 'em was named Patricia, but I don't remember the other two's names. I've never seen peoples that could sweat like those four. And you talk 'bout peoples that could eat, they sure could put some groceries away. Sometimes I told Archie I believed those four could eat they own weight in fried chicken, and that was somethin' considerable.

"But they could sure sing, they sure could. Sounded like a little bit of the heavenly host right down here amongst us. So we called 'em the Jacob's Ladder Chorus. I told the peoples they music was a sweet soul-savin' connection between Heaven and down here where we is. They sure could sing, yes sir, sweet as Heaven itself.

"So we got us quite a name back then, and we was doin' all right. We traveled all through Louisiana, Miss'ippi, up into Tennessee, a little bit in Alabama, even over into Arkansas. My boy Joseph was with me then, went with us on the road 'til he joined the Army, but that was later, durin' World War Two, when he turnt eighteen.

"One summer evenin' in Tuscaloosa, Alabama, we had so many peoples wantin' to hear the preachin' that we had to hold services at the Negro League baseball field. Archie told me they was nearly four thousand peoples there, all crowded up into the bleachers behind home plate and halfway up the first base line.

"He might have been stretchin' it some, but not by much; I had to stand on home plate and yell at 'em through the screen fence. I preached until the sun went down, and then them folks just sat there in the dark, listenin' to me preach, and listenin' to them big women sing. They didn't have no lights at the baseball field, or I would've preached some more. We took up a whoppin' big collection that night, must've had a couple hundred peoples give theyselves to Jesus. Archie got drunk as hell that night, just drunk as hell; I had to go get him out of the Tuscaloosa County Jail.

"We thought we was really somethin' then, boy, we was really somethin' extra special. Next mornin' we started talkin' 'bout leavin' the tent and goin' just to baseball stadiums, just goin' to the big towns. Archie was talkin' big then, sayin' we was ready to hit the big time. The war had started in nineteen and forty-one, and peoples was lookin' for a little hope, and the fields was ripe for harvest. Oh, yes sir, Buddy, we dreamed us some big dreams that day, some real big dreams.

"I tol' Archie to cancel the next few stops, and then I caught the afternoon train west. I set out right for home, takin' all my hopin' and dreamin' with me. Joseph wanted to come with me, but I told him I needed him to stay there, and look out after Archie.

"But really, the truth was I wanted to talk to Chantille by myself. I thought she'd be proud, I thought at last she'd be happy with me. I wanted to see what she had to say 'bout me now, see was she satisfied with her man. I figured it may be I could take her with me, if we was goin' to the big towns, I thought I ought to see did she want to go. I was hopin' this could make things right between us. Things had been pretty bad for a real long time by then.

"By the time the train got to Vicksburg, I had wrote up a list of where I was goin' to take her: Birmin'ham, Mobile, Baton Rouge, Jackson, and Memphis. We'd spend a few days extra in Memphis, stay at one of them big fancy downtown hotels. And after that, we might even go to New Orleans. I always wanted to go to New Orleans, sure did. Yes sir, we was dreamin' some big dreams then, we sure was.

"I rode that train all night, and got into Vicksburg in the middle of the mornin'. I tried to call Chantille from the train station, but she didn't answer. A man I used to know saw me and asked me did I need a ride, said he was goin' to Beaumont anyways. He said it may be I could just surprise her at home. And I sure did, too—I sure did.

"That fella carried me out to the ol' house, took me right up to the driveway. I thanked him and offered him some money, but he didn't want none. The sun was shinin', the birds was singin', it was a beautiful spring day, seemed like ever'thing was just the way it ought to be.

"I stopped in the yard to pick her some flowers, some sort of yellow flowers growin' there in the yard. And I went up on the porch, tryin' to walk quiet so I could surprise her. Then I opened up that door and I heard her voice, sayin' some things I ain't goin' to tell you. She was with another man. You understand that, boy? It'd be like your mama kissin' somebody that ain't your daddy, you know what I'm talkin' 'bout?"

It was hard enough for me to imagine my mother kissing my father, but I nodded so Jake would keep telling his story.

"I crept on up to the door of the bedroom as quiet as I could on that creaky ol' floor. The door didn't shut all the way, hadn't for years. They was a gap up near the top of the door. Back when we used to have relations, we worried could Joseph see us through that crack between the door and the frame. But we was all messed up a long time before he was tall enough to look through it."

Right about then, while I was still wondering what "relations" might be, I heard something out in the dark night, snagging at my awareness. I suspected I might need to pay attention to it, but just then I was caught up in the story, so I ignored it, and Jake, who didn't look like he'd heard anything, kept talking. He told me that he tiptoed to the door and looked in, and that his wife was having relations with a man who worked at a bank in Vicksburg.

"I rared back and kicked the door as hard as I could. I was tryin' to break the door down and bust in, like I'd seen in a movie one time. But all I did was make a lot of noise and twist my ankle. Then they was yellin' and tryin' to get up and get dressed, and I got up and turnt the doorknob and opened the door.

"The man was tryin' to put on his silly-lookin' underwear, big ol' white shorts with red dots all over 'em, an' hoppin' around on one foot. Chantille had the sheet pulled up over her to her chin. He looked at me and yelled, 'Who the hell are you?' She yelled out, 'Oh, God, no!' But they wasn't no God there, no sir, not there, not then. I tried to say somethin', but I couldn't. I was tryin' to remember somethin' from a movie to say, but it didn't really feel like a movie—seemed like it wasn't as real as that. Mostly I s'pose I was just glad for a excuse to finally be free of Chantille. Still, here was my one chance to hit a man, and feel good and righteous 'bout it."

The something I'd heard was getting closer, louder. It seemed to be more than one noise, maybe two or three woven together. I looked to Jake, unsure if he wanted to keep talking, but it didn't seem like he'd heard anything at all.

"So, I figured, what do I have to lose? He done stole my wife away already. I walked right up to the man. By this time he was tryin' to get his pants on. He asked me again who the hell I was. I didn't make no answer, and was just 'bout to decide I wasn't goin' to hit him after all, when he turnt to Chantille, and asked her, 'Is this your daddy?' When he looked my way again, I hit him as hard as I could with my fist, catchin' him right 'bout here." Jake pointed to the left side of his face, above the eye.

"I knocked him down, sure did, and broke my right hand to boot. He sat on the floor stunned for a little while, then got up and put his pants on. He carried his shoes and shirt out, and then he was gone. I sat on the bed that used to be mine, but now belonged to that white man, and I thought I ought to cry. I knowed it would be good for me, but I just couldn't make it come. All I could do was hold my right hand in my left, hang my head down over my belly, and wonder what was I goin' to do next."

5

Now You Got to Decide

Now the noises were voices, and I could hear what they were saying. "Buddy! Buddy? *Buddy!*"

It was Lee, his friend Clayton, and the Calhoun brothers, out looking for me and calling my name. And I was conflicted.

I have to admit I felt a distinct sense of satisfaction that Lee was worried about me, after I'd been so grievously mistreated by him and his friends on the campout. More deeply than I'm comfortable admitting, I cherished the possibility that maybe he loved me after all. I was also keenly aware that they were out in the rain and I was warm and dry. But that happy moment was all too brief and was soon replaced by a bitter and unwelcome stab of conscience, knowing that I was the reason for their discomfort.

I said, "Excuse me, sir?"

Jake had gotten his pipe back out and was scraping away at the inside of the bowl with his pocketknife, his story and his guest momentarily forgotten. He looked a little surprised that there was someone talking to him, but he recovered himself enough to reply with some nonchalance. "Hmm?"

"Well, it's just that . . . that's my brother Lee and his friends, yelling for me."

"All right."

"Do you hear them?"

"Been hearin' 'em."

"Why didn't you stop?"

"I'm just gettin' to the good part."

"Why'd you stop now?"

"I figured you was 'bout to interrupt me."

"Oh." He was right about that, and now that I had started the interruption, I needed to get on with it. "I need to tell them I'm okay, and then I'll be right back."

"Well, now, I'd just as soon you didn't do that."

"But they're looking for me."

"It ain't goin' to hurt 'em none to keep on lookin' for a while."

"But don't you want them to find me?"

"Well, sure I do, sure I do. But it'd be fine with me if they find you in the mornin'." He saw my uncertainty, and added, "I ain't all that interested in them boys knowin' where I live, you understand?"

"Yes sir. I'll just run out and tell them I'm fine, and then I'll come right back."

"An' you think your brother just goin' to let you wander off into the dark? You think he goin' to say to his friends, 'My brother's okay, so let's go'? That ain't the way it'd be. They goin' to have to know where you been. They goin' to want to get out of the rain."

"Yes sir, but—"

"And then them boys would know where I live. Them same boys who threw mud on me when I was fishin' would be up in my house. Them same boys who been kickin' over grave markers 'cause it's 'only niggers' buried up there. Hell, I'd have to go find a new place, build a new house. No, thank you."

"But it's raining hard out there! They're out in the rain because they're looking for me!"

"The way I see it, I rescued you from a lot of rain and a long night with them mean boys, too. I'll take you in for the night, but I don't want none of them up in here. Now you got to decide where you want to be—out there with them or in here with me."

It was a difficult, critical moment. On the one hand, the idea of letting Lee and his friends just walk on by made me feel miserable, deceitful. My parents had drilled it into each of their children that we stick together, that we take care of each other. This was more than letting Lee walk around out in the rain; it seemed like disloyalty to my family. On the other hand, a different part of me newly born desperately wanted to stay with this man, to hear his story. I've often wondered how different my life would have been if I'd gone back out into the rain right then.

I didn't know what to say, so I was surprised to hear myself talking. As it happened, I got more than I bargained for. "How come you're okay with me knowing where you live?"

"'Cause . . . well, 'cause I trust you, Buddy. I ain't sure why, but I just do. You ain't like them other boys. They ain't no meanness in you, they sure ain't. You ain't one of them. You know it, and I know it, and there it is. I trust you, is all."

I was completely overwhelmed by the idea of being different from the other boys. Looking back on it, I should have been flattered, but at the time it felt threatening, like I would never fit in no matter how hard I tried, like there was something wrong with me. But even as he said it, I knew it was true.

I sat quietly, wrestling with all that, and he said gently, "Buddy, you think your brother or them other boys would be worryin' 'bout you if you was out there and they was in here?"

The absurdity of it drove his point in deeply enough to cause me pain. I was different. I didn't fit in. I had known it for a long time, but now someone had said out loud, and that made it real. I tried to sulk. "But you don't even know me."

"Well, that may be. But I see you, and I do know some things 'bout peoples. I can see you got a good heart. I 'spect I know who you are more'n I know you, really. Let's us see what I might know, you want to?"

With some apprehension, I nodded, fearful and excited, wondering what there could be to know about me. I don't think I knew that much about myself right then.

"Let's see here. I bet you don't like it when them other boys fight and fuss, do you?"

"How do you know they fight?"

"'Cause they's boys, and fightin' is just somethin' most boys seem to want to do. But I bet you'd ruther not fight if you can help it. Is that right?"

This had been something of a sore subject with me for a long time, something that had set me apart from the other guys: when an argument erupted between them, it was usually about something I didn't think was critical—whether the ball was in or out, whose turn it was to swing on the vine, whether we should play war or kickball. As hostilities inevitably began to escalate, I almost always stepped back. Part of this was because most of the boys I played with were older and bigger, but there was more to it than that. I tried not to take sides, even though that often meant everybody was mad at me for not siding with them. I just wanted everybody to get along.

"Yes sir," I admitted.

"And I bet other boys make fun of you because they say you're too nice, don't they?"

I nodded, and Jake went on. He opened me up, went to the table of contents and read me like a book.

"Sometimes you play with your sister, even though your friends poke at you about it."

He was right, and I nodded again.

"I bet you don't like scary picture shows."

This was true; every year when *The Wizard of Oz* came on television, I had to go into the kitchen to make a sandwich when the trees threw their apples at Dorothy and the Scarecrow. Then I'd have to get a glass of water when the Wicked Witch sent her Flying Monkeys after the four friends, and I went to the bathroom when she had them trapped in the castle. I had to listen carefully from afar, because I didn't want to miss the Witch's death soliloquy. One year a poorly timed flush made me miss that wonderful moment when she says, "I'm melting, melting! Oh, what a world, what a world!"

Jake puffed on his pipe and continued, "You spend a good bit of time alone, thinkin' your own thoughts. You like to write down some of your ideas and whatnot, but you don't ever want anybody else to read 'em.

"Sometimes you think of somethin' so funny it makes you laugh out loud. Or somethin' so sad it makes you want to cry.

"I bet when it's time for lunch at school, you'd ruther sit off a ways and see who might come and sit with you than to sit down amongst a bunch of your friends. I bet you spend most of your time talkin' about what they want to talk about, instead of getting them to talk about what you is interested in.

"I bet the boys you play with at school is boys nobody else wants to be around. I bet when you do get in a fight, it's to look after somebody like that, somebody smaller than you."

He was right on all counts, and I felt naked, exposed. It is an amazing thing to be known so fully, to be understood, to be trusted. I felt like I'd been given a precious and frightening gift, and I knew I'd made the right choice by staying. I listened to the boys' yelling as it became more and more distant, and I hoped that I wouldn't have to worry about it much longer.

Jake took another deep pull on his pipe. "How am I doin' so far?"

"Pretty good. How do you know all this?"

"Well, I spunt a fair amount of time at the Parchman Prison Farm"—I tried to turn my shocked gasp into a cough, but I don't think I was especially convincing—"and you got to learn how to read them mens up in there, or you'll get kilt. Most nights we didn't have much to do but play poker, and you got to read peoples, know who they are and whether they's lyin' to play poker, or you'll lose your shirt. So like I said, I don't really know you, but I see you. I know peoples, I know who you are."

"Was it scary in Parchman?'

"Yes sir, it sure was, 'specially at first. They's some tough mens up in there, they sure is. But after a while I found me some mens who was lookin' after one another, and they let me join up with them."

"Were they criminals?"

He laughed at that. "Yeah, they was criminals. But they was just mens, too. After a while, some of 'em came to be my friends."

"Is that who you played poker with?"

"Yes sir, most times it was with them. Sometimes I'd get in with some other mens, and then it wasn't 'bout playin' for fun: then we was playin' for loot."

"What's loot?"

"Well, in prison they's all kinds of loot. We'd play for money sometimes, but mostly for cigarettes or booze."

"What's booze?"

"Booze—you know, whiskey, gin, wine, and whatnot."

"You can get whiskey in prison?"

"You can get pretty near whatever you want at Parchman Farm. Everything 'cept a good friend, somebody you can really trust."

I wondered about Lee and how long they would search before they gave up. When I imagined how far they would walk down in the woods, I remembered it was one of my grandfather's favorite riddles: "How far can you go into the woods?" The answer is "halfway," because if you keep on going past halfway then you're on your way back out. I laughed out loud at the thought of it, and Jake nodded, his point made manifest by my laughing at my own thoughts.

I said, "You think Lee and them'll be okay?"

"Them boys? Sure they will, sure they will. Listen, Buddy—they wasn't goin' to get no sleep tonight noways, campin' out in all this rain and thunder and whatnot. Hell, they wasn't goin' to be much drier if they'd stayed in them little tents. At least this way they're not tryin' to be comfortable." I guess I didn't look convinced, and he went on. "They just goin' to walk around for a while, 'til them other boys talk your brother into givin' it up. Then they goin' to go back to where they tents are and see that everythin's all wet. Then they goin' to spend a great deal of time tryin' to start a fire, so they can dry everythin' off. They might even get one goin', I ain't sure 'bout that. Then they goin' to spend a great long time tryin' to figure how they goin' to explain all this to they parents, how come they was out in the woods on a night when no parent would let they chillun go campin', and how come they lost you. They goin' to be thinkin' the police is goin' to have to be called."

He paused a moment to draw some smoke through his pipe. It floated around a little before getting organized enough to go up the chimney. "They thinkin' they goin' to be asked some hard questions, and they need to get they answers straight. They ain't goin' to be in no hurry to go back home. Tell you what, how 'bout if we let 'em fret with it until sunup, then we'll go find 'em and let 'em know you doin' just fine, all right? We'll tell 'em you found someplace warm and dry and slept like a baby all night. How 'bout that?"

The tide of conflicting thoughts and emotions rushed back: satisfaction that Lee would be worried and guilt at my pleasure in the thought of it, but mostly relief that he'd be okay. A little discomfort on my behalf I could live with, but I didn't want him to be hurt or in any real trouble. I nodded, unable to speak and aware that Jake was watching me, reading me. I tried to will myself not to tear up because it would prove again how completely he knew me, but I didn't have much success.

6

When It's Dreadful Dark

To be honest, I don't remember what else Jake might have said that night. But over the years, the story he told became my favorite story to hear. I'd beg him to tell it again and again, and he'd use the same words and phrases, so that I could tell it along with him. After he told about hitting the banker in the silly-lookin' underwear, he would continue.

"When I looked up, Chantille was gone, too. I ain't never seen her again, and don't know whatever happened to her.

"I walked around in the house for a while that afternoon, just goin' into one room after the other. That night I caught a ride across the river to a place called T.C.'s Lounge, got as drunk as I could stomach, and hired me a woman who didn't want to talk too much. I don't guess I ever even knew her name; if I ever did, I don't remember it now.

"I woke up the next mornin' sittin' with my back up against the outside wall of T.C's. 'Parently they'd kicked me out and I couldn't think of no place else to go. My wallet was gone—all I had was a headache and a throbbin' right hand I didn't think me or Jesus could heal. By the time I got back to the Miss'ippi side, back home, Chantille had been back to the house and taken ever'thing she could find worth anything at all. By the time I thought to get to the bank in town, she had cleared out our account. It may be I owed that money to her anyways, I don't rightly know 'bout that. It don't matter, it don't matter at all.

"I found a telephone and called Joseph, waitin' for me in Tuscaloosa. I was callin' partly for some help, and partly because I was afraid Chantille might be tryin' to call him and her lowlife brother Archie soon, and I didn't want Archie to run off with all my money. I thought she might want to turn my Joseph against me, and I knew I couldn't have stood that.

"Joseph told me he hadn't heard from his mama, and he didn't know where his Uncle Archie was. He said he hadn't seen him since right after I left.

"I was relieved, but I knowed I was goin' to have to put a heavy load on my boy. Joseph was just sixteen when all this happened, none of it his fault, a heavy load for such young shoulders to have to carry.

"I told him his Uncle Archie was a drunk, and that he was probably in jail. I told him it would be best if he'd just leave Archie there, least 'til I got back. I told him his mother had herself another man, and she and I wasn't married no more, and I didn't know where she was. I told him not to give Archie no money for no reason. I told him to find out where they was a Western Union office, and told him to get two hundred dollars of our money out of the money box and wire it to me over the telegraph. He was confused, of course, off his balance. He asked me had I spunt all the money I took with me, and I had to tell him that I'd lost my wallet. It wasn't the whole truth, I couldn't . . . I never did tell him the whole truth. The boy needed somebody to believe in, even if it was only just me."

"Later on that afternoon, the money came, and I got on the train to go back to Tuscaloosa. I had nowhere else to go. By the time I got there, Archie had 'parently talked to his sister and must've figured that his road and mine had come to a fork. Leon was gone with him, which I was glad of, and so was them big fat sweaty women singers. I was sure glad I didn't have to feed them no more. I don't rightly know whatever happened to that piano player, I never was sure 'bout him, no ways.

"Nobody was waitin' on me but my boy Joseph, and he met me at the train station, met me like he used to when he was a tiny small boy, runnin' out to meet me in the yard. Now he was pretty near a growed-up man, but he still reached out and hugged me good and tight . . . and then I cried, yes sir, cried like a baby in the night, like I wasn't never goin' to stop.

"We went back to the hotel there and had us a long talk. I had to tell him what had happened and whatnot, and it wasn't easy, not for neither one of us. I didn't tell him 'bout T.C.'s, or that woman who stole my wallet. Joseph took it all pretty well, better than I think I could've. He stayed with me after that. I don't believe he ever saw his mama again.

"Next day we took off again, just him and me in our old truck with the tent in the back, just like me and my daddy had done back when I was a boy. But it was just different somehow, somethin' was missin'. I wasn't missin' Archie or Leon or nobody else; it was somethin' missin' inside of me.

"We stopped to set up the tent in a pasture outside of Eutaw, Alabama, I remember, and Joseph walked into town to put up the flyers to let folks know who we was, and why we was there. I hauled that big new tent out the back of the truck and onto the ground, and spread it all out on a level place, then went to get the canvas bag that held the stakes and the big hammer that drove 'em in. It had been years since I'd done that part of the ministry; I'd been leavin' it up to Archie and his help. I was lookin' forward to doin' some good honest hot hard work.

"In the bag I found Archie's last bitter gift to me: wrapped in a towel, a Mason jar of moonshine whiskey, almost full. I thought 'bout throwin' it away, into a ditch, down a hole. I knowed it was trouble, that whiskey. I thought 'bout pourin' it out, so Joseph wouldn't find it and mess hisself up. God, I wish I'd gotten rid of that damn whiskey! But I didn't. I hid it away somewhere in the truck instead.

"That night, a crowd came in and sat down in the chairs we'd set up for 'em. They knowed who I was, they'd heard of me, heard me on the radio. When most of 'em was there, I got up on the platform, stood up behind the lectern, and looked out on 'em, a couple hundred faces lookin' up at me, lookin' up to me to tell 'em 'bout the grace of God, the love of Jesus, to tell 'em they could have a little hope. They was hopin' in me, waitin' for me to give 'em somethin' precious. But I couldn't think of nothin' to say. That was what was missin'. I just didn't have nothin' to say no more.

"Oh, I mumbled around and preached some stuff, welcomed 'em, told 'em I was glad they was there. I sort of preached some things I'd used somewhere else before, and they responded pretty well. They'd never heard it, I guess, and they just ate it right up. So I went on with it, and preached little bits and pieces of sermons I'd preached in other places. But I didn't much mean it, just didn't have it in me. You understand, Buddy? Somethin' was missin' inside of me.

"Next night, a bigger crowd came in, and I preached again. I had all the right words, the things I knowed they was wantin' to hear, but I didn't feel it like I had before. I started to pay more 'tention to what I could say in my preachin' that would help the collection plate, and stopped payin' much mind to what I really thought or believed. I remembered that woman at T.C.'s Lounge right then, and I knowed I was just like her: just doin' it for the money.

"The third night a man came up and asked me could he be healed. He said he had a heart problem. Right then and there I knowed that whether I'd ever had any sort of healin' power before, I didn't have it no more, just didn't have nothin' no more. I should've just sent him to the hospital, but I was lookin' to make a big collection. You hear what I'm sayin', boy? I knowed right then I was just preachin' for the money. I put my hand on his chest and commanded the demons to come forth out of him. The crowd really liked that little bit of flourish. I told myself that was how Jesus would've done it, but I knowed I was lyin', lyin' to the peoples in the tent, lyin' to myself. Them peoples might believe it, but I didn't, I didn't believe nothin' no more.

"I drank up that whole bottle of homemade whiskey that same night. I drank that one and a good many after it on a good many other nights, just to ease the pain and the shame a little bit, just to let it ease. I didn't never drink so's Joseph would catch on, didn't never get loud or into no trouble. Mostly I just had a drink or two right before I lay down to sleep, just so's I could find me a little peace in my mind. They was a lot of folks makin' moonshine back then, and it was easy to find, yes sir. It was real easy.

"So that's how it was for a little while, me and my boy Joseph drivin' from town to town, mostly in Alabama and Miss'ippi, a little here and there in Louisiana and Arkansas, once or twice over into Texas, stayin' a couple of nights most places, three in some. The crowds was usually pretty good, and the money was comin' in steady. I was glad to be with my boy, that was the main thing, just glad to have Joseph with me. He was pretty near all I had then, pretty near all I had. I was still preachin' 'bout hope, that's what the peoples really needed to hear back then. But I didn't have no hope, not much noways. All I had was Joseph.

"Wasn't too long after Joseph turnt seventeen the Pearl Harbor was bombed, and we was all in a war. It was a terrible, scary thing, that war, and more than anything else I was scared for Joseph. It was like I knowed what was goin' to happen the whole time.

"Joseph enlisted when he turnt eighteen, joined up with the Army. It was November, and we was in Monroe, Louisiana. It was rainin', as I recall. I put him on the train to go to Jackson, where he was shipped off for trainin' somewheres. We told our goodbyes there at the train station in Monroe, and somehow I just knowed I wasn't never goin' to see him again. I hugged him real tight, and even though he was a growed man then I told him I loved him, and kissed him right on the jaw. And he hugged me, too, but not long enough, couldn't never have been long enough.

"I watched the bus drive off, followin' the rain east, takin' my boy away so's I'd never see him no more. I watched the bus 'til it was gone, and then kept on watchin' for a good while after that. Then I went back to the truck and sat behind the wheel and cried. I cried 'til I didn't think I could cry no more, and then I just sat there a while, didn't have no place to go, didn't have nothin' to do. My insides felt all empty.

"I prayed then, sittin' in the rain in the cab of that ol' truck, the first real prayin' I'd done in a good long time. I asked God to show me what I ought to do, where I ought to go. I asked Him to send me a sign. I told him I was goin' to put my life in His hands, let Him be in charge for a while, see could He do any better with it. And after I was through prayin', I looked up through the raindrops runnin' down the windshield, and sure enough I saw me a sign.

"The sign was across the street from the train station, in front of a liquor store. It read, 'Stanton's Package Store.' It was just below another sign: 'George Dickel Sour Mash Whiskey.' It was the first time I ever bought any Federal whiskey, and it was sure smooth, that sour mash. I drank the whole bottle right there in the truck, drank the whole damn thing dry, just tryin' to fill up the emptiness left when my boy Joseph went off to war.

"Next mornin' a policeman woke me up. I guess I'd passed out and slept in the cab of the truck. We'd wrote 'The Rev. Jacob J. Jefferson, Prophet, Preacher, and Healer' right there on the side of the truck, and the policeman was real polite. He had to smell that liquor, I s'pose, but he didn't never say nothin' 'bout it. He told me they didn't like nobody sleepin' in they vehicles, and that I needed to move on. He asked me did I have any money, and I told him 'course I did. I didn't know nothin' 'bout bein' a drunk then. But I sure found out, I sure did.

"I went and got me some strong Louisiana coffee, and choked down some eggs and grits with it. After a while I started to think what would I do next. I decided to go on, down into south Louisiana, it may be even on down to New Orleans. I ain't never been to New Orleans, but I hear it's a fine town. I didn't know nothin' but preachin', so that's what I knowed I'd have to do. But before I left town I bought me six more bottles of that George Dickel Sour Mash Whiskey.

"So I kept on at it, drivin' in the day, preachin' in the evenins', drinkin' to go to sleep. They was a lot of miles put on that old truck then, a lot of tiny small towns, a lot of old womens with sore knees and achin' backs, a lot of passin' the plate, a lot of whiskey.

"All that time I didn't keep up with nobody, and couldn't nobody keep up with me, except my sister Pearlie. She done stayed in Beaumont her whole life, with her husband Jimmie Lee and six or seven chilluns. Ever' so often I swung back by home, and I'd stay with them—get some good home-cooked food, and see had I gotten any mail. Or if I was gone for a good long while, I'd call 'em up on the telephone, see what was goin' on. She was a good woman, my sister Pearlie, and Jimmie Lee a good man. She's passed now, but she was a good woman, she sure was, a damn good woman.

"One hot summer night outside of Brookhaven, Miss'ippi, I called up Pearlie on the telephone. It had been several months since she and me had talked, and almost a year since my Joseph went off to war. Soon as she picked up the telephone I knowed somethin' was terrible wrong. She tried to tell me, but I couldn't make no sense out of it, with all that blubberin' and tryin' not to cry and whatnot. The only thing I could understand was that somebody had died, and then she couldn't talk no more. She gave the telephone to Jimmie Lee, and he asked me where I was and told me I needed to come on home. I asked him what the hell was goin' on. He said, 'Jake, it's Joseph.'

"Joseph was dead, kilt in a battle 'bout a bulge, in Germany or some place over there. He was not even nineteen yet. Jimmie Lee told me I'd got a telegram from the United States gover'ment, said my Joseph died a hero, fightin' for his country, said he died bravely in combat. But all I really heard was that Joseph was dead. My tiny small boy, the best and only thing I ever had, was gone, and wasn't never goin' to come back at all, just like I knowed. The letter said they buried him over there, with a whole lot of sons of other fathers who won't never see they boys no more, neither.

"Truth to tell, I don't really know what happened then. I was on my way somewhere, but I don't think I ever got there. I know I got pretty drunk, but I don't remember buyin' the whiskey or drinkin' it, or anything else for a few days. Hell, it may have been a few weeks. You got to understand me now, boy—I just didn't have nothin' to keep goin' for, no reason to pay no 'tention to nothin'. Joseph wasn't never comin' back no more.

"When I woke up, when I got sober enough to wonder where I was, I was in the Forrest County jail, in Hattiesburg, Miss'ippi. The jail keeper told me I almost died, said he thought I might just up and stop breathin'. Said I was in jail for disruptin' the peace and being a public drunk. Said I could call somebody to make bail for me, get me out of jail. But they wasn't nobody to call, and wasn't no reason to—Joseph was dead.

"I was, too, pretty much.

"So I sat there in that jail for thirty days. A preacher came in to talk to me, told me how drunkenness was a sin in the Bible, told me how they's a Hell, and I was on my way to it if I didn't repent. I told him I was already there, thinkin' I'd tell him 'bout Joseph. But he didn't ask me nothin' 'bout myself, though, all he cared 'bout was what he had to say. So I let him talk 'til he stopped, and then I told him I wanted to see him again the next day. He sort of perked up some then, I guess thinkin' he'd made a convert, he'd saved a poor wretched soul.

"All that night I thought 'bout what it was I was goin' to say to that preacher when he come back. He didn't know who he had taken aholt of. I didn't want to talk 'bout the Book; I wanted to talk 'bout God.

"He came back the next mornin', and brung two of the ladies of his flock with him, I guess so's they could witness the conversion and 'preciate they preacher. I asked 'em to come in and sit down, and I told the preacher that I was grateful for what he was tryin' to do, more than he could know. But I told him it was too late for me. I told him either God was a cruel son of a bitch who lets chilluns die thousands of miles away in wars they don't know nothin' 'bout, or they wasn't no God at all, just somethin' preachers had made up a long time ago so they could make money tellin' other folks what to do. I told him either way I didn't want nothin' to do with it, nothin' at all.

"That preacher didn't know what to say. He was embarrassed; I 'spect I caught him off his guard. He told me I was decidin' to go straight to Hell, that they is some things God is not goin' to forgive. I guess he was talkin' 'bout me callin' God a son of a bitch right then. One of his ladies got all mad, and seemed terrible distressed she'd come to see a conversion that didn't play out right. She left my jail cell in a fluster, with the preacher followin' right behind. But that other lady, her eyes all filled up with tears, like she really cared about me, even though I didn't repent like I was s'posed to. What she said that mornin' I been thinkin' 'bout ever since. She said, 'And the light shineth in darkness; and the darkness comprehended it not. St. John

One Five. The Light shines on, friend, even when it's dreadful dark, even we can't see it.'

"And then she was gone, too, just left me there all by myself to think 'bout the trap I'd tried to set. I tried to think 'bout the darkness and the light, 'bout whether God was up there or not, but all I really knowed was that Joseph was dead, and that I wanted a drink.

"A few days after that I got out, promised the jail keeper I'd leave town and wouldn't never drink no more. Then I went straight to a liquor store and bought the biggest bottle of the cheapest whiskey I could find. I went right behind that store and drank as much as I could, threw up ever'thing I had in me, and drank some more.

"The next mornin' when I woke up, the bottle was all empty, and the liquor store was closed, so I got up and started walkin'. I thought I ought to go find my truck, but I didn't know where the hell it might be, and I didn't really want to do no preachin' no more noways. It was 'bout the first time in my whole life I wasn't preachin.' It felt strange. I felt free.

"After that I walked and hitched rides from one little town to another, doin' yard work and odd jobs to get enough money to buy me a bottle for the night. For a spell there I'd go into a town and hit up all the churches. I'd tell the preachers I was on my way home to see my poor ailin' mother, that I just needed enough money to get me to Memphis, or Tupelo, or Mobile, or somewhere I figured would get me enough money to buy me some booze.

"The time passed on that way, without anywhere to go and nothin' to look for but the next bottle of whiskey. Then the night before the Fourth of July nineteen and forty-five, I went into a liquor store in Grenada, Miss'ippi. The Catholic preacher there had a big heart and a big bank balance, and gave me twenty dollars. We was through fightin' the Germans, but still worried 'bout the Japanese. In the package store I was lookin' careful, seein' could I get somethin' extra special to get me July Fourth celebratin' drunk. I was terrible sober, but I was lookin' to fix that.

"They was a white man in there, even though it wasn't his part of town. He looked pretty drunk already. Him and me both came up to the counter at the same time, and I let him go first. He didn't say nothin' to me. But to the little colored girl behind the counter he said somethin' 'bout havin' a brand new twenty-dollar bill just for her if she'd treat him nice. She told him she wasn't interested, and he said he couldn't believe she'd charge more than twenty. She told him she didn't want to do nothin' but sell him some whiskey. And he reached right over the counter and grabbed her by the collar of her blouse. Next thing I know I'm beatin' that white man over the head with a fifth of Wild Turkey whiskey, like to have kilt him. I thought that bottle would break, like you see in the movie shows. But it never did, though.

"Somebody must've pulled me off him, I don't remember that part, and I was arrested and took to jail, which I don't remember, either.

"The girl from the liquor store come to see me in jail there when I was waitin' for my trial. She told me the man I beat up was still in the hospital in Memphis, but he'd be gettin' out pretty soon. She said he was married to a cousin of the deputy sheriff in that county. She said she'd taken up for me, but that her boss told her she best stay quiet or she'd be lookin' to find a new job in another town. She told me she came to see me to tell me why she wasn't goin' to speak for me at the trial. She said she was sorry, but she had chilluns at home to feed, that she needed her job. I told her I understood.

"The trial didn't take long, I don't believe they was much to it. If you don't have much money you don't get much of a lawyer, and mine didn't have much to say. Most ever'body was talkin' 'bout a town in Japan we'd bombed with a new atom bomb, not payin' too much mind to a trial of an old black man in Miss'ippi. On the same day we dropped the second bomb, I was taken to the Parchman Prison Farm.

"Parchman Farm is in the Miss'ippi Delta, flat as a table, green in the summer, gray in the winter, wind blowin' most all the time. It was all fences and barbed wire and guards with dogs and shotguns, sleepin' in your sweat when it was hot, with all your clothes on when it was cold. We all had jobs, to 'earn our keep' there. I worked in the laundry for a while, then in the kitchen. I never had to go out to work on the road gangs, or pick cotton or hoe sweet potatoes, thank the Lord; they let the young bucks do that. Wasn't none of it easy, but I believe that might have been too much for me.

"I was one of the older mens in my camp; the other mens sort of looked up to me. I wasn't never one for fightin' and whatnot, but I didn't never let on to the guards who done what. It was the first time in my life I ever felt like I belonged to a group of peoples, like they was some folks who needed me. They was one of 'em who claimed that he'd seen me preachin' in a tent one time, that he recognized me. I told him that was all behind me now, and asked him to stay quiet 'bout it. But word got out anyhow, and even though I didn't never do no talkin' 'bout God, they respected me. They called me Preacher Jake.

"It was a hard life, I ain't goin' to tell no lies 'bout it. And the whole time I was in prison, I was countin' the years, the months, the days, 'til I could get out. Somewhere in there I decided I wasn't goin' to drink no more when I got out. I decided I wasn't goin' to preach no more, neither. I figured I'd get out and get an honest job, work at somethin' I could be peaceful with, and live until I died.

"I had a twenty-year sentence, and served near twelve years of it. When I got out I came right here. We had us a shop there at the Farm, where some of the younger mens was taught some what they called 'vocational skills' so they could get a job when they got out. I was friends enough with one of the trustees that he let me use some of the tools to make a headstone for my boy Joseph. He got buried over in that Europe somewheres, and I knowed I couldn't never go over there to see where he was restin'. But I needed someplace over here to do right by his memory, and I wanted it to be right next to his granddaddy. I made him a tombstone out of pine boards, and covered it with the metal they made license plates out of, used they press to write out his name and his years. I had lots of time to write somethin' else, but couldn't never think of nothin' else to say.

"When I got out, I came straight to the graveyard you boys were playin' in tonight, and stood up his tombstone, side by side to where I'd buried my daddy. I thought I ought to preach a sermon or at least say a prayer, but I didn't have none in me.

"Next mornin' I started to work on this house, used up the last of the little bit of money the prison give me to buy some fishin' tackle and lines and whatnot. I been fishin' ever since, sober, watchin' out over my daddy and my boy Joseph."

Then, like the rain that had blown through earlier that night, Jake's story was done, and there wasn't much else to say. As we got ready to go to sleep, I remember thinking that I knew this man much better than I knew any other person I'd ever met. I still think it's a privilege to be trusted with someone else's story.

We slept in his hut the remainder of the night, as the breeze outside blew gently and the trees rustled and murmured. When the sun came up, I drank the first cup of coffee I'd ever had. I can't truthfully claim to have enjoyed it, but that's all he had except water, and it seemed oddly appropriate. I was a lot more grown up that morning than I'd been the morning before.

After a breakfast of fried bologna and beans out of a can, Jake and I went back to the graveyard, where I got my sleeping bag, which was heavy, soaking wet. In the cemetery he showed me two markers, the two larger ones under the large tree, one for his father and the other for his son, the first made out of stone and covered with lichen and moss like all the rest, and the other looking something more like a license plate.

Then, as we had discussed, he pointed his shotgun up and fired it. He said, "Them boys'll come runnin' now. Take care of yourself, Buddy."

In a few minutes the other boys came puffing up. They wanted to know what had happened to me. I'd given this some thought and had my answer ready. At first, I'd planned to tell them about Jake, that he was an honorable man, and that I was never in any danger at all. But I knew if I did, the big boys would make fun of me, call me a darkie-lover, and eventually they'd find his little home and ruin it. I answered, "After you sissies got ascared and ran off, I stomped down as hard as I could on that old man's foot and ran like hell. He chased me but I lost him, then doubled back and got my sleeping bag. I took it up the hill over there and made a shelter out of some sweet gum branches to stay dry, and waited for y'all to come back."

Durant spoke up. "Didn't you hear us yellin' for you? We were walkin' around for hours!"

I knew it wasn't really true, but I relished the idea of it anyway. "No, I guess I must've slept through it."

This won a modest murmur of envious admiration, a precious and rare moment of appreciation for one of the younger boys. It didn't last long, of course, but I still remember how gratifying it felt.

Purvis wanted to know if there had been a shotgun fired. I told him I'd seen a hunter, and I'd heard the shot fired, too. Then we started lining up what we were going to tell our parents.

It was an intricate structure of lies, and I was worried about remembering it all, but I was saved the trouble of it. By the time we got home, Mama had already talked to the mothers of the homes Lee and I were supposed to have stayed the night in, and we were in trouble. I don't remember that particular punishment of all the various punishments of my childhood; all I remember is thinking how odd it seemed that our house was just the same as it was when I'd left it. I had certainly changed, and it didn't seem right for everything else to have stayed the same.

7

Mourning the Death of a Chipmunk

After that, I spent as much time with Jake as I could. A lot of days, I'd go down into the woods and fish with him after school, and more often than not, I'd spend a large part of the day with him on Saturdays. Sometimes I worried about spending too much time with him, working with the often-proved assumption that I was getting in the way if I was ever in one place for too long. But Jake always seemed glad to see me, to listen to me, to give me his point of view.

Jake treated me differently, not like my parents or teachers or other adults, who talked down to me, assuming I couldn't understand; and not like the other kids, always trying to get something or prove something. Jake talked to me in a way that showed that he respected who I was, as I was. He trusted me to tell him if I didn't understand what he was talking about, and so I did. He treated me as an equal. Sometimes he needed my help, but more often I needed him. I still do. He was a wonderful friend, and I will always miss him.

He told the most wonderful stories. Some were about his life, some were from the Bible, and some he'd heard his father or someone else tell. Some were strictly true, he claimed, and some I suspect he improved a little. More than once, when I told him that I'd liked a story, he would say, "In the end, our stories is all we is."

Still, I didn't tell anybody about Jake, not even my mother. She and Dad must have thought it was a strange for me to be spending so much time down in the woods alone, but I think they were having some real trouble with Lee and my older sister Kathleen, who'd both hit adolescence fairly hard. I wasn't ashamed of Jake; in fact, I was quite proud of our friendship. But I didn't think other people would understand. And if I didn't tell anybody, it was as if he was mine, and I wouldn't have to share him.

Jake was a musical person, in his way. It seemed like there was always some music in the air around him, as he whistled or hummed or played his harmonica. One tune was peculiarly mournful and triumphant at the same time; he said it was a church song, but I didn't know it. There were other tunes, too: not hymns, exactly, but not quite the blues, either. Later, I came to think of them as laments.

The spring of my eleventh year, it was time for me to be confirmed in the Episcopal Church. Mama's family had been Episcopalians for generations over in Alabama, and Dad had some Episcopal branches in his family tree, so we were all brought up spending every Sunday morning in pew number nineteen at Holy Trinity Episcopal Church in Vicksburg. It was an old church, built just after the Civil War, and the pews still had the numbers on them from the days when the pews were rented. Number nineteen had a velvet-covered armrest, no doubt the gift of a previous patron. The four Hinton children—Lee, Kathleen, Buddy, and Kelly—went to war every Sunday to determine which of us would be able to rest his or her right arm, smug in the knowledge that no one else in the whole place could rest their arm, and haughty with the advantage gained over the other three siblings.

I'd been baptized there when I was just a few months old, and officially received the blessing and curse of my name: Judah Bennie Hinton. Actually, I'd already been baptized; my mother was concerned that her third child was puny and sickly at birth, so much so that the relatives were called in to see me before I died. So the night after I was born, just after the nurse introduced the idea of "a failure to thrive," when Mama was nursing me late at night all alone, she dipped her finger in her little hospital water glass and baptized her baby in the name of the Father, and of the Son, and of the Holy Ghost.

They thought I was going to die because I was long and thin, and because apparently I had a negative reaction to something in my mother's milk. Assuming my impending death, they named me Judah after a long line of Judahs in my mother's family, and after Bennie, my dad's favorite uncle. Mama asked him if he wanted to name me Benjamin, but Dad told her that his uncle's given name was Bennie, which they later found was not the case, but it was too late for me. When I was a kid, sensitive to the slings and arrows of the other kids who called me "Chewed A Penny," I used to comfort myself with the hope that if they'd thought I was going to make it, they would have named me something more regular, like Paul or Jeff.

After it became clear that I was going to survive after all, they had something of a struggle to figure out what they were going to call me. Dad couldn't see calling me Judah, which was "too Jewish" for him. Mama was willing to call me Ben, or Benjamin, but Bennie was just too . . . common. "Bennie is something you call a taxi driver," she pleaded. Somebody suggested they call me J.B., which I think they tried for a week or so, but they decided they didn't have it in their hearts to call a baby by his initials. So for a few weeks, Mama and her family called me Judah, proudly remembering several Judahs from that family and thinking that the name would surely catch, and Dad and his family held their ground and called me Bennie. Finally, my brother Lee settled it, as the story goes, one day when he allegedly announced at the age of three, "I don't care what his name is, he's my Buddy." Since everyone was desperate for a compromise, the name stuck, and I've been Buddy ever since.

So by the time I was baptized Judah Bennie Hinton, I was already safely Buddy. Eleven years later, it was time to be confirmed in that same church. I wanted to be confirmed so I could be an acolyte; I wanted to be an acolyte so I wouldn't have to sit with the family in pew number nineteen and pretend so hard to pay attention. My brother was an acolyte, and I was envious of his freedom, his mind wandering at will, out of our parents' reach.

The new rector of the church scheduled a sixth grade confirmation class after school on Thursday afternoons. There were six of us in the class: a couple of guys I had known and disliked from our years together in the same Sunday school class; a couple of girls I'd met but didn't actually know; the rector's son, Andy, whom I'd never met before our Thursday afternoon classes began; and me.

One of the guys I'd known for years was Ricky Livingston. His father was a wealthy lawyer in Vicksburg. Ricky always had everything, and was never bashful about letting you know what all he had that you didn't. He always wore the right clothes, always knew the right thing to say and the right name to drop. The girls fell all over themselves for Ricky. My mama loved him, and thought I would do well to be more like him, which made me hate him all the more. He was a little guy, quick with words. His main defense well into high school was Chip Johnson.

I've forgotten Chip's given name; his father was whatever-it-was Junior, and Chip was whatever-it-was the Third. He was a big guy, and for the most part affable. I liked Chip well enough when Ricky wasn't around; we were friends then. But he tried so hard to earn Ricky's favor, that when he was around, Chip wasn't my friend. We both understood; it's just the way it was. Sometimes Chip was my friend, and sometimes he wasn't. It wasn't determined by either of us but by where Ricky was. It was Chip's chief delight in life to take up for Ricky.

The two girls in the class were Mary Edward O'Keefe and Hope Thomas. Mary Edward was sweet and friendly, and, more important, she was already showing signs of puberty. At that time, I didn't know what puberty was, but I knew that there was a difference between girls and women, and that Mary Edward was well on her way to leaving the former and becoming one of the latter. I also knew that she made me breathe sort of funny and that I was always a little nervous and especially awkward around her, and I liked it.

Hope was a smaller girl from a Lebanese family, less developed, and quietly satisfied for Mary Edward to get all the attention. She was smart, too, with straight A's in school, and she always knew all the answers to the questions Father Simmons asked us. I suspected her of studying all that stuff between Thursday afternoons.

Father Simmons was our rector. He'd recently come from a larger church in New Orleans, where he'd been an assistant. He wasn't all that well liked in the church, I think; we certainly didn't like him much in our confirmation class. And he obviously didn't have much use for children, even though he had a few of his own.

Andy was the younger of his two sons, a funny, overly energetic kid, more worldly and sophisticated than any of the rest of us, which admittedly was no great accomplishment. He was what I later learned to call "street smart," having come from New Orleans. His sense of humor must have come from his mother; we didn't see any of it in his dad. Andy went to the Catholic school and didn't come to Sunday school, so none of the rest of us knew him. (One of the things the older church ladies did not like was that Mrs. Simmons didn't make her children go to Sunday school.) If there was any discussion as to whether Andy would be confirmed, Father Simmons must have won, and Andy must have lost, because he was there every Thursday afternoon, obviously against his will.

Andy could imitate his father, and he did so to our great delight when Father Simmons had to leave our classroom from time to time. He had the voice reasonably well, and the mannerisms were perfect. He stayed up late at night and watched Johnny Carson, and he could do Carson, too. I didn't know who Johnny Carson was, so I just tried to laugh when the other kids did. His older brother Pete had a few albums by Redd Foxx, and Andy had them memorized. I didn't understand a good bit of that, either, but I could still tell they were comical in a naughty, forbidden sort of way.

In class, Father Simmons was strict on us all but especially tough on Andy. The first Thursday afternoon our class met, Father Simmons was writing something on the blackboard in our little Sunday school classroom, something profound and vital to the Faith, and of no interest to us whatsoever. Ricky wadded up a piece of paper and threw it at me, knowing Father Simmons wouldn't know who'd thrown it. The paper took a ricochet off my shoulder and bounced over to Father Simmons's feet. He turned around in a sudden rage.

"Andy!" he bellowed. "Get out of this room right now!"

Ricky giggled, and Chip predictably followed suit. The girls froze. Andy got up to leave, not nearly so happy about his expulsion as I would have thought he'd be.

Father Simmons took Andy's chair out into the hallway and told him to sit there until he allowed him to get up. Then he came back in and continued to write.

Before I could think about it much, I heard myself say, "Father Simmons, Andy didn't throw that piece of paper."

"Who did, then?"

Ricky glared at me; Chip stared menacingly; Hope looked into her Prayer Book. Mary Edward smiled, and I found new courage. "I did, sir," I lied. Ricky checked the rector's response; Chip checked Ricky's; Hope continued to look at the catechism. And Mary Edward beamed her approval. My face was flush and red, an invigorating mix of fear and excitement.

Father Simmons went out into the hall to get Andy, who came in and sulked for the rest of the class. After we were through, and I was waiting for my mother to come get me, Andy came up to me.

"Thanks, man." He was the first person I ever heard say "man" like that, and I thought it was cool. "Did you really throw it?"

"Uh, no. Ricky threw it at me."

"So why did you take the rap?"

"Huh?"

"Why did you take the blame for throwing the paper if you didn't throw it?"

"Oh. 'Cause I didn't think you ought to get in trouble for it. And if I ratted on Ricky, I'd have to fight Chip, and sometimes he's my friend."

"Oh. Well, thanks, man."

"You're welcome . . . man."

After that, Andy and I became friends. We sat next to each other in confirmation class and passed notes back and forth, drew pictures of monsters and futuristic cars and military machinery, played tic-tac-toe. Andy started coming to Sunday school, and I went over to his house to play a couple of times. Then Mama suggested I ask him over to spend the night. I think Mama thought he'd be a positive influence for me, being the rector's son and all, and I imagine Mrs. Simmons hoped I might be of some value for her son, too.

So Andy came and spent a Friday night at our house. Lee was away at a Boy Scout campout, so Andy slept in his bed. We stayed up late into the night and sneaked out of my room to watch the *Tonight Show.* One of Johnny's guests was a buxom Latin woman named Charo, and we greatly enjoyed their conversation, especially when she stood up from time to time to do what Andy called the Jiggly Dance.

After that, we quietly opened the back door and slipped outside. There was no moon in the clear sky, and the stars were bright. We lay on our backs in the warm spring air and looked up. I was glad to have a friend I was comfortable with. I was ready to continue to speculate about Charo, or for Andy to entertain me, but I wasn't ready for what came next. The night sky brought out a philosopher where I thought there wasn't one.

"Buddy, do you believe in God?"

"What do you mean?"

"Y'know, do you think there really is a God, and that He's up there watchin' us?"

"Yeah, I guess. Do you?"

"Naw, man. I think it's all just a trick to make us do what they want us to do, like Santa Claus. It's all just a bunch of crap."

I was horrified. It had been hard enough for me to let go of Santa Claus, even though the evidence was clearly against him. But to think of God as a fictional character, as a gimmick invented for crowd control, was too much.

"Naw, man. God's not like Santa Claus."

"Oh, sure He is. You know: 'He knows when you've been sleeping, He knows when you're awake, He knows if you've been bad or good, so be good for goodness' sake.' 'Cept the church says, 'Behave the way we tell you to or go to Hell.' God is like the big boogie man in the sky, man, just waitin' to get you when you screw up."

"But what about the Bible?"

"Who do you think wrote the Bible? God? Naw, man. The people who wrote the Bible just want to keep us under control. They tell us that God wrote the Bible, or some saints or somethin', but it's just more of their mind-control crap."

I was even more astounded. "You don't believe in the Bible?"

"Naw, man. It's supposed to be some sort of magic book, everything in it is the whole truth, and nothin' but the truth? It's all crap, man. Even my father doesn't believe all that crap. If it's all true, let me ask you a question: how many animals did Noah take on the ark?"

I remembered coloring a picture of this in Sunday school and was glad to have the answer. "Two of each kind, I guess."

"Well, that's what it says in one place. But in another place it says he took seven pairs of some kinds of animals, and only one pair of some others. So which is it—two kangaroos, or fourteen? Even the lists of Jesus' disciples don't all agree; check it out sometime. It's all crap, if you read it."

I had not read the Bible, not because I thought it was crap but because it was so boring. I asked, "Have you read the Bible?"

He replied, "Hell, no, man—it's all crap. Mind-control crap."

"Then how do you know all this stuff?"

"I hear my parents talking about it."

I was silent. I didn't want to seem unsophisticated, but I couldn't accept this line of thought, either. I felt like I needed to talk to Jake.

We sat for a while in uncomfortable heretical silence until Andy asked, "Hey, Buddy, ever ride the rails?"

"What?"

"Did you ever hitch a ride underneath a train car? There are these rails, see, under a boxcar, and you get on 'em when the train is stopped, and lay on 'em to catch a ride. But you got to hang on, and stay on 'em 'til the train stops. If you fall, or try to get off, the train'll run over you."

My reaction to this intrigues me still. I knew that I would never do such a thing, but it sounded exciting, scary, thrilling. "No, I've never done that."

"Aw, man, you got to do it! Me and Pete used to ride all the time when we lived in New Orleans. Pete told me him and some of his pals're gonna ride the Bridge. You up for it?"

This time I knew exactly what he meant. The bridge over the Mississippi River was long and narrow. For me, it was scary enough to ride across in a car. To ride hanging on to something underneath a train car was crazy. Suddenly I was not so comfortable with my friend.

"No, thanks."

"Whatsamatter, man? Scared?"

"Sure I'm scared, Andy. That's the kind of thing we're supposed to be scared of."

Andy laughed and slugged me in the shoulder, and I slugged him back. After a while we talked about the stars, and UFOs, and the existence of life on other planets, and I was more comfortable, until it was a real effort to stay awake. We sneaked back inside and went to sleep.

The next morning, we played down in the woods until lunchtime, and then Andy went home. Sunday afternoon, after church and lunch, I went to see Jake. It was a gorgeous day, warm and bright and breezy. Jake never fished on Sundays; he was taking a nap in a hammock he'd made out of some soft cotton rope Mr. Howell at the fish house had given him. I sat on the fallen tree and tried to whistle, but I only succeeded in waking Jake up. He came and sat on the tree with me, and tried to explain whistling for a while. He showed me how he held his lips, but I couldn't make it work, and I gave up well before he did.

After a while, I asked, "Jake, do you believe in God?"

Jake looked at me as if I were somehow dangerous, like I was a snake. "What you talkin' 'bout, boy?"

"Well, you know, do you think there really is a God up there?"

"'Course I do. Who you been talkin' to?"

"My friend Andy. He says he doesn't believe in God. He says God's just somethin' like Santa Claus, somethin' somebody made up so they could make the rest of us do what they want us to do. He says the Bible is just mind-control crap."

"Where the hell he get ideas like that?"

"I dunno. His father's the priest at our church."

"Oh," said Jake, as if that explained something. "Listen, Buddy. You listen to what I tell you, and try to remember it. God is up there, sure is. For a while I thought He may not be, but now I knows He's there.

"How else you think we got here? You think peoples made the world? If we was in charge, you think they'd be anything beautiful, anything perfect? No sir. Hell, no—if we'd made the world, it would be all wrong and ugly. Ever'thing would be at least a little bit messed up.

"Look here, boy, look at"—he looked around—"look at this leaf." He pulled a new spring leaf from the fallen sweet gum we were sitting on. It was soft, bright green, with five points like a star. "You think this leaf could be any better than this? No. You think we could make a tree like this one, that kept on livin' even after it got blowed down? If they ain't no God, how did birds get to be so pretty, and sing so sweet? How did them squirrels get to where they can climb and jump from tree to tree and whatnot? No sir. God must be up there, 'cause it had to be God made the world.

"Now listen. Me and God ain't been on speakin' terms for a few years now. I think He done me wrong, and I 'magine I done Him some, too. I don't understand God, but I knows He up there.

"I used to think I knowed ever'thing they was to know 'bout God, back some time ago. But now I knows better; now I knows ain't nobody knows ever'thing 'bout God. We ain't s'posed to know ever'thing 'bout God. Some church peoples think they own God. Don't nobody own God, ain't nobody got Him all figured out. But that don't mean He ain't there.

"Sounds to me like your friend's got a problem with his daddy, and he's got God all confused up in it 'cause his daddy's a preacher."

I was much relieved and tried to whistle again for a bit, until I remembered something else. "Jake, how many animals did Noah take on the ark?"

"Two of each, I believe."

"Andy told me that somewhere in the Bible, it tells how he got seven pairs of some animals, and another place says it was just one pair."

"Ah," he said, nodding. "Now you is on to somethin' sure 'nough important. Peoples mess up thinkin' the Book was all wrote by God.

That's what you hear preachers and they peoples sayin' sometimes, but it ain't true. The Book was wrote by a whole lot of peoples, peoples writin' down stories they had passed along for a long, long time. The Bible ain't nothin' but stories, just like the stories you and me tell. And just like our stories, some of 'em is better than others. Some is truer than others.

"Sometimes they tell the same stories in the Book two or three times. So one ol' boy tells the story of Noah and the Ark so that he takes two of every animal, just enough so they can have babies, so life goes on after the Flood. But later it's important to somebody else that the animals is different, see, some is clean, and others is unclean. Them Jews long time ago was real serious 'bout which animals was clean, which meant they could eat 'em, and which was unclean, which meant they couldn't."

I was still confused, and I told him so. He could see it on my face anyway.

"Pigs was unclean, see—Jews don't eat no pig meat, no pork, no bacon. So somebody was tellin' the story and wanted to tell that ol' Noah must have knowed that, bein' a godly man and all. He must've saved only just two pigs, since we still have pigs around, but he must've saved more of the better animals, clean animals like cows and chickens, stuff they could eat."

This was a lot to chew on, but I could tell it was important, so I told him I'd think about all that. Then I told Jake all about the confirmation class, the kids in it, and about Ricky and Chip, about Father Simmons and Andy. He seemed particularly amused when I talked about Mary Edward O'Keefe.

"Look here, boy. Don't let them two snooty boys bother you, not one tiny small bit. These is the peoples you'll have to struggle with all your life: peoples that believe they better than ever'body else, that convince the rest of us we're somehow less because we don't know the right peoples, wear the right clothes, talk the right talk.

"And I've allowed myself to believe it, the whole time knowin' all that don't make a damn. But not no more, no sir, not no more. I ain't never goin' to let myself think I am worth no less than nobody else, never again.

"Needin' to be better than somebody else is an ailment we all catch. It ain't nothin' but bein' selfish, what the preacher calls sin. You ain't never no better than nobody else, Buddy, but nobody else ain't never no better than you, neither.

"The worst of it is when the top dogs invite you in, just for a little bit. That's what's happenin' to your friend Chip. The big dog invitin' him in. Not all the way in, of course . . . them that's all the way in don't never have to be invited. The top dogs invite you in 'cause they can use you for a minute or two, 'cause you can do somethin' for 'em. And you sittin' there so hungry to belong that you let yourself get took in, like your friend Chip, even though you know they ain't goin' to let you stay long. And then you back on the outside, and they laughin'. No sir, ain't nobody no better than you or me, not Ricky nor Chip nor nobody else. You remember that, Buddy, you hear?

"Look here: ain't but two kinds of people: takers and givers. The takers just take whatever they can get, and keep on takin' 'til somebody tells 'em no. The givers just give, never 'spectin' nothin' back. And that's good, 'cause they ain't never goin' to get much back. Most peoples think the takers is the winners in the world, but they ain't, 'cause a taker ain't never satisfied, a taker always wants more. You a giver, Buddy, always will be. Just like me.

"Let me put this another way here. In the swamp, you got the alligator, and then they is ever'thing the alligator eats. Big ol' alligator can eat ever'thing else in the swamp, but ain't nothin' goin' to eat him, not 'til he dies. That makes him the boss, and ever'body else has to live with that and get out the way, or be gator food.

"They's some peoples who you don't want to mess with, but they goin' to mess with you. With them, you got to either get out the way or leave the swamp, 'cause unless you an alligator, too, they goin' to eat you up. And you ain't no alligator, Buddy, not you nor me. You a giver, and you goin' to pay the price for that, you sure is, but that's what you s'posed to be."

"But Jake, what do I do when the takers are mean?"

"Well, yes sir. That is a problem. You can run from 'em, but they goin' to find you. You can fight back, but you ain't never goin' to be no good at it, it just ain't in your soul. Or you can just try to put the love of God on 'em."

"What does that mean?"

"It ain't no easy thing to do, it really ain't. You just got to look in they eyes, and tell yourself that this mean alligator is a child of God just like you. They ain't no better'n you, and you ain't no better'n them. It don't matter why they bein' mean, you just got to love them best you can. But be careful, they still goin' to try to bite off your damn hand!"

"Does that work?"

"Well, Buddy, I believe it's like this right here. Runnin' and fightin' ain't no good. If you try to put the love of God on 'em, it may not do 'em no good, but at least you know you was tryin' to do the right thing."

"Are you just making this up?" I had to ask. I'd never heard anything like what he was saying before.

"Hell no, I ain't makin' it up. It's all in the Book. Ain't you ever heard what Jesus told his friends? 'But I say unto you, That ye resist not evil: but whosoever shall smite thee on thy right cheek, turn to him the other also.' Matthew five, thirty-nine. And Saint Paul wrote 'bout this, too; I used to preach a pretty fine sermon on it. 'Therefore if thine enemy hunger, feed him; if he thirst, give him drink: for in so doing thou shalt heap coals of fire on his head. Be not overcome of evil, but overcome evil with good.' Romans twelve, twenty and twenty-one."

"So when somebody's being mean to me, you're saying I ought to love him?"

"That's what Jesus told his friends they 'spose to do, ain't it? 'Ye have heard that it hath been said, Thou shalt love thy neighbor, and hate thine enemy. But I say unto you, Love your enemies, bless them that curse you, do good to them that hate you, and pray for them which despitefully use you, and persecute you; That ye may be the children of your Father which is in heaven: for he maketh his sun to rise on the evil and on the good, and sendeth rain on the just and on the unjust.' That's in Matthew chapter five, I forget which verses, but

I guess it don't matter none. Jesus knowed that hatin' somebody's like somethin' that eats away at you."

"Haven't you ever hated anybody?"

"'Course I have. I hated Chantille for a long time, and that stupid fool man I caught her with, too. I hated some German I ain't never even seen for shootin' my boy. But it didn't help me none, and it didn't do them no harm, so I gave it up. Hatin' was killin' me, and wasn't hurtin' them at all. 'Cause hate is like . . . ah, hate is like a cavity in your tooth, Buddy, eatin' it away 'til they ain't much left but a rotten smelly hole. It don't do nobody no good."

This was all too much for me, and I told him so.

"Yeah, well. You likely be workin' on that for the rest of your life, figurin' out the givers and the takers, who is alligators and who ain't, and how to deal with them. It's hard to love some of our brothers and sisters, I know it is. I believe love is more powerful than hate, but I know how hate can reach out and pull you in. But you is askin' is they a God. Good Lord, child, what a question. Of course they is!"

We sat and thought for a few minutes, and then Jake apparently decided to move us along. He opened his eyes to reveal a mischievous sparkle and teased, "Say amen, brother Hinton."

I said, "Amen." I said it "Ay-men," with a long "A," not "Ah-men" like we said it in the Episcopal Church.

Later, I tried to tell Andy what Jake had said, putting it into my own words, but I never could make it sound right. It didn't seem urgent at the time, especially compared to whatever business was at hand. Usually Andy and I were too busy killing enemy soldiers for theological discussion.

We fought most of the major battles of most of the American wars in the woods behind my house, just the two of us alone against the British, the Mexicans, the Germans, the Japanese. We didn't know anything about the Koreans, so they were safe. The wars and the enemies changed from day to day, but some things remained constant. We were always "cut off from our platoon," "hopelessly outnumbered," and "low on ammo"; at least one of us was shot but never "mortally wounded"; and we always, always won.

In addition to having a fairly sharp wit and a big-city attitude, Andy had another quality that was greatly appreciated by boys our age: he could make great battle sound effects. I could almost see the mortar shells whistling in over our heads, landing nearby with deafening explosions. His machine gun tat-tat-tat-tat, the bombers dropping their loads, and the sounds of the enemy soldiers dying when we "lobbed a grenade" were simply masterful.

One Saturday morning, we were in the ravine behind my house, holding one of the hills of Vicksburg against the invading Yankee army. Losses to our regiment had been staggering, and only the two of us stood in General Grant's way, protecting the city on the bluffs overlooking the river. We were fortunate to have confiscated several repeating rifles from dead Union soldiers, at least one of which sounded suspiciously like a machine gun in the heat of battle. We must have killed thousands of Billy Yanks, and we were confident of victory. When we played Civil War, which was one of our favorites, we always won, even though we always fought for the Confederacy.

Andy was starting to get bored, but I wasn't done. I yelled, "It's General Sherman!" as I pointed off to our right, down the hill. "He's leading the charge!" General William Tecumseh Sherman was a favorite villain; I couldn't imagine ending this battle of Vicksburg without taking a few shots at him. He usually got away so he could go and burn Atlanta, but it was still a noble effort every time.

Andy was ready to do something else, I guess; he wasn't interested in General Sherman. We'd found a piece of a board, a two-by-six about eight inches long, a special weapon we always saved as last resort. Ending our game, Andy picked it up and pulled the pin out of what had anachronistically become a hand grenade, then lobbed it at the Yankee commander. It sounded like a great explosion, and we agreed that there was no way Sherman could have survived. The battle was over, the villain was killed, the day and the city of Atlanta were saved.

Andy went to get the board and cried out in anguish. "Oh, no! Buddy! C'mere!"

When I got there, he showed me a chipmunk, mortally wounded by a piece of two-by-six. One of its little back legs kicked a few times, and then it moved no more.

Now chipmunks are terribly cute, but they were definitely a nuisance at our house. We lived on the edge of a gully, and the pesky chipmunks dug little holes in our yard that the rain ran through, eroding the land. This caused my father to get a truckload of dirt dumped in our front yard every spring, and he made Lee and me haul the dirt to the backyard in a wheelbarrow, one load at a time. We had to dig out the holes and fill them with dirt, tamping the dirt in tightly. It was hard, sweaty work that we hated, so we hated chipmunks. Cute as it was, I couldn't say I was sorry to see this one go.

But Andy was mortified. "Oh, my God," he wailed, "I've killed it!"

"It's okay, Andy, it's just a chipmunk."

"I wasn't trying to kill it. I'm sorry. Poor little thing. I'm sorry!"

So, only a few minutes after killing thousands of Yankee soldiers and at least one famous Union general, I stood next to my friend Andy, mourning the death of a chipmunk. For all of his big-city toughness and sophistication, his little twelve-year-old heart was broken.

There was no consoling him until I suggested that we bury the chipmunk. Lee and I had buried several birds and a squirrel back in one of the corners of the yard, next to the path that went down into the woods, and I told him we could bury the chipmunk there, too. It went against his callous pretensions, but I could tell he sincerely wanted to do it. I went to get my father's shovel, and by the time I got back, Andy was trying to put two sticks together to make a cross, "just to mark the grave." I dug a little hole, and Andy put the chipmunk in it. I covered the furry body with the dirt, and Andy put one of the sticks into the dirt behind the chipmunk's head.

He said, "You can tie the other stick on later, if you want to."

"All right."

"Shouldn't we say something?"

I was surprised. "What, like a funeral?"

"Well, yeah."

"Okay." I waited, but he didn't say anything, so I prompted him, "Go ahead."

"No, you do it."

"You're the priest's kid!"

"What does that have to do with it?"

"Well, I mean you hear this kind of stuff more than me."

"Yeah, but I killed the poor little thing. And you're the one that believes in God, man."

"Yeah, but you're the one that wants a funeral for a chipmunk!"

"Just say something, Buddy. Please."

I looked at my friend and saw him in a new light. Andy was actually a sweet, compassionate kid, in spite of himself. He couldn't say anything without compromising his nonreligious principles, so that left it to me. It was my first time to officiate at a worship service.

"All right, Andy, I'll say something. But don't make fun of it, okay?"

"Okay."

I don't actually remember what I said, but I'm pretty sure I asked the Lord of Heaven and Earth to provide plenty of acorns in the chipmunk's afterlife. I do remember ending with, "In the name of the Father, and the Son, and the Holy Ghost," because it sounded like church, and both of us saying, "Amen."

A tear had blazed a muddy trail down Andy's dirty cheek and fell from his chin. He wiped his face on the back of his arm and looked at me unashamedly. "Thanks, Buddy."

Mama always said that for some people, it takes a death to realize the importance of religion. Maybe even the death of a pesky chipmunk, I thought that day.

8

More Than Our Mamas

A few weeks went by, a few more Thursday afternoon confirmation classes were endured, and then one Wednesday afternoon when I got home from school, Mama met me at the door. Something was terribly wrong; I could see it in her face.

"Buddy, I have to tell you something."

I stared at her, dreading whatever it was.

"Andy Simmons was found this morning. He'd been missing for a couple of days. I didn't want to tell you. He's . . . he's dead, Buddy. Nobody knows what happened. Nell and the Reverend are just crushed, of course. I thought you would want to know, sweetheart. Oh, Buddy, I'm so sorry."

My first thought was this must be a joke. It was the kind of prank Andy would have loved; it flashed through my mind to wonder how he'd gotten my mother to go along with it. I looked at her hard to see if she was going to smile, and was frightened by the pain in her eyes. I realized that my mom wouldn't joke about something like that, which meant Andy was dead.

Andy was dead.

It didn't make sense; it wasn't fair, it wasn't right. I swallowed hard and knew that I could easily throw up.

Mom said something else, but I was having difficulty hearing her.

"Buddy? Are you all right? Buddy?"

I walked out of the house in such a fog that I didn't notice my brother, Lee, until I almost ran into him.

He said, "Buddy, did you hear about Andy Simmons?"

I mumbled that I had, and he continued. "Aw, man! Can you believe it? I heard both his feet were cut off, and one of his hands. They found him just floatin' down the river."

I said, "In the river?"

"Yeah, over on the Louisiana side."

We stood there for a moment, neither of us knowing what to say. Finally he said, "Buddy, what happened?"

"I don't know."

"Everybody's talkin' about it. He was a weird kid, though, wasn't he?"

"He wasn't weird!"

"Aw, c'mon, man—he *had* to be weird. He didn't have any friends but you, always actin' funny, sayin' strange stuff. He's the priest's kid, man—he had to be weird."

I had no idea what was happening and couldn't think about anything but Andy dead. I looked into Lee's eyes and said, "He was my friend, whether he was weird or not."

I must have sounded fiercer than I felt; Lee said, "Okay, man, he was your friend." And then, "Hey, look, Buddy—I'm sorry, okay?"

I think I nodded. I walked down into the woods. I don't think I decided where I was going. My feet just took me down the hill, along the shoulder of the ridge, over the little creek I'd dammed up years before, past the waterfall, through the canebrake, across the broad field, beside the bayou to the wide place where we'd seen Jake fishing, and then over the hill and up to Jake's.

I guess it was the place I needed to go to make sense of what was happening. If anybody could help me understand, it would be Jake.

He'd just gotten back from the fish house and was putting away some canned food. He saw me as I was about to come into the little hut, and he stopped and came out. "What the hell's the matter with you, boy?"

I couldn't talk. I knew what I wanted to talk about, but I couldn't think of how to start, couldn't make the words come out. Jake motioned to the fallen tree and said, "Go sit down, boy. I'll fetch you some water."

I sat on the tree, and after a minute or two Jake came with one of his lumpy cups, filled with cool water. "Somebody die, Buddy?"

I nodded, still dumb. How could he know that? How could he tell?

"Who? Who died, Buddy?"

I remember looking at him and wanting him to somehow make it better, then being angry that he wasn't able to fix it. He'd been a preacher. Didn't he have any influence? I knew at the time that this was unfair, but it was how I felt.

"Buddy, look at me," Jake persisted. "Who died?"

Finally I sobbed it out. "Andy."

"Oh, Buddy. I'm sorry, son." He put his hand on my shoulder, and I buried my head in his dirty gray shirt and cried.

After a long while, I stopped crying, and he brought a wet rag and washed my face. While my breath was still erratic in the aftermath of sobbing, Jake asked, "How did he die?"

"They don't know. He was found in the river, over on the Louisiana side. Lee said his feet were cut off—" As I said it out loud, I realized what must have happened. "It's because he let go, Jake. He let go and the train ran over him and cut off his feet and his hand!"

"What you talkin' 'bout, boy?"

"He was ridin' the rails, Jake. You know what that is?"

"I know."

"He was ridin' the rails across the bridge, and somethin' must've happened, and he let go, or fell, and the train cut off his feet and hand, and he fell into the water and he died. He wanted me to ride with him, but I told him I was scared."

"Well, hell yeah, you scared; of course you scared!"

"But I should've talked him out of it, Jake. I should have made sure he didn't do it."

"You thinkin' you coulda stopped him?"

"Or maybe I should've been with him, to help him hang on. Oh, Jake, I've never known anybody that . . . that died before. It's not supposed to be like this!"

"Like what, Buddy?"

"So that kids die. That's not right!"

"It's a damn shame, that's for sure. But it ain't your fault, you understand me? You can't take this blame, it ain't yours."

"But I could've . . . I should've done something."

"Look here, Buddy. Peoples goin' to do what they want to do. You ain't never goin' to stop peoples from doin' foolishness. I don't know why young peoples got to die before they time, I sure don't. But they do, sure as the world, and they ain't nothin' you and me can do 'bout it."

We sat there for a minute or two, with the birds and squirrels and various insects carrying on as if nothing had happened. But the world had changed; they just didn't know it. When I put together the question I needed to ask, I asked it.

"Jake, how could God let this happen?" I wonder now if Jake had been waiting for me to ask this; he was quick with his response.

"Why you ask it like that?"

"Huh?"

"Why you goin' to ask why God let this happen? God didn't choose this; Andy did."

"But God could have stopped it, right?"

"He could have, sure could. He could make it so nobody ever did things that's stupid, or hurtful. But we would be less than His chilluns if He did."

I suppose I must have looked confused; that's certainly the way I felt.

Jake continued, "Look here, Buddy, this is a hard thing. They's lots of grown-up peoples don't understand this. I might be wrong on it my own self. But I believe God lets us do what we choose. He don't get in the way or make us do what He wants us to do. It may be that's part of what it means that we created in the image of God, that we all free to make our own choices."

I still wasn't buying it, so Jake kept on. "Listen now. You and Andy used to play like you was in the army, shootin' soldiers and whatnot. Play somethin' with me for a minute, all right? Play like God Almighty was creatin' the world and all, long time gone now, and He asked you and me to help him get things all set up. We goin' to play like, all right?"

I nodded.

"Play like He all done made the heavens and the earth, the sun and the moon and the stars. He all done made all the fish in the sea, and the birds of the air. He all done makin' 'the beast of the earth after his kind, and cattle after their kind, and every thing that creepeth upon the earth after his kind: and God saw that it was good. And God said, Let us make man in our image, after our likeness.'

"Now God looks at you and me, and says, 'All right, boys, I said I'm a-goin' to make man in my image and likeness. What you think about that?'"

I was caught up in the idea that I had been appointed to the Committee on Creation, and my mind was just starting to wander out into things I'd have done differently, starting with Andy's death but moving quickly to the elimination of mean kids, spiders, and sticker-bushes.

Jake knew he'd set my imagination free, and he watched for a while as my mind roamed. Then he chided playfully, "Buddy, God done asked you a question. You think it's a good idea for God to make man in His image and likeness?"

"Oh . . . I don't know. What does that mean?"

"Yes sir. That's the very question I'm tryin' to get you to wonder about. What do you think it means for us to be made in God's image?"

"That we should look like Him?"

"How you goin' to make somebody look like God? What do God look like?"

"Well, He's real big, I guess, and old. He's got long white hair and a beard."

Jake chuckled. "Where the hell do you get all that?"

I'd colored a picture in Sunday school that had God looking down on Noah in the ark with all the animals. Two giraffes, two elephants, two zebras, and the rest. God was behind the clouds, and He was an old man with long white hair and a beard. I'd colored the sky and the water two shades of blue but left the clouds and God's hair white. The skin on His face I'd colored with a crayon labeled "flesh." Sometime after our conversation, I wondered what color Jake would have used.

Jake asked again, "Where did you get what God looks like?"

I guessed, "From the Bible?"

"That ain't in the Book, Buddy. God don't look like nothin,' just like the wind don't look like nothin,' just like love don't look like nothin.' God didn't never have no body, 'cept Jesus. But that was later. Now, God is busy creatin' the world, and He's askin' us is it a good idea to make peoples in His image."

I saw my chance and took it. "You tell Him, Jake."

He chuckled again, looked up into the trees above us, and spoke to God. "Me and Buddy think you is doin' a great job so far, Lord. We 'specially like the animals you done made, fish to catch, birds to listen to, squirrels to play in the trees up above us. We love to see your sun comin' up in the mornin,' and settin' down in the evenin.' We love to see your moon slidin' across the night sky, or to see all them stars up there winkin' at us. We is glad it ain't hot all the time, Lord, nor cold all the time, neither. We's thankful for your rain when it comes, and thankful when it stops rainin', too. We is mighty grateful, we sure is.

"Now you wants to make up some peoples, and we think that is a good idea, too. It would be terrible lonely if me and Buddy is the only people they is. You want to make peoples in your image, and in your likeness. That's a little confusin' to us, 'cause we think a image is how somethin' looks, and you don't look like nothin.' You a Spirit, Lord, but we is tryin' to make you into somebody just like us. We is spirit, too, but we mostly don't know that, 'cause we got bodies, too, and they's easier to pay 'tention to.

"Lord, you can't make our bodies like yours, 'cause you ain't got no body. You can't make us look like you, 'cause you don't look like nothin'. I 'spect you best make our spirits to be like your Spirit. Let us be like you in our hearts. Make us to love, and hope, and imagine.

"Now, Buddy, play like the Lord says this, he says, 'That's just what I was gonna do. But listen here, Buddy and Jake. If I do that, we goin' to have to choose one of two ways. I can either make peoples so they is free to make they own choices, like me, or I can make them so they does what I tells them to do all the time. Which way you boys want it?'"

I repeated, "You tell Him, Jake."

"No sir, you tell Him this time." And I knew Jake had come to the point, and that it was an awful choice. Should God make His people to be free, or to do what He tells us to do?

I said to Jake, "If He makes us so that we do what He says, there would be less trouble."

"They sure would."

"There wouldn't be any mean people."

"That's right."

"And Andy would be"—I choked on the words—"be alive."

"That's right."

"Maybe that's the way it ought to be."

"Well, maybe. But we wouldn't really be peoples, if we couldn't make no choices."

"Could we just choose the good stuff? Y'know, always choose the right thing?"

"If we was choosin' between one good thing and another good thing, it wouldn't really be no choice, you think? We'd be more like trained dogs than peoples. We'd stay when He told us to stay and bark when He told us to bark. We'd be less than His chilluns if we wasn't free."

"So we need to tell God to let us be free, so we can make our own choices. Even stupid choices."

"That's what I think, too. But listen: if we is free, peoples is goin' to do things that hurts other peoples. Peoples is goin' to do things that hurts they selfs. You understand what I'm sayin?'"

"Yes sir."

"If we is free to make our own choices, Andy is free to ride the rails."

"Yes sir."

"And God ain't goin' to stop him, or Andy ain't free."

"Yes sir."

"But that's what you is goin' to tell God? That He ought to make us free?"

I paused, reluctant to see the truth of it, before I muttered, "Yes sir."

"All right, then. That's why God lets things like this happen. He don't choose it, but He lets us choose it. He done told us what we ought to do, but we goin' to do as we choose. God loves us enough to let us do what we choose to do, even when it's wrong."

"Even if it kills us."

"That's right, Buddy, even if it kills us."

"Jake, I need you to tell me the truth now, not ideas or sermons you used to preach. Do you *really* believe in God? Do you think people go to Heaven when they die? Do you think Andy's okay? He didn't believe in God, you know."

"All right, now, all right. Let me tell you now, Buddy. Let me tell you. I believe they is a God, I sure do. He don't always do what I think He ought to do, but I knows He up there. And I do believe in Heaven. That's where my Joseph is, I know that, and my daddy, too. But I don't believe Heaven is a place, like you could get into a rocket ship and fly there. It ain't a place, no. It's when somebody is with God.

"Sometimes, not very often, we can catch a tiny small glimpse of Heaven, even when we is still alive. It don't last long, mostly, just a little snatch of it sometimes when the moon is full and bright, or when the sun's comin' up and the coffee smells good and strong, or when I remember my boy Joseph huggin' me, or . . . or when you laugh, Buddy, sometimes I know God is there. And I get just a little peek into Heaven, 'cause I knows God is with me then. And I knows I'm with God then, even though I'm still mad at Him.

"Used to be peoples would ask me who was goin' to go to Heaven, and who was goin' to Hell. That was back when I thought I knowed, but now I knows better. Used to be I could tell 'em, yes sir, just like I really knowed. But now I think I'll just leave that up to God, yes sir. I believe I'll let God worry 'bout the hereafter and all that."

He must have seen the worry still in my eyes, so he continued. "But this boy Andy, he a friend of yours, right?"

"Yeah."

"Well then, if he a friend of yours, he got some good in him, even if he wanted to keep it hid. You think he ought to go to Heaven or to Hell?"

This stunned me. "Huh?"

"I mean, if you could choose should Andy go up to Heaven or down to Hell, which one you goin' to choose?"

"Uh, Heaven."

"Why?"

"'Cause he's a good kid, 'cause I . . . I liked him a whole lot, 'cause he could make just about anybody laugh. And he was soft, too, not just hard all the time. Jake, I don't want to believe in God if God sends Andy to Hell."

"You think he could make God laugh?"

"I don't know. If anybody can, Andy can."

"Yeah, well, I believe God laughs pretty easy. Listen, Buddy, if you can see somethin' in Andy that's good and right, don't you think God can, too?"

"Yeah, but . . ."

"But what?"

"But he didn't believe in God, remember? He said He was like Santa Claus, just something to keep us in line."

"Well, hell—I wouldn't believe in that God Andy talked 'bout, neither. The God I believe in is a whole lot better than me. If somebody did somethin' to me, made me mad, hurt me, and if I was God, I'd send that person to Hell quick as I could. But God is better than us, and better than that. We all hurt God, we all mess up, every damn one of us. And God keeps on lovin' us, no matter what. He ain't like Santy Claus, who just brings chilluns presents when they good, and he ain't out to get us. He's most like your daddy or your mama. He just want to love his chilluns, that's all. We is all the chilluns of God, and he loves all of us, no matter what. God loves us more than our mamas do."

Incredulous, I asked, "More than our mamas?" It was hard to imagine being loved more than my mama loved me.

Jake nodded. "One time Jesus was talkin' to His friends, and he asked them, 'Who would give his son a stone if he'd asked for some bread? Or a snake, if he'd asked for a fish?' I think it's in Matthew's Gospel. And then, and this is the thing I want you to hear, Jesus said, 'If ye then, being evil, know how to give good gifts unto your children, how much more shall your Father which is in heaven give good things to them that ask him?' God loves us more than our mamas.

"I believe, when it gets right down to it, when we get to them Pearly Gates, it ain't goin' to be a matter of what did we believe, but how did we love, and did we let somebody love us." Here Jake lapsed into a sort of easy singsong; it was the first time I'd ever heard him preach. "It ain't goin' to be what church did you go to, but how did you treat your fellow man. Mmm-hmm, and it ain't goin' to be do we believe in God, but do God believe in us. Mmm-hmm, and it ain't goin' to be do God choose Heaven for us, or do God choose Hell for us, but do we choose to serve God, mmm-hmm, or do we choose to serve our selfs."

Jake was rocking on the fallen sweet gum tree, his eyes closed, feeling the old rhythms of the preacher and hearing his preaching tones. I sat quietly, saying good-bye to my friend Andy, as sure then as I am now that he is in the presence of God.

Jake looked into the late afternoon sky. "You'll see him again, later."

I didn't understand what he was talking about, didn't know how I'd ever see my friend again, but something in the way he said it didn't encourage me to ask.

The funeral was two or three days later. I'd never been to a funeral before, and Daddy thought I shouldn't go to this one, either. But Mama thought I needed to go. "After all," she told him, "his mother said Buddy was Andy's closest friend."

Mama came to pick me up at school and told the teacher I would have to miss class. Andy would have liked that, I thought: anything to miss school. On the way to the church, I asked, "Mama, do they know how Andy died yet?" I was feeling guilty about knowing what he'd been doing, when some people who really should've known didn't.

"No, sweetheart," she answered. "The sheriff's department is investigating, but we may never know."

We went and sat in the church, always cavernous and solemn, but especially so this day. We sat behind Andy's classmates from the Catholic school, sitting all huddled together, leery of their Protestant surroundings. The rest of the crowd filed in quietly, until the church was as full as I'd ever seen it.

The organ was playing sad songs in a hush. It wasn't quite enough to make you cry, but enough to make you feel like you could. When the time came, the acolyte led the coffin down the aisle. The family followed, Father Simmons holding up his wife, who was holding him up, too. Father Simmons was just wearing a suit, not his robes. Behind them were ten or twelve more priests, friends of his, I guess, all in their robes, all trying to look like they could make sense out of this if a person could stand to listen long enough.

The last one in the procession was the Bishop, whom I'd seen before. He was an old, short man, bald as a cucumber, and he looked like he could be mean when he needed to be. I was scared of the Bishop; mostly I was scared of his hands. When the Bishop came, he would bless those of us who couldn't take Communion when we came up to the altar rail with his big, scary hands, big knuckles with veins bulging out. His hands looked so unlike my hands that I had to wonder if he and I were the same species.

He was in charge of this service. When he started into the Prayer Book, my mind automatically began to search about for something to occupy it. I looked up to see who the acolyte was, and I was shocked to see that it was Pete, Andy's brother: Pete, who let his little brother ride the rails in New Orleans; who told Andy that he and his pals were going to ride the rails across the bridge; the only other living soul who knew exactly how and why his brother died.

The Bishop talked about the Purposes of God, dragging it all out for quite a while, and we sang some sad and stately hymns. We committed Andy's soul to the mercy of God; I remember that part. Then the service finally ended. Mama was talking to some of the ladies of the church, and I told her I'd be right back. I went to the room where the acolytes put on their robes.

"Pete."

"Yeah, squirt?" He always called me that; I always hated it.

"Andy was riding the rails, wasn't he?"

Pete was shocked. "How did you—" He stopped, weighing how much he could trust me. He closed the door to the little room. "Yeah, he was riding the rails. Dumb kid. I was just kiddin', y'know? I didn't think he'd ever do it, y'know? Oh God, Buddy, you gonna tell?"

I'd already thought about this for a long time, as the funeral dragged on and on. "No, I'm not gonna tell. What for? It wouldn't bring Andy back, and it wouldn't help you or your folks. Pete, I'm sorry Andy died. He was a good kid. He loved you, man, he really did."

"I didn't think he would do it."

"Did you?"

"Did I what?"

"Did you ride the rails over the bridge?"

"No, man, I swear. Me and some of my friends all pretended we did, y'know, but we didn't. We lied, and Andy believed us."

"But you told Andy you did?"

"Yeah." Pete sat on a folding chair, actually collapsed into it, as if his bones all went soft at the same time. He held his head in his hands and let out a sob I could tell he'd been holding in for a long time. After that he cried for a while, and I didn't know what to do, so I just stood there. He whispered, "I bragged about it, and the next thing I know, he was missin'."

After a while I spoke. "You gonna tell your folks?"

"No! It would kill 'em, man."

"Yeah. I guess. You think you can keep it a secret? I mean, that's a pretty big secret, y'know?"

"I can't, man. I can't tell Mama that I made Andy ride the rails over that bridge."

I agreed with him. I couldn't have, either.

A few days later, I went to see Jake. The Bishop would be coming back the next Sunday to confirm us, but it didn't seem right anymore. It seemed to me that going through with the confirmation, as if nothing had happened, was somehow being disloyal to Andy. I found Jake sitting on the fallen sweet gum tree, playing his harmonica. I told him I was thinking about not being confirmed.

"You goin' to stop livin' 'cause your friend died? Must not have been much of a friend, if you think that'd make him happy."

"No, but Jake, I know what happened, how he died. It makes me feel terrible, like I can't look at Father Simmons or his wife."

"It ain't your place to tell, Buddy. That boy Pete needs to tell his mama, his own self."

"Aw, Jake, it would kill her."

"If he don't, it's goin' to kill him. He needs to tell her for his own self, so he can start to get over it. Look here now, livin' ain't about never messin' up. The trick is when you mess up, you got to get up and keep goin'. If you ain't confirmed, it's like you ain't gettin' up."

The next Sunday, the Bishop was back. It was Palm Sunday, and I was about to be confirmed. Dad had let me grow my hair long enough to hold a part, just for the occasion. I remember wearing a pair of red polyester pants with a white belt, a light blue jacket, a white short-sleeved shirt, and a wide blue-and-red-striped clip-on tie. My younger sister Kelly told me I looked like a walking flag, and I think she was probably right.

Mrs. Simmons saw me before the service started, and she came over and gave me a big hug. She told me how much it meant to them that Andy'd had such a close and trusted friend, and that I was a fine boy. I wanted to tell her that she was wrong, that I could have stopped him, that I was lying to her, that I knew how their son died. But I didn't.

Pinned to everyone's shirt or jacket was a palm cross one of the Sunday school classes had made. Those being confirmed, five sixth graders and two adults, sat up front so the Bishop could look at us when he was preaching. I wanted to sit next to Mary Edward, but Ricky was quicker: she sat between him and Chip. I had to sit next to one of the adults, Mr. Nash, who taught algebra at the white high school. I'd heard one of the ladies of the church tell Mama that Mr. Nash wasn't married, in such a way that meant she thought something must be wrong with him. He seemed a little too clean to me.

The organ played, the service began, and we all sang and mumbled through the prayers the way we always did. And then the Bishop preached.

I don't remember much of what he said, exactly, but I know he talked about responsibility, and all of us having gifts and talents. He talked about Andy, and what a loss it was to us that he was dead, and how precious life is, and how precious our faith is, and how we ought to use our time and talents to the fullest. He said the people being confirmed, and at this point he looked right at us, were giving themselves to the work of God, giving our lives and our gifts.

I guess it was the first sermon I'd ever actually felt like I needed to listen to. And somewhere in the middle of it, it seemed obvious to me that I ought to be a priest. I started thinking about that and began to cry. Mr. Nash must have figured I was crying because of Andy, and he put his arm around my shoulders and whispered kindly, "It's all right, Buddy. It's going to be all right." But I knew it wasn't. Right then it seemed to me that allowing the possibility that I might have to be a priest was going to thoroughly mess up my whole life.

Then the time came for the confirmations, and Father Simmons motioned for us to stand in front of the whole congregation, and called each of us by our whole name. When our names were called, we were supposed to kneel before the Bishop, who would put his big-knuckled, vein-bulging hands on our heads and say a prayer. Then we'd get up, all confirmed.

The two adults went first, of course, followed by Ricky, of course, and Chip followed like a puppy eager to please. Then Father Simmons intoned, "Angela . . . Hope . . . Thomas." Hope kneeled down, and the Bishop pressed down hard on her head and said the prayer. "Mary . . . Edward . . . O'Keefe" was called next, and she knelt and was confirmed. And finally Father Simmons droned, loud enough for everybody to hear, "Judah . . . Bennie . . . Hinton." I saw Ricky and Chip look at each other in great mirth at my name, and read Ricky's lips saying, "Chewed A Penny." But I didn't care. I also felt a tear run down my cheek, and saw it fall onto my red polyester knee as I knelt to receive the laying on of hands that were suddenly no longer scary, just old and wise.

As I got up, I looked back at my mama and dad in pew number nineteen, to see if they were proud. They were, of course. Mama was beaming, and even Dad was proud, though he didn't want to be too obvious about it. Lee made a face, trying to get me to laugh. My sisters both looked uninterested: Kathleen, just a few months into being a teenager, had been practicing her apathy to the point that it seemed convincing, and Kelly was just plain bored.

And way behind them, way in the back of the church, I saw what looked like a dark silhouette of a man, putting on a gray hat and getting ready to leave. I couldn't clearly see who it was, but I knew. After the service was over, I heard people talking about the man in the back of the church, using words I didn't know, like "gall" and "audacity" and "uppity," when I thought I ought to be hearing how glad they were to have this man with us.

I had a lot to learn.

The next afternoon, I went down into the woods to see Jake, who was fishing, three cane poles stuck in the mud beside the wide place in the bayou. I asked him if he'd been in my church the morning before. He smiled his big, wonderful smile. "Well, it was a big day for you. I wanted to be there, just to see it, to be part of it. Didn't mean to make no big stir."

"What big stir?"

"Some of them folks didn't take too kindly to me bein' there, me bein' colored and whatnot, with the Bishop in town to make a big to-do and all. Some of them folks didn't like it too much, no sir, not too much at all."

"Oh, Jake. I'm sorry."

"Ain't your fault. I don't 'spect nothin' more than that. Peoples always glad to have somebody they can feel better than. And I'm just the man for the job!" He laughed.

I was relieved. "You don't mind?"

A sudden storm on his face betrayed the emotion buried deep below the surface. "Mind? Would you mind if peoples treated you like you wasn't a person? If they treated you like you was less than a dog? If they just 'spected you to be stupid, and no-count, and lazy, and worthless, just 'cause you look different from them? And if you wasn't all that, if you didn't fit in that box they put you in, then they call you uppity? Mind? Hell, yeah, I mind, boy. 'Course I do. Anybody would. I didn't say I didn't mind. I just 'spect it, that's all."

We watched the quills a little. One had a nibble, but it didn't go under. Jake told me I needed to put another worm on the hook. As I was impaling the squiggling worm, I asked, "Jake, what's 'uppity' mean?"

He thought for a moment and said, "When you was little, did you ever color in a colorin' book? My boy Joseph used to love to color in his colorin' books. And your mama or somebody told you to stay inside the lines, ain't that right? I believe peoples put colored folks in between some lines that they think is where colored folks ought to be, and when you color outside them lines, when you someplace they think you ain't s'posed to be, you uppity. They never stop to think them lines might not be the right ones for you, they just see you goin' outside they lines.

"Some white folks think a colored man goin' to a white church is colorin' outside the lines, see? Like it's they church, 'cause they pays the preacher. But it ain't they church, is it? Hell, no!"

"It's not their church?" I said.

He laughed a little, but I thought it was sad for a laugh. "If the church makes any sense at all, and that's a pretty big consideration, it's 'cause it belongs to God. Who the hell are they, to say somebody can come into they church, and somebody else can't? Like it's they church. Hell, no!"

We watched the quills ride the still water again, not even a nibble. After a while, Jake chuckled. "I 'spect I am uppity sometimes."

I replied, "I'd be uppity, too, if somebody else put down lines I had to stay in all the time."

"That's right," he said, and looked at me as if he was trying to see inside me. "Buddy, you is a wise man." I thought he was kidding me then, but he wasn't.

When it was time to quit, Jake started getting his poles and tackle together. He was putting the fish in a bucket so he could take them to Mr. Howell at the fish house. His back was turned to me when I said, "Jake, somethin' happened to me in that service."

"You was confirmed."

"Yeah. But more than that. I think maybe I'm supposed to be a priest."

I expected Jake to be surprised, to whip around from facing his tackle box and have some sort of strong reaction, to laugh, or tell me he was proud, or that I was silly. But I was the one who was surprised. Jake didn't turn around, not right away. He slumped a little, as if some of the air was let out of him, and murmured, with his back still to me, "That's right."

I thought maybe I didn't hear him clearly. "What?"

He turned around and looked into me. "I said that's right. I think you s'posed to be a preacher, too. And I think you is a wise man, too wise to be just eleven years old."

"But Jake, is it wise for me to be a priest? I've never known a priest I liked, except you, and you're not a preacher anymore."

"It is wise to be who you is s'posed to be." And then, picking up the bucket of fish and motioning for me to pick up the poles, he added, "But I am glad I ain't a preacher no more, I sure am."

9

Inherited Wisdom

Life continued, as life does. I have the same stories many people have: first love; athletic triumphs and failures; sibling rivalries; problems with school, parents, friends, girlfriends. I survived junior high school and puberty with no small amount of self-conscious self-doubt, just like most of us did; I came through high school, the beginnings of romance, and trying to see what would be next for me with excitement, frustration, pain, and joy.

And Jake was there through all of it, listening to my ideas, telling me what he thought, laughing with me, crying with me. With great patience, he did eventually teach me how to whistle, showing me how to hold my lips and blow, and how it touches the soul. He taught me what he could about playing the harmonica, until we agreed that I just didn't have it in me. He showed me how to consider both sides of an argument, how to think fairly. The adults around me at school, in church, at summer camp, often mentioned how mature I seemed to them. At first I thought it was because I was larger than most of the other kids my age, but after a while I realized it had nothing to do with size. Jake claimed it was because I was wise; I thought it was because of Jake.

In May of 1973, I graduated from South Vicksburg High School, three years after Mississippi schools had been forced by a Federal court order to desegregate. Public schools in the early seventies in Mississippi were tense, but we made it through with just a bomb threat or two. With graduation coming up, I invited Jake to come to the ceremony. I told him it was about time for him to meet my parents.

"No, I don't believe so," he said.

"Why?"

"All that whatnot just don't mean that much to me, Buddy. I . . . I'm sorry. I'd just be out of place."

"But Jake—"

"Buddy, I don't want to come. Please don't make me feel all guilty 'bout it."

I didn't pursue it, but it left a bitter taste in my mouth. I didn't want to force him or manipulate him, but didn't he know how important it was to me that he was there?

Finally, the big night came. Several times I looked back into the crowd there at the Municipal Auditorium where we graduated, hoping to see Jake in the back, as he had been for my confirmation, but I didn't see him. I graduated without distinction, and without Jake. It wasn't just that he wasn't there; there was a hole inside me where I felt he should have been.

That summer after graduating from high school, I went to work at the Episcopal summer camp, north of Canton, Mississippi. That's a whole different set of stories to tell, and they're interesting enough but have little to do with this story. At summer camp, I had my first experience with people who are mentally and/or physically disabled, which taught me a great deal about life, and I met some Episcopal priests I liked, people I thought I could try to be like, and that was a relief to me. Out of the reach of my father, I also let my hair grow, realizing for the first time in my life, at age seventeen, that it's wavy.

The day before I went off to college, I went to see Jake, to say good-bye. It was terribly awkward. I wasn't sure if I would ever see him again. Jake seemed just as awkward as I was. We talked about my hair, about the St. Louis Cardinals, which he loved to listen to on his little transistor radio, about the town of Starkville, the home of Mississippi State University, where I would go to school. He had preached outside of Starkville a few times. And then the time came for me to go back home, to get packed, to go to college.

I stumbled out, "Jake . . . uh, thanks. Thanks for everything, for all the time you spent with me. Thanks for being my friend, all these years."

He replied, "Well, look here, boy. I ain't 'bout to die or nothin'. It ain't like you ain't never goin' to see me no more, is it? Hell, we don't have to get all mushy up in here. Now listen. I want you to do somethin' for me. Will you bring me your address at college? I'd like to write you a letter, if you don't mind. Will you do that for me?"

"Sure. I don't know what my address will be yet, but when I get it, I'll bring it to you, the first time I come home for a visit."

He stood up then, and it was time for me to go. I started to say something, but he stopped me. "Hush, Buddy. I been meanin' to tell you: sometimes you talk too damn much." There were tears in his eyes and a smile on his face. He held out his arms. "Come on now, give an old man a hug before you go."

I stepped into his embrace and held on for a long while. I started to say something again, and again he stopped me. "Hush. Go on, boy, get on home."

I remembered him saying that the day I met him, the day the doe died. Then he patted the side of my neck, and with his voice choked with emotion he whispered, "Don't forget me, boy."

I found I couldn't say a word; I could only shake my head, and turn and walk down the hill. I was going back to the house I'd grown up in, but it felt like I was leaving home.

I took him my address at Mississippi State the first time I came home to visit, along with some paper, envelopes, and stamps. I figured he'd write one or two letters and then quit, especially as there was no way I could write him back, since he didn't have an address. We sat on the fallen sweet gum and had a long talk, about life in the dorm, which he said sounded a lot like prison, and fraternity rush, which he thought sounded like an easy way for mean people to be mean. Most of the awkwardness was gone, and I was relieved and glad to be able to say I'd see him again, and know it to be true.

I was delighted to get the following letter a few days later. It was printed in pencil, with a great deal of smudging from repeated erasing.

I was lucky enough to keep all of the letters Jake wrote me in a shoebox. I didn't intentionally set out to collect them; I just couldn't bear to throw any of them away. The various letters from Jake that follow are almost exactly as they were written. He had no sense of paragraphing, which I thought was odd at first, until I realized he'd never read much other than the King James Version of the Bible, which doesn't use paragraphs. It also doesn't use contractions or quotation marks, so he didn't, either, for the most part. He didn't write in the same way he talked, as his knowledge of the written word came only from his study of the Bible.

September 23, 1973
Sunday

Dear Buddy,

I thank you for bringing me this paper and whatnot so I can write you this letter.
I do not imagine it might mean all that much to you but it does for me.
It means I can feel like I am in touch with you.
Like you ain't so far away and that I ain't so all alone.
You know I do not do much work on Sundays, and I hope I will be able to look forward to writing you a letter every Sunday.
I have always tried to be honest with you as I can be.
I did not tell you the whole reason why I did not want to come to your graduation.
Because I was not honest I believe we been pushed apart a little bit.
I am very sorry for that.
I want to tell you the reason now in this letter so that it may be we can be close in our hearts even though you is far away now.
The reason I did not want to come to your graduation is really two reasons.
The first is that I did not want to meet your parents.
I did not want to know in my heart that you had a daddy that was not me.
I know that in my head but my heart wanted to have room to pretend.

I wanted to leave it just like that.

I thought you would think that was something a silly old man might think so I did not want to tell you.

The second is that my real son Joseph did not ever graduate from high school. Because I took him away from his mother and then he went to war.

I carry some considerable guilt because of that.

Going to your graduation would have put me where I would have to face up to that and I was too selfish to do that.

And there was another reason too so that makes three.

I did not want you to graduate and leave me down here all by myself.

It was not lonesome before I met you or I did not notice it.

But now you been here and you is gone and I ain't never felt so alone.

I reckon I just did not want you to grow up.

You are a good boy Buddy.

Do not do too much foolish things like I know they do in college eating goldfish and whatnot.

Do not let your hair get too long.

Be careful with them womens up there.

They can sure bring some trouble.

When you come home to see your mother and father I hope you will forgive me enough to come back to see me, too.

Your friend,
Jacob Jefferson

I opened that letter in the post office and stood before my PO box, crying. I had long known that Jake felt like a father to me, but seeing it on paper, in his careful, painstakingly printed handwriting, brought it to the surface so I had to acknowledge it. It didn't lessen any feelings for my father, but I was clearly like a son to Jake. He needed to hear that; I needed to say it to him. I began calling around to find a ride home that weekend, since I didn't have a car. But before I could get there, I got another letter.

September 25, 1973
Tuesday

Dear Buddy,

Well, I guess I made a fool of myself with that other letter you probably already got up there at college.
I saw it was a mistake just as soon as I let it go into the mail box.
I am just an old silly man. I scared to be alone now that I am getting old.
But do not feel no pity for me.
I am living the way I choose to live.
I caught a great big catfish yesterday, must have weighed near ten pound.
Mr. Howell gave me three dollars for that one fish alone.
I been putting a dollar back here and there so I could buy me a new pipe.
That big fish got me enough money to buy it and I did.
It is a brand new Dr. Graybow and it smokes real good and cool.
I got me some new fresh Prince Albert pipe tobacco too.
I hope you are having a good time up there at college.
You probably do not need no advice from a used up preacher but I want to tell you this right here.
Do not let alcohol take you over like it did me.
I know drinking is a big thing at college but it can sure kill a man.
Please stay away from drinking too much.
You may be able to drink a little. It may be it will not bother you or take you over.
Just be careful please.
Buddy I do think of you as my kin.
I know that ain't right but I do just the same.
I hope you will come see me soon.

Your friend,
Jacob Jefferson

That weekend I went home, much to the consternation of Laura, a girl I'd met at a fraternity rush function. I had gone to a few parties, but I'd never had any intention to pledge. I'd let the Greek system go, but I was trying to hold on to Laura. She had shown a little interest, and we planned to go to the big football game on campus, but I had to break the date. I didn't want to tell her anything more than I needed to go home. She got a date with some fraternity guy, and she never returned any of my calls after that, which was probably just as well.

I got home on Friday evening in time to enjoy some of Mama's cooking that I'd taken for granted all my life and was missing sorely. Saturday morning, I got up early and headed down into the woods. I told Mom and Dad I was going fishing, which I knew they thought was sort of odd, but they didn't stop me.

It was cool, gray, and drizzling, so I was generally damp when I got to Jake's. He was inside, smoking his new pipe and reading. He was surprised to see me, and glad, though it seemed to me that he was a little embarrassed.

"Hey, boy! Hey! C'mon in here, come on in! It's good to see you. I didn't know when you might be comin'. It's *good* to see you. Come in, come on in."

I stooped and made my way in. His hut seemed much smaller than it had the last time I was there, but of course it was exactly the same. I was glad to see the fire, and made my way over to it to warm up and dry out. I looked around his home. He and I had never really spent time there together after that first night. He didn't stay in the hut except at night, or when the weather was bad, times when I wouldn't have been there. I'd been in it several times over the years, but just to fetch something or put something away. So I'd never actually spent much time in his home. It seems strange, I know, but then, he'd never even been to my house at all.

"What are you reading, Jake?"

"The Book." He held up the worn book in his hand. "Genesis."

"Oh."

He seemed sheepish that I caught him reading the Bible, when he had made such a show of being angry with God. Then, trying to lighten the mood and thinking I'd make a joke about Genesis being the first book of the Bible, I quipped, "Starting over?"

He didn't smile; in fact, he was deadly serious. "Yep." There was a long, heavy pause. Then he asked quietly, "You get my letters, Buddy?"

"Yeah. That's why I'm here, in fact. Listen, Jake—"

"Well, uh, I didn't mean nothin' by all that talkin' 'bout you bein' my son and whatnot. I—"

"Jake, hush. Just hush a minute, and listen. Talk about somebody who talks too much. We've both known for a long time that you and me are like a father and a son in some ways, we just never have said it out loud. You *are* like a father to me; in some ways you're even better than a father, because a boy has to become a man with his father trying to help but sometimes just holding him back. You've taught me so much, and I owe you so much, Jake, and I think . . . maybe we're related, but just not by blood, you know what I mean?"

"Yes sir. I know."

"Okay. Okay. Well uh, well then . . . okay."

"Can I talk now?"

"Yeah."

"Buddy, I don't know how it happened, but somehow or another you is a wise man."

"If I am, if I have any wisdom at all, I got it from you."

"How you get it from me?"

"I must've inherited it."

Jake laughed at that, and everything was all right again. "No sir," he answered. "I sure didn't make nobody wise. It sure ain't inherited wisdom, not inherited from me. See, I wouldn't have been foolin' with you to start with 'less I seen you was wise."

We talked for a while about the fishing business, and about the World Series, and the Cardinals' chances for the next season. He told me I needed a haircut, and I told him my other father had already told me that. When we were quiet for a moment, I asked, "Jake, who's that in the picture over there?" I nodded toward the framed picture, still on the Coca-Cola crate shelf by his sleeping bag where I'd seen it that Halloween night years before.

He smiled a deep, satisfied sort of smile, and crawled over to get it. He took the picture off the shelf with tenderness, dusted it on his shirtsleeve, and handed it to me.

It was a small black-and-white picture of a young black man dressed in an Army uniform. His piercing eyes were the same as his father's. "That's the only picture of him I ever had," Jake said. "The Army took this picture, and sent it to me when he died."

I looked at him then, to see a tear crawling down his broad, dark face, beaming with pride and love and deep sadness.

"He was a nice-looking young man, Jake. I think I'd have liked him, if I'd ever met him."

"Yep, I 'spect so. Yes sir, you a lot like him, sure are. I wish I had another picture, but that one there is the only one I ever got. Chantille got all the others."

Reverently, he put the picture back on the shelf next to where he slept, and fumbled around, putting his pipe in his pants pocket. After a while he said, "Buddy, I'm gettin' old now."

"How old are you?"

"I was born in Nineteen and Oh-Five: one two three oh five, my Daddy told me."

"So you're, um, sixty-eight."

"Sixty-eight! Why the hell somebody want to be sixty-eight years old? Sixty-eight, good Lord. I'm gettin' old faster than I thought." Just at that moment, he looked as old as he was; I'd never noticed it before. "I 'spect it's goin' to be a cold winter."

We talked for a while about whether the hut would keep out the rain and keep in the heat, whether he had enough firewood, whether he had enough money saved up to make it through the winter when the fishing was slow. I asked him if he needed any money, which hurt his pride a little, but he understood what I was trying to do. He didn't want money, and I didn't want to argue. So when he went outside to get some water to make coffee, I slipped a twenty-dollar bill my grandmother had given me into his Bible.

Then it was about time for lunch, and I wanted to get home so I could listen to the football game with my dad. We said our good-byes, and I promised we'd see each other soon. I had no way of knowing then how long it would be before I came back to his home.

I returned to college. A week passed without a letter from Jake, and then another. I was busy with school and campus life, and a month went by. About the time I'd decided that Jake's initial enthusiasm of writing unanswered letters had faded, I got the following letter. It was addressed to me, with the return address printed on the envelope: "Mississippi State Penitentiary; Parchman, Mississippi." I ripped it open.

October 28, 1973
Sunday

Dear Buddy,

I guess you figured out I am back in jail.
I did not want to tell you for a while but they would not give me no envelope that did not have Parchman wrote on it. I forgot the envelopes you give me at home.
I did bring my pipe though and the picture and the Book.
So I reckon I got what was important.
And I got that twenty dollars you left for me.
It started me thinking.
My first thought even after all these years was that I could buy a real fine bottle of whiskey with it.
That scared me.
I started thinking about what I was doing and what I ought to do.
I thought about it all that Sunday until I had me a plan.
They ain't no reason for me to stay down there in the woods now.
I done what I wanted to do there.
I want to be needed.
I cannot preach no more but I figured they would need me back in here in Parchman.
And I knowed the rain would not get in and I would not be cold neither.
So I took the money you give me and some other money I had put back and went and bought me a little pistol.

I believe somebody got it when they was in the war, it was that kind they call a service revolver.

I bought it from some sneaky looking boy in Beaumont for 34 dollars.

It was probably stolen I believe.

So that's good, cause the police can have it back now.

I went into Vicksburg to the bank hoping to find that man that had been with Chantille, long time ago.

But he was not there.

That was too bad. I could have give him a pretty good scare.

I walked up to the little glass window and talked to the lady bank teller.

She looked nice but not too happy to be a bank teller.

When she asked could she help me I told her she could.

I took the pistol out my pocket and told her to give me all the money she could put her hands on.

The bank guard come up behind me and put his pistol right in the middle of the back of my head and told me to drop the gun.

I did not want to drop it. I was afraid it might shoot.

So I put it on the counter instead.

The lady bank teller picked it up and pointed it at me.

I was afraid she was going to shoot me.

There wasn't nothing I could do to stop her if she wanted to so I just looked at her.

She put the gun down like it was burning her hands and the guard told me to lie down on the floor.

The police came directly and put handcuffs on me so my hands was behind my back and told me to stand up.

I could not stand up with my hands behind my back like that but I did not want to make nobody mad so I tried.

After a little while they helped me get up and took me on down to the police station.

The police put my fingers in ink and made me make fingerprints on some paper.

They asked me could I tell them what happened and I did.

I told them I needed some money and that was why I bought me a gun for $34, and that was why I came to the bank, to rob it.

They asked me what was I going to do with all the money I got at the bank.

I had not figured they would ask that.

I had to think about it for about a second or two.

Then I told them I was going to buy me the biggest bottle of George Dickel Sour Mash whiskey I could find and get drunk as a monkey.

They smiled at that like I told them something they already knew.

And then they took me off to the jail cell.

There in the city jail I was warm. I got three pretty good meals a day.

The other mens in there was complaining but I was glad to be eating food I did not have to catch nor cook nor clean up after.

It rained outside some of those days but I was dry. I was grateful for that, too.

After some days, a lawyer came to see me.

He had been sent by the judge to make sure I got a fair trial.

He was what they call a court appointed like that man in Grenada.

This one was young and just out of law school at Ole Miss. He really wanted to do right by me.

Of course, I did not tell him I wanted to go to Parchman the whole time. I believe it pained him to lose my case.

I had been through this once before as you recall.

The judge asked me how did I plead. I said I was guilty.

He asked me some other questions, and my lawyer tried to stretch things out some.

I told the judge I wanted him to let me go but I could not promise that I would never try to rob the bank again.

He told my lawyer my trial would be in a few weeks.

Me and the other mens in the jail played dominos some and cards but mostly I watched the TV set.

This is the first time I had ever saw one.

You had said something about TV a couple of times before but I think I could not imagine it.

It made me a little sick to my stomach at first, with them peoples in there but looking all flat like that.

But I got used to it and enjoyed it very much.

I had to learn how to watch it so I could see the World Series on TV.

Some days passed and my trial came.

It did not take long.

The judge told everybody there that because I had been to prison before and because I was an alcoholic and because I said I was guilty, I would have to go to Parchman.

He looked real sorry when he said it like he did not want to hurt me.

I put my head down on the table so they would not know that is what I wanted the whole time.

After a few days I came here.

It is all right.

I am in a camp with 23 other mens.

Because I am the oldest and because I have been here before they accepted me almost right away.

Sometimes some of the other mens argue or fight, but they do not mess with me none.

Buddy, I am safe and warm.

The food is not all that good. But it is regular and I am not particular.

They is a TV in here too.

I saw most every game of the World Series.

The Cardinals weren't in it but I purely enjoyed watching the Athletics beat the Mets.

I did not never know that the Athletics wore them ugly green and yellow uniforms but I did not mind that.

You know I always like it when somebody beats the Mets.

And the mens in here, they need somebody to listen to them.

I used to think being a preacher was mostly talking but most peoples need somebody to listen to them.

I reckon listening is likely more useful than talking most of the time.

The mens up in here need somebody to bring them some way to hope, like you done me.

And I am glad to be needed.

I hope you understand why I done what I done.

And now that I am up in here you can write me a letter.

These mens get letters all the time up in here.

I'd be glad to get one from you.

The address is on the envelope.

You need to write my prison number on it, or I will not get it.

Well I had best stop here.

Buddy, I'm sorry for any worry I might have caused you.
Write me a letter if you get the time.
But do not come up in here. This ain't no place for you.

Your friend,
Jacob Jefferson

I wanted to go see him. I felt like I needed to go and be sure that he was all right, but I didn't have a car. It wasn't too difficult to get a ride to Vicksburg; there were lots of people at school from there. But to Parchman? Truthfully, I didn't even know where it was. But still, my closest friend was stuck in prison. Jake was my father, if not in body then at least, in some large part, in spirit, in soul. I had to go.

I thought about hitchhiking, which was more noble but also more risky. I thought about riding the bus, which I considered to be too expensive, and tacky.

One of the guys on my floor in the dorm had a car, a 1965 Ford Mustang convertible, light blue. Trey Swayze and I had met the day we both came to the dorm and had gotten along fairly well, mostly because neither of us liked our roommates. He was a big sports fan, had played football for his little high school team, but wasn't big enough to play in college. When I told him I didn't actually care about football all that much, but that I was a big baseball fan, it was as if I'd mentioned in passing that I didn't love my mother, or that I was thinking about becoming a Communist.

"Baseball?" he sneered. "I thought only Yankees and wimps watched baseball."

Trey lived and breathed and dreamed Mississippi State Bulldog football. He idolized the coach; he envied the players and despised their opponents. He was as fanatical a fan as there could be. For me, Mississippi State football was a noble cause, like the Alamo, the United Nations, speeches on tax reform, or the Confederate States of America: noble and doomed. There is something compelling about effort made in the face of inevitable failure, the romance of being willing to hope made only sweeter with the sure knowledge that it will never work.

The 1973 season was typical. While I waited for baseball season, my friend Trey dared to hope and believe, only to have his dreams dashed on the hard reality of the Alabama Crimson Tide, the Tigers (from both Auburn and LSU), and the supremely hated Ole Miss Rebels.

He and I shared a couple of classes, and sometimes we went to eat at the Union together. As long as we steered the conversation away from football or religion, we were comfortable with each other. He was terribly uneasy any time we touched on the subject of religion, so I figured out early on that I wouldn't bring it up.

The Saturday after the Wednesday I got Jake's first letter from prison was November 3, a difficult game for the Mississippi State faithful. The dreaded Alabama Crimson Tide was coming to town, a team the Bulldogs hadn't beaten since 1957. At lunch together in the Student Union, Trey said he couldn't bear to go to the game, that he was going home instead. His parents lived in Riggsville, a tiny town in the Mississippi Delta. I asked him where that was, and he told me it was just ten or twelve miles from the Mississippi State Penitentiary at Parchman.

I asked him if he'd ever been to the prison.

"Naw," he said. "My daddy has to go out there every once in a while, and comes back tellin' terrible stories about why those men are out there, and the things they do to each other. I know some people that work there, and they say it's awful. Why?"

"Just wondering."

"You want to go?"

"Uh, yeah. I'm interested in that sort of thing, prison systems, criminology, stuff like that."

"Well, I think I'd just read about it, and not go in there."

"Yeah, well. I'd really like to go visit."

"Oh. Well, different strokes, huh? I hope you get there someday."

"Actually, I'd really like to go this weekend."

"Oh." Trey kept eating his hamburger and reading the sports page, not taking any hints. I decided it was time to bite the bullet, before we started talking about the average weight of Alabama's offensive linemen.

"Listen, Trey—I was wondering, since I'd like to go to Parchman, and since you live pretty close to there, and since you're going home this weekend, and since I don't have a car, uh, maybe I could go home with you this weekend."

"Oh." He was suspicious; he could tell there was more to the story than I was saying. He waited a moment, maybe to see if I would tell him anything more, but when I didn't, he said, "Okay. Sure. I'd be glad for you to visit. Just be careful around my father, okay?"

"Hey, great, thanks. I'll be careful," I promised, not sure what that might mean.

As we talked about it, we both realized that we would have to do something we didn't want to do. I couldn't keep avoiding the truth; I would have to tell Trey the real reason I wanted to go, to see Jake. Trey would have to go out to Parchman, to take me at least to the gates. And then there was something I had not anticipated: Trey told me I would have to go to the Sunday morning service at the First Baptist Church of Riggsville and eat Sunday dinner with the preacher. Again, I agreed, thinking, "What's the worst that could happen?"

10

Folks You Don't Much Fit in With

That Friday afternoon, we put our stuff in his car and headed west. After we'd been riding for a while, I said, "Thanks for letting me come home with you, Trey."

"Hey, no problem. Most of my friends don't want to come home with me."

If I'd been paying attention, I would have wondered what that meant, but I was working up the nerve to tell him about Jake. "The real reason I want to go to Parchman," I finally admitted, "is that I need to see somebody who's in prison there. A friend of mine, from home."

"Oh." Trey paused, as if trying to think how to ask what he wanted to ask. "Somebody you were in high school with?"

"No. Look, man, I've never told anybody else this, what I'm about to tell you." I took a deep breath. "It's not really a secret, I guess, I've just never told anybody about this guy. His name is Jacob Jefferson, and I've known him for most of my life. He used to be a preacher, then he was an alcoholic, then he went to prison almost thirty years ago for beating up a county sheriff's cousin in a liquor store. When he got out, he was a fisherman for a while, and lived down in the woods down behind my house, which is where I met him. Now he's back in prison because he wanted to go back there, because he feels needed there. Jake has meant a lot to me growing up, and I just found out he was in prison, and I want to go see him. I have to be sure he's okay."

I waited for Trey to make what would surely be an indignant response, and was surprised when he said, "Cool!"

This was not what I had expected. "What?"

"I just think that's pretty cool, man. When you go visit, can I go with you?"

"Uh . . . no."

"How come?"

"Well, I … uh, I don't know. I just don't think it would be a good idea." We rode a while, and then I asked, "Do you really want to go?"

"I've never been out there. I guess I've never had a reason."

"And now you want to go?"

"Well, sure. I think it's cool that you're sticking with this guy you knew when you were a kid. It's a pretty scary place, and if you want somebody to go with you, I'd be glad to go along."

Trey was turning out to be much more than I had thought. More than just a convenient ride, he was becoming a friend. I replied, "Thanks, man. I'd be glad for you to go."

We drove on into the sun, into the flat Delta fields of cotton and soybeans, through little Mississippi farming towns.

Riggsville was about as unimpressive as a town can be and still be a town, but I'd grown up in Beaumont, so I was accustomed to being underwhelmed. The main feature of the town was the First Baptist Church of Riggsville, a disproportionately big red brick building right across from the Riggsville Town Hall. I wondered how there could be enough Baptists in the whole county to support such a big church.

We turned off the highway onto Main Street and then left on Elm. I was surprised to see what looked like a pretentiously large red brick house down the block; it looked out of place in the neighborhood. I laughed, and when Trey looked at me I asked, "Can you imagine living in a house like that?"

He didn't say anything right away, but pulled the Mustang into the driveway of that house and then answered with a funny sort of smile, "Welcome to the parsonage."

"What's a parsonage?"

"This is my home. The church owns this house for the preacher to live in."

"The preacher? You're kidding! This is your house? Your father is the preacher?"

Flashing that funny smile again, Trey replied, "C'mon in."

Trey's mother came out on the porch as we were getting our stuff together, waited patiently for her son to notice her, and then smiled brightly when he exclaimed, "Mama!" He dropped his laundry bag and suitcase and jumped up on the porch to hug her. Right then I realized I'd missed my mom, too, and I wondered for a moment why I was here instead of there, in Beaumont.

Trey said, "Mama, this is my friend Buddy Hinton. Buddy, this is my mother, Mary Claire Swayze."

She was a gracious woman, handsome in a motherly way, with graying hair put up on her head and dark eyes that looked like they ought to sparkle, as if the sparkle had been there and left the laugh lines around her eyes, but the laughter was gone now. She welcomed me to her home, told me she was glad to meet a friend of Trey's and that the Reverend would be home shortly. I noticed her face seemed to darken a little at the mention of the Reverend. Trey was picking up his laundry bag, and I couldn't see his face to figure out what was going on. Neither of them mentioned the Reverend again.

It was the biggest house I'd ever been in, with a wide hall opening into a foyer decorated with portraits of severe ancestors looking distantly disappointed, and two sweeping, curved staircases leading up to various bedrooms and other rooms I couldn't even imagine beyond. I was relieved when Trey told me I'd be staying in the downstairs guest room, and not just because I didn't want to have to carry my stuff up the stairs.

I didn't want to get lost.

I lugged my stuff into the room, tested the huge bed, combed my hair, washed my face and hands, and brushed my teeth, and just as I was wondering where Trey was and what I was supposed to do next, there was a knock on the door. Before I could say "Come in," the Reverend did.

He was a little man, shorter than Trey, and wiry. His face had settled into a smug scowl, and he carried himself with an air of superiority that made me wonder how he could be related to his son. But his chief feature was his hair, jet black and meticulously coiffed into a waxy helmet. It was the kind of hair that sent a message. Part of the message was that no hair on that head would dare be out of place. I was glad I'd combed mine and acutely aware that I probably needed a haircut. It was the early seventies; I was on my way to making a statement of some sort, but at this point I just looked scruffy.

I smiled as winningly as I could, and offered, "Hi."

I was about to go on and introduce myself, maybe tell him what a beautiful house he had. But his stern face cut me off short. "So you're Trey's friend," he said.

"Yes sir."

He looked at me hard, and I got the strong sense that I was being measured and coming up short. Then he said, "I expect no trouble from you, young man. I know you're a college boy, but all those shenanigans are far removed from this town and this house."

"Yes sir," I replied again.

"Dinner is at six-thirty," he declared.

I said "Yes sir" one more time, figuring it was my part in this conversation, and then he was gone.

Trey came in soon after. "So you met Father."

"Yes sir." I laughed, and, after a little bit, he joined me. "He's not at all what I expected."

"Really?" Trey raised his eyebrows. "Well, from now on, you'll know what to expect."

Not sure what he meant, I asked, "So is he always like that?"

Trey smiled a sad smile and answered, "Yeah. The people at the church all think he's a wonderful man."

Something in his tone invited me to ask the question: "Is he?"

"Is he what?"

"A wonderful man."

"Yeah, I guess . . . I don't know. I think he's skillful at what he does. But . . . aw, I dunno." After a pause, he added, "He's in control, no matter what, wherever he is."

"Listen," I said, "we don't have to talk about this if you don't want to. I'm not trying to put my nose in where it doesn't belong, okay?"

"Okay. Thanks. It's, uh, it's nice to have a friend. I think most of my life, most everybody I've ever known has liked or disliked me because I was the preacher's kid, y'know?"

"So you didn't want me to know who your daddy is, right?"

"Well, yeah. I guess I figured you knew. Everybody's always known, all my life, that I'm, y'know, Brother Swayze's boy. They all put me on a pedestal, up there with Father."

"Hey, listen, man, it's okay with me. I don't really care who your dad is. I'm not a Baptist."

Trey looked at me like I'd told him I didn't care that much about football, like I listened to baseball on the radio, like he'd just found out that I was from a different planet. It occurred to me that everybody he'd ever known was a Baptist. "You're . . . are you a Methodist?"

"No, I'm—"

"You're not Catholic, are you?"

"No."

"Good. Father hates the Catholics. One of the things that gives him the most satisfaction in his life is that he thinks they hate him, too. Uh, Church of Christ?"

"No. Episcopal."

"What?"

"I'm an Episcopalian."

"Oh. Is that something they started out there in California?"

I knew what he meant. It had always seemed like the oddest ideas came from California. "Well, no. It started in England."

He wasn't sure what to make of that. "Is it some kind of religion?"

Now we were both confused. "What?"

"Is Epis . . . is that what you are, like a religion?"

"Well, it's a denomination. Like Baptist or Methodist. It's the Church of England, but in the United States."

"Oh. So it's like Baptists?"

"I don't think so, but I'm not sure. I've never been to a Baptist church."

He gave me the suspicious-of-planetary-origin look again. "Oh."

I didn't blame him. In Mississippi, it seemed like nearly everybody was either completely or at least partially Baptist.

Maybe to make sure I wasn't kidding, he asked, "Never? Not even for a funeral, or a wedding?"

"No. I guess I've only been to just a few weddings, and only one funeral. That was mostly for relatives, and I don't think I'm related to any Baptists. My brother and sister went to a revival with the kids next door one time," I offered, trying to soothe his disbelief.

"Did they like it?"

"I guess. Lee told me the preacher started yelling about how everybody was all sinners and stuff, and my sister started crying and joined the church. She just walked down the aisle and gave her life to Jesus. I remember they came home and Lee told my mom and dad that Kathleen had joined the Baptist church. It was the only time I ever heard my father cuss, except for when he was fishing. We couldn't play with Lewis and Lucille for a few weeks after that."

"Who?"

"Uh, Lewis and Lucille Graham. The kids next door. The ones who invited them to come to the Baptist church."

"Oh. Hey, listen, Buddy. Is this why all your ideas about religion are so strange?"

"I guess so. It's part of why my ideas about religion are different from yours, anyway." I paused then, again weighing how much I was willing to trust him. "But the main reason my ideas are . . . different . . . is because of Jake. He doesn't have much to do with church, but he's a very religious person. Sort of."

"Your friend, the one who's in prison? Oh, yeah, in the car you mentioned he was some sort of preacher. Is he a Epispal—whatever you are?"

"No. Jake's not an Episcopalian. I don't guess I've ever thought about him as a part of any denomination. He was a tent preacher, y'know, one of those guys who goes from town to town, setting up a tent and preaching for a few days, and then moving on."

"Oh, like a revival preacher."

"I guess. All I know about revivals came from that time when Lee and Kathleen got all caught up in one."

"Man! You don't even know about revivals?"

I was about to tell him about the Episcopal Church, and how I was considering becoming an Episcopal priest, when his mother called out to us. "Boys! Time for dinner!"

Before going to dinner, I made sure my hair was combed, forcing as much order into it as I could, anyway.

Trey and I came into the dining room, a cool, dark, stiff-feeling place. Mrs. Swayze stood at one end of the table, and the Reverend at the other. It was a long table, with six chairs matching its dark wood, but only four places were set: one at one end of the table in front of the Reverend's chair, the only chair with armrests, another by his wife at the other end, and the other two opposite each other next to her. I felt like Trey's father was watching us from a distance, and I guess he was.

When the Reverend sat, we all sat. When the Reverend bowed his head, we all bowed our heads, too. I was expecting that we'd all say, "God is great, God is good, let us thank Him for our food," but the Reverend launched into a long and extensive prayer. It went on for a while, and covered some ground that didn't seem to have anything to do with the meal we were supposed to be giving thanks for. I don't remember most of it, but I know it included the phrase, "And Lord, we just thank you, Lord, for being our Lord." It became a joke between Trey and me that the Reverend had claimed ownership of the Almighty.

In due time, the blessing ended, and we all said "Amen." Actually, the Reverend kept his head down a little longer, as if he had even more to say to *his* Lord, things the rest of us apparently didn't need to know about or couldn't understand. As soon as he pronounced his "Amen," a woman came in, pushing a little cart with steaming dishes of food and a pitcher of tea on it. She was short and compact, a little heavy, a black woman wearing a white uniform. She looked like someone you'd want to have on your side, somebody who does things while everybody else is wondering what to do. On the cart was a platter of ham, bowls of mashed potatoes, green beans, and boiled okra, and a basket of cornbread. It had been weeks since I'd had any home-cooked food. Overlooking the okra, which is way too slimy for me, I was betting the woman who brought in the food was an excellent cook, and I was hungry.

The Reverend nodded and directed, “Mabel, you can just set that right here,” indicating some of the space at his end of the table. She put all the food within his reach with the practiced ease of years resigned to his authority, and we passed our plates around for him to serve up portions. I briefly considered telling him that I wouldn’t care for any okra, but decided I ought to take what I got. Being glaringly un-Baptist was suspicious enough without having to admit to a family in the Mississippi Delta that you don’t eat okra.

We ate for a while in awkward silence until the Reverend spoke. “So, Buddy.” There was an uncomfortable pause. “Trey tells me you’re from Vicksburg.”

“Yes sir.”

“And which church does your family attend down there?”

“Holy Trinity.”

His eyes lit up at that, like the look of hawk closing in on a rabbit in the open. He took a deep breath, cleared his throat, and accused, “Catholic.” It was an indictment, and he looked at me as if I were a puzzle now solved.

But that look was replaced with frustration when I answered, “No sir, Episcopal.”

The Reverend, apparently not immediately prepared with something else to say, and clearly not comfortable with the experience, muttered, “Oh.” And then, “I see. Well, I suppose we can’t control who Trey chooses for friends now that he’s away at a secular college.”

Mrs. Swayze asked, “Would you like some more tea, Buddy?”

But before I could answer, the Reverend continued. “Oh, no, no tea for an Episcopalian. The Whiskeypalians teach that whiskey and beer are just fine with Jesus, isn’t that right, Buddy? Why, you even serve wine in your church services, I believe.”

“Yes sir, we do. I think that’s because Jesus drank wine at the Last Supper.”

“Well, now, that’s quite an assertion. Is that what your High Priest tells you?”

“I think it’s in the Bible, sir.”

Mrs. Swayze looked a little anxious about the path of the dinner conversation. As if hoping to redirect our energies, she asked Trey, "How's school, honey? How about some more ham?"

The Reverend deliberately put his fork down and took a deep breath. I could see him arranging his thoughts, preparing to engage the heathen in his house. But before he could begin, Trey started talking about the football games that weekend. The Mississippi State Bulldogs were at home playing the Alabama Crimson Tide. He said the Dogs didn't have a chance, but that he and I would listen to the entire game on the radio because that's what True Fans do, that Ole Miss was playing that night, too, and that he felt sure they'd lose to the LSU Tigers, which was a good thing.

The moment passed, and theological crisis was averted, but the divide was sharply drawn. The conversation drifted into safer and warmer waters, and I couldn't help noticing that the Reverend lost interest early on.

After he'd finished his plate, he announced, "Well. I must retire to my study for the evening. We have something special this Sunday, and I want the sermon to be particularly powerful. You will all excuse me, I'm sure."

Nobody objected. In fact, the mood of the room lightened almost visibly with his departure. Mrs. Swayze waited until she heard the door to the study close, and then nodded to Trey, who got up and went toward the kitchen. Trey opened the door and said, "It's okay," and then came and sat back down.

A few seconds later, the door opened again, and Mabel the cook came out, this time carrying a plate of food that she set down at one of the empty places.

Mrs. Swayze said, "Buddy, I want you to meet my dear friend, Miss Mabel Robinson. Mabel, Buddy Hinton."

I smiled, glad this lady was on our side. "It's nice to meet you. I enjoyed dinner very much."

"I'm glad you liked it," she replied, "but I know you ain't done. I see you ain't much for okra."

"No ma'am. I sure would like some more ham and green beans, though. And another piece of that good cornbread."

Miss Mabel rewarded me with a big smile and more ham, green beans, and cornbread than I had started with, and the conversation relaxed. Trey filled them in on life in college, and they filled him in on the latest news and scandals in Riggs County and caught him up on the latest about his high school friends at other colleges.

Mrs. Swayze asked me what I was planning to study, and how I knew Trey, and if I was as big a football fan as he. I told them I didn't know what I was going to study yet, maybe either marine biology or psychology, that Trey and I lived in the same dorm, and that I didn't care for football all that much. Out of nowhere, Miss Mabel asked if I was in some kind of trouble.

I answered, "No ma'am."

"Your girlfriend leave you for a basketball star?" she asked.

"No ma'am," I said, "I don't have a girlfriend."

She eyed me suspiciously, and I waited for Mrs. Swayze or Trey to come to my rescue, but they didn't move a muscle. Miss Mabel did not relent. "Somethin' don't add up here. You ain't tellin' us the whole truth, are you?"

"What do you mean?"

"I mean, why you are here, in Riggsville, Miss'ippi, up in here among folks you don't know and don't much fit in with? You and Trey ain't such good friends that you would come here without some good reason." Then she looked at Mrs. Swayze and avowed, "He ain't tellin' the whole truth, I know he ain't."

Mrs. Swayze looked at me sympathetically and then turned to her friend and scolded, "Mabel, he has his own reasons, now, and I'm sure it's none of our business." She turned back to me and began, "Buddy, I'm sorry. You don't have to—"

But I had to interrupt. "No ma'am, I'm the one who needs to apologize this time. Miss Mabel, you're right. I haven't told y'all the whole truth."

Miss Mabel sat back vindicated, and Mrs. Swayze leaned forward, suddenly interested in the mystery of why I was there.

"A friend of mine is in the prison, and I needed to come and see him. I don't have a car, and Trey was kind enough to give me a ride."

Both women issued sighs, and Miss Mabel had a little smile.

"A friend of yours from high school?" asked Mrs. Swayze. "Someone from the college? Is it drugs?"

"Oh, no ma'am. This is an older man, somebody I've known most of my life, from Beaumont, where I grew up."

"How you gettin' out there tomorrow?" Miss Mabel asked.

I'd assumed Trey would be taking me, but I didn't want to get him into trouble. My face must have betrayed my concern, and Miss Mabel continued, "I'll take you." It sounded more like a proclamation than an invitation.

Trey announced, "I was thinking I'd go, too."

Mrs. Swayze was obviously a woman accustomed to controlling her emotions, but I could tell was on the edge of losing control now. "Now just a minute! Trey, you know how your father feels about your going out to the prison."

"Yes ma'am."

She nodded then, as if she thought the matter was settled, and was about to turn her attention to Miss Mabel. But then Trey continued, "If it's going to upset him, maybe we don't need to tell him. But I'm planning to go out there with Buddy tomorrow."

Miss Mabel hummed at that—"Mmm-hmm"—but I could tell she was proud of Trey.

He went on, "Mama, Buddy's my best friend at Mississippi State, and he's not my friend because I'm Brother Swayze's son. He doesn't care about any of that. He doesn't know what he's getting into out there, and I want to be there for him, that's all. Mama, *please*."

Mrs. Swayze considered a moment. I imagine she saw her little boy taking a step toward becoming a man. Or at least I think that's why she had tears in her eyes when she addressed me. "Tell me about this friend of yours."

I paused, unsure how much to trust, wondering how much to keep secret. I looked at Trey, who nodded reassuringly. "His name's Jake Jefferson. I've known him since I was a little kid. When I met him he was a fisherman, but he used to be a tent preacher "

Miss Mabel leaned in to put her hands on the table, as if she was holding on tight while something in her world shifted. "'The

Reverend Jacob J. Jefferson, Evangelist, Elder, and Prophet.' Preacher Jake is your friend?"

I was surprised she knew all that, and said with some misgivings, "Yes ma'am."

Miss Mabel was looking at me as if I'd just appeared there, like I was new to that spot. She said in a hushed tone, "You his friend Buddy."

It was too late to back out now. "Yes ma'am."

Trey and his mother looked completely lost. Mrs. Swayze said, "Mabel, what are you talking about?"

Not taking her eyes away from me, Miss Mabel answered, "Preacher Jake. Long time ago, I saw him heal a woman who'd had a bad back for ten, twelve years. I thought it was just some tomfoolery, y'know: a show for people who wanted to have something to believe in. But I knew that woman, knew her all my life. And she was sure enough healed. I mean, she just straightened right up after he touched her that night. It was . . . it was a miracle. We waited for him to come back, but he never did. Now he's in Parchman. He works in the kitchen with my man Cornelius."

I knew Mrs. Swayze was concerned for her son to go out to the prison, but I could also tell she wanted to trust him, and she did trust her friend Mabel. She looked at me for some sort of help.

"He was a traveling preacher for a long time," I explained, "until . . . until he lost his son in World War Two and became an alcoholic. Then he got in trouble with the law and went to prison."

"And he's been in prison for all that time?" Mrs. Swayze asked. "No, that can't be right—you knew him down in Beaumont, didn't you?"

"Yes ma'am. He got out of prison and came back to where he was from, in Beaumont. He was catching catfish for a fish house when I met him."

"So," Mrs. Swayze paused. She didn't seem to be able to find the right words.

Miss Mabel murmured, almost to herself, "I heard him preach one night, Jake Jefferson. He was good, too, he was real good."

"So why is he back in prison now?" Trey's mother finally asked.

"He just wants to be needed, and he needs somebody to take care of him. A few months ago he pretended to rob a bank so he could get arrested and put back in prison. He says they need him in there."

"Lord knows that's true," Miss Mabel agreed. When we all looked at her, she said to me, "He talks about you all the time. I know he'll be glad to see you. But it's a bad place in there, Buddy, a tough place."

"I figure it is," I said. "What does your husband do there?"

Miss Mabel stiffened a little and answered, "He's my man, you understand? He works at the prison, supervises the inmates who work in the kitchen."

I didn't understand, but I had enough sense to leave it alone. Later, Trey explained to me that they weren't actually legally married, not in a church, but that they had been together for a long time. It was something of a sensitive point for Miss Mabel, especially since she worked in the parsonage.

Mrs. Swayze came to my rescue again. "Well, boys, have you got time for a piece of Mabel's pecan pie, or have you got big plans for the night?"

Trey laughed, and I was happy to hear him say, "We don't have any plans at all, but even if we did, they'd have to wait 'til after we had some of that pie."

11

A Rose Blooming in the Swamp

The Reverend wasn't at breakfast the next morning; there was some sort of meeting at the church, according to Miss Mabel. We had ham and scrambled eggs, with wonderful thick grits and huge flaky biscuits smothered in milk sausage gravy. I ate way too much, and Trey ate more than I did, but still Miss Mabel clucked around us both, fussing about fast food restaurants and how young people today have no appreciation for good food. After we helped her wash the dishes and put them away, Miss Mabel was ready to go to Parchman.

She and Trey had decided we ought to go in her car, since it had her man's employee sticker in the window. It would also lessen the risk of the Reverend finding out that Trey had gone to the prison, as they reasoned the Mustang was too conspicuous. He sat in the back seat so he could duck down out of sight if he needed to.

Riggsville was no more impressive in the daylight than it had been the night before. On ground so flat it couldn't be distinguished from any of the miles and miles of flat ground all around it, it seemed to me that somebody decided a long time ago that they wanted to put a town there, and that was the only reason for its existence. I later found out that a wealthy cotton planter named Mr. Riggs had gotten an inside tip that the railroad would be coming through the area, and he built a store, a schoolhouse, and the Baptist church in anticipation. The track missed the ambitious little town twelve miles to the east, but the town struggled on. Riggsville had never declined; it had just never amounted to much.

We were riding in Miss Mabel's '67 Chevrolet Impala, the windows down in anticipation of what would be a warm day. Trey sat hunched over until we were out of town. It didn't take long.

Soon we were surrounded by miles of land bearing cotton or soybean fields as far as you could see in any direction. Looking ahead into the distance and a little off to the left, just off Highway 61, we saw a clump of tall trees. In the midst of the relentlessly level agriculture, those trees were visible for miles.

Over the lack of a working muffler and a variety of other automotive squeaks and grinds and noises I was afraid to ask about, I pointed toward the trees. "Miss'ippi State Penitentiary, Parchman, Miss'ippi," Miss Mabel said in a tired voice. "That's what they call the Farm."

It was the bleakest sight I could have ever imagined, even from a distance, and the closer we got, the bleaker it looked. The clump of trees was near the highway, next to the offices and chapel. The rest of the prison was treeless, surrounded by a ten- or twelve-foot-high fence topped with vicious, curling barbed wire.

"This is a God-forsaken place," Trey moaned.

I agreed. If any place was truly God-forsaken, it would have to be there.

Miss Mabel pulled the car up to the gate, and the pot-bellied guard inside the little white house groaned stiffly to his feet and came out to say hello.

"Hey, Miss Mabel, how you doin'?"

Miss Mabel seemed relaxed. "I'm fine, Rusty, how are you?"

He looked over at Trey and me and asked, "Who've you got in there?"

She answered, smooth as silk, "This is Buddy Hinton, a student at Miss'ippi State University. He's a friend of Trey Swayze, Brother Swayze's boy; you know Trey in the back seat there. Buddy's staying at the parsonage for the weekend. He's writing a paper on prison conditions, and . . . what was it, Buddy?"

I had a moment of panic before she continued, still smooth, "And Correctional Systems Reform." I could hear the capital letters the way she pronounced it.

The guard nodded and turned his attention back to Miss Mabel. They talked about how they ought to make the food better, largely based on his contention that the food for the employees should be cooked differently and separately from the food for the inmates. Miss Mabel had been a cook for the warden, Trey told me, before the Reverend hired her at the parsonage. Now she listened appreciatively, as if the man were telling her something she sincerely needed to know. After he waved us on and went back into the little house, she murmured, "He's been talking that same talk the whole time I've known him."

She parked the Impala under the shade of one of the trees I had seen from miles away. It was a huge, spreading oak, with its lowest branches almost touching the ground.

"What do we do now?" I asked her. "Do I need to go to some sort of visitors' area?" I had prison movies in my mind, where I would talk to Jake over a telephone, looking through a glass window.

Miss Mabel shook her head and smiled a secretive smile. "No, honey; you boys just come with me. Stay close, now." There was no reason for her to tell us that last part; we walked right on her heels.

She headed into the heart of the prison toward what looked like the largest building, which stood in the middle of a cluster of buildings. Trey and I followed, both scared and fascinated, walking a little closer to each other than either of us thought manly. She looked back to check on us and smiled a little. All the buildings were the same dirty white brick and wooden trim; the building we were heading for was much larger, with a shed by the backdoor for the mops and brooms.

We went around the back, where we saw two truck bays for delivering supplies to the kitchen, under the shade of another ancient oak. An old man, dressed in blue overalls and light blue inmate work shirt under a dirty white apron, leaned against the cinder-block wall. His number was printed over his left breast, where most shirts would have had a pocket. "Hey, Mabel, how you doin'? Hey, who you got there?"

"Mornin', Freddie. This is Trey Swayze, Brother Swayze's boy, and this is his friend, Buddy. Trey, Buddy, meet Freddie Jackson. Freddie's worked in the kitchen here for, what, Freddie, fifteen years, twenty?"

"Yes ma'am, 'bout that. Been knowin' ol' Cornelius that whole time, too." Then he looked at Trey and me, saying, "Mornin', boys. How you?"

I didn't know what to say or do. This was a real live convict, a criminal. He was here because he had committed a crime; clearly this was someone my mother would warn me to stay away from. Did he murder someone? Or was it rape, or just a simple robbery? There was no way for me to know what he had done, and no way to find out. I glanced over at Trey. He was clearly as uncomfortable as I was.

"Hi," I said.

Freddie chuckled, and Miss Mabel shook her head. She told him, "This is their first visit to prison. They're a little nervous, I 'spect." Then she assured us, "You're all right, boys. Freddie's a friend of mine."

I felt the red in my face and decided I would have to do something. I held out my hand to the convict before me. "I'm pleased to meet you, Mr. Jackson."

The old man looked surprised, but he took my hand and cut his eyes toward Miss Mabel.

Still shaking her head but smiling broadly now, she said to Freddie, "They got a lot to learn, but they goin' to be all right." Freddie nodded, and shook Trey's hand, too. Miss Mabel continued, "Buddy's here to see Preacher Jake. You seen him anywhere?"

Freddie looked at me again, and his eyes went wide, as if he were seeing me for the first time. "You Buddy! You Preacher Jake's Buddy, ain't you? Buddy Hinton."

"Yes sir," I answered.

He laughed again. "You sure is, Buddy Hinton, just like he talked about; you *Buddy*."

"Have you seen him today?" I asked.

"Yeah," Mr. Jackson said excitedly. "He in the kitchen, right here. You can go in right here. Yes sir, Buddy Hinton, c'mon in here with me." He led me to a screen door and held it open for me like I was somebody important. I looked at Miss Mabel, and she nodded toward the door. Trey stood a little behind her, trying to act nonchalant and failing miserably.

I went to the door, put my hand on the handle, and paused. Would Jake be embarrassed for me to visit him? Would the other men in the prison give him a hard time? Why else would he have written that I shouldn't come? Would he be mad at me? What would I say? I didn't want things to be awkward between me and Jake.

Miss Mabel was just behind me, crowding me toward the screen door. She whispered, "Go on, Buddy. I know he'll be glad to see you."

I opened the door and went in alone. It was a huge kitchen, with tremendous pots and trays and all sorts of oversized spoons and utensils hanging over a long table. There were six or seven men doing various jobs, all of them wearing blue overalls and blue shirts with white aprons. They worked at their tasks with well-practiced ease, each of them in their own area, using tools they were well accustomed to. I heard the whistling before I saw him, that plaintive, mournful, triumphant music blown through his lips from his heart to mine, and there he was off to my right, chopping something into small pieces with a big knife.

I hesitated, then slowly walked over to where Jake was. Everybody stopped what they were doing to watch. He finally looked up and saw me. I couldn't catch my breath for a few seconds, worrying about how he would react to my being there. When his face broke into that grin I loved so much, it was like the sun breaking through storm clouds.

"Buddy!" he said, beaming. "Hey—look here, it's Buddy!" There were tears running down his face. I walked into his open arms and felt the tears on my own cheeks, too, as I put my face against his chest. I remember dreading the end of the hug, because then we'd have to talk, and I still wasn't sure what I wanted to say.

When he finally let me go, I had to let him go, too, and I became aware of the other men in the kitchen, all of them black, all of them staring at a white college boy whom an old black man had been holding as if I were his son. I blushed, red and hot. But Jake announced to all the men, "Hey, y'all! This is Buddy, my Buddy. Buddy Hinton. This is my Buddy I been tellin' you 'bout." And the men in the kitchen put down their rags and spoons and knives, clapping us on the shoulders and making me feel welcome.

Every once in a while, you get the sense that you're home. It comes in a smell, in a memory, in something so deep down inside that it's hard to know what's going on. There in that prison kitchen, surrounded by some of the most dangerous thieves and felons in the great state of Mississippi, I had that feeling: being with Jake was coming home.

"Buddy," Jake said, "I want you to meet my kitchen brothers." One by one they came up, some bashful, some curious, all polite. Each of them already knew who I was, and about my friendship with Jake. The first was a tall black man who carried himself with a natural dignity that would have shamed the Queen of England. His eyes had the look of a man who had seen more of the world than he wanted to remember. "This is Earl Cook. Earl and me was good friends the first time I was up in here. He been up here the whole time." Jake leaned in close and continued, "Big Earl is one of the main reasons I come back here. I want to make sure he know the Lord pretty good. He older than he looks, and I just wanted to be sure 'bout him."

I held out my hand, and Big Earl took it solemnly, as if he and I were entering a commitment of some sort. "It's nice to meet you, Mr. Cook," I said.

A shorter, heavier man came up next. He had nothing like the dignity of Big Earl, but he made up for it with an evident sweetness.

"This my friend Roscoe Burrell," Jake said. "Roscoe's from Vicksburg, too, just like you, Buddy."

"I'm proud to meet you, Buddy Hinton, I sure am. You got family still livin' in Vicksburg?"

"Yes sir."

Several of the men snickered, and I was quick to say, "Well, Beaumont, really." They kept on smiling like somebody had told a joke that I didn't get. Then I realized that all the men were tickled that I would say "Yes sir" to a black man, and to a convict on top of that.

But the truth was, I couldn't have just said "Yes" to save my life.

"Where your daddy work?" Roscoe asked.

I told him that my dad worked for the Waterways Experiment Station, with the Corps of Engineers.

"He a good man?"

"Yes sir."

"A man be proud to have a boy like you."

"Thank you."

There was a growing line of other men to meet, more than there were in the kitchen to start with, I think. I suppose word got out that Preacher Jake's friend Buddy had come to visit, and whatever he'd been saying about me drew something of a crowd. I've forgotten most of those men now, but I knew when I met him that I'd never forget Eugene.

Eugene was simply huge. When I was seventeen, I was probably six feet two or three, and Earl Cook and a couple of the other men I met that day were at least that tall. Eugene towered over us all like a straight pine in a grove of dogwoods. He was easily six or seven inches taller than me, but that's not what made him huge. He had a massive chest, a neck like a bull's, and arms as thick as telephone poles. Eugene was the most human I had ever seen in one pair of shoes.

He came up to me with his eyes looking down, watching his feet. Several of the other men were pushing him, gently and cautiously, toward me. I was surprised to realize that this giant man was not only shy but also scared. "And this is my little brother, Eugene Jefferson," Jake said. The rest of the men laughed comfortably at the probably well-worn joke of using the word "little" in any connection with this giant man.

I replied, "I'm pleased to meet you, Mr. Jefferson," and I held out my hand to shake his.

He took it gently, like he was picking up a kitten, and muttered, "Yes sir. Pleased to make your 'quaintance."

Just for the briefest of moments, he risked looking up, and my eyes met his. It occurred to me that here was a man who could be dangerous. Jake put his hand on my arm and squeezed both assurance and a warning. I had seen somewhere, in some movie or book, that you should never ask anybody in prison what he did, but for some reason I wanted to know more about this man. "How long have you been here?" I asked.

Eugene answered in a low, soft voice, "I couldn't say, Mr. Buddy. Been a long time, though. A long time. 'Most all my life, I believe."

Jake pulled at my arm, tugging me away. I let myself be pulled, not fully comprehending what was going on, either in the kitchen or in my heart.

Jake declared, loudly enough for everyone to hear, "C'mon over here, Buddy, let me get back to work 'fore the Boss comes up in here."

Jake picked up his knife and went back to cutting celery. The other men grabbed their rags and knives and found other things to do, but they all stayed close enough so that they could see me and Jake.

"Jake," I asked, "what did you tell these guys about me?"

"Just the truth, boy, just the truth. I told 'em you's a good boy, that you brung me back to livin' my life. I told 'em 'bout your friend Andy dyin', and how you took that pretty hard. I told 'em you up at the State College now, and how I went to your confirmin' at the church. It sure is good to see you, Buddy, sure is, damn good."

Then he looked away and lowered his voice to whisper. "But you should not be up in here, Buddy. Parchman Prison ain't no safe place for a boy like you."

It struck me then that it was strange to see him in there, this wonderful, kind, wise man in such a desolate place, surrounded by dangerous and frightening men. It was like seeing a rose blooming in the swamp.

"Jake, are you okay in here? This place . . . it's rough. Aren't you scared?"

He laughed then, as if my question was silly but harmless. "No, Buddy, I ain't scared. I'm fine. These mens is my friends. They all got troubles, they all done things they wish they hadn't, but that's how it is. Ever'body got troubles in here, out there, too; we all done things we feel bad 'bout later. Up in here, I'm somebody important. They call me Preacher Jake, they listen to what I got to say. They need to hear what I got to say. *It's all 'bout hope, Buddy.* That's what I got to give, and that's what they needs to hear. I got hope to share, thanks to you, you understand that, Buddy? You brought me hope, now I got hope to share. That's what I tell them 'bout you, that's why they all want to see you.

"But listen here, Buddy—hear me now. Ain't ever'body wants hope. Some of these folks got a different way, an' all my talkin' 'bout God's got 'em messed up. That's why you should not be here."

I was used to feeling bewildered with Jake. I knew he would straighten me out; it was just a matter of asking the right questions. "You mean some of them aren't Christians?" I ventured.

"Aw, hell, Buddy, we ain't worried 'bout all that up in here. No, some of 'em ain't Christians, but they's more to it than that, more than I know how to explain. Listen here, Buddy: They's mens up in here that hate God, hate love, hate life. It messes up how they understand the world. They is sad men, sick men, but they's powerful, too. They tell the other mens that God ain't nothin' but lies. They tells 'em life ain't nothin' but fightin', fightin' to see if you is goin' to control other peoples, or is they goin' to control you. They tells 'em every man got to fight for his own self. They ain't no way interested in me comin' up in here talkin' 'bout the love of God, and how our hope is in Jesus, whatnot like that.

"But they's scared, Buddy, scared somebody goin' to prove 'em out to be liars. That's why they's scared of me; they want to shut me up."

"Do they want to hurt you, Jake? Are they gonna try to kill you?"

"No. My kitchen brothers don't never let me go nowhere by myself. They protectin' me all the time." He laughed then at the thought of it. "Hell, I can't even take a leak by myself—they tryin' to go with me to the john! And them other mens don't really want to hurt me, noways. They just wants to keep me scared; they needs to keep me alive so they can prove I'm wrong, see."

I was horrified at the idea that they might prove him wrong, and I told him so.

He just laughed again. "They can't prove I'm wrong no more than I can prove I'm right! But they's sure goin' to keep tryin'."

Long before I had figured all that out, he asked, "How's your mama and 'em?"

I told him my family was all fine, that nothing ever changed. He asked me about school and whether I had a girlfriend yet. I asked him if he needed any money or if I could do anything for him. He assured me he was fine. "So when are you going to get out of here?" I finally asked.

"Hell, I don't know. It don't matter: reckon if they put me out too soon I'll have to rob another bank or whatnot. This is where I need to be, Buddy, where I'm s'posed to be. It's my work, you understand?"

I didn't understand, but I was trying to. I knew it had something to do with his relationship with God, and with finding hope even after all that had happened to him. I guess I didn't realize exactly why that was important, but I could tell it was.

After a while, he handed me a knife and showed me how to cut the celery. We chopped for a while in comfortable silence, until I realized that he didn't seem as comfortable as I was. "Is something wrong, Jake?"

"Buddy, it ain't safe for you up in here," he said again. "These mens right here is my friends, but they is other mens here who won't want you here. They's dangerous, and they got nothin' to lose. They goin' to hear you're here, and they goin' to come lookin' for trouble. If they don't find none, they'll make some. Buddy, I am glad to see you, you just don't know. But you got to go."

"I just needed to be sure you were okay."

"I know it. It means the world to me that you came to see me, I hope you know it does. But sure 'nough now, you got to go. I don't believe I could forgive it if somethin' bad was to happen to you."

I told him I'd leave, and he made me promise not to come back. He told me he'd write and that he'd let me know if he needed anything. He started to herd me toward the door, and all the men in the kitchen, more now than before, it seemed, came to say good-bye. I shook all their hands and wished them well.

The last one to come up was Eugene. Again, Jake seemed to tense up, ready to protect me from the huge man. He put his hand on my arm, just above the elbow, pulling me gently. I didn't understand. Eugene didn't seem menacing there in the prison kitchen. He was just big.

He came up to me without anybody guiding him, and I figured he had gotten over being shy of me. He was looking at his feet, but I held out my hand to him and said, "Good luck to you, Mr. Jefferson." I happened to remember his last name because it was the same as Jake's, and Jake had made the joke about him being his little brother.

Eugene looked at my hand as if he was making a decision. Then he looked up, looked me in the eyes, and asked, "You love Preacher Jake?"

"Yes sir."

"You believe what all he say?"

"Yes sir."

I couldn't place his expression. It was like he was trying to solve a puzzle nobody else could see. Wanting to help him, I asked, "Do you?"

Jake tightened his grip on my arm as Eugene leaned down to me and whispered, "I believes him when he talkin' to me, but I believes Eddie when he talkin', too. I don't know who I believes when they ain't nobody around."

Before I could ask him who Eddie was, Jake urged, "Eugene, Buddy's got to go now. It's time for him to go." Then to me he murmured, "C'mon, Buddy, I'll walk you out."

One of the men opened the screen door in the back of the kitchen, and we walked out into the shade of the huge oak. Trey and Miss Mabel were waiting for me, and I motioned to Trey.

"Jake," I said, "I'd like you to meet my friend Trey Swayze from college. His parents live here in Riggsville. Trey, this is my friend, Jake Jefferson."

They shook hands, and Jake asked, "You Preacher Swayze's boy?"

Trey looked uncomfortable with the ease of this identification, but he nodded and replied, "Yes sir."

Jake smiled his wonderful smile and joked, "Your daddy's pretty full of hisself, ain't he?"

Trey smiled, too, and answered, "Yes sir."

Jake nodded and turned to Miss Mabel. "Thanks for bringin' my Buddy and his friend," he told her. "It was fine to see him, tonic for my heart. But now he needs to go, before they's any trouble. You understand."

"I understand, Preacher Jake. You need anything?"

"No, no. Ever'thing's fine. Just get my mule-headed boy out of here."

Then he opened his arms and I stepped into them. It was like sitting on your mother's lap when you have a skinned knee. We hugged a long time, without saying a word, but then much too soon Jake was insisting again that I had to go, and we were back in Miss Mabel's '67 Chevrolet Impala, moving down that flat, straight Highway 61 toward Riggsville.

On the way back, Trey asked what time it was; his watch was broken. As for me, I had decided in Philosophy 101 that I didn't want to be constantly reminded of the passage of time, so I'd told myself and others that was the reason I didn't wear a watch. The real reason, though, was that I'd gone through three or four of them in high school, smashing them into things or forgetting to take them off before I got in a shower.

I shrugged. I never knew what time it was.

"It's a quarter 'til eleven," Miss Mabel answered. "I got to get back and start on something for lunch."

I couldn't believe it. We'd gotten to Parchman a little before nine o'clock; it didn't seem possible that I'd been in that kitchen for nearly two hours.

As we turned the corner onto the street where the parsonage stood, Miss Mabel said, "He's home."

"Who?" I wondered.

But Trey just said, "Let us out here."

Miss Mabel pulled over, and we got out. She told us we'd been for a walk, that Trey had been showing me the town. She told us we'd be home in about a half an hour, just in time for lunch, and we knew she was going to be right.

12

The Kind of Drivel They Teach

We walked up the front porch steps just as Mrs. Swayze was coming out of the house.

"Good morning, boys," she said. "Mabel tells me you've been out for a walk. Seeing the sights, Buddy?"

For a moment I was confused. Mrs. Swayze knew where we had been. Then I realized that the Reverend could be listening, and that we were playing a game to protect ourselves. "Yes ma'am," I answered.

In a quiet voice she warned Trey, "Your father's back from his meeting. I think it didn't go well. He's in his study."

"Yes ma'am," Trey replied, and it seemed to me that they were both battening down hatches I couldn't see. She put her hand on the back of his neck, as if to lend him some of her strength.

Miss Mabel came out on the porch, too, and beamed. "Hi, boys. Trey, were you showing Buddy around?"

She, too, was helping us get our stories together, preparing us to meet the Reverend.

"Yes ma'am," I affirmed, joining the game. "It was a good tour. I—I'm glad Trey could show me around." I nodded to Miss Mabel as I said "Trey," trying to include her as well.

I was beginning to appreciate the risk they had taken to go with me, and I wanted to thank Miss Mabel for driving us. These three lived under the thumb of a tyrant, and I realized what they had done for me that morning.

"It's almost time for lunch," Miss Mabel announced. "Boys, y'all need to wash up." In a quieter voice she said to me, "Buddy, you got to do something with that hair."

We washed up. I tried for a while to bring my hair under some sort of control, and we went into the dining room to eat.

The Reverend and Mrs. Swayze were waiting for us. He paused, assessing each of us, and again I felt like I was somehow inadequate. When he sat down, we all sat; when he gave the blessing, we all bowed our heads. This time it was much shorter, almost terse. Again, after the "amen," Miss Mabel came in with our lunch on her little cart: ham sandwiches, corn on the cob, and yellow squash casserole. The Reverend ate almost as quickly as he had prayed and spoke only when he excused himself to go back to the church. The rest of the lunch was very enjoyable—except for the squash casserole, which they allowed me to ignore.

That afternoon, Trey and I rode around the town, and I saw the high school, its battered sign out front proclaiming it "The Home of the Riggsville Raiders," a proud if faded memory of a state football championship back in 1961. We listened to the football game on the radio and didn't miss a play, even though we both knew the Mighty Bulldogs of Mississippi State could not prevail. I was surprised that Trey sang the "Star-Spangled Banner" along with the radio, until I realized that the whole reason to sing the National Anthem at a ball game was so you could yell, "Go to Hell, Ole Miss!" over the last notes.

Trey was feeling guilty for not being there in person, as if he'd somehow failed the Bulldogs, and as I listened with him, I began to understand some of his passion. It was the first time I'd ever listened to a whole football game, and Trey explained the finer points. He also taught me that there is no shame in losing to the Alabama Crimson Tide, but that people who go to Ole Miss are evil, smug aristocrats, worthy of nothing but our scorn. Thus Trey expanded my understanding of the game, and I felt the passion of it as I never had before.

When the game ended, we consoled each other, saying that losing 0 to 35 to Bear Bryant's boys was not all that bad, that it was actually closer than the score showed, and (this one was true) that it could have been worse.

After supper, Trey and I sat on the porch, shelling purple-hulled peas with Mrs. Swayze and Miss Mabel. I listened contentedly as they talked about their town and their family—comfortable, familiar talk about people and things they knew and loved. Eventually, both of the women left us, and we listened to the Ole Miss game. State had lost convincingly, and we rooted for Ole Miss to lose, too, to soothe our pain. LSU graciously obliged, beating the Rebels gloriously. The boys from Baton Rouge scored more than fifty points that night, and Trey and I celebrated every one of them. I had never realized it until that night, but the sports fan's fervor is fueled not only by love of his team but also by hatred of its rivals.

We rocked in the rocking chairs on the front porch for a long time that night, talking about our dreams, our loves, and our fears. Trey told me he wanted to be a football coach; I told him I thought I would like to be an Episcopal priest. We talked about my family, and I said I hoped he could meet them someday. We exaggerated our romantic histories, both of us understanding that the other was stretching things.

After a while, it occurred to me that the only sound I heard was tree frogs and cicadas. I had dozed off, and so had Trey. I gave him a nudge, and we agreed it was time for bed.

A few minutes later, I went into the kitchen wearing my cut-off sweat pants to get a glass of water. I was surprised to find the Reverend there, his head down on the round oak table. If I didn't know better, I'd have thought he'd passed out. I asked if he was okay.

He looked up at me then, searching me with his red, tired eyes. He looked sad: a forlorn, lonely, vulnerable man. He was the Reverend, a great man in the eyes of many, but other than the church, other than the Bible, other than the façade of Brother Swayze, it didn't seem like there was much more to him.

"Are you okay?" I asked again.

Narrowing his eyes, he said, "Do you believe you're saved, son?"

And just like that, I was hauled into a theological discussion. I sat at the table, opposite the Reverend, and answered, "Yes sir, I do."

"But do you *know* it?"

"I know that God loves me."

"Well, of course He does. But are you saved by the Blood of the Lamb?"

This was unfamiliar territory, not the way we talked at my church. I searched for an appropriate response, and an interesting thing happened. I remembered Jake distinctly, as clearly as if I were watching a scene in a movie. This might have been the first time something like that happened, when I remembered and relied on words Jake had said. It certainly wasn't the last.

I remembered him sitting on the fallen sweet gum tree after Andy died. I remembered how he preached a little sermon. "When we gets to them Pearly Gates," he said, "it ain't goin' to be a matter of what did we believe, but how did we love. . . . And it ain't goin' to be do God choose Heaven for us, or do God choose Hell for us, but do we choose God, mmm-hmm, or do we choose ourselfs."

"I'm saved by God's grace," I answered.

"But have you accepted Jesus Christ as your personal Lord and Savior?"

"My personal Lord? I believe Jesus came for all the children of God."

"Ah, a universalist. You've fallen into the liberal trap. And everybody's going to heaven, I suppose?"

"I . . . don't know. Maybe if God had His way, I suppose we all would. But we don't all choose God, we don't all choose love. Some of us choose to serve ourselves."

"Are you saying that we can thwart the will of God Almighty? There is no warrant in Scripture for such idealistic speculation."

"Well, sir, you might be right. But in the story of Adam and Eve, did God want them to eat the forbidden fruit?"

"No, of course not. It was God that forbade them."

"Exactly. But they ate it anyway. You think God could have stopped them?"

"Of course He could have stopped him."

"But He didn't. He let them have their way, honored their choice, even though it pained Him and cost them."

"It certainly did not pain God for Adam and Eve to disobey Him!"

"Sure it did. He was ticked off, and He cursed the ground or something."

"'Ticked off?' I'm not going to sit here and argue with a liberal young fool! You have no idea what you're talking about, young man. You think life is all about blue jeans, easy sex, rock and roll, and smoking drugs. And you have the temerity to preach to me in my own kitchen! I know you. I see you in all your glory. Get thee behind me, Satan!"

I stood up then, stunned and bewildered at the turn in our conversation, and made my way for the kitchen door. Then an odd thing happened: I was filled with an unreal sense of serenity. It was as if I was willing to accept whatever punishment he might dish out. I turned and said with deliberate calm, "Brother Swayze, you don't know me at all. You certainly don't know what I think about life or anything else. But I'll tell you a little of what I believe: I believe the gospel is about love." I paused, wondering if I had the courage to say what I wanted to say next. Then, figuring I couldn't make things much worse, I concluded, "It's *not* about control."

Then I left and went to the guest room, closed and locked the door, and waited for the Reverend to come and throw me out of his house. I put my clothes back on, just in case, and fell asleep listening for his footsteps.

The next morning, Trey knocked on the door to wake me up. I was surprised to find I'd slept in my jeans, until I remembered that I'd more than half expected to be tossed out of the parsonage during the night. He told me I needed to hurry if I wanted to get a shower before breakfast, that church started at 10:30. I understood that skipping church was not an option, even in my new role as Brother Swayze's embodiment of Satan.

I took a shower and wrestled with my hair. I thought about tying it back into a ponytail, but it wasn't quite long enough. Besides, I didn't know how the Reverend would react, and I didn't want to make life worse for Trey.

I was greatly relieved to find that the Reverend was not at breakfast; he was already at the church, of course, preparing for the day.

We had thick, spicy sausages and pancakes with Log Cabin syrup, and Miss Mabel sat and ate with us. We talked about my visit with Jake at Parchman, and Miss Mabel assured me that her man Cornelius was watching after him. "Preacher Jake'll be just fine, don't you worry," she cooed.

The Sunday morning service at the Riggsville Baptist Church was long, made almost tolerable by the singing of several patriotic hymns. The service was interesting enough in its own way, but I was glad when the sermon blew itself out and the service ended.

We went to the Riggs County Country Club for Sunday dinner. The family lunched there every Sunday afternoon, an opportune moment for the Reverend to display his wife and son and continue to schmooze the congregation. It also allowed Mabel to go to her church with her family. As we got out of the car and walked across the gravel parking lot, Trey prepared me for what was coming.

"Now, when he gets here, Father will ask what we thought of the service. It's not a good time to make any criticism, even if it's valid or constructive or clever. Usually by the time church is over on Sunday, he's ready to fight, and I learned a long time ago that it's better if it's not me that he fights with."

"So what should I say?"

"As little as possible. Tell him you liked it. But mostly, just stay quiet."

We were seated in the middle of a large room full of buffet tables heavy laden with fried chicken, fried fish, roast beef, and all sorts of vegetables and bread.

The Reverend chatted and back-slapped his way to our table, flashing a smile at everyone he met. He kissed his wife on her cheek—the first affection I'd seen between them, which was clearly for public consumption—and sat down. We had saved him the seat next to the wall so he could watch his flock grazing on the Country Club buffet. I was, appropriately enough, seated opposite him.

He looked at me like a pitcher looking into the eyes of a slugger he's had a hard time with, and greeted me with what seemed an accusation. "Buddy."

"Sir," I replied. I figured that was safe. And safe was what I wanted to be.

He looked at Trey and continued, "It's good to have you home, son, back where you belong. What did you think of the service?"

Trey looked aside at me before saying, "It was great, Father. I loved it."

The Reverend followed his glance over to me, but, with a will, he turned to his wife instead. "Mary Claire?"

"It was wonderful, Stewart. And your sermon was very moving. How did you think it went?"

He smiled winningly and waved at someone behind me as he murmured, "The choir director almost ruined the whole thing, showing off as usual. And Shelton—did you hear Barney Shelton's closing prayer this morning? I thought he was going to preach my whole sermon all over again!"

I agreed with him that this would have been a terrible development, but I kept it to myself, playing it safe.

We went through the buffet line, where I took several pieces of fried chicken and some mashed potatoes. I thought I should get squash or okra, just to create the impression that I was a true-blue, all-American Southern boy, but I knew my cover was already blown.

We ate the majority of our meal with only polite conversation, largely carried by Trey and his mother. I was lying low, and the Reverend's smile never reached his eyes. It seemed glued on, in case one of his flock was looking.

We'd all gone back to get a piece of pie (apple for each of the Swayzes, lemon icebox for me) and settled back at our table (coffee for the Reverend, tea for Mrs. Swayze, milk for the boys), when the Reverend, noticing that the room was almost empty, turned his raptor glare on me. He looked at me for a moment, as if expecting me to look away.

But that odd sense of tranquility from the night before returned; I didn't look away at all. I tried to show no expression, but I wasn't going to look away.

I was remembering what Jake had told me about the givers and the takers, and I realized that the Reverend had been a taker for most or all of his life. I saw that Trey and his mother had no choice but to be givers. And it occurred to me that I was leaving that afternoon, that I didn't ever have to see this jerk again, and that I didn't have to give him anything.

I was looking at the biggest alligator in the swamp, but it wasn't my swamp. So I glared back, as best I could, and waited for him to speak.

"And what did you think of the service, Buddy? Different from what you're accustomed to, I imagine."

"Yes sir." I wasn't going to back down, but I'd take a way out if it were presented to me.

Of course, Brother Swayze didn't let it go so easily. "How did you like the sermon?" He was clearly enjoying the moment.

"Well, like you said, it was different from what I'm used to."

"And what are you used to?"

"Sir?"

Obviously impatient now, the Reverend pressed on. "How is what you're accustomed to different from this morning's service?"

Trey and Mrs. Swayze studied what was left of their pie with resigned looks on their faces. I could tell they knew there was no hope for me.

But I knew I had nothing to lose. And that, I figured, made me dangerous. Brother Swayze, on the other hand, was somewhat vulnerable. I damned the torpedoes and plunged in where angels fear to tread: arguing with a Southern Baptist preacher over his apple pie at Sunday lunch.

I thought for a moment and then said, "My experience is that the church ought to encourage people to think for themselves, to work out their own salvation in fear and trembling, as St. Paul wrote."

"Philippians, chapter two and verse twelve," cited Mrs. Swayze quietly, to the amazement of the rest of us.

Brother Swayze was furious, fuming, and frustrated.

I noted that Mrs. Swayze submissively studied her pie again, but Trey looked at me when I glanced at him. He winked, and then his eyes went back to his now-empty plate.

I was concerned that I was making trouble for Trey and his mother. Trying to back out into something we could all agree on, I said, "Look, it's about love, right?" I remembered a part from the Book of Common Prayer service at my church that I always liked, and said it from memory: "Thou shalt love the Lord thy God with all thy heart, and with all thy soul, and with all thy mind. This is the first and great commandment. And the second is like unto it: Thou shalt love thy neighbor as thyself. On these two commandments hang all the Law and the Prophets.'"

"Are *you* quoting Scripture to *me*?"

And since a response came quickly to mind, I eased back in my chair and said it. "I hadn't realized it was exclusively yours to quote."

"Of all the nerve!" he sputtered. He looked to his wife as if to see her sharing his shock. But her face betrayed no shock. It was more like satisfaction.

And it occurred to me that I could be wrong, which at that moment was not altogether a happy realization. It struck me that the Reverend could be correct, and I could be completely and totally mistaken. After all, he had been doing this for a long time and had a library full of books to back him up. All I had was the freedom of having nothing to lose and remembered wisdom from an old black man sitting on a fallen sweet gum tree.

Then I realized that I could use this realization to my advantage. "Of course, I could be wrong," I offered.

Trey and his mother both looked up sharply. There was a wounded look in Trey's face. Mrs. Swayze frowned at me, as if she were trying to understand what I was doing.

The Reverend was momentarily confused, and then he agreed, with justification dripping in his voice, "Yes, I believe you are." Clearly, he thought that would be an appropriate place for the conversation to end.

But I wasn't done. "I didn't say I was wrong. I said I could be. I certainly don't pretend to know everything about God, or Christianity, or faith. It's not for mortals to know everything there is to know. And that means, Brother Swayze, that *you* could be wrong, too."

He was speechless. I had the strong sense that it wasn't a condition he'd experienced often, or at least not often enough.

"You have to admit," I pressed, "that there is at least a possibility."

The Reverend tried to rally. "No. I am not wrong. I *could not* be wrong, because what I say is based in Holy Scripture, written for our edification by the Lord God Himself. 'All scripture is given by inspiration of God, and is profitable for doctrine, for reproof, for correction, for instruction in righteousness.'"

"Does that include all the Bible?"

"Of course it does!"

"The Old Testament, too?"

"Certainly."

"How many animals did Noah take on the ark?" It was abrupt, and seemed completely out of the blue. But I knew where it came from, and I silently thanked my dear friend Andy for asking it.

I could tell the Reverend thought it was a trick question. Cautiously, he ventured, "Two of every kind of animal, according to the book of Genesis. I would have thought even an Episcopalian would have known that."

I had him, and I knew it. He didn't even know what was coming. "What chapter and verse is that, Reverend?"

"Why, I'd have to look it up. It's early in Genesis, of course, chapter five or six, I suppose."

"Do you have a Bible with you, sir?"

"Of course I do. I always carry the Word of God with me."

"Could you look it up for me?"

"Well, the Bible I carry with me only has the New Testament and the Book of Psalms. Where are you going with all this?"

"It's just that I think the Bible was inspired, but not like you say. The Holy Ghost didn't dictate the words to somebody to write down."

"Is this the kind of drivel they teach you in Episcopal Sunday school?"

"No sir. A friend of mine told me that."

"A preacher?"

"Well, yes sir."

"And what did this liberal preacher tell you?"

"I don't think he's particularly liberal, sir. He believes the Bible is stories written by a lot of different people over a long period of time. He told me that some of the contradictions in the Bible are just two different people telling the same story in two different ways."

I could tell that the Reverend was enraged. "There are . . . no *contradictions* . . . in the Bible, young man."

"But in another place it says that Noah took seven pairs of animals on the ark. If God wrote the whole thing, He'd have gotten His facts straight, don't you think?"

"What are you talking about?"

"I don't know. That's what I was asking you; look it up. Something about clean animals and unclean animals." I'd never looked it up myself, and I actually hadn't thought that particular point since Jake and I had talked about it. But I knew it was there; Jake told me it was.

I decided this would be an appropriate time to go, that I ought to get out while the getting was good. I thought it probably wouldn't be getting any better than it was at that moment. So I stood up and said, "Mrs. Swayze, I thank you for your gracious hospitality, and I apologize for causing any trouble. Trey, I think it's time for us to go."

Mrs. Swayze stood, too. "Thank you for coming, Buddy. We enjoyed having you, and you are more than welcome in my home any time."

Brother Swayze sat with his mouth agape, and his wife continued. "Trey, I'll give you boys a ride home so you can start packing up and getting ready to go." To her husband, she said, "I'll see you later, dear." And then she walked out, without giving her husband so much as a peck on the cheek, but with her head held high. Trey followed close behind.

I turned to the Reverend, almost sorry for him, in the same way I'd felt sorry for that snake Lewis and I had jabbed to death years before. His mouth was still wide open, and he looked like he was about to say something. I waited, but he had nothing to say.

I held out my hand then, as I had when I'd met him. "Thank you, Brother Swayze, for your hospitality. You have a fine church."

This time he took my hand. He was dazed, probably still trying to figure out what had happened. He muttered, "Thank you" in a voice that seemed to come from a great distance. And then, almost as if he realized what he was doing, he looked at me with sharper eyes and saw me more in the light he had the night before. In a sterner voice, closer to his natural self, he said, "Good-bye." The note of finality was not lost on me; he never wanted to see me again.

I turned and walked away through the maze of tables and out into the parking lot, where I climbed into the car. I sat in the front passenger seat; Trey was in the back. I looked at Mrs. Swayze and said, "Whew."

"You said it, kid," she replied.

And Trey added an exclamation point, saying "Amen" with a long "A," as he was a Baptist.

13

The Great Parade of Pagans

We rode away quickly, as if lingering might change something that had happened, as if the Reverend might catch me in the parking lot and somehow prove me wrong.

After we were safely away, Trey and his mother seemed to let out their breath. I guess I wasn't in the position to appreciate exactly what had happened there at the Country Club, and what it meant for them. They were elated that somebody had put Brother Swayze in his place, but they knew that there would be consequences and repercussions. The Reverend was not the kind of man who could let something like this drop.

Mrs. Swayze encouraged us to pack up quickly and hit the road. All of us expected the master of the house to return at any moment, and we thought it would be best if Trey and I were heading east when he did. Some of Trey's laundry was still wet, but they decided to put it in a garbage bag.

"Clothes dry in Starkville, too," his mother assured us.

She walked us to the car, almost pushing us in her graceful, gentle way. She hugged her son and told him to call when we got there, and then she came to me. I was surprised that she hugged, me, too, but I managed to hug her back.

"I hope I haven't caused you any trouble, Mrs. Swayze," I offered.

She chuckled. "Oh, there's always something that has him upset. He'll rail and pontificate about your impertinence and audacity for a while, and then you'll be lumped in with the great parade of pagans and idolaters who don't do what he thinks you ought to do. I'll hear a few extra sermons about the corruption of innocence, and the ravages of drugs and rock and roll music, the terrible waste of the youth of America today, that sort of thing, but I've heard them all before. It'll be nice to put your sweet face on it. I'll smile when I think of you."

I was flabbergasted and didn't know what to say.

"You didn't do anything wrong, sweetheart," she assured me. The term of fondness reminded me of my mother. "All you did was say what you believe, and answer his question. He'll get past it, but for right now, you two have got to go."

I thanked her again, told her to tell Miss Mabel thanks, and we left. I looked back and saw her going up the steps on the porch, back into her house. I'd come to visit one prison, but I wound up visiting two.

Trey and I went back to school without incident, but with several retellings of the conversations between me and the Reverend. As the days and semesters rolled by, we became inseparable friends. We ate together at least once a day, went to all sorts of sporting events together, studied together, and just hung out together. All through high school, Jake had been my only real friend. And all through high school, Trey had been Brother Swayze's boy. I understood now how both things would get in the way of deep friendships with other guys our age.

A few days after my visit to the Delta, I got the following letter:

November 4, 1973
Sunday

Dear Buddy,

It sure was good to see you boy.
It warmed up this old man's heart powerful.
But you should not come back up in here again.
All my kitchen brothers was very glad to meet you. They thought you was real nice, too.

Sometimes when I talk to them I say your name and they just about think they knows you, too.

A few minutes after you left, a sneaky-looking fellow named Eddie come into the kitchen.

He said he wanted to meet you.

I was glad you was gone.

He is a dangerous man and my main adversary here.

He wants the mens here to think they is all his servants.

He wants them to think that he is running the show in here with fear and what Saint Paul called hardness of heart.

But he ain't.

You said this is a God-forsaken place but it ain't.

There is love, and hope, and joy even in here.

Eddie ain't running this place no more than I am.

Just so you will know, Eugene the great big man I called my little brother, ain't a bad man. But he is very dangerous though in his own way.

He killed two or three other mens in a fight in Jackson I believe.

So that is why he is up in here.

I think they was drugs involved and Eugene was working for somebody all mixed up in that.

Eugene will do whatever he is told to. He was just listening to the wrong person and that is why he is here.

Something ain't quite right in his brain I think.

He talks to me in the kitchen almost every day, about God and his mama and what is right and wrong.

But he is in the same camp with Eddie. Eddie talks to him at night.

Eddie keeps him all confused and angry.

I am glad you met Miss Mabel.

She is a fine woman.

Her man Cornelius is the boss here in the kitchen and a good friend to me.

I spend a good bit of time in the kitchen here and I feel I am safe with Cornelius.

Him and Mabel is good Christian peoples.

I hope I did not make your friend Trey mad by saying what I said about his daddy.

A young man ought to love his daddy even if his daddy is a prideful fool.

I believe I'd stay away from Brother Swayze if I was you.
He comes in here and preaches every month or so and works hard to get everybody all riled up.
He prides his self on taking a narrow view.
It may be you remember that I am reading Genesis, starting over.
I thought I would read the whole Book all the way through. I ain't sure.
I got a little small book called a commentary about Genesis that is slowing me down pretty much.
I tell you the truth, I did not ever know they was so much to think about in that one book.
Alright that is enough for one letter, my hand is getting all tired.
Write a letter to me back and tell me all about your college and what all you is doing.
Say hello to your friend Trey.

Your friend,
Jacob Jefferson

I did write Jake a letter, the first of a long series of letters. I didn't make a copy of the letters I sent him, of course; it's his letters to me that carry the magic of his joyful wisdom.

In that first letter, I told him about my classes, especially the course in Comparative Religion I was enjoying, and about Laura, who was in my Psychology 101 class. Judging from appearances, it didn't take her any time at all to move past our relationship, but I was having a hard time getting over her. She remained the One That Got Away, a title she retained until I lost a couple more and she was replaced, if never completely forgotten. I told him about the pageantry of college football, and about the beer joints halfway to Columbus.

When I went to the post office to mail that letter, I was surprised to find another letter in my box. There was a brief but intense moment of panic when I saw that the postmark was from Riggsville, Mississippi, until I realized the letter was from Mrs. Swayze and not her husband. It was written on expensive-looking light blue stationery, and her handwriting was as gracious and handsome as she was.

11/5/73

Dear Buddy,

I'm not altogether sure of my intentions in this letter, except to express my concern for you. I know my husband can be a very difficult person to deal with (who could know that better than I?), and I hope that you won't think less of me or Trey because of him.

I have long ago surrendered the idea that I should defend or explain my husband's actions or words. I assume you have a fairly accurate picture of the kind of man he is, but I hope that you will not think ill of Trey for being his son, or of me for being his wife.

Trey had no choice in the matter, of course, and I think he is developing into a fine young man. His father wanted him to go to Mississippi College, which is where he himself went, and where we met. But I was afraid that if Trey went there, he would fall into step with his father's limited, regimented way of thinking. A young person needs to see a broader spectrum of life, and be confronted with things to make him think. Mississippi College would only have supported what he's been told his whole life, and in the same words and phrases. We had several difficult and heated discussions on this matter, but Trey and I eventually won, and Trey went to Mississippi State, for which I am grateful. I'm grateful he found such a good friend in you.

Stewart wasn't always who he is now. When I married him, he was a seminary student, and had such love for the Lord. He wanted to serve the Church, and bring people to the Truth. Our first church was in Itta Bena, near Greenwood, and we were so happy there. That's where Trey was born.

But as we went to the next church, and then the next, his focus shifted, and he became more concerned about keeping the Board of Deacons happy, and making sure the money came in. He forgot about the spiritual part of his job, and concentrated on the business of the Church. Success has increasingly been measured not by telling the Truth, but by the numbers: attendance and budget.

Each year has made him more inflexible, narrower, and more bitter. He seems to get angrier each week. I'm so glad Trey is out of the house, seeing more of the world, and being exposed to new ideas, and away from his father.

You are certainly welcome to come and visit any time; I'd love to see you. Of course, if you do come, you'll need to deal with Trey's father, and that may be more of a price than you'd like to pay. If that's the case, I'll certainly understand.

Love,
Mary Claire

I showed the letter to Trey, and we talked about it for quite a while. I wanted to do something to help Mrs. Swayze, but I couldn't think of anything. Trey told me his parents simply had their system worked out, and there was nothing to do about it. It seemed a shame to me that such a fine woman was trapped in a difficult marriage, but Trey assured me that his father wasn't always such a bad guy.

"As long as you can avoid politics and religion, he's really okay. The trouble is, politics and religion are pretty much all he ever wants to talk about."

We agreed that it wouldn't be advantageous for anybody if I went back to Riggsville. I had no reason to go back, since Jake clearly didn't want me to visit him at the prison again. That worried me. I knew his reasons were connected to Eugene and a man named Eddie, but there was more to the situation than I could understand. Jake had told me he was safe, and I was glad Cornelius was there to look out for him, but that was all I could do about it.

I wrote Mrs. Swayze a reply later that same day, telling her again how much I appreciated her hospitality and graciousness. I told her that it didn't seem likely that I would come back to Riggsville, but I was grateful for her welcome and hoped to see her again. I didn't say, or need to say, that I wasn't hoping to see the Reverend any time soon.

I continued to pine over Laura, who continued to have forgotten that she'd ever spoken to me. The Mighty Bulldogs had a sub-mediocre year, winning four, losing five, and tying two. Ole Miss did better, winning six and losing five, but still had nothing to brag about, except of course that one of their W's was one of our L's. Just in case somebody outside the Deep South ever reads this, that's a big deal in the Magnolia State.

I went home for Thanksgiving, and again for Christmas. It was strange to be in Beaumont without Jake down in the woods. I went to see how his hut was faring without him, and it all looked much the same. I thought about taking something from the hut so I could mail it to him at Parchman, but there wasn't anything to take aside from a couple of pots, his old cast-iron skillet, and those lumpy clay cups. His fishing tackle was right where he'd left it, the only thing there worth stealing, so I felt fairly sure that no one had been there. Really and truly, unless you knew what you were looking for, Jake's hut was almost impossible to find. On an impulse, I rubbed some cooking oil on the skillet and wrapped it up as tightly as I could with paper towels and garbage bags. When I left, I was sure I'd never see that place again, but I knew that Jake treasured his frying pan, and preserving it was the least I could do for him.

A new semester started, and life progressed. I was starting to get comfortable with college, and I was looking forward to baseball season. Baseball had been the main athletic success at Mississippi State for years, and I couldn't wait to explain some of the intricacies of the game to Trey, the football fan. He still thought baseball was not a game for *real* men.

Classes continued. The Comparative Religion class took us through a whirlwind tour of Buddhism, Hinduism, Judaism, and Islam, and I marveled the number of ideas they all have in common. I mentioned the idea in a letter to Jake, and he wrote me back.

February 10, 1974
Sunday

Dear Buddy,

It was good to get your letter.
Thank you very much for writing.
Every thing is fine here.
It is raining outside yesterday and today.
I am glad to be in out of the cold and rain.
But I do miss being alone sometimes and being quiet.
They ain't no place to be quiet or alone here.

They ain't much to tell about what is going on.
It is pretty much the same every day, every week.
I do not know nothing about this Buddha or Mohammed or Krishna.
They just ain't part of what I know but I do not know everything.
I do not know nothing about most of the things you is talking about in your letter such as reincarnation and karmas and whatnot.
I looked up reincarnation in the prison library dictionary.
We got us a big old dictionary in there.
It is as big as two or three Bibles and it has tiny small print.
I wrote down what it said about reincarnation so I would not forget it.
Rebirth in new bodies or forms of life.
It had another meaning, too.
Rebirth of a soul in a new human body.
They ain't nothing in the Book about no things such as that, that I know of.
The prophet Jeremiah and Saint Paul both talk about being called before they was born. I do not know how they would know such a thing.
They do not say nothing about being alive before they was born, anyways.
The Gospel of John tells about Jesus living before He was born as the Word but I expect He is a special case.
I sure do not know every thing they is to know, not even about the Book.
But I do not think they is anything about reincarnation in the Bible.
I do know a little about the Jewish religion because Jesus was Jewish, and the Old Testament is Jewish.
I do not think the Jews believe in this reincarnation.
Peoples used to ask me was the Jews and whatnot going to Heaven.
Back when I thought I knowed every thing a body needed to know about God I told them only the Christians was going to Heaven.
I'd tell them "Jesus saith unto him, I am the way, the truth, and the life: no man cometh unto the Father, but by me."
I told them everybody else would just have to go to Hell.
But now I think I was most likely wrong.

I imagine that no flower grows but by the warmth of the sun. I don't think the flower has to believe in the sun to bloom.
It don't make no sense for God to make a man a Jew and then damn him to Hell because he is Jewish.
I expect that goes for some of them other religions too.
Cornelius says he has knowed some Hindu Buddhist or Muslim or some such here in Parchman.
He says some of them was pretty nice and some of them was not just like all the rest of us.
But look here, Buddy.
I know God loves all His children not just us Christians.
I know we all has a lot to learn about God.
All of us can learn from each other even when it does not look like we can.
Just look at what you and me has taught one another.
God knows we all need all the help we can get.
We are all given a tiny small spark of the Light of God to shine.
We need to put all them sparks together so we can make a light and see what we are doing.
But instead church peoples hide they little spark to protect it so nobody else can even see it. Not even other church peoples.
And they tell other peoples that if they spark is different, it ain't no good.
That ain't right, but just foolishness and vanity.
So listen to what your professor has to say.
But remember what you believe.
Look for the Truth, and the Light.
Do not be afraid to hear new thoughts or to think new ideas.
But do not forget the ideas you was raised with neither.
There is more to the world than I am able to know.
Write to me again, and let me know more about all this.
It gives me something to think about while I am cutting onions and celery and whatnot.
I hope you are well, learning a lot and having fun.
But not too much fun.

Your friend,
Jacob Jefferson

I showed the letter to Trey, who shook his head in disbelief. He'd heard all his life that Jews were going to Hell, and had accepted it without ever truly thinking about it. I'd never heard the idea, never even thought about it. We talked about it for several days, spinning old ideas and new ideas around and around until we were both theologically dizzy. Trey talked about what his daddy said, and I talked about what Jake said, and we both wondered about what the Buddhists and Hindus say. I wondered, and considered saying out loud, how I could be tolerant and sympathetic of other world religions and so intolerant and judgmental about other denominations of Christianity, and especially the Reverend—but I kept this to myself.

Trey got a little testy somewhere in our discussions. I remember him arguing, "Well, if just anybody can go to heaven, what's the point of being a Christian?" It reminded me of my mother telling us we'd have to eat our vegetables if we wanted to have dessert, but Trey didn't appreciate the analogy.

Somehow the conversation spilled out of its banks like a river flooding in the spring, and we wound up talking about the Jews who'd been executed in the Nazi prison camps in World War Two. Trey's American History class was just finishing WWII, so he knew all about it.

"And there were millions of Jews killed," he said. "Men, women, and children. And not just Jews, but gypsies, too, and homosexuals. The Germans gassed 'em and burned 'em by the hundreds and thousands."

"I guess that Hitler is the most evil man who's ever lived," I said. "You think?"

"I guess so."

"He sent millions of Jews to their deaths, just 'cause they were Jews."

"And gypsies, Negroes, and homosexuals."

"But you're telling me that God is going to send those same Jews to Hell? That God is going to burn these poor people forever? That makes God worse than Hitler!"

Trey looked at me with the expression of a young man who had too many thoughts and ideas competing for brain space at the same time.

I knew the feeling. “Theological traffic jam?” I asked.

Trey nodded weakly.

14

We Is All Sinners Most of the Time

One Thursday morning between classes I was sitting at the student union, working a crossword puzzle from the *Tupelo Daily Journal.* I had an early class on Tuesdays and Thursdays, with a little over an hour and a half break before my next class. People usually left newspapers all over the chairs, so I had gotten into the habit of picking up a paper and working the puzzles.

I was just about finished with my first puzzle of the day, one of the easy ones, when a girl came and sat down in the next chair. This in itself wasn't unusual; sometimes the place got crowded, and someone would come and sit next to me. The girl was looking at me with what seemed to me to be undue interest.

She was attractive, but not what I thought of as beautiful. Her eyes seemed a little older than the rest of her. She had disorganized dark blonde hair cut short, and wore no make-up. She was wearing jeans and a peasant shirt, and the kind of sandals that I've always associated with Jesus. She was what I had thought of as "Bohemian."

She didn't look away when I looked at her, so I looked away instead, and I was surprised to see that there were lots of places to sit. I looked back at her, and she was still looking at me, with an odd expression on her face, a dreamy sort of look, as if she was just about to sigh.

This kind of thing had never happened to me, and although it was quite exciting, I didn't know what to do or say. I wanted to play it cool—but not too cool. I looked back at the crossword. I was stumped by the puzzle and by the girl, and lacking anything whatsoever to say, I asked, "What's a six-letter word for warriors or companion?"

"What have you got?"

"It begins with C, and the fifth letter is R."

She answered, "Cohort." It fit; I wrote it in.

I said, "Hi."

She said, "Hi.

"My name's Buddy Hinton."

She held out her hand for me to shake and said, "Eleanor Logan."

I shook her hand. That had gone smoothly enough, but now I was out of conversation. She asked, "What's next?"

"Next?"

"To solve the puzzle."

"Oh. Let's see—I need a six-letter word for riddle. It's blank, N, blank, blank, M, blank."

"Enigma."

We worked that puzzle quickly and found a harder one that we both had to work at, and I relaxed a little. All in all, she wasn't an easy person to relax around: she talked too fast and with undisguised intensity, her eyes always scanning the room around us looking for something more interesting. I found out she'd been born and raised in a little town in New Hampshire, near Lake Winnipesaukee. When I asked her how she'd gotten to Mississippi, she said she'd graduated from a private Christian high school there that she was afraid had scared her away from Christianity forever. She had enrolled at Mount Holyoke College in Massachusetts, but lost her scholarship—not because of academics, she assured me, but something to do with boys from Dartmouth and a little bag of marijuana. After that she felt a need for some distance between herself and her disappointed parents, and she headed west. It took her almost two years to run out of highway; it took her just a few months to decide that waitressing in San Francisco was not her destiny. She continued to work as a waitress in Santa Clara, California, and worked her way through a bachelor's degree at Santa Clara University. After she graduated, she applied to graduate schools in English literature, and was as surprised as anyone to find herself at Mississippi State, which had offered her the best scholarship and graduate teaching opportunities.

She told me all this with a rapid-fire New England accent while we finished the more difficult puzzle, and then it was time for me to go to class. I told her that I was there every Tuesday and Thursday at about this time, and she promised she'd see me Tuesday.

I'd never met anyone who'd ever even been to New Hampshire, never heard of Holyoke College, never really considered that California could be a place that existed in reality. A lot of people from Mississippi grow up with the understanding that being connected in any way with California explains all sorts of strange ideas and behaviors. And, more mystifying than any of that, she seemed interested in me. In time, Eleanor Logan would become a cohort of sorts, but she was an enigma from the very start.

All weekend I thought about it, alternating between the fantasy of my irresistibility and the reality of my insecurity. The more I thought about it, the more beautiful Eleanor became in my imagination. I had convinced myself that she was smitten with me, and it was exhilarating to speculate where her passions might be taking us. I was completely thrilled to imagine a graduate student could be attracted to a freshman.

Finally Tuesday morning came. After my eight o'clock class, I hurried to the union. She wasn't there. I didn't want to look anxious—or like I was waiting for her—so I tried to work the crossword, with one eye watching for beautiful blonde graduate students.

I suppose I got a little caught up in the puzzle, because I didn't see her come in, didn't know she was there until she sat beside me. Again, she just looked at me, with a frankness that was . . . unsettling. I said, "Hi."

She said, "I'm thinking of giving up on Buddhism. What do you think?"

I said, "I have no idea what you're talking about."

So began a series of Tuesday and Thursday conversations with Eleanor that lasted for the rest of that semester. They were sometimes enlightening, sometimes embarrassing, often odd and generally disconcerting. Her attraction to me, as it turned out, wasn't physical, but spiritual. It was more disappointing than you might think.

She told me she'd seen the brightness of my aura from across the room, that she'd never seen an aura like mine, that it was a bright yellow.

I said, "My what?"

"Your aura. Surely somebody has told you about your aura!" She seemed indignant that the rest of the world had failed to bring this to my attention.

I told her I'd never seen an aura at all, that I had never heard of such a thing. She told me I did know about auras, and I told her I did not. She asked me if I believed in Jesus. I began to wonder if this whole conversation was an evangelical trick.

Trying to be cagy, I asked, "Why?"

"Have you ever seen an image of Jesus?" she asked with exaggerated patience.

"Like in a stained glass window?" The church I grew up in has beautiful stained glass windows.

"Right—exactly. Have you ever seen an image of Jesus in a stained glass window?"

"Sure. The church I grew up in has—"

"Does he have a halo around his head?"

"Yes, in some of the—"

"That's an aura."

"You're saying you saw a halo around my—"

"What color is His halo?"

"What?"

More exaggerated patience: "What color is the halo around Jesus' head in the stained glass window in the church you grew up in?"

"Uh, yellowish, I think."

"Exactly."

"Exactly, what?"

"That's why I came to sit with you"

I was completely lost. "Why?"

"Because your aura was so bright."

She told me she'd learned how to read auras when she spent the summer in San Francisco. That confirmed something for me: she learned about auras while she was in California. She told me that everybody has an aura, and that she saw mine from a distance because it was so bright. So she came to sit beside me.

I was still having a hard time letting go of the fantasy that there might be some romantic attraction involved, so I guess I wasn't ready to hear that she was just attracted to my aura. I don't know if anybody is ever ready for that kind of thing, but I know I wasn't ready for it right then.

I asked her if she was just making all this aura stuff up, and if she really believed what she was saying. She told me that she didn't really know what she believed any more.

I didn't know what to say, so I didn't say anything, and I think she appreciated what she perceived as patience. Finally she said, "Oh, you know—I was trying to hide from God, or I thought I was. But it turns out that I've just been avoiding the Church. Not the part of Church that I like, just the judgment, all that condemnation."

There was a pause, and I felt like I needed to say something. "Well, I don't know about—"

"And fear."

The pause resumed, and I tried again, "Well, I don't—"

"And the relentless threat of everlasting damnation!"

The pause dared me to try again, but I kept my silence. I didn't know what I was going to say, anyway. The pause lengthened, and she continued, much more slowly and softly, "I've done things . . . things I'm not proud of."

I didn't know how to respond, whether to ask what those things were, or why she'd said that in the first place. I thought I'd wait until she said something else, but she didn't, so I said, "I guess we all have."

Too late I realized that a door had been opened for just a moment. I didn't see it while it was open; I only knew it after it was closed again.

But then it was too late. I decided to mention it in my next letter to Jake.

She said, "You're a good listener."

"I didn't know what to say."

"Buddy, do you believe in everlasting damnation?"

"Well, I don't know much about that. I suppose if somebody would rather not go to heaven, God wouldn't make them."

She lit up as suddenly as a light bulb. "Yes, exactly!" She closed her eyes, remembering, and then recited

> Never fear. There are only two kinds of people in the end: those who say to God, "Thy will be done," and those to whom God says, in the end, "Thy will be done." All that are in Hell, choose it. Without that self-choice there could be no Hell. No soul that seriously and constantly desires joy will ever miss it. Those who seek find, to those who knock it is opened.

I was dumbfounded, both by the idea itself and by the fact that somebody could just walk around with things like that to say. I said, "Yeah, something like that."

Her intensity was unabated. "No, exactly like that!"

I asked, "Was that a quote? Where did it come from?"

"Of course. I'm an English major, remember? It's from *The Great Divorce.*"

"A divorce?"

"The book, silly—*The Great Divorce* by C. S. Lewis."

"Who?"

"C. S. Lewis."

"Is he from California?"

Later that day I went to the library, a building I'd so far made a habit of walking past without ever actually entering, and found books by C. S. Lewis.

I'm sure I learned a lot that semester from whatever I was supposed to be studying—Western Civilization, Biology One-Oh-Something, Spanish literature—but what I remember from that time is Clive Staples Lewis—and Eleanor. I read *The Great Divorce* and *The Screwtape Letters*, attempted (and failed) to read *Mere Christianity.* Eleanor and I had more than enough to talk about for the rest of the semester. She never mentioned again the things she'd done that she wasn't proud of, but sometimes I could hear echoes of it, or see the pain of it in her eyes.

March 3, 1974
Sunday

Dear Buddy,

You sure has got your self all mixed up with some people to make you think about many different things.
I tell you true that shame and guilt will eat a person all up if they let it.
I hope you will tell your friend Eleanor that they ain't nothing she could have ever done and nothing she is ever going to do that will put her outside the love of God.
They is times when people give up on God but I do not believe God will ever give up on us.
You do not need to know what all she might have done.
She could not have done nothing that God will not forgive.
Then the problem is will she forgive her self?
I think many Christians and their preachers do not really believe this.
They just cannot believe that God could really love us whether we deserve it or not.
So they make up rules and laws and try to keep God under their control.
Or it might just be somebody trying to explain something they do not understand.
I believe that is mostly what a lot of religious talk is, just peoples trying to explain things they do not understand.
Many peoples like to have somebody to believe they is better than.
Many white peoples think they is better than colored peoples but they ain't.
Many rich peoples think they is better than poor peoples but they ain't.

Peoples in New York City or Chicago might think they is better than peoples in Mississippi but they is wrong about that too.
If somebody is doing something that you could not stand to do then you might want to let your self feel better than him.
If you ain't doing that thing you might want to believe that it is wrong.
Especially if you can think you is better than that person because he's doing it and you ain't.
You might even stand up all righteous and tell people that is something bad sinful.
But none of that has nothing to do with God.
The best sin to preach on is one that you have never done nor ever been tempted to do.
It ain't no wonder peoples do not believe in God if this is how peoples that believes talk about Him.
I believe that sin is when somebody chooses to do what they know ain't right or ain't what God wants them to do.
Sin is when somebody puts what they want to do in front of what they think God wants them to do.
Eddie got Eugene all worked up and he made a fight with several mens in they camp.
The fight broke out at breakfast in the mess hall so I saw the whole thing.
One of them mens is in the hospital in Memphis now and they say he ain't doing so well.
I might have known that man but I ain't sure.
When the guards got up in there to break up the fight Eugene hit one of them square in the face and broke his jaw.
The guards beat Eugene down with they sticks.
After he fell they all come in and kicked him until he hollered he was sorry.
They put him in solitary which I understand he hates that.
He was in solitary a few years back for another fight and he told me one time that it was scary to him to be alone like that.
He does not like to be alone.
Eddie did not get hurt at all of course.
He did not get in no trouble neither.
And the mens he wanted hurt was hurt.
One of them was hurt pretty bad.

All the mens up in here know that Eugene is going to do what Eddie tells him to do.
That makes Eddie more powerful than he ought to be.
They all afraid of Eddie because of Eugene and fear is a powerful thing.
Nothing else ain't going on up in here.
I saw Mabel the other day and she asked would I remember her to you.
She says you is a fine young man.
Tell Trey hello from her too.
Buddy I have been writing and writing a long time and it looks like I ain't said much at all.
So I best stop pretty soon.
Tell Eleanor we is all sinners most of the time and that God loves us all anyways.
All the time and forever.
That is all that really matters when it comes right down to it.
Ain't none of us ever good enough to earn the love of God.
And tell her that shame will eat her up if she lets it.
It will suck all the joy out of her life if she is ashamed of her own self.
We all got to be who God made us to be, as much as we can.
We all got to play the cards we was dealt.
If somebody lives his life trying to be somebody else he is just natural bound to fail.
Buddy what you and me have to offer is the love of God.
It is the Light of Christ that we have to shine.
If it is some part of the Gospel message to preach about punishment and damnation, I will leave it to some other preacher.
Gospel means good news.
Did I ever tell you that?
It ought to be good news not threats and not fear.
Fear is a powerful thing but only when we let it run us.
Do not let fear run your life.
So I want to talk most about what I believe Jesus talked most about.
Jesus talked most about love and hope and forgiveness.
That is the Gospel I believe.
Not telling peoples they is going to Hell because they is doing something the preachers do not like.

Just remember that the Gospel is about love and forgiveness and that is the main thing.
Thank you for your letter.
You sure is leading an interesting life up there in college.

Your friend,
Jacob Jefferson

I took that letter to the Union to read to Eleanor, and when I was finished there were tears on her cheeks. It was the only time I ever saw her speechless, and when she recovered she whispered, "Thank you, Buddy. And thank Jake for me." I told her I would, and then she said, "I'd love to see *his* aura."

15

You Got to Be Careful Who You Is Naked With

Before long, I had a couple of other things to think about, less important, perhaps, but more pressing, and more important to me at the time. First, it was baseball season at Mississippi State. The Bulldogs were ranked in the top ten nationally, the campus was excited, and the games were crowded. Second, I fell in love, or at least in deep infatuation.

Kate was beautiful, and it was intensely exciting for a few weeks. I thought it was love at first sight, but I think for her I was a project, sort of a romantic fixer-upper.

We met in our Statistics for the Behavioral Sciences 101 class, required for and dreaded by both of us. She had been sitting next to me for a couple of weeks, but I hadn't dared to talk to her; she was too pretty. One day she laughed at a cartoon I'd drawn, poking fun at our Middle-Eastern professor, whose command of statistical formulae far surpassed his command of English. At least I assumed it did; I didn't completely understand the formulae or his English. We talked after class, and I was surprised that she was genuinely a pleasant and friendly person. I think she was surprised that I could talk at all. I walked her to her next class (I would have walked her to Chicago if she'd asked me to), and she told me I should call her. I called her, we went to a movie, and for a few precious weeks, we were dating. We were young, it was gloriously springtime, God was in His heavens, and all was right with the world.

But alas, she was a member of one of the snootier sororities on campus, and some of her sisters pressured her into telling me that I was just going to have to cut my hair and improve my wardrobe if I was going to be seen in her company. In the mid-seventies, hair was more than just hair; mine was long enough to reach my shoulders, and well beyond curly: it was altogether undomesticated. As much as I wanted to please her, I didn't feel like I could cut my hair for her sorority and keep on being me. She didn't think she could back down without disappointing her sisters. Eleanor, no respecter of social conventions and no friend to sorority girls, told me I should drop Kate like a hot potato. By the time Jake got the letter I'd written to tell him I was in love, I was writing another to tell him my heart had been broken.

So Trey and I threw ourselves into baseball with renewed enthusiasm while I nursed my wounds. He told me there were plenty of other fish in the sea, but I decided I was giving up women forever. It was a decision I would make from time to time for years, usually a little too late.

When the Dogs were playing on campus, we'd take his car and park it just beyond the left center field Cyclone fence, pulling the front bumper up so that it almost touched chain links. When our boys were in the field, we sat on the hood and were very polite and encouraging; but when the other team took the field, we stood at the fence and yelled at them without mercy, trying to distract the outfielders.

Trey made it a point to learn where the opposing center fielder was from, and kept up a steady harangue, talking about the guy's college, hometown, girlfriend, mother, whatever he could think of. The opposing team's center fielder did his best to ignore us, but sometimes even they had to laugh at some of Trey's antics.

That year we played Ole Miss at home, in Starkville. For the Saturday afternoon game, the outfield was packed. Trey took advantage of the quiet during a change of pitchers to yell at the Rebel center fielder, whose first name was listed as Mike on the official roster.

"Hey, Mikey!"

No answer.

"Hey, Mikey!"

The center fielder's hands were on his knees, and he seemed very interested in watching his new pitcher warming up.

"Hey, Mikey! Does your girlfriend know the difference between having dinner and having sex?"

No answer. But then, what could he have said?

"Hey, Mikey! Does she know the difference between having dinner and having sex?"

No answer. But it was an intriguing question; most of the people around us were waiting to hear the answer.

"Hey, Mikey! Does your girlfriend know the difference between having dinner and having sex?" Trey asked a third time.

A couple of guys over to our right put their voices together: "She doesn't know!" Everybody laughed, and when the laughter died down, they yelled again: "What's the difference?"

The center fielder stood up, and took a couple of steps back, steadfastly ignoring all of us but wanting to hear the punch line.

Trey waited until almost everybody was quiet. Then he yelled again, "Hey, Mikey!"

No answer.

"Hey, Mikey! Can I take your girlfriend to dinner after the game?"

Mike the center fielder never turned around, but we could all see his shoulders bumping up and down as he laughed with us.

The Diamond Dogs had an exciting season that year, and it was a beautiful spring. Just as Trey had taught me to appreciate the passion and power of college football, I taught him to love the beauty and intricacy of baseball. Eleanor read me Tennyson's famous line: "In the Spring a young man's fancy lightly turns to thoughts of love." Somewhere in there, my fancy turned to baseball, and the pain of lost love eased.

April 21, 1974
Sunday

Dear Buddy,

I sure am very sorry that girl and you did not keep on with it.
Romance is a powerful thing and can make a man feel as he is on top of the world.
It can also make a man feel like he ain't worth spit.
I been thinking about this for a day or two now seeing do I have anything smart to say about womens.
It may be that I do not.
I done told you several times to be careful with them but I know that ain't enough.
You can't be scared of them or you will never get no love from none of them.
That would be a shame.
The reason it pained you for her to leave out of your life is because you let her come so far into it.
Somebody said we only hurt the ones we love.
I think it was in a song or some such.
I believe that the only ones we is able to hurt is the ones we love and they is the only ones can hurt us.
Because to love somebody is to trust her.
As I say I been thinking about this and this is what I come up with.
If it don't make no sense just let it slip on by.
But see does this make sense to you before you give up on it.
Imagine if you was a house.
I ain't talking about your body being no house but if your soul was a house.
If you was a house you might be on a busy street with peoples passing you by all the time.
Most of them is strangers who just ride on by too fast for you to see did you know them or not.
These is peoples who you got nothing to do with and don't need to worry about.
You don't know them and they don't know you.
Some others would be walking by.
These are peoples you see from time to time.

They is peoples in your classes and whatnot.
You don't know them but you are used to they faces.
A few might stop at the fence around the house of your soul and speak.
You don't know they names but they say hello before they move on.
These are peoples who have made your acquaintance.
A few but not as many can come up inside the fence into your yard.
These are friends of yours.
You know they names and they know yours.
It may be that you and them has done something together and share the memory of it.
You might be in the stories they tell and they might be in yours.
A few but not as many you might invite to come up on your porch.
These is friends you can sit with.
You know they mama's names and they know your mama's name too.
A smaller number than that can come on in your house into your soul.
These is your good friends.
These is peoples you want to keep up with.
A smaller number than that can come up in the kitchen of your soul in the heart of the house.
These is your best friends.
They is peoples you love.
They is peoples you can cry with.
They ain't many peoples up in the kitchen of your soul.
These are friends of your heart.
They is peoples who know about things you is proud of and things you is ashamed of.
Trey is one of these peoples for you and so am I.
But you don't want to ask no more than only just one person up in your bedroom of the house of your soul with you.
Because in the bedroom is where you are naked.
I ain't talking about your body being naked.
I reckon you might be getting old enough for me to talk to you about that but it ain't my place anyhow.
That ain't what I am talking about anyway.
What I am talking about is when your feelings are naked.

In the bedroom of your soul you let your walls down.
You ain't protecting your self in the bedroom of your soul.
The further you let peoples get into the house of your soul the more you trust them.
The more you trust them the more you let your walls down.
So that is why the peoples you love is the only ones who can really bring you pain.
Some of them peoples who just pass on by they can't hurt you none.
It don't matter what they say or what they do.
They can't hurt you cause you don't care about them.
Only the peoples you love can hurt you.
I ain't saying you ought not to love somebody.
I ain't saying they ain't no women you can trust.
I am just saying you got to be careful who you is naked with.
It don't matter how pretty a girl is.
If you can't trust her with being who you are you best just keep on walking.
A good friend is a gift of much value.
You are lucky to have a friend like Trey.
And I am lucky to have a friend like you.

Your friend,
Jacob Jefferson

And one more thing I just thought of.
I ain't been thinking on this but just a few minutes but I believe it makes sense.
It may be they is one more room in the house of your soul.
This is a tiny small closet that you don't go in much off the bedroom of the house of your soul.
This is where you keeps all the memories of things you done that cause you shame now.
This is where you keep the memories of your darkest day.
It smells bad in there Buddy.
It stinks like shame.
Most of us keep the door closed and locked on that room most all the time.
Most of us hate that room, and stay well clear of it.

But that is where we meet our Lord in the dark smelly room in the house of our soul.
I believe He is sitting in the middle of all that junk.
And when you takes a peek into that room He says It sure stinks up in here.
You need to go ahead and get rid of all this stuff.
He says I already forgave all this junk.
It's just pure arrogant to hold on to something that Jesus has let go.
Now you need to let it go.
That is what our Lord says in the shameful room in the house of our soul.
Let it go.

Your friend,
Jacob Jefferson

16

Deuces and One-eyed Jacks

The semester ended, and Trey and I went our separate ways for the summer after agreeing we'd find an apartment together in the fall. Trey had a summer job working as a deckhand on a towboat on the river. His mother's uncle owned the company, and he was looking forward to it. I went back to work at the Episcopal Church camp where I'd been a counselor all through high school. This would be my second summer on the permanent staff there, one of the college kids who got to work at the sessions all summer long.

The Episcopal camp in Mississippi is a beautiful spot, with over five hundred wooded acres of rolling hills and a small lake. We had seven sessions, each lasting a little more than a week. Each session brought in a new set of counselors, adult staff members, and a session director, who was almost always a priest. The session staff stayed in the cabins with the campers; the Permanent Staff was in charge of the various program areas. As you might imagine, the Permanent Staff was the envy of all the counselors and a challenge for every director. I loved being a part of it.

It was the most wonderful job imaginable: I got to play with kids all day, but I didn't have to sleep in the heat and humidity with them at night. There's a limit to how many nights a guy can lay listening to fifth grade boys passing gas and giggling, and I felt like I'd done my time in the cabin. In the big house down the road, which with no imagination at all we called the Big House, we sat up and played cards, drank beer, and talked about the session staff.

And then there were the girl counselors, who all thought the Permanent Staff was cool. My first summer brought me several summer romances—nothing serious, either emotionally or physically, but mostly fun. The second summer, those girls came back. Unfortunately for me, they weren't as well distributed as they had been the first summer. During the first session that year, three of my previous year's girlfriends all came back at the same time. I stayed at the Big House every night that week instead of going down to the camp after lights out as I usually did.

The Diocese of Mississippi had started a session for people with mental and physical disabilities in 1968. There were other camps in Mississippi for people with disabilities, but in 1968 ours was the only one that took black campers as well as white campers. I'd been a counselor at one of these special sessions when I was still in high school, in 1971.

By the time I geared up for my second year on the Permanent Staff, I'd attended several more special sessions, all of them adventures, all of them educational, and almost all of them great fun. There are hundreds of wonderful stories to tell, stories I'll tell for the rest of my life, but those are for another book.

The second session that summer was a special session. One of the groups came from a residential center in south Mississippi. There was a mistake somehow, and the bus driver had left the box with all their medicines back at the center. We knew we were in trouble that first afternoon, when several kids had epileptic seizures during the free time before supper. The director phoned the center, and someone there found the box and called back to tell him they'd get it to us as quickly as they could. The director asked the Permanent Staff to help in the cabins that night, which we were glad to do.

I was assigned to the boys' cabin furthest away from the rest of camp. One of the campers was a young man named Paul, a moderately challenged new camper from that center in south Mississippi. The nurse had asked me if I would sit with that cabin and especially keep my eye on Paul.

I told her I would, and then asked, "Until he goes to sleep?"

She shook her head. "All night. One of you needs to be awake and aware of Paul all night." She told me that he was supposed to be taking an extra large amount of epilepsy medication, and that she didn't truthfully know what would happen since he hadn't had any all day. She suggested that I talk with the adult in the cabin and set up a way to keep watch. If Paul had a seizure, one of us would have to come get her .

Each cabin held fourteen people in seven sets of bunk beds, with an additional room for an adult. The adult in that cabin was a priest named Phil, who'd never been to a special session before. He'd served in the Navy, though, and was tough and squared away. He and I gave ourselves permission to disregard the bell signaling lights out in the cabin, given the special circumstances; Phil told the guys they could go to bed whenever they wanted to. The campers and counselors all thought that was an accommodating idea, and Phil asked if I would get a couple of decks of cards and some uncooked macaroni from the kitchen.

I did, and by the time I got back, half of the campers were already snoring. The rest were listening to Phil, who was explaining how to play poker. Without cards or chips, he wasn't making much headway, but they all looked entertained.

One of the counselors had brought twenty or thirty long-play record albums, which we laid on his bed to make something like a table, and everyone still awake gathered around. Phil and I counted out fifty pieces of macaroni for each player, and then he dealt the cards and called the game: "Five card draw, deuces and one-eyed jacks wild."

I sat a little behind Paul, and he asked me what to do. I'd never played before, but I wanted to help Paul, so I had to figure it out quickly. Over and over, Phil had to repeat the order of winning hands: "One pair, two pair, three of a kind, straight, flush . . . ."

Paul held out the cards so we could both see them, and he and I whispered our idea about which cards he should keep, how many cards to ask for, how many pieces of macaroni to bet, when to fold. We lost the first few hands, but after a while we were holding our own. Before long, we'd sorted ourselves out so that five of the campers were playing, three of them assisted by counselors.

Father Phil continued to play, and he soon collected a huge pile of macaroni. I thought about trying to give him a hint that he needed to let the campers win, until I realized that Phil was treating them with more dignity by playing for real. Every once in a while, Phil would slip a camper a handful of macaroni to keep him in the game. When Paul won an especially big hand and was raking in the macaroni, Phil proclaimed, "Our friend Paul here is a card shark—Card Shark Paul."

Paul beamed. You'd have thought he'd won the Publishers Clearing House sweepstakes.

We played for hours that night. One by one, the campers "cashed in" their macaroni, and finally Card Shark Paul, the last camper at the table, had to call it a night. We counted his macaroni, almost two hundred pieces of precious elbow pasta. Phil had more, but we didn't count his. Phil told Paul that he was an expert poker player, and they shook hands. It was a great moment for Paul, and for Phil.

After everybody was in bed and quiet, with a counselor keeping an eye on things inside the cabin, Phil and I went to sit on the front porch. Phil lit a cigarette and let out a deep breath. By the light of a yellow bulb orbited by moths and June bugs, Phil told me that in the Navy he'd been on a ship with a guy who was manic depressive, and that one time when he ran out of medicine, a commanding officer had told Phil to keep the guy's mind off of it until they could get more. They'd played hour after hour of poker that night, and Phil told me he couldn't think of anything else to do tonight in the cabin.

The medicine arrived at three or four in the morning, and the nurse came to our cabin to give Paul his dose. She gave the rest of it out at breakfast. Most of the campers were all right, but for a few it took a couple of days to restore their medicated balancing act.

The last night of that session, we had the Big Dance, as we did the last night of every special session. It was hot in the chapel, the heat from over a hundred dancers quickly overcoming the air-conditioning system. I was taking one of the campers to the ice machine near the kitchen to get a paper cup of ice when I heard voices inside the dining hall. I'd been somewhat perturbed with some of the counselors who seemed more interested in each other than their campers, and I went to see if it was some of them.

I heard Paul crying and saw Phil with his hand on his shoulder. Phil caught sight of me and warned me off with his eyes. As I turned to leave, I heard Paul wail, "But why did God have to make me a *retard*?" I closed the screen door quietly, wishing I could stay to hear Phil's answer.

I saw Phil later that night, and asked him what had been going on. It seems that Paul had asked another camper to dance, and she had told him that she didn't want to dance with him, because he was a retard. Paul was terribly upset and had found Phil to ask him what that meant, and they'd gotten into the discussion that I'd almost interrupted.

I told Phil I'd heard Paul ask the question, and that I'd love to know the answer. Phil said he would, too. He said he'd given Paul some kind of response, but he didn't honestly have a sufficient answer. Phil went on to say that it was the problem of evil, which theologians and scholars had been writing about for centuries: if God is loving and benevolent, why is there evil in the world? Why are there tornados, why do people die young, why are some born with cerebral palsy or mental retardation? I speculated on the role of karma in all this, but I decided that Phil had enough to worry about.

The next time I wrote to Jake, I told him all about it. He wrote back with an especially long and thoughtful response.

July 21, 1974
Sunday

Dear Buddy,

You do not have so much time when you is at camp to write to me as when you is at college.
I hope you have enough time to read all these letters I am writing.
It sounds like that preacher Phil is a good man.
The mens up in here plays a lot of poker.
They is other card games too but poker is always my favorite.

They is some mens who play for serious money but I do not ever play at they table.
Me and my friends just play for nickels and dimes mostly, sometimes for cigarettes.
A few weeks ago I won enough to buy me a big can of Prince Albert tobacco for my pipe.
I already had enough money to buy it anyways but it tasted sweeter knowing that I had won it playing poker.
You say Paul asked Phil why did God make him a retard.
That is a worrisome question, all tangled up with itself.
Did God make him that way or was it something gone wrong in his mother's belly before he was born?
Did God make something bad to happen or did He just let it happen?
It is troublesome either way.
It may be that part of the problem is that we think God is in control in a way that he is not really.
Paul might be thinking he is like he is because it is something God did to him.
He figures God must have done this to him cause he thinks God is in control.
Now if you or me was God, we would be in control.
The world would be in a terrible mess, but we would be in control of it.
I ain't so sure God is in control, not like we mean it, anyways.
It may be He don't need to be in control like us peoples do.
We got mens up in here at Parchman in control.
We got the warden, the bosses, and guards.
We got Eddie who is in control more than he ought to be.
Peoples is very serious about control in Parchman Farm.
But let me ask you something.
Who is in control of that fishing hole back at my house?
God? Or is it just the biggest fish in the water?
Who controls how many frog eggs hatch there?
Who controls how many tadpoles get eaten before they become frogs?
Jesus said in the Gospel of Matthew that not even a sparrow will fall to the ground without God knowing it.
But do a fishing hole need to have somebody in charge?

Or do everything in there—fish and frogs and bugs and snakes and turtles and whatnot—do they just all live they lives without nobody in no control at all?
When my Joseph died I asked them same questions.
I have thought about it from time to time ever since.
Why does God just sit up there and let bad things happen?
Or does He make them happen?
Why is they evil in the world if God made it, if God is in control, and if God is good?
If God loved me why did He let my boy get killed?
One time when I was preaching a woman brought her son to me in a wheel chair to heal him.
He was drooling on his self. He could not walk nor talk.
She told me he had been like that since he was born.
We prayed over him. I put my hands on him but nothing happened.
She whispered to me that he was all messed up like that because she had cheated on her husband. She thought God was punishing her.
I whispered back to her that I did not believe that.
I told her I do not think God works like that.
But she did not believe me.
She said she just wanted her boy to be normal.
I told her God loved her and her son just like they was.
I believe that is true with all my heart.
She did not believe me that time neither.
As I say I been trying to loose up this knot for 30 years or more.
I will not pretend I know the answer.
But I believe some of this has to do with God letting us make our own choices.
You and me have talked about this before when your friend Andy died.
It may be you remember we played like God was asking us should peoples be free to choose or should we be made so that we all do what God tells us to do.
Sometimes I believe I would have chosen to make peoples so they would just do what I told them.
I would have told them to love me and they would have because they did not have no choice.

But when I write it down I know I would have been wrong.
It is a good thing I ain't God.
You cannot make somebody love you.
For it to be love they has to choose to love you.
If you make somebody love you it ain't really love.
It is fear or guilt or something else.
It is forced some how or another.
If peoples cannot choose to not love, they cannot choose to love.
I hope that makes sense to you.
God is most interested in love so He lets us choose.
He always has let His peoples choose.
Just like Eve and Adam, they chose to disobey.
But if they did not have no choice, they could not choose to disobey or to obey.
I have thought about this too so read this careful, and tell me what you think.
It may be that they was not really peoples until they was able to choose to obey or not obey.
I think it may be that they was not really in the image of God until they could choose.
I believe this might be the great truth of this story.
It may be that part of being created in the image of God is that we is free to make our choice between good and evil.
Or it may be that I don't know what I'm talking about.
Some peoples is all concerned that we came from monkeys or some such and it may be we did.
It may be that the story of Adam and Eve is about the first peoples who made they choice to disobey God.
I ain't getting real excited about that.
God made us and everything else they is.
If He made us in a week or a million years don't make no difference to me.
Before anything was made, they weren't nothing and they was not nobody but God to make it.
God made the world and everything in it.
That's all they is to that.
To really choose you have to have some things to choose between.
It ain't enough to choose between this good and that good.

You have to be able to choose to obey or disobey, not between obey like this or obey like that.
You have to have bitter so you know something else is sweet.
You have to have darkness so that you can know what the light is.
If it was all light, or all sweet, we would not know it.
I believe we have to have evil so that we can treasure good.
These is high and lofty ideas like a professor would write. They look like they ain't honest or whatnot when I write them.
And I expect they work better in your head than they do in a real life.
I suppose if I kept on walking down this same path of thinking, that I could have told that woman that her son was not normal so we could know what normal is.
I could have told my self that Joseph died so we would treasure life.
But them grand thoughts seem to ring all hollow when a person is hurting and wondering why.
I do not know why they is evil in the world.
Does God punish us?
They sure is a lot of stories in the Book of God doing things to punish his children.
Peoples make the story of Noah and the Ark a cute little story for children, but it ain't really.
If you read it in Genesis, God repented that He done made peoples in the first place and decided to destroy every living thing.
God destroyed Sodom and Gomorrah because the sin of the peoples there was very grievous.
God hardened Pharaoh's heart and killed all they firstborn Egyptian children, and all them soldiers in the Red Sea.
It was not they fault they was Egyptians, nor that God hardened Pharaoh's heart.
Did God punish them because of Pharaoh?
Because He hardened Pharaoh's heart?
That does not seem fair to me.
They is only one story in the Book that I can think of that is talking about somebody who is born messed up somehow.
In John's Gospel chapter nine it tells the story that one time Jesus and His friends was walking outside the Temple and they saw a man who was born blind.

And his disciples asked him saying Master, who did sin, this man, or his parents, that he was born blind?

Jesus answered, Neither hath this man sinned, nor his parents: but that the works of God should be made manifest in him.

Well Jesus made a little mud out of dust and His own spit, and healed the man.

The rest of the story is all about the Pharisees being upset because Jesus did this on the Sabbath.

They was angry that Jesus broke the law about working on the Sabbath.

The disciples wanted to know who was God punishing—the blind man or his parents.

Jesus said that man was born blind so that the works of God should be manifest through him.

Jesus said the man was born blind so that he could be healed of it.

But that does not help us understand why is people born messed up today, when we can not heal them.

It may be that did not help as much as I was hoping.

But I done wrote too much to start over now.

So leave that story alone if it does not help.

It does show that peoples have been thinking about this for a long time.

It might be if they was an easy answer, Jesus would have told His friends, and they might have wrote it down.

Or maybe He told them the reason, but they did not understand it.

I wonder how much Jesus might have said that His friends did not understand, and so they never wrote it down.

These is good questions to ask, Buddy.

I expect that being faithful has more to do with asking questions than having answers.

Some peoples can not stand to have questions without answers, so they either do not ask the questions or make up some answers for them and play like they is true.

And it does not seem to matter to them that they answers is foolish.

Just having an answer is enough for them.

I think these peoples is more interested in being in control than looking for the Truth.
I ain't sure what we mean when we say God is in control, but I am sure that we ain't in control.
I believe being faithful is looking for the Truth.
We have to remember that God is a mystery without no limits.
One more thing, and then I have to stop writing.
I have a friend who is a guard.
His name is Boss Charlie.
Twice now, when the sky was clear at night and they was no moon, Boss Charlie has come to open up my cell door, and took me up to sit on the roof of the jailhouse.
They ain't no trees any where around, as you might recall, and it was pretty dark.
We looked at the stars, and smoked our pipes, and talked.
Boss Charlie is a Christian, or trying his best to be.
But he sees a lot of meanness up in here, in the prisoners and the guards.
He is trying to make sense out of all that.
I hope it helps him when we talk.
I hope he comes and gets me again.
I know it helps me to see the sky at night.
It does me much good to see all them stars.
It helps me know that I am a very small part of some thing much larger than I can understand.
My daddy used to look up at the sky at night sometimes after the peoples left the tent, and we would sit and look up at the stars.
He would point out the Big Dipper and the North Star and such as that.
I asked him a lot of questions, how many stars they was, and was they other peoples out there and whatnot.
He told me it was a good thing to ask questions, even if he did not have the answers.
I remember he used to say, The mysteries is ever before us, boy.
That is where I got that saying.
You might remember I have told you that a time or two.
Some things will just have to be a mystery.
I choose to leave them to God, and trust that He loves us.

I can not do no better than that.
Do not drink too much beer.
And be careful with them womens at camp, too.

Your friend,
Jacob Jefferson

17

Laissez les Bon Temps Rouler

The summer of 1974 ended, as summers always do, and I went back to Mississippi State. Trey introduced me to a friend of his from Riggsville who was a member of a small fraternity called Acacia. I had gone to a couple of rush parties for the large frats as a freshman, but it didn't seem like where I ought to fit in, and after that I decided I'd do better without any of it. But these eight or ten guys at Acacia seemed like a group that I could belong to. Some of them were boneheads, and a couple were just gross, but they were like brothers to each other.

Trey had joined Acacia, and they invited me to come live in the house. So instead of renting an apartment together, I moved into the Acacia House, which was fine with me. Trey eventually became an officer, but I just paid my share of the rent, which was cheap. They had great parties, they were happy to accept anyone who would accept them, and it was a little community to be a part of. And we had a running poker game every Thursday, Friday, and Saturday night. It was strictly nickel, dime, and quarter, but most weeks I won enough to buy lunches through the week.

I also had a series of jobs through college. Permanent Staff at summer camp didn't pay much, so I worked during the school year, too. I was a potato cook and dish washer for a steak restaurant, I worked in an aquarium shop, and I was a cashier for a convenience store. The summer after my junior year, I stayed in Starkville and took several courses, especially the pesky required class in Statistics that I'd tried several times before, only to drop it before I failed it. All those numbers couldn't find a place to rest in my head.

Trey and I went to as many football and baseball games as we could, enjoying the moments of glory together, consoling each other in the times of anguish. I met a young lady named Ann in Biology lab; she was beautiful and smart, wonderful in every way. She met Trey through me, and we both pursued her in our own ways, each of us respecting the other's efforts, neither of us having any skills or clues what to do. I was eventually the best man in their wedding at the First Baptist Church in Eupora, her hometown, experiencing glory and anguish all in one afternoon. Brother Swayze preached the sermon, all about resisting temptations and the wife's duty to her husband, and gave me a series of menacing looks throughout the weekend. It was great to see Mrs. Swayze, though.

In December of 1976, I graduated without distinction but a semester early, with a bachelor's degree in Sociology. I'd already talked with the Bishop of the Episcopal Diocese of Mississippi about going on to seminary. He'd told me that I shouldn't just go straight from college to seminary, that I needed to take a break. I'd graduated a semester early, thinking that would be enough of a break, but the Bishop told me I'd need to sit out another year to gain a little life experience before going back to school.

So I made my way through another set of temporary jobs: managing a seafood shop in Oxford, working in a residential center for people with developmental disabilities, doing a little construction and roofing, and finally as a deckhand with the Mile Wide River Towing Company. My brother Lee had worked for them a couple of summers before that, and the owner went to church with my parents. So they gave me a job.

The deal was that you could work two six-hour shifts a day on a towboat for thirty days and then be off for fifteen. The pay was inviting, the food was excellent (of course, to me this meant lots of steaks and hamburgers with few vegetables), and there was no place to spend the money you made. It was hot, hard work, and Jake wrote that it seemed right that I could do some honest work before I went off to seminary.

The *Martha Ray* was powered by two huge diesel engines, pushing four barges lashed end to end with thick steel cables that the deckhands tightened with winches pulled by hand. We were heading south to New Orleans to fill the barges with diesel and unleaded gasoline. After we were loaded with petroleum products, we'd push the tow north to Memphis, where we'd unload and head south empty again.

I got on the *Martha Ray* in Vicksburg with two other guys, both of whom had been on before and were coming back, having finished their break. We got on the boat together, and they showed me to the cabin where we would all sleep. Moe was tall and muscular, with long brown hair tied back in a ponytail. (I'd gotten mine cut short to interview at the seminary, and even shorter when I was working for a roofing company.) Moe told me he'd been in the Marines until he'd gotten into a dispute with a commanding officer, which resulted in his being sent to Leavenworth for six months. He said he would have gotten a year, but he remembered to say "Sir" after he told a lieutenant to go to Hell. He reminded me of a boxer bulldog. Peewee was small and slight, with stringy blond hair and a nervous laugh. He'd dropped out of school to work on the river; he'd been on the boat for years and probably still is. If Peewee were a dog, he'd have been a stray.

I was put on the forward shift, which meant that I was on with the captain from midnight to six a.m. and noon to six p.m., and I did whatever the captain told me to do. The second shift, from six to twelve, was supervised by the pilot. Peewee and I were on the forward shift; Moe was on the second shift with another deckhand named Charles.

The captain's name was Lamar. Captain Lamar was an immensely fat, short man who had a cigar in his mouth or his hand every time I saw him. I never saw the cigar lit; he told me he just chewed on them since he'd quit smoking. His sideburns went down onto his neck, he had a white crew cut, and he always wore a white T-shirt several sizes too small, blue jeans, and pointy-toed cowboy boots.

Everybody on the boat did what Lamar commanded, because he was the captain, because everybody hated him, and because he was rude and loud and arrogant. He smelled bad, he never brushed his teeth, he made unappetizing noises when he ate, and he told long, offensive jokes that were not funny. He must have known we all hated him, but that seemed to be the way he wanted it.

The work of a deckhand varied from day to day, but it was mostly some combination of keeping the barges tied together, mopping the decks, polishing everything made of brass, and trying to stay out of the way. The pilothouse had a whistle that you could hear over the engines, anywhere on the boat. On my first day, Captain Lamar told me that when I heard the whistle blow four shorts, I needed to come and see what he wanted.

Captain Lamar didn't particularly like any of us, as far as I could tell, but he seemed to have a particular dislike for me. A week or so into our cruise, Peewee told me that Captain Lamar had given several college boys working the summer a hard time; Lamar believed that college students thought they were better than people who work for a living. I'd already made the mistake of admitting to somebody that I'd graduated from college, and Captain Lamar went out of his way to make life difficult for me. I heard four shorts many, many times, so that I could get him a cup of coffee, recoil a rope, or tighten a cable that was already as tight as it could be.

Captain Lamar rotated off about a week after I got on; nobody was happier than I to see him walking up the ramp and off the boat. In his place came a short Cajun man named Captain Jimmy.

Captain Jimmy was as neat as his predecessor had been slovenly. A trim man of medium height, he wore blue or tan short-sleeved jumpsuits that zipped up the front, a New Orleans Saints baseball cap, and new white Keds tennis shoes. I found out later that he had two identical pairs of Keds, which he washed once a week. He had tattoos on both forearms, one from the Navy and the other of a hula dancer. But the most prominent and memorable feature was his eyes, clear and bright and ready to laugh at any moment. Captain Jimmy exuded a sense of calm strength that called for your respect; I knew it from the first moment I saw him.

Everybody loved Captain Jimmy, even more than we'd all hated Captain Lamar. We wanted to do what Captain Jimmy said, not because he was the captain but because he was Captain Jimmy. He spoke with a thick Cajun accent that was fun if sometimes difficult to follow. He couldn't remember anyone's name, so he gave everybody nicknames. On earlier trips, he'd named Moe and Peewee, and because I was tall and fairly strong, I became Hoss. But he didn't always remember the nicknames, either, so from time to time he called everybody "partner" or, as he pronounced it: "podnah." He started a lot of sentences with a word I didn't know: "Mais," which, as far as I could figure, was about the same as "Well"; so he'd say "Mais aw rat," which meant "Well all right."

The noon to six p.m. shift was usually busy, keeping things shipshape. But from midnight to six a.m., there were long stretches with not much to do. The four barges at front of the tow were removed from the diesel engines' constant roar and as close to quiet as could be found. Sometimes, lacking anything that needed doing, I'd go and sit up at the front.

One night around three, I was sitting at the front, and the whistle sounded four shorts. Captain Jimmy needed me. I ran as fast as I could, wondering what had happened, hoping I wouldn't be too late to help. Everything looked okay as I ran the length of the barge closest to the boat, no problems visible. I ran up the ladder and into the pilothouse and panted, "Yes sir?"

Captain Jimmy was calm, listening to some odd music that seemed to employ an accordion and a washboard on a little cassette player. I'd never heard of zydeco.

"How y'all are, Hoss?" the captain asked.

"Yes sir. Is everything all right?"

"Hoo yeh, podnah, ever t'ing's jus' okay. I didn't whistle you up here rat now because I got somethin' for you to do, non. I jus' whistle you up because dey ain't any t'ing for either one of us to do. Mais, I jus' saw you sittin' you self out on de front of de tow by you self alone, and t'ought you and me we could maybe jus' talk some little. I don' know you none at all, non. It ain't no use dat both of us be sitting all alone by our selfs. How 'bout a little chat, hah?"

"Oh. Okay, sure."

"Cap Lamar he tol' me you done already finish up wit' your school. He tol' me you done already graduate from college. He tol' me he want him to know what de heck you doing on dis boat. He tol' me he want him to know rat now. I tol' him, me, I don't know. I tol' him it ain't really my bidness, non. But I jus' been sittin' my self here wonderin', 'til I t'ought maybe I jus' come on an' ax you."

Actually, I'd been waiting for somebody to ask that question, and dreading it. Captain Lamar didn't like to have college boys on the boat because they were short-termers. He resented the idea that he'd teach a guy how to do all this stuff, and then in a month or two he'd be gone. He also resented that the college kid was more educated, and that in a year or two the kid would be out of school making more money than he by not working nearly as hard. So while Captain Lamar had the kid under his power, he would make him work as hard as he could. I know he did a reasonably thorough job of it with me.

In the case of a college boy, it was understandable that he'd leave at the end of the summer; he had to go back to college. But I was out of college; I didn't have to go back. What was I going to do, and why wasn't I out there doing it already? I guess they weren't real sure about me.

I dreaded telling anybody that I was about to go and work on a master's degree. I was worried what they'd say if they found out I was trying to become a priest. I had already concocted a fanciful tale about being on the boat for a few months and then pushing off to explore the West. If Captain Lamar or Moe had asked me, I'd have told them that. But when Captain Jimmy asked, I couldn't lie to him.

"I finished at Mississippi State over a year ago," I said. "I've just been working a few different jobs here and there before I go back to graduate school, starting this August."

He indicated that I should sit down. I sat in a little vinyl-covered chair with strips of duct tape almost holding the cracks in the vinyl together, and studied the impressive array of dials and lights and switches between the large wooden steering wheel and the tall window looking out over the river. I was especially interested in the radar screen that revealed the contours of the riverbanks before us and showed what was beyond the next bend.

"You t'ink you goin' back up to dat state college in de fall, hah?" Captain Jimmy asked.

"No sir, I'm going to a little college in South Carolina called Becket."

"Becket, hah?"

"Yes sir."

"Me, I ain't never heard of it, non."

"Most people haven't. It's very small."

"So what kind of t'ing do dey teach up dere at Becket?"

It was the moment of truth. He was watching the river now, coming up on a big bend. You had to be careful in the bends, he told me, because the sandbars were always shifting, and you didn't want to run aground if you could help it. He was watching the river and the radar screen, but he was listening for my answer, too.

"They have a seminary there," I said. "I'm going back to school to study to become a priest."

He was surprised. "Oh."

We sat for a while, neither of us knowing what to say next. He got us through the bend, and he relaxed. He stepped away from the wheel and said, "Mais aw rat, Hoss, I gotta take my self a leak. You take a holt on to de wheel, I'm gonna brought my self rat back." And he walked out, through the door and down the narrow steps before I could even think of a protest.

I put both my hands on the wheel, at ten and two like I'd learned in driver's education, and held on tight. We were on a long, straight stretch, plenty of time for him to do what he needed to do and get back.

After he'd been gone for what seemed like a long time, I started to wonder if something had gone wrong. Another bend was coming up, and I didn't dare take my eyes off the river.

Just before the calm part of me agreed with the fidgety part that this would be an appropriate time to panic, a voice from behind me said, "She out too far now, podnah. Move her to starboard, jus' a hair. Jus' a lil' blonde hair." Apparently he'd been standing there for some time.

I was still trying to remember which way was starboard when he continued, "Dat's to de right, Hoss." I turned the wheel a little with no appreciable effect, and he chuckled behind me. "A boat, she like a woman, Hoss," he said. "You got to hold her gentle, but move her firm, see?" He turned the wheel at least a quarter turn to the right, and we went starboard a few points. I hadn't noticed that my knuckles were white until it came time to let go of the wheel.

He took the wheel back, and I was glad to reclaim my seat. After a while, he asked, "A priest, hah? I don't t'ink you ain't Catholic, non."

"No sir. Episcopal. Our priests can marry if they want to. We also don't pay all that much attention to the Pope."

He laughed, "Mais, shoo—our priest, he don't pay dat much 'tention to de Pope, too, and he some Catholic, dat fo' sure." He thought about it for a minute, then continued more quietly, "Dat make sense 'bout dem gettin' married too, yeh. Pere Antonio he ought to be his self married jus' like dat, sure."

He got us through the next bend while I stayed quiet. "Is it t'ree years in de seminary, hah?" he finally asked.

"Yes sir."

"And den what you gonna did wit' you self, podnah?"

"Then I'll be out, and be a priest for some Episcopal church in Mississippi."

"Hoo boy! Can you preach?"

"I don't know. I've never tried. It looks pretty scary."

"I guess you gonna found dat out at de seminary, hah?"

"I suppose so."

We talked about the church, and what he thought was wrong with it, what the Pope needed to do about it. We talked about my call to the priesthood. He asked me if I knew the Bible, chapter and verse; I told him I figured I had three years to learn what I needed in seminary. He said Father Anthony, his priest in Thibodeaux, Louisiana, didn't know much about the Bible, either, but he knew what the Pope or the Bishop said, whether he paid them any attention or not.

Captain Jimmy was a very religious man, in his way, even though he was not as involved with his home parish as his wife Marie wanted him to be. He told me he was a recovering alcoholic, and that Alcoholics Anonymous was his true community of faith. And he wanted to know about me, what I thought and believed. He listened when I talked, like Jake had, in a way that older people often do not. So we talked for a long time, until the sky began to lighten.

He said, "Mais aw rat, Hoss, you better get you self down on dem barge and make you self sure all dem cinches is tight 'fore you frien' T-Joe get his self up out de bed and t'ink he maybe find one got loose. An' t'anks for de chat, podnah."

T-Joe was Captain Jimmy's nephew, Marie's sister's son. I learned that quite a few Cajun boys or men are named "T"-something. The "T" comes from the French word *petit*, which means little. T-Joe's father's name must have been Joe. He was the second shift first mate, and he loved to find things wrong with the way the first shift had done our work. Some people just love to keep things stirred up, and T-Joe was one of them.

But he didn't give me any trouble that day. I tightened all the lines, even though none of them were loose. The second shift came on, and I went to the galley, had some breakfast, and went to bed.

After that, more nights than not, four shorts would call me up to the pilothouse, and Captain Jimmy and I would talk and watch the river. Sometimes, in a straight spot, he'd ask me to hold the wheel, sometimes he'd tell jokes or stories he'd heard, and sometimes we'd talk about religion or politics. I'd thought politics in Mississippi were a mess until I heard about politics in Louisiana.

Sometimes we just sat together and enjoyed the view. On dark nights, we watched the stars reflected in the mile-wide river, and I wondered if Jake was watching those same stars on the roof with Boss Charlie.

One night Captain Jimmy asked me if I drank much, and I told him that I didn't, just some beer in college. He said, "Mais yeh, podnah, I t'ink I done spilt more beers dan you ever drunk." He told me he'd wasted many a year drinking too much, and almost lost his wife, whom he always called "my sweet Marie." He told me that, for him, being on the boat was like being at an AA meeting, because it was a firm company policy that there was no alcohol on the boat. He said some of those other rules might be bent from time to time, but this was the only rule he cared anything about: No Alcohol on the Boat.

Another night he saw a small herd of deer swimming the river. He cut the engines back so we wouldn't hit them, and trained the spotlight on them until they made it across to Louisiana.

"Dey gonna like it much mo' better over in Louisiana, hah?" he teased.

With a straight face, I told him they'd swim back to Mississippi if they had to listen to the Louisiana deer speaking Cajun. He laughed until he couldn't catch his breath, and then he said, "You all right, Hoss."

A few days before my first thirty-day shift was up, the electrical generator blew. We'd been pushing upriver, twenty miles north of Baton Rouge, when something came loose and the whole thing exploded. It was about 10:30 at night, and I slept through the whole thing.

Apparently the generator ran off the power of the engines and provided electricity for the boat. The steering system depended on the electricity the generator produced, so when the generator blew, the pilot cut the starboard engine and ran us aground. We rammed into the mud shore on the Mississippi side, almost throwing me out of my bunk.

Peewee came to wake me up and told me that Captain Jimmy needed me in the engine room. I pulled on my jeans and slipped on my tennis shoes, and we went out into the dark, still night.

Our bunks were right next to the engine room, and I'd gotten used to the howling of the two 3200-horsepower diesel engines all day and all night. After four weeks, I hardly even heard them anymore. But now, with the engines off, the silence was oppressive. Instead of the familiar diesel roar, we heard frogs, big ones, and cicadas, millions of them. There was no moon, or not much of one, and the stars were hidden behind a layer of clouds. We were dead in the water, surrounded by the dark and the creatures that dwelt therein.

Captain Jimmy shined his flashlight at my belly to avoid blinding me, and motioned me over to where he stood with Moe by the ruined generator. The engineer, a small man we all called Pops, who had white wispy hair with a life of its own, stood off to one side holding an ancient flashlight, looking dejected that there was something broken that he couldn't repair or rig up somehow. It looked like Pops was taking the situation personally.

Captain Jimmy was upbeat, totally at ease. "Aw rat, podnahs, I tell you what we gonna did. Hoss and Moe, you gonna took dat skiff on back down to Baton Rouge. It gonna took you 'bout almos' one hour 'fore you got dere, aw rat? When you did got dere, you gonna found dis place called Broussard's, hah? It's rat dere on de river, on de wes' side, rat south of de Rainbow Bridge. Mais, den you gonna took you selfs in dere an' call on de telephone dis man. He got de name Elmo Guidry, aw rat? I got you his name an' his telephone numbers rat cheer on dis lil' piece o' paper I got in dis hand I'm gonna gave you. Hoo, he some fine electrician, I'm gonna tol' you. You gonna brought him back wit' you so he gonna got us goin' pretty quick again. You gonna tol' him what hoppen, how dis generator done give up her ghos', and he gonna brought us a new one, jus' like dat. Aw rat?"

Moe and I answered together, "Yes sir."

Captain Jimmy yawned and handed me the paper with Mr. Guidry's name and number. "Aw rat, den. Me, I'm gonna took my self back up to my bed and make some sleep 'fore dat sun come up. It gonna be hot hot in de mornin', shoo yeh."

Pops made sure we had all the right information about the generator, the manufacturer and model number. T-Joe made sure everything in the skiff was squared away, and he told us several more times how to get to Broussard's. He and Moe had used the skiff for something once before, and T-Joe was obviously ticked that he didn't get to go again. Moe told me to get my wallet, and we were off.

The ride down to Baton Rouge was marvelous. The skiff was about twenty feet long, with an 80-horsepower Evinrude outboard motor. It felt like we were flying compared to the speed of the *Martha Ray*, but we probably weren't going any more than twenty-five miles per hour or so. We had running lights and a powerful flashlight, but it was mostly pitch-black dark. I sat in the front with the flashlight, watching for floating logs and trying to show Moe which way to go.

A little before midnight, we saw the glow of the lights of Baton Rouge in the distance. Finally, we came around a bend and saw the city. We went under the Rainbow Bridge and saw Broussard's off to starboard, right where Captain Jimmy said it would be. Moe pulled the skiff up to a floating dock, and I got out and tied the front rope to a cleat. Moe got out, too, pushing his shoulder-length hair into some order, and we made our way up the pier.

Broussard's Grill and Bait Shop was stocked with a curious assortment of people, men and women taking a little time off from the hard lives they lived. It was the first time I'd ever seen tattoos on women or earrings on men.

They all looked up when we came in, but as we did nothing to hold their interest, they ignored us after that. Moe went to the bar, and I went to find a pay phone. It was well after midnight, and Mrs. Guidry didn't seem happy to hear from me, but Mr. Guidry didn't seem to mind my waking him up. I told him what had happened, told him it was Captain Jimmy on the *Martha Ray*, gave him the name of the generator manufacturer and the model number, and he told us to stay at Broussard's, that he'd meet us there.

When I found Moe, he had two bottles of Pabst Blue Ribbon beer sitting on the bar in front of him, one full and the other almost gone. He told me he'd bought the first round, and it was almost time for me to buy the second. I picked up the full beer and took a long drink of it; it was as fulfilling as beer on the television ads. I told Moe what Mr. Guidry had said, and that we'd just have to wait. Moe was delighted.

Moe got the attention of the man behind the bar and ordered two more beers for us. He told the man, who was wearing a plastic nametag that read "Alphonse," that I was buying the second round. When Alphonse brought the beer, Moe asked him what kind of po'boys they had. I got a ham and cheese, no tomato, please; Moe wanted a soft-shelled crab po'boy, but it wasn't the right time for softshells, so he settled for a po'boy with crawfish. That was fine with me; I'd seen somebody eat a soft-shelled crab sandwich once, and it looked like he was eating a big spider, with the legs hanging out over the bread. In a few minutes, our sandwiches came with two bowls of gumbo that we didn't order, but that Alphonse assumed we'd want. And as it turned out, he was right.

When Alphonse came back, I made a point of thanking him for the gumbo and told him I was enjoying it tremendously. I'd never actually had gumbo because I don't like okra, which is a principal ingredient. But I tried this gumbo, and it was great. Alphonse wasn't nearly as excited about it as I was, and he droned with weary sarcasm, "Laissez les bon temps rouler."

I was stunned. I watched Alphonse walk away, and Moe explained, "Lay-zay lay bon ton rule-ay. 'Let the good times roll.' Truer words were never spoken, Hoss, what you got there is your basic words to live by: Laissez les bon temps rouler."

Moe got the third round, and I got the fourth. I was starting to get a little concerned that if Mr. Guidry didn't get there soon, we were going to have to sleep off our late-night snack. Moe started talking about buying another round, and I started trying to tell him that I didn't think that was such a smart idea, and somewhere in there he said, "I just feel so sorry for Peewee, though."

That seemed to me to have come out of the blue, and I asked him what he was talking about. He looked disconsolate. "Poor Peewee is back on the boat, just sweating through the night, while you and me are sitting here drinking beer and letting the good times roll. Doesn't seem fair, does it?"

I had to agree that it didn't seem fair, and Moe went ahead and ordered another round. I was getting to the point where I couldn't feel my lips. That probably affected my ability to talk, although it didn't seem that way at the time. I told him there was nothing we could do about Peewee's misfortune.

But Moe had a different idea. "Well, Hoss, think about it like this. If me and Peewee had brought the skiff to Baton Rouge, and you'd had to stay on the boat, and if me and Peewee had a few beers, and then out of the goodness of our hearts if we brought you one, you'd be grateful, wouldn't you?"

I told him that I probably would, and I was about to tell him that it still wouldn't be ethically justifiable, because of Captain Jimmy and the No Alcohol on the Boat rule, but I couldn't seem to get all that to come out of my mouth. Moe, who seemed much more practiced at letting good times roll, could still speak distinctly, so he did.

"I'll tell you right now: it's gonna be a day or two before we get going again. That generator we're replacing must be forty years old. I'll kiss your pink ass if Guidry has the right generator the first time. Hell, I'll kiss my own ass!"

I remember trying to think about that, but I couldn't picture it. Or maybe I didn't actually want to. Moe didn't let the image linger.

"And it's gonna be some kind of hot, too, Hoss. All day tomorrow we're gonna be lookin' for somethin' cool to drink. And here we are with a cold beer in our hands, and ol' Peewee's gonna be drinkin' lukewarm Gatorade. It just doesn't seem fair, does it?"

Mais podnahs, the longer Mr. Guidry looked for the appropriate generator to make Moe pucker up, and the less I could feel my own lips, the more Moe talked about the tragic unfairness of Peewee's severe lack of suitable beverages, and how it was our duty to come to his aid. By the time Mr. Guidry finally arrived, Alphonse had sold us two six-packs of Pabst Blue Ribbon beer and a big white Styrofoam box to keep them cool. We also bought several large bags of ice, some bread, sandwich meats, and cheeses, and two jars each of Hellman's Mayonnaise and Zatarain's spicy mustard. Hoo boy, yeh: it was looking like those bon temps were just bound to rouler.

The trip from Baton Rouge back to the boat was not so memorable, partly because the sky was getting lighter so we could see, and partly because I probably dozed at least some of the way. Mr. Guidry rode with us, sitting by the new generator in the middle of the boat, in front of the middle seat. Moe and I put our contraband behind it.

We got back to the *Martha Ray* at about seven that morning, and it was already getting warm. We helped Mr. Guidry and Pops carry the generator into the engine room, and then I went to bed. When I woke up a little after noon, T-Joe and Pops had already taken Mr. Guidry and the generator in the skiff back to Baton Rouge. Moe had been right; it wasn't the correct generator. But Mr. Guidry was sure that he would find the right one, and all we had to do, and all we could do, was wait.

A few mosquitoes found us and went back to alert all their mosquito friends and relatives that the *Martha Ray* was now an all-you-can-eat buffet. They came in swarms, clouds, flocks, and herds. Inside the boat, the heat was stifling; outside, the mosquitoes were threatening to carry us away, and all we could do was wait and wait some more.

Later that afternoon, T-Joe and Pops brought Mr. Guidry back with another generator that didn't work, either. Pops was completely disgusted, but Mr. Guidry remained cheerful about the whole thing. Peewee and Charles took him back again, with T-Joe telling them to return with three or four generators this time. It was not unlike trying on shoes, said the cheerful electrician; we just needed to find a right fit.

Still later, I'd fixed a sandwich and was sitting in the shade in the starboard stern of the boat when Moe came up and handed me something wrapped in a yellow bandanna. It was one of our outlaw beers; he had another wrapped up in his other hand. I looked around for Captain Jimmy, but Moe was cool. "Captain Jimmy's in his room, T-Joe's asleep, and nobody else cares. We got 'em wrapped in these insulating wraps, nobody'll even see 'em."

He told me Peewee had indeed been grateful, and that Charles had had a couple. When I'd gone to my bunk, Moe had taken the groceries and put them in the galley refrigerator with all the ice. He'd put the beer way in the back, so they were hard to see. Each time the skiff came back, it brought more ice. Moe said everything was just fine.

I relaxed a little, ate my sandwich, and drank my beer. I can't think of anything I've ever tasted before or since that was any better than that cold Pabst Blue Ribbon beer after a long, hot day of swatting mosquitoes.

Then I asked Moe a question that had been bothering me. "You and T-Joe took the skiff before, but last night Captain Jimmy asked me to go with you. I think it ticked T-Joe off, y'know? I was just wondering why Captain Jimmy didn't ask T-Joe to go with you that time."

Moe laughed a little, and told me that he and T-Joe had taken the skiff into Memphis one night almost a year before, when the boat had gotten stuck on a sandbar. Captain Jimmy had sent them to get some ice and groceries, but they'd had wound up drinking a few beers and getting into a fight with each other in a night spot. He told me the sheriff had called Captain Jimmy to come get them out of jail. Moe said Captain Jimmy had blamed T-Joe, who had apparently been involved with some drinking and fighting before, and that he hadn't spoken to his nephew for months after that.

After a while, Moe took off his T-shirt, shoes, and jeans and slipped into the water over the side of the boat in his boxers. He figured the mosquitoes wouldn't be able to get him so well if most of him was in the water. The mosquitoes were having no trouble at all finding me. I asked him if he was worried about snakes or snapping turtles, but he told me he hadn't even had a nibble, and suggested I ought to come in, too. I was just about to take off my shoes when he started telling me how wonderful it would be if we could float in the Mighty Muddy with a Pabst Blue Ribbon in our hands. He said there were only two or three left, and that if we didn't hurry, Peewee or Charles were sure to drink all our beers. He said he would've gone in to get them, but he didn't want to be dripping around the galley in his boxers.

So I took the insulating bandannas and went to the galley. Moe had told me where the beer was, that it was pushed to the back of the refrigerator. I was trying to see behind the lettuce and tomatoes when I noticed the toes of two white shoes under the refrigerator door. Two very white, recently washed Keds tennis shoes.

I closed the refrigerator door and faced Captain Jimmy. The sparkle was gone from his eyes, and I knew in that one terrible, clear moment that I'd broken the only rule of the boat he cared about, the rule that kept him safe. I had brought alcohol onto the boat. With disgust dripping in his voice, he said, "Mais, I ought to kick your tail, dat fo' sure, boy."

I couldn't have agreed with him more. I needed to have my tail kicked; I wanted to kick it myself. Some part of me wanted to blame it on Moe, but it didn't hold up, even in my own head. I had knowingly done something I knew was hurtful to Captain Jimmy, a man I respected and loved, and I knew I had no real defense at all.

"I'm sorry," I said.

He looked sad more than angry, and took a step back. "Yeh, I know. Mais, we always sorry when we done got cotched, hah? I ought to kick your tail, but I won'. I ain't nobody to do no kickin', non. I gonna tol' you what you gonna did rat now. You gonna took dem beers and t'row dem in de river, hah? Den we ain't never gonna said nothin' else about dis, aw rat?" I looked up at him, to see if it was going to be all right. He looked hurt, and hard. "But I don' forget, Hoss. If you ever gonna did somethin' else like dis' again, den it's gonna be jus' you and me, and I t'ink it gonna be mos'ly me."

I said, "Yes sir."

Captain Jimmy turned around and left the galley. There were four beers left, and I took them and threw them as far as I could into the river off the port side. Then I went and told Moe.

"You threw them *all* in?" he asked.

"Every damned one of them," I affirmed, and I left Moe in the water and walked out to the front of the tow, alone with the sun, the mosquitoes, and my shame.

Mr. Guidry didn't get the right generator in place until the next day. We worked our way out of the mud and continued upstream, reaching Vicksburg just before twilight. Captain Jimmy told me it was time for me to get off. I must have looked alarmed, because he laughed and reminded me that it was time for my two-week break. He told me to get my check at the office, and that he'd see me after his break was over.

"Captain Jimmy," I began, "I'm sorry about the bee—"

But he cut me off.

"Aw rat now, Hoss, we ain't talkin' 'bout dat, hah? But lissen, podnah—only one man ain't never messed up. An' shoo, look what we done to Him." He smiled, we shook hands, and it was time for me to go.

Moe, Peewee, and I went up the ladder to the office and got our checks. I'd never been paid so much at one time. I called home, and my father came up from Beaumont to get me. Peewee called a sister and was waiting for her when I left; Moe just walked off into the night.

The next couple of weeks went slowly. I had a hard time sleeping without the roar of the diesel engines in the background. My internal clock had become accustomed to working and sleeping in six-hour increments. I thought about going to Parchman to visit Jake, but decided against it. He had warned me many times about coming to visit, and I didn't have any way to get there. One of the reasons I was working on the river was to save up enough money to buy a car. I'd gone through college with only a bike, but it didn't seem reasonable to think I'd be able to catch a ride to and from Becket University in South Carolina.

I went to check on Jake's hut, and everything was fine. I found a patch of black-eyed Susans in a clearing on my way, so I picked a bunch and put them on the graves of Jake's father and son. I sat on the fallen sweet gum for over an hour, whistling. I wasn't nearly as skillful as Jake, but I'd had some time to practice on the boat, and it was starting to sound like there was a tune in there somewhere.

The morning came when my father would take me back to the dock in Vicksburg. I put the books I'd gotten with all my other stuff in my old Army Navy Surplus duffel bag, met Peewee and Moe at the office, and waited for the boat.

Captain Lamar was in the pilothouse, and each of us went up to tell him we were back. I went last, in no hurry to see him spilling out of Captain Jimmy's chair. "Ah, here's the professor!" he sneered. "Hell, I'm surprised you come back. We'll see if we can keep you busy before you go back to school, show you how working men work for a living. You're four shorts—keep an ear sharp for it."

I hadn't even unpacked my stuff before I heard four shorts. It was time to be underway, and Captain Lamar was yelling to cast off. I untied some of the ropes from the dock and coiled them; Charles and Sonny, a guy I hadn't met, checked the tow, tightening all the winches. By the time we were pushing up toward Memphis, it was after noon, and the forward shift had begun. Captain Lamar was true to his word, and he found several things to keep me busy. I was counting the days until Captain Jimmy returned.

Captain Lamar was at the wheel when we ran aground the next day; I was on top of the pilothouse scrubbing the roof, getting ready to paint. We were north of Greenville on our way to Memphis completely loaded, so we were heavy and deep in the water, and moving slowly. Still, as I was kneeling on top of the pilothouse with a bucket of soapy water and a sponge, the hit almost knocked me off. If I hadn't caught the flagpole with my hand, I would've fallen into the water. As it was, I got a scary-looking cut on my left knee when it went over the side of the pilothouse, and it was bleeding profusely by the time I dropped down onto the pilothouse deck.

Captain Lamar told me to go down to the galley and get my knee cleaned up. That's where the first aid kit was. He told me Cook would help. Cook was what we called all the cooks, one of a series of different women, all of them hard and loud and overweight, all of whom I'd taken some pains to be friendly with, with no appreciable difference in their attitude toward me. I made my way to the galley, resolved that I could handle this without Cook's nursing. I doused the wound with hydrogen peroxide and pulled it together with a couple of bandages. I didn't want anybody to know, but it hurt like hell.

That night at supper, Captain Lamar handed me a piece of white paper. At the top was written "Mile Wide River Towing Company Accident Report." There were blanks to fill in, indicating the time of the accident, who was piloting, who was involved, and a description of the injury, along with a place for me to sign at the bottom. Captain Lamar had filled in his part and had to have my signature so he could file it. Under the description of the injury, he'd printed: "Fell off pilothouse and scratched knee." There was no mention of his running the boat aground.

A few days later, Captain Lamar got off the boat without a word to me or anyone else, as far as I could tell, and Captain Jimmy came back on. We all breathed a little more easily. The first couple of days, he didn't whistle me up during the early-morning shift, and I was afraid I'd ruined an important relationship for two six-packs of beer. The third night Captain Jimmy was back, though, I heard four shorts at about 1:30, and I got up to the pilothouse as fast as I could.

"Mais aw rat, Hoss. How y'all are?"

"I'm fine, Captain Jimmy, how are you?"

"Hoo, me, I'm okay fine, good as I can stand my self. Cap Lamar he tol' me you done got you self a pretty bad cut, hah?"

The cut on my knee had left an impressive scab, but it was well on its way to recovery. "Yes sir," I replied. "It's getting better."

"Mais yeh. Things heal, sure. Jus' don' pick at it, it gonna got some better pretty quick."

"Captain Jimmy, I'm sorry about the beer. I shouldn't have—"

"Aw rat, Hoss. We ain't gonna said nothin' 'bout this one more time. Things heal. Jus' don' pick at it, it gonna got better. Aw rat?"

"Yes sir." We watched the river for a moment, and I continued, "It's going to leave a scar, though."

He laughed, and I saw the twinkle in his eye. "Hoo, sure, podnah, you gonna got you self a lot of more scars before you all done, dot's for dam' sure."

18

All Them High and Lofty Professors

August 6, 1978
Sunday

Dear Buddy,

I thank you for the letter.
It was so good to hear from you.
I am sure glad you is off that boat so that you will be safer and also so that I have someplace to send you a letter.
Send me your address up in South Carolina when you get there, please.
And thank you for telling me about Captain Jimmy.
He seem like he a good man.
It look like Captain Lamar is shaky about his own self, and hates peoples he thinks is smarter than him.
They is more peoples like that than they is like Captain Jimmy.
Now I ain't going to preach here but I do want to say this right here.
What happened to you is what Jesus meant when He was talking about forgiveness. You was caught red-handed like the woman caught in adultery, in the very act.

And what Captain Jimmy did was to give you a second chance.
Like Jesus gave the woman caught in adultery.
Like the father of the prodigal son.
And here is the thing.
It ain't enough for somebody else to forgive you.
It ain't even enough to ask God to forgive you.
You got to forgive your own self.
They is a lot of mens up here who need to know this.
If somebody is forgiven, he need to let it go, or he will have to drag that around with him the rest of his life.
I believe it is just prideful to hold on to something God has let go of.
Mens up in here keep on punishing they selfs for what they did, even when they is saying God has forgiven them.
They need to let it go, and move on.
We do not need to punish our selfs, because Jesus has already took the punishment for us.
The prophet Isaiah told it like this: He is despised and rejected of men; a man of sorrows, and acquainted with grief: and we hid as it were our faces from him; he was despised, and we esteemed him not.
Surely he hath borne our griefs, and carried our sorrows: yet we did esteem him stricken, smitten of God, and afflicted.
But he was wounded for our transgressions, he was bruised for our iniquities: the chastisement of our peace was upon him; and with his stripes we are healed.
All we like sheep have gone astray; we have turned every one to his own way; and the LORD hath laid on him the iniquity of us all.
All we like sheep have gone astray, they ain't nothing we can do about that.
But Jesus was wounded for our transgressions, and with His stripes we are healed.
So when we refuse to forgive our selfs, we might just as well tell God that His Son's death was just for nothing.
When we do not forgive our selfs we is the ones Jesus is despised and rejected of. We is the ones who is hiding our faces from Him.
The trick to living ain't that you never mess up but that you get up and start over when you do.
Everybody messes up.

That is just part of what it mean to be human.
Being forgiven which is forgiving yourself too, is part of what it mean to be a Christian.
But you is right, too.
It is going to leave a scar.
And I do not mean just the one on your knee.
Me and Boss Charlie was up on the roof one or two of them clear nights when you and Captain Jimmy was watching the River.
It looks funny to see it wrote down, but I miss you more when I know I cannot write you a letter you will read.
I think you might want to come up here and visit me before you go up to South Carolina. I hope you do not.
It is best for me if you do not come up in here.
I would love to see you but it might stir up things in here pretty bad.
Several of the mens have told me that Eddie is waiting for you to come back.
I believe he would like to hurt you if he could.
Eugene listens to me, just like he listens to Eddie.
Eddie would hurt you to hurt me if he could or if he thought it would make me look bad to Eugene.
I do not know if that make any sense to you but that is the way it is.
Eddie ain't got nothing to lose. That makes him a dangerous man.
It will be enough to send letters.
I hope you learn a lot at the seminary.
It may be someday you can teach me like I tried to teach you.

Your friend,
Jacob Jefferson

I entered the School of Theology at Becket University in August 1978. From a friend of my mother's I'd purchased a 1971 Mercury Comet, which required a quart of oil every time I filled it up with gas. I named the car Bill, after Sam Gamgee's horse in *The Lord of the Rings.*

On my way up to Becket, somewhere in Tennessee, I had to stop the first time I saw that the road had been cut through the mountain stone, just to look at it. Growing up in the dirt and mud of Mississippi, I'd never seen real stone before, just the gravel in some roads.

Becket is a beautiful place, with old stone buildings and huge ancient trees. Built just after the Civil War by wealthy landowners who didn't want their daughters to have to mingle with Yankees to get a good education, the school was later expanded to include a seminary for Southern gentlemen seeking ordination in the Episcopal Church. They modeled it after an English university and named it for Thomas Becket, the famous English martyr whose shrine Chaucer's pilgrims to Canterbury were going to visit. The first time I saw the school, it looked like I imagined Robin Hood's Sherwood Forest must have looked; I wouldn't have been surprised to see Little John or Will Scarlett leap out from behind a tree and twang me.

We had twenty-five students in our class. I was surprised that almost all of them were considerably older than I. Our first night there, the incoming class all met in a big room at the seminary, on the first floor of the seminary building. I had a dorm room on the third floor of that same building with the other single students.

The dean welcomed us and told us the kinds of things we should expect. He explained that first-year students were called juniors, second-year students were middlers, and third-year students were seniors. He told us where to look for schedules and other posted information, and explained the weekly routine. We sat in a circle and introduced ourselves. Some of my classmates took a while explaining who they were and why they were there. I was nervous about speaking in front of a group of people I didn't know and kept it short. I still remember my whole speech; I'd rehearsed it over and over in my mind before I had the chance to deliver it.

"Hi. I'm Buddy Hinton, from Beaumont, Mississippi. I'm glad to be here."

I later learned that several of my classmates would have something to say every time there was an opportunity, as if they wanted to be sure everybody knew they were there. On our first night, one of them asked if we would need to wear coats and ties to class. Apparently, this guy had been doing his homework already and knew that it was a tradition among the male undergraduate students at Becket to wear ties and coats—some of them with shorts or tattered jeans. The dean answered that we could, and that some of the professors would, but that it wasn't required. We would need to dress appropriately for some university functions, matriculation, and convocations. A few of my classmates wore ties to class for the first couple of days, but they soon gave it up as a hot and bothersome affectation. After we'd been there a couple of weeks, I bought a tie that didn't clash too much with my one coat, just so I'd be ready.

We had Morning Prayer every day, which was optional, but the dean was always sitting in his seat, aware of who was there and who wasn't. I went nearly every morning, not only so the dean would see me but also because the preacher was a different seminarian each time. Either middlers or seniors gave most of the sermons, with a few professors or visiting priests or bishops tossed into the mix. If the sermon was meaningful or profound, which was rare when a seminarian preached, or just goofy, which was more common, it was the topic of discussion for the whole day. So if you missed the sermon, you were out of the conversation that day.

After Chapel we all went to Morning Curriculum, which for the juniors was usually Old Testament, for two hours. Then we had a forty-minute break in which we usually went next door to the Bishops' Commons, sort of a Student Union building, and had a cup of coffee with doughnuts or bagels. After that we had more Morning Curriculum until lunch. In the afternoon we had electives. I took Hebrew for a little more than a month before I dropped it. My second semester, we had New Testament in the morning; in the afternoons I took Greek until I dropped it, too. Neither language was required, and I knew I'd never have enough Hebrew or Greek to replace the work of the scholars who wrote about the nuances of adjectives and the conjugation of verbs in our textbooks, but I was glad to at least learn the alphabets and appreciate the difficulty of translating from ancient languages into a language normal people can understand.

Most mornings in my junior year, the Morning Curriculum was an introductory course in either the Old or New Testament, but some days we had something else. Some mornings we had liturgics, all about the proper way to conduct the services, or phenomenology, which isn't easily defined but was "designed to blow our minds," and we talked about visions, dreams, appearances of the Virgin Mary, and UFOs, among other things. Despite the arrogance of the professor, Dr. Sprague, whose book I had started but couldn't force myself to finish, I was enjoying the class quite a bit.

Then one morning I surprised us all by joining in the discussion. I quoted Jake, telling them a wise man once told me, "There is more to the world than I am able to know."

Dr. Sprague was tall and delicately thin, balding with a white fringe, and wore thick black glasses: sort of like Ichabod Crane in a clerical collar. He looked at me like I was something he needed to clean off his shoe, and, glancing at some of the other members of the class, he said, "How . . . droll." Everybody but me thought that was funny; I blushed so hard my ears burned.

After that I didn't say much of anything in any class, not for a long time.

The Episcopal Church had officially voted to ordain women as priests in 1976, although there were some spectacularly rebellious pioneers before that. In 1978, we had four women in our entering class, the largest group of female seminarians Becket had ever had. We repeatedly blundered into what would later come to be thought of as violations of politically correct patterns of speech, being reminded to say "he or she" rather than just "he," or "his-slash-hers" rather than just "his." One of the women in our class took it upon herself to help us with gender-appropriate pronouns; I don't know how well she did with her grades, but she was constant and relentless in her crusade for precise pronoun use. After only a couple of weeks of that, I wanted to slap her.

One of my classmates, a retired civil engineer, computed that the average age of our class was 36.3 years. I was 22; my friend Scott from Florida was about two months younger. He and I lived on the third floor of the seminary and quickly became steadfast friends. Scott was gentle, musical, and idealistic with a wonderful sense of humor and a healthy sense of wonder; he'd been a youth minister between college and seminary, and had longish, straight hair and a wispy, beatnik sort of beard.

Scott and I were two of the three single students out of the twenty-five juniors in our class; the rest were older, married with children, and exploring a second career. The pedagogy in place seemed to be based on instructing a group of young single men, as apparently had been the case throughout much of the history of the church. The faculty was trying not to adjust to the new situation of dealing with older students or women, holding on to the way things had always been done. This is not unusual. It only takes one Episcopalian to actually change a light bulb; the others are there either to mix drinks or to complain that they liked the old one better.

In our study of Genesis, I learned about source criticism, a way to look at the Bible while considering who might have written the different parts. Jake had prepared me for this years before in our discussion of Noah and the ark, but some of my classmates were greatly upset by the idea. One of them, a good old boy from south Alabama, kept saying loud enough for the back rows to hear, "What does this have to do with Jesus?"

Every Wednesday, all the seminarians and the professors walked to Cranmer House, a hotel for parents and dignitaries with an adequate restaurant. It was just down the street from our classrooms, a good place for us to have lunch together as a seminary community. It was a time each week for the classes to mingle, for the dean to make announcements, and for the hot dogs and suck-ups in each class to report on the various conferences and conventions they had attended. None of my friends was ever invited to represent the seminary at these impressive gatherings, and neither was I.

On Friday afternoons we had feedback groups, in which we met with five or six of our fellow students and two members of the faculty. The idea was that these would be informal discussions to absorb the learning of the week. The informality and rate of absorption had diminished years before when, in an effort to encourage more participation, the faculty had changed feedback groups into something for which you received a grade. I decided I'd leave most of the discussing to the hot dogs, my classmates who would run over anybody or anything to make an "A" in everything; I decided I'd be content with a "B" and just talk when I genuinely had something to say. I didn't quote him, but I remembered that Jake had told me several times that listening was more important than talking. So I let them talk.

It was also in feedback group that junior students preached their first sermons, starting in the second semester. The plan was for a student to stand behind a little podium and give a sermon, and then sit in front of the podium so his or her classmates could jump in with brotherly and/or sisterly love and make criticisms. Finally, the faculty advisor would pronounce the verdict, which also carried the weight of a grade. One of the faculty advisors in my feedback group happened to be our homiletics instructor, who was charged with teaching us how to preach or, as she put it, be a "preacher teacher." So the first sermon in our particular feedback group was an especially big deal for all of us.

It was a nerve-wracking process, a determining factor on our grades that semester, and it affected our standing among classmates. The hot dogs went first, of course, and delivered extensively researched and painstakingly written treatises on the Scripture passages assigned for that week in the Lectionary. I was the last to sign up, and I got the last assignment, which gave me more time to dread it. Preaching was the thing in seminary that scared me the most.

When my time came, the Scriptures included the Gospel passage on the story of the Prodigal Son. I told them the story of Captain Jimmy and the beer, and finished with Jake's admonition that we ought to forgive ourselves if we want to honor Christ's gift of penance on the cross.

I sat down and waited for the sniping to begin. There was only stunned silence. Eventually, our faculty advisor, the homiletics instructor, broke in.

"Buddy," she said, "that's the finest sermon I've heard in seventeen years here." My classmates were much more stunned by what she'd said than what I'd said, and she continued, "From any student or member of the faculty."

"Well, all right!" my friend Scott exclaimed.

It was the best thing that could possibly have happened to me. After that, I wasn't so afraid of preaching, and I started to talk a little more in class. The dean asked me for a copy of my sermon at our weekly seminary lunch, in front of the whole school. My stock soared, and my confidence went with it. I wrote and told Jake all about it, and sent him a copy of the sermon.

March 25, 1979
Sunday

Dear Buddy,

I am very glad you had a good sermon so you know you can preach.
I am very proud of you.
Do not let it go to your head.
It is good that you told them a story instead of just shuffling the words in the Book around.
Jesus told stories to preach, too.
But please be careful that you do not become prideful.
Preaching ain't nothing to be proud of and I will tell you why.
If you pay too much attention to peoples telling you how wonderful you is you might soon forget that it is God you is supposed to be pointing to and not your own self.
I knowed you would have the gift of preaching, I knowed it for a long time.
But remember who gave you that gift and what you is supposed to do with it.
I am likely being too hard on you. I am sorry for that.
I just have seen too many preachers who listen to peoples telling them how wonderful they is until it ruined them.
No preacher worth his salt lets hisself be the star of the show.
It ain't supposed to be about the preacher.
It ought to be about God and His people.
I would love to see you up there in seminary. My Buddy sitting with all them high and lofty professors and whatnot.
But even they have something to teach you.
Just keep looking for the Truth however He comes to you.
Eugene was in the camp hospital for a few days this week.
Boss Charlie took me in to see him.
We had a good visit.
He was afraid, said he felt like he was going to die.

He just had the flu Boss Charlie said.
Eugene told me he was sorry for everything he ever done.
He said he was a bad man.
I told him he was a child of God who had done some bad things.
I told him God would always love him no matter what.
He smiled at that.
If I could just keep him away from Eddie I believe he would be all right.
Boss Charlie told me he would talk to one of his bosses to see could they move Eugene into my camp.
I hope they can.
I best go now.
I will let you know about Eugene.
You let me know about your preacher school and whatnot.
And remember what Saint Paul wrote in his letter to the Romans.
For I say, through the grace given unto me, to every man that is among you, not to think of himself more highly than he ought to think; but to think soberly, according as God hath dealt to every man the measure of faith.

Your friend,
Jacob Jefferson

I wanted to argue with him and tell him I wasn't getting to prideful, but I couldn't unless I drove to the Mississippi Delta. The more I thought about it, though, the more I realized he was right, which made it even more difficult to swallow.

I had a great deal to learn that first year—about my various courses and about myself. That summer I went to C.P.E., Clinical Pastoral Education. The program takes seminarians and other people, makes them chaplains in hospitals and prisons, and has them interacting with other seminarians and supervisors to discuss the work they're doing in interpersonal relations groups. This was something like the feedback groups at Becket, in that you earned points with the supervisors if you criticized your peers.

Most of my classmates wanted to stay close to home, with families to consider. Being young and single, I could go anywhere, so I applied for two places in Massachusetts and one in California, just because I'd never been to either place. I was accepted at the Massachusetts State Hospital for the Chronically Ill in Tewksbury, Massachusetts. It was a nine-week program, so I had a week to get there and a week to get back before my middler year began in August.

On my way to Massachusetts, I drove the Comet through Columbia, South Carolina, to visit Tiffy, a girl I'd been dating at Becket, where she was an undergraduate. She told me she got her name from her mother, whose maiden name was Tifton. In Columbia, I met her parents and spent the night in their huge antebellum home. In our tearful parting scene, Tiffy and I pledged our undying love and fidelity before I drove up the East Coast. I knew without a doubt that she was the woman of my dreams. I was even able to reconcile myself to the idea of marrying someone named Tiffy.

I got impressively lost in Boston, and stopped to ask directions in a neighborhood where people apparently spoke only Portuguese, of which I knew not one word. Finally I found my way to Tewksbury, about ninety miles north of Beantown. In Maryland, I'd bought a case of oil, and I kept my eye on the gauge. By the time I got to the Massachusetts State Hospital for the Chronically Ill, Bill the Comet looked like it was smoking as much as the truck that used to come down Ridge Road once a week when I was growing up as it fogged for mosquitoes.

Eventually I found the appropriate building and met the other people in the program. The supervisors were all Catholic, but the seminarians were mixed, from Methodist to Jewish to Universalist Unitarians. That first night, several of us found the China King, a Chinese restaurant that served strong drinks at a reasonable price. I had my first gin and tonic and my first egg roll on the same night, greatly expanding my view of the world. A group of us went to the China King almost every night after that: warm spicy food and potent cocktails on a budget. I learned how to eat with chopsticks.

Most of the folks in the program were from up there somewhere; one of them told me she'd been as far south as Philadelphia, Pennsylvania. They were forever asking me to say things again, just to hear my accent; it made me feel like Gomer Pyle. And they talked so fast that I could hardly understand them. After a week, I started telling people to slow down, that my ears didn't hear that fast.

My closest friend that summer was a Catholic seminarian from Chicago named John. Or that's how he spelled it; he pronounced it "Jan." His last name was something Polish that I couldn't have spelled or pronounced, whether in Chicago or Mississippi speech. John was as sweet a person as I had ever met.

A couple of weeks into my New England adventure, I got a letter from Tiffy in Columbia. Her old boyfriend was home for the summer, and she was dating him again. She wrote that he was transferring from Duke to Becket for their senior year, and they were talking about getting married when they graduated.

That night at the China King, I offered a toast to undying love and fidelity. All my celibate Catholic friends commiserated as best they could, but the Methodist guy wanted me to write Tiffy back and tell her what a cold-blooded witch she was. I told them I hoped she was happy, which was mostly true. At least, I wanted it to be true.

John lifted his wine and made another toast: "To Tiffy, God bless her, and to our friend Buddy. Take it from a guy whom God is apparently calling to be celibate: 'Tis better to have loved and lost, than never to have loved at all."

We all raised our glasses and drank. The Methodist guy shook his head and muttered, "You people are crazy."

July 22, 1979
Sunday

Dear Buddy,

Thank you for the letter from Massachusetts.
A letter going from Massachusetts to Mississippi has a lot of spelling to do on the envelope.
I am sorry about that girl Tiffy.
I know you feel like you has lost something but she is the one who has lost out.
I expect her boyfriend is rich with a big fancy car.
So it may be she was more interested in that.

Well it is best to know now than have her deeper in your heart and find out later.

I have not never had much experience with womens, as you know, and most of that was not good.

And now in Parchman we don't hardly ever even see a woman except on television.

I know they is different from mens not just in they bodies but in the way they think and feel.

So it is hard for us to understand them or for them to understand us.

But when things is good between a man and a woman it is like a tiny small glimpse of the love of God.

Undying love—like you is talking about—is where God is.

It is rare and wonderful in this life but it is the substance of life with God in the next. So I am glad that you had you a girlfriend even if it was only just for a short time.

You got to step up to the plate and take your swings, if you are ever going to get a hit.

Even if you strike out three times out of four you still got to swing at them if you is ever going to get a hit.

One of these days the right girl will come along and pitch one where you can really hit it.

She going to be a lucky girl, she sure is.

When you get you a girlfriend you best make sure she is at least as hard-headed as you.

Do not let them peoples up North make you think they is any smarter or better than you just because they talk faster than you.

I ain't never had no Chinese food.

Cornelius said he heard they eat dogs and cats some times and fish heads and whatnot.

I thought he must be joking with me but he was serious.

You best be careful what you eat up there.

It might say pork on the sign out front but they ain't no telling what it really is.

Your friend,
Jacob Jefferson

19

The Problem of Evil

In Massachusetts, the girl I'd been dating dumped me, I had an impacted wisdom tooth extracted, Bill the Comet had his rings and valves replaced, and I learned to juggle on Harvard Square during a visit to Boston. I also survived the Clinical Pastoral Education process without notable incident and with minimal damage to my ego. In the middle of August, I packed up the car and headed back South, home to Beaumont.

I spent a few days at my parents' place, and then it was time to go back to school. I left early on a Friday morning and traveled up Highway 61. This wasn't the quickest way to Becket, but I had some extra time and wanted to swing by Riggsville and Parchman Prison. I hadn't seen my friend Trey since his wedding. He was working in Riggsville at one of the private schools, teaching science and coaching football and baseball. I'd called him from Beaumont, and he'd invited me to come have dinner with him and Ann, spend the night and catch up a little.

And I thought I could put together a care package for Jake. Mom made brownies and cookies, ostensibly for me to take back to school. I bought Prince Albert pipe tobacco, pipe cleaners, chocolate bars, a baseball magazine, two new decks of playing cards, and a carton of Kool cigarettes. Jake didn't smoke cigarettes, but he had mentioned in a letter that Kools were the real currency at Parchman, more useful than money. I also wrote him a note and put it in the box.

I got to Riggsville around lunchtime. The town looked smaller. The First Baptist Church was there on Main Street in all its red brick glory. It hadn't shrunk like the rest of the town; if anything, it looked larger and more imposing than ever.

Trey had told me he wouldn't be able to get away from the school until after five that afternoon. School hadn't actually started, he said, but two-a-day football practices had begun, with one early in the morning and another in the late afternoon. I thought about going out to the prison and trying to talk my way in, but I didn't want to make things worse for Jake. His friend Boss Charlie had not been able to move Eugene into Jake's camp, and I didn't want to give Eddie any reason to cause an incident.

So I went to see if Miss Mabel was still at the Swayzes' house, and she was. She welcomed me with a big hug and told me that the Reverend had gone to Jackson for some kind of meeting that day. Mrs. Swayze was at a ladies' luncheon at the church, but Miss Mabel knew she would want to see me. We had leftover fried chicken for lunch, and I asked her about Jake.

"Oh, he's doin' fine." Then, more carefully, she said, "Preacher Jake was pretty sick for a couple of weeks, had him a cold that turnt into pneumonia. Did he write and tell you that?"

I told her that he had not, and she shook her head. "I didn't think he would. He don't want to be no worry to people. And while they had him up there in the prison hospital, they found out he got the high blood pressure, too." She looked at me to gauge my reaction before concluding, "I bet you didn't know that, either."

"No ma'am."

"Well, he's doin' all right now. They got him on some several pills and medications and such, and he has to get his pressure checked regular. My man Cornelius keeps after him about it. That Preacher Jake, he's a rascal."

"Do you think you could get me in to see him?"

"Oh, honey, I knew you'd ask me that. It ain't safe up in there, Buddy, it 'specially ain't safe for you. They's a bad man up in there, name of Eddie, who thinks he's runnin' the place. He got him a gang of mens doin' what he say do, and a great big strong boy named Eugene workin' for him. My man Cornelius says that this fool Eddie has some kind of problem with Preacher Jake. He says anything Jake loves, Eddie gonna hate. You best not go into the prison with Eddie runnin' things. Somethin' ain't right about Eddie. Me an' Cornelius don't know what it is, but somethin' ain't right."

I knew all of that, but it was interesting to hear it from someone else. I hadn't expected to be able to visit Jake, so I wasn't too disappointed. In truth, I was somewhat relieved.

"But Jake is safe, isn't he?" I asked. "You think he's all right?"

She smiled and assured me, "If anybody could ever be safe up in there, Preacher Jake is safe. It's a terrible bad place. But he got mens around him all the time. Eddie hates him for some reason, but Preacher Jake's got a lot of friends in there, mens who wants to protect him. No, honey, he all right. And my man Cornelius is lookin' after him, too, don't forget."

"Well, could you get Mr. Cornelius to take something to him? I've put some stuff in a box, things I thought he might like."

She assured me that she'd get Cornelius to take Preacher Jake the box, and wanted to see what was in it. Then she served me a cup of coffee, and we had a big slice of pie, and after a while, just after Miss Mabel had convinced me that one piece of pecan pie was simply not enough, Mrs. Swayze came in. She gave me a big hug and then stood back and looked at me questioningly.

"Just stopping by to see Trey and Ann—"

"And he done brought Preacher Jake a package," Miss Mabel interrupted, pointing to the box on the table.

Both women nodded appreciatively, and Mrs. Swayze hugged me again.

"It's so good to see you, Buddy," she said.

"It's good to see you, too. Is everything okay with you?"

Miss Mabel started to say something, but Mrs. Swayze warned her away from it with a look. "Oh, it's about the same. Trey and Ann are doing well, talking about giving me a grandchild." Her face was almost shining with that thought, but the next one put the light out:

"The Reverend is the same, getting involved in the politics of the Baptist Convention now, just as happy as he can be, ranting and railing at this person and that resolution. I try to stay out of it."

Miss Mabel broke in, ignoring Mrs. Swayze's look. "She been offered a job, directing the kindergarten at the Presbyterian Church, but Brother Swayze say he forbids it. Says her place is in the home. She ought to slap that man, I been tellin' her so for years."

This was obviously a topic worthy of spirited discussion, none of it any of my business. Trying to be innocuous, I offered, "I'm sure you would do a good job if you took it, Mrs. Swayze."

"She sure would," Miss Mabel said with a grin.

Mrs. Swayze gave a small smile and conceded, "Well, we'll see."

Then she told me all about Trey's work and the football team, the trials and tribulations of being employed by a private school. Ann, she said, was working at a bank and doing well. We chatted about Riggsville, the public schools, and life in a small Delta town. She asked me about seminary, and I told her all about my classes and professors, Clinical Pastoral Education, and my summer in New England. Then it was time for me to go.

They both walked me to the door, and I hugged them good-bye. Mrs. Swayze had given me detailed directions to Trey's house, and it didn't take long to get across town. I got there before he did, and when I got out of my car, an English bulldog started barking and slobbering at me through the chain-link fence. I went over to see if he'd let me pet him. Right away, he rolled over on his back for me to scratch his belly. I was still rubbing him when Trey drove up.

"Hey, Buddy! It's great to see you. Welcome to Riggsville. I see you met Roscoe."

"Yeah, that's some ugly dog," I said, standing up and wiping my hands on my pants.

"I'll have you know that dog is a cousin of Bully, the Mississippi State mascot. I always wanted a dog, but Father would never let us have one. So Roscoe is a reminder that I can do whatever the hell I want now. He's got a better pedigree than either one of us, and I've got the papers to prove it."

"Oh. Well, then, that's a different story. He's getting prettier already."

He showed me around his modest home, and then we chatted a while and lit the charcoal to grill chicken when Ann got home. She came in a little later, and we grilled and ate and talked late into the night. It was great to see them both, wonderful to see for myself that they were happy and well.

The next morning, I left Riggsville and headed toward Becket. I went right past the prison, and slowed down, but didn't stop.

My second year in seminary, my middler year, was much more challenging academically. We had a series of papers to write on a variety of subjects, all meeting page requirements and deadlines, with proper observation of footnoting and bibliography standards. We had five major papers called locus papers, which were to be typed, with three copies to be handed in, which meant putting carbon paper in my typewriter, a major pain in the neck. The papers were titled "The Doctrine of God," "The Doctrine of Man," "The Doctrine of Revelation," "The Doctrine of Sin and Redemption," and "The Doctrine of Sacraments." These papers were graded by different professors, according to the subject matter.

In addition to the locus papers, we were to work with an assigned professor on a larger paper in which we were to research a particular area of interest to us and show that we could produce a work of scholarly integrity. This middler project, roughly the equivalent of a Master's thesis, was graded by two professors, the one who was assigned and another chosen by the seminarian. It was to be a minimum of one hundred pages long, typed, double-spaced, with footnotes and bibliography.

One night during the first week we were back, I saw Tiffy outside the dining hall. She fluttered up and gave me a big hug, as if she'd never broken my heart. Then she introduced me to her fiancé, Rushton, a tall, handsome kid with scruffy blonde hair. I told him I was glad to meet him, which was a lie, and that I hoped they were happy, which was true.

Tiffy kissed me on the cheek and beamed. "See, Rush? I told you he's wonderful!"

I didn't feel wonderful, though, not at all. I'm sure it is better to have loved, but to lose my girlfriend to a rich kid with a verb for a name seemed like more than I could stand at the time.

I was scheduled to preach at Morning Prayer about a month after school started. I don't remember the Scripture passages, but I told the story of playing poker with the campers at special session. The point was treating people with dignity, and seeing past appearances and labels. I thought it went over reasonably well; most of the listeners laughed when I thought they ought to laugh, some of them were moved when I thought they ought to be, and I think they understood what I was trying to say.

That same day, just before lunch, I walked past Dr. Sprague's office. He saw me walking by and called to me in the hall.

"Mr. Hinton."

I poked my head into his office. "Yes sir?"

"I just wanted to tell you I enjoyed your performance," he said.

I couldn't tell if he was kidding or not, and didn't know what to say. But it was clear that he wasn't going to say anything else, and it also seemed as if that was not the end of the conversation.

"Sir?" I asked.

He motioned me into his office and indicated where I should sit. I'd never been in his office before.

"Yes sir?"

He took off his thick Buddy Holley glasses and spoke deliberately, as if he were talking to a child or someone very old. "I simply wanted to tell you that I enjoyed your act."

"Sir?"

"Your sermon this morning. I enjoyed your act."

I didn't know whether to thank him or take offense. He watched me, enjoying my confusion with no intention of helping me out of it.

I replied cautiously, not knowing what to say. "I hope it made sense."

He closed his eyes and leaned back in his chair. It occurred to me that I could probably get up and leave his office before he knew I was gone. But then he said, "I couldn't tell if you were trying for Will Rogers or Huckleberry Finn. Or is it Huckleberry Finn only for stories on the Mississippi River? Can you do Jerry Lewis, too?"

Since I was still there, I felt like I needed to say something. "Dr. Sprague, I'm afraid I'm not following you. I just talk the way I talk."

"The persona you'd like to project is simple, uncomplicated, innocent. But of course it's all a fabrication."

"No sir. I'm not sure what you're talking about, but there's no fabrication."

He opened his eyes, put his glasses back on, and looked at me for a long moment. "Mr. Hinton, no one is as untainted and virtuous as you pretend to be. For your own good, I will find and expose the chink in your spotless armor before you leave this school."

He'd laid all his cards on the table, and I still didn't understand the game we were playing. The thought came to me that this could be some sort of push-him-'til-he-breaks mind game, but it seemed more personal than that. I didn't think I ought to argue that I was tainted or that I lacked virtue, but I didn't want to let him think that I was being false, either.

"Sir, I'm sorry you thought what I said was a show of some sort. I told a story to make a point; it's just the way I talk. I'm sorry if you didn't like it, but please don't think I was faking anything."

He turned to face the window and seemed interested in something outside. "We will see," he said. And then, after a pause, he dismissed me, saying, "You may go, Mr. Hinton."

I should have stayed. I should have had it out with him then and there. I should have taken the matter to the dean. But I didn't do any of those things. I was just glad to leave, so that's what I did. I left his office and sat in my room on the third floor until I stopped shaking.

I told Scott about it, and he told me that Dr. Sprague was a jerk. I thanked him for his highly trained psychological evaluation, and it felt like a restoration of sorts to laugh. Scott told me Dr. Sprague considered himself a fine preacher, and had been threatened and jealous the year before when the dean had asked for a copy of my sermon about Captain Jimmy and the beer. He reminded me of Dr. Sprague's reaction to my comment in Phenomenology, and wondered if it was because Sprague was so fragile and somehow he thought I was strong. Or maybe it was a question of age. Or maybe he was drunk. In any case, we agreed that we didn't understand Dr. Sprague.

September 30, 1979
Sunday

Dear Buddy,

That Dr. Sprague is a puzzle to me.
Of course he ain't the kind of man I ever had much dealings with but still a growed man ought not act that way.
They must be more to this than you has told me or more to it than you know.
If he is drinking that could explain a lot.
A man will do and say all sorts of foolish things when he is a drunk.
Ain't much I can say I really know but I know about drinking too much, and how it can make a fool out of a man.
We got a guard here at Parchman that sounds like the way you talk about Dr. Sprague.
His name is Boss Wade.
He is a short little fellow who likes to keep his billy club in his hand, talk loud and tell all the mens what to do.
Boss Wade comes into the kitchen and tells us to sweep it up, or mop the floor, or whatnot.
He don't care about the kitchen, he just likes to use his authority.
He is just a little man with a stick.
They is peoples just that way.
You remember I told you long time ago that peoples is either an alligator or something an alligator eats?
Well, this Boss Sprague sounds like he ain't nothing but an alligator and you best just stay away from his teeth as best you can.
Of course it is his swamp you is swimming in so that might not be easy.
One more thing too.

Some peoples is so twisted up on they selfs that they think every body else must be that same way.

Some of the meanest mens at the Parchman Prison Farm really thinks every body else is just as mean as they is.

Some times you see it the other way around—not in here but out there—so a person who is nice and sweet think everybody else is nice and sweet just like them.

But either way it is a mistake.

We ain't all the same neither good folks nor bad.

Only a fool figures everybody else is just like him.

The cigarettes you give me is all gone now. I am still smoking that good Prince Albert pipe tobacco.

I give them cigarettes to some of the mens who do not have nobody looking out after them.

I know you said in your note that I could use them like money but I got enough.

So I just give them cigarettes away.

I hope you do not mind.

I tell you the truth I am glad they is gone so I can tell mens I do not have no more of them.

Some of them mens pestered me to no end to get a cigarette.

When I just had three or four left, they was two mens almost got into a fight over them, even though I already told both of them they could have one.

Cigarettes is an addiction I believe, just like alcohol or drugs.

It may be smoking a pipe is, too.

I expect there are worse things than addiction to tobacco.

But addiction is a terrible thing.

Some peoples is addicted to power and control.

That is what I believe is the problem with Boss Wade. It may be with Dr. Sprague too.

It may be that is the problem with Eddie now that I think on it.

But I think they is probably more to that than I can see, too.

Eddie is getting more and more powerful.

He got fifteen or twenty mens he is herding around now.

Ain't none of them as big as Eugene of course. But some of them is pretty big.

Some of the mens call him Boss Eddie but not to his face.

Even the guards is scared of Eddie.

But I know something about Eddie.
He is just a sad scared little boy whose mama never loved him.
I knowed his mama and she was just as sorry and mean as he is.
He has chose his own road.
But Eugene has not ever had the chance to choose.
Other peoples been making his choices for him all his life.
Now Eddie is making Eugene's choices. I'm afraid Eugene is going to get hisself hurt.
Well, that is enough.
You got better things to do than read long letters from me.
Take care of your self.
And stay away from alligators.

Your friend,
Jacob Jefferson

I couldn't tell if Jake got a little confused, or maybe he was making a joke. But the label "Boss Sprague" so perfectly described my professor that it stuck with me. I showed Scott the letter, and he wanted to know all about Jake. At first I was reluctant; it seemed strange to talk about him. But I'd told Trey, and that had turned out well. The more I talked about Jake, the more cheerful I felt—and stronger somehow, more rooted.

Life went on, and studies continued. For the most part I did well, or better than I thought I might. I was surprised to enjoy Church History, especially after I realized it was like a long story with hundreds of characters. Also, some of my classmates had decided that maybe I wasn't just a kid out of place after all, and that helped to bolster my struggling self-esteem.

I did my best to stay clear of Boss Sprague.

The Monday before the Christmas break, the dean gave us our assignments for the middler project. The topic was ours to choose, but each middler was assigned to a member of the faculty who would serve as an advisor, as well as one of the two graders. The various members of the faculty had set aside times for the seminarians to come and meet with them about their projects, beginning that Thursday at four. The dean posted the list of assignments and first appointments on the bulletin board outside his office. After the crowd cleared, I looked for my name.

My blood chilled. "Hinton—Dr. Sprague. Thurs. 4:00 p.m."

I asked one of the hot dogs standing nearby how the faculty assignments were made, and he said, "I think the faculty just chooses the students they want to work with. Why? Who'd you get?"

"Sprague."

He groaned, "Oh, that's rich! I bet he'll love that."

"Why? What's the deal with Sprague?"

"Oh, you know. Every few years some seminarian comes along that just really gets under his skin. It's like he needs someone to be angry with sometimes. A few years ago it was a guy from my diocese in Atlanta, and he wound up withdrawing from school. He's a Methodist minister now. And now you're it, Buddy. Surely you knew that!"

I told him I'd never heard of such a thing; he couldn't believe I didn't know it already.

Later on the third floor, I told Scott about it, but he'd never heard of Sprague's "whipping boy." One of the seniors happened by, and I asked him.

"Oh, yeah," he said. "I've heard that. I think he was pretty rough on some guy from Atlanta four or five years back. The dean supposedly told him to knock it off. Why are you asking?"

Scott told him that we thought I might be his new target. The senior went on to tell me that the buzz in his class was that Dr. Sprague was drinking again. He had been recovering for a few years but had fallen off the wagon.

"Now," he said, leaning toward us conspiratorially, "his wife has left him. Again. So I guess you could say he's got some anger issues."

All that day and the next, I dreaded my appointment with Boss Sprague. But time slipped by, as it does sometimes when you'd like it to stand still, and "Thurs. 4:00 p.m." was upon me all too soon.

It wasn't until I was standing in the hall facing his door that I realized I had no idea what my middler project would be about. I figured it would be a difficult and painful experience no matter what, so I picked the name of a theologian I felt sure we'd study next semester in Church History. Armed with that name, I knocked on the door.

"Come in."

"I'm here for my middler project appointment, Dr. Sprague."

"Ah, Hinton. Your given name isn't Buddy, is it?"

That took me altogether off guard. "No sir."

He peered at me through his thick glasses and waited.

"That's just what I've always been called," I said.

"I see," he responded. He had my file from the dean's office before him and had it lifted slightly off his desk so I could see what he was holding. "What is your real name?"

I knew he knew my real name; he must have had it in my file, right in front of him. And he knew I knew he knew; it was part of the game. "Judah Bennie Hinton," I told him. "I was named after—"

"Mr. Hinton," he interrupted, "I'm sure it's a delightful story, but I don't want to hear it. Faulkner or Twain could have done wonders with it, I'm sure." He picked up his teacup, dunked the tea bag a few times, and threw the bag away. "You have an idea for your project, I trust?"

"Yes sir. I'd like to do my middler project on St. Thomas Aquinas."

He had taken a sip of tea, something imported and British, I'm sure, and almost had to spit it out in exasperation. When he recovered, he puffed, "Thomas Aquinas! Good God, why don't you just do your paper on Jesus, or Creation?"

"What do you mean?"

"Do you even know who Thomas Aquinas was? He was the greatest theologian of the Church; he wrote thousands and thousands of pages of theology, much of which still form the basis for most modern thought." He took another sip of tea before continuing, "Not Aquinas. What else did you have in mind?"

I was in full rout. All I had in mind was wondering what it would be like to be a Methodist minister, having no other ideas for a middler project. "I don't know," I admitted weakly.

He chuckled, as if my confession confirmed something that he already knew. "Well," he patronized, "what part of Christianity are you most interested in?"

Grasping at another straw, since St. Thomas Aquinas had failed me, I said, "I'd like to read about why there is evil, if God is good."

That took Dr. Sprague by surprise. He looked at me as if he might have missed something. "Ah, theodicy: the Problem of Evil. Very good, very good. I'll tell you what, Judah Bennie. Let's approach this from both ends, shall we? Perhaps you would be interested in looking at the writings of Thomas Aquinas concerning the Problem of Evil. What do you say to that?"

I told him that would be fine with me, and he advised me to look in the seminary library for a little set of books called *Summa Theologica*, which would get me started. He asked if I had any questions, which I did not, and he dismissed me.

That night I went to the library and looked up Thomas Aquinas. He had apparently written a great deal, but it was not difficult to find the *Summa Theologica.* The "little set of books" Boss Sprague referred to was a collection of twenty-two thick books with small print and no pictures. Overwhelmed, I picked up a smaller book about Aquinas's life and sat down to look through it. Much to my surprise, the more I read, the more I was relieved to find that I have a definite affinity for St. Thomas Aquinas.

The accounts of the lives of the saints are a mixture of fact and fiction, but still interesting reading. St. Thomas Aquinas has had almost as much written about him as he himself wrote about his God, which was prodigious.

Thomas was so humble and meek that his instructors thought him dull-witted and called him an ox. But when Albertus Magnus, the most renowned professor of the order, heard him defending a particularly difficult thesis, he declared, "We call this young man a dumb ox, but his bellowing in doctrine will one day resound throughout the world."

As an adult, Thomas applied Aristotle's logic to the *Sentences* of Peter Lombard, which he'd studied during the year that his family held him prisoner (in their attempt to prevent him from becoming a

Dominican priest). This formed the basis for his first series of books, the *Summa Contra Gentiles*, a remarkable work with which he was not satisfied, and which led to his writing the *Summa Theologica*, an ordered summary of the faith. He was called on by bishops and consulted with popes, and was extremely well respected.

On the Feast of St. Nicholas, December 6, 1273, Thomas Aquinas said his mass, and afterward he had an ecstatic vision for three days. This revelation was of such power that he stopped writing altogether, even with his *Summa Theologica* not yet finished. His secretary, Reginald of Priverno, urged him to continue, but Thomas said, "I can do no more; such things have been revealed to me that all that I have written seems to me as so much straw." He died a few months later.

I wrote that down, about the straw. I liked the idea of the greatest scholar and theologian of all time coming to the end of his life and saying that everything he'd written was worth no more than grass now that he had seen the glory of God. I thought Jake would like that, too.

It seemed particularly appropriate that I settled on this project on the Feast of St. Nicholas: December 6, 1979.

Over Christmas break, I checked out some of the more pertinent volumes of the *Summa Theologica* and took them home. Mom and Dad were mightily impressed that their boy was reading that sort of thing; I tried to act nonchalant, like I was accustomed to spending hour after hour with big fat books revealing the mysteries of God. I made pages and pages of notes, exploring and explaining the saint's views on the problem of evil, defending the righteousness of God in view of the existence of evil.

He had basically five different ideas to explain the existence of evil: that evil is God's punishment; that evil is necessary if the universe is to exist in all degrees of goodness; that evil is nothing more than the privation of good, as a shadow is the privation of light; that evil exists to create a greater good, as the death of an apple plants the seeds of apple trees; and, finally—and this was my favorite—that this kind of stuff just sort of happens, for reasons we don't understand. Like the bumper sticker sort of says, evil happens.

I read and wrote, wrote and read. I stretched, expanded, enlarged, extended, and stretched some more, trying to meet the target of one hundred pages. I figured that a page of my handwriting was about the same as a typewritten, double-spaced page. Each day my pile of pages got a little higher, until I figured I had about seventy-eight pages. I needed more stretching, expanding, et cetera ad nauseum. It was an exercise in academic filibustering, and I hated every page, paragraph, line, word, and syllable of it.

Somewhere in there, I remembered the camper Paul asking his poker-playing friend Phil why God had made him a retard. That was the question I wanted to ask. I wrote down that story as an introduction to my paper, and started over, trying to fit the answers of St. Thomas Aquinas into it. This approach felt much better, suited my soul, fit my karmic requirements if not the requirements of the seminary. I typed it on my mother's old Blackwood manual typewriter: twenty-nine pages.

20

Odd Sacraments

After Christmas, when I got back to school, this letter was in my box.

December 16, 1979
Sunday

Dear Buddy,

I do not know if you will get this letter before you go to Beaumont for Christmas.
But I will go ahead and send it.
I already got the Christmas package you sent me and opened the tobacco and sports magazine.
Thank you very much.
I will not open the stocking until Christmas morning just like last year and the year before so Santa will have something to come up in here and fill.
It looks pretty full already but I am sure he will bring something to add to it.
It sounds like you sure in the alligator's mouth now.
I wonder did Dr. Sprague try to get hisself put with you or was it just bad luck for you?
It does sound like he has picked you out.
I do not understand that.
But I might have an idea.

You know how I have a lot of time to think up in here.
You wrote me about a paper you wrote up there about how peoples is.
You put in that paper about a Buddhist idea called yin and yang, that peoples is both good and bad.
I am not real sure why you would want to use a Buddhist idea in a Christian school. I reckon you will know more about that than I do.
As I understand it the shadow in us contains some light and the light in us contains some shadow.
I been thinking about that for a few months now. I wonder if it is so.
I am sure that you is right about every one being good and bad.
I am sure they is bad in the best of us and good in the worst of us.
But is they good in the evil or evil in the good?
In the last chapter of Genesis when Joseph was talking to his brothers after they cast him down into a pit in the wilderness he said But as for you, ye thought evil against me; but God meant it unto good, to bring to pass, as it is this day, to save much people alive.
Joseph's brothers was being mean because they was jealous, but God used it to do something good.
It may be that some good might come out of your working with Dr. Sprague on this paper.
It may be that some good will come out of Boss Wade's pushing mens around or Eddie twisting Eugene up in knots.
We will have to trust God with it though because I sure do not see it.
I believe Dr. Sprague has problems you cannot do nothing about.
That is a mess you did not make and cannot clean up.
And while I am thinking on such things and what you call the problem of evil, I will ask you this.
What do you reckon Jesus meant when He told His disciples to pray to God to lead us not into temptation, but deliver us from evil?
Is Jesus telling His friends that God might lead us into temptation?
Is He telling them that God might control evil?
I know they might not be an answer but it is just some things to think about.

Cornelius has been telling me that I need to see a doctor up in here who helps the mens with they eyes.
I did not want to do it but he set me up a time this week for me to go and see the eye doctor.
Cornelius says it may be I need to wear glasses.
It may be that they will help.
I tell you the truth—if that doctor can make me some glasses that will make your letters look more clear, it will be a good present for Christmas for Santa to bring me.

Your friend,
Jacob Jefferson

It wasn't my usual pattern to turn in work before the deadline, but when I got back to school, I turned in the paper I'd written in Beaumont. It wasn't due for a couple of weeks, but I went ahead and turned it in so I wouldn't chicken out and type up the seventy-one pages of erudite baloney. Retyped with a little embroidery on the story, a couple of paragraphs on the petitions in the Lord's Prayer on evil and temptation, with a more generous placement of margins and footnotes and bibliography, my paper was forty-three pages. But it was honest and real, and it did a fair job of covering St. Thomas Aquinas's arguments on the subject of evil. I was hoping that might count for something.

One of the single students, a tall skinny guy named William, had gone to the General Convention of the Episcopal Church that summer and met a couple of priests from New Orleans, Morris and Carlos. They'd invited him to come down for Mardi Gras, and offered a place for him and his friends to stay. So William told a married couple, Jenny and James, whom we all called Smitty, and talked them into going with him. They decided they had some extra room in William's car, so they asked me and Pat, a first-year student, to come along. Most of my class was putting the final touches on their middler projects, and it seemed like the right time for me to get out of town.

I'd been to Mardi Gras twice when I was in college and knew what to expect. None of the others had ever been and had no idea. I told them all to get a costume together before we went down, as I knew from years before that on the day of Mardi Gras, or Fat Tuesday, the day before Ash Wednesday, you needed to have a costume to fully enjoy the experience.

We all crammed into William's gold Dodge Duster on a Saturday morning and drove down together, listening to two Pink Floyd tapes all the way through Tennessee, Alabama, Mississippi, Louisiana, and into New Orleans. We alternated all that Saturday between *The Dark Side of the Moon* and *The Wall*, but William turned up the volume every time it played "Another Brick in the Wall, Part 2." We sang as loud as we could, so the faculty could hear it back in Becket:

> We don't need no education
> We don't need no thought control
> No dark sarcasm in the classroom
> Teachers—leave them kids alone
> Hey! Teachers! Leave them kids alone!
> All in all it's just another brick in the wall.
> All in all you're just another brick in the wall.

We got to New Orleans and found the way to our host's house by late afternoon. Wearing old blue jeans and a black clergy shirt, not tucked in, he met us as we drove up and introduced himself as Morris. I liked him immediately. The rectory was a block from one of the parade routes, and he was delighted that we'd come. The three single guys would stay at his house, and Smitty and Jenny would stay with Carlos, his Cuban assistant. Carlos, whose wife was out of town, was coming over that night to watch the parade; he and Morris were boiling up a pot of shrimp and crawfish to celebrate our arrival.

William had stopped on the way in to buy a case of Dixie beer because I had told him it was the official beer of New Orleans and Mardi Gras. Carlos came a few minutes after we arrived, a small, dark man with kind eyes, bearing an ice chest full of crustaceans and more beer. And so our party started.

We ate and talked and drank and talked, and then we ate and drank and talked some more. After supper we went down to Canal Street for the parade. We all caught bead necklaces, and Pat and Jenny caught doubloons, quickly jumping into the spirit of things. Looking at the people on the floats, and most of the people in the crowd, I thought it was obvious that their party had started several days before ours.

After the parade, we went back to Morris's house and ate and drank and talked some more. We talked about seminary life, the ordination of women—a passionate issue back then—and the new Prayer Book of 1979, which had just been released. The variety of opinions expressed were more interesting then and there than they are here and now, so I'll just leave them in the past where they belong.

I asked the two priests, both of whom had gone to seminary at Becket, if they knew Dr. Sprague, and Morris scoffed, "That son of a bitch is still up there? Is he drinking?"

We assured him that Dr. Sprague was very much in evidence, and Jenny broke into the conversation. "He's taken a special interest in our friend Buddy," she told them.

I was surprised that she knew about my situation, but I didn't have much time to think about it, because Morris said, "Well, Buddy, you're gonna have to confront him, stare him down. That's the only way he's gonna get off your back." Carlos nodded.

Pat answered for me. "But Buddy's not going to. He's gentle, meek and mild."

And before I could even register a protest, William suggested, "That's why Sprague has him in his sights. He's a bully. He's not going to pick on somebody who fights back. Buddy's going to have to become a little more confrontational."

Confrontational was the buzzword *du jour* at the seminary; it was considered a great virtue to confront someone when you felt wronged. For the most part, it seemed to me like whining and needless bickering. I had so far chosen not to be confrontational if I could help it.

We sat there, with everybody waiting for me to say something, and with me thinking of a way to change the subject, until Jenny did it for me.

"I'd just kick him in the mustn't-touch-it if I were you."

Smitty and William knew the term and howled in laughter, and the rest of us had to be let in on the joke: "mustn't-touch-it" was her

West Texas family's expression for genitalia, either male or female. We all laughed, got another beer, and moved on to other topics, much to my relief.

But the image of kicking Boss Sprague in the mustn't-touch-it had a certain appeal, even to someone described with regrettable accuracy as gentle, meek and mild.

The next morning, we got up and went to church at Grace Episcopal on Canal Street, where Morris was the rector and Carlos the associate rector. About one hundred and fifty people showed up for the Sunday morning service, maybe a third of them Hispanic. The gospel was read in English and again in Spanish. Some of the music was hymns I had grown up singing, but guitars accompanied other songs with a Latin beat. The mixture was interesting, in the same way that it would be interesting to put a burrito on the same plate with egg rolls, but it wasn't something I wanted to do with any regularity. Morris preached, and introduced the five of us from Becket as "seminarians making a pilgrimage to the largest religious festival in the United States." He then explained that the season of Mardi Gras is a time for boisterous living before the rigors and discipline of Lent, which would start that Wednesday. His parishioners must have heard something similar every year, but the five pilgrims from Becket were distinctly impressed.

That afternoon we took the streetcar down Canal Street and walked into the French Quarter. This is the oldest part of the city, an odd mix of Spanish and French cultures. We strolled around Jackson Square, had café au lait and beignets at the Café du Monde, and explored Bourbon Street. We saw people everywhere, in different degrees of contentment and excitation: some passed out, some running or yelling and laughing, some just watching. And we saw church people working the crowd. Some handed out religious pamphlets illustrating the threat of hell and the need to repent. One team preached at us through a bullhorn, blaring out the love of Christ and warning us of the danger of damnation. Another time we saw a heavy, life-sized cross being dragged through the streets. I was impressed with it until I saw that they had little wheels on the bottom to make it easier to pull. They had posted a sign near where Pilate probably put his:

"Jesus died for YOUR SINS!" The word "YOUR" was printed as if it dripped with blood.

I remember thinking that these evangelists were a textbook example of what Jake had written about good people trying to do something right, but actually causing harm.

That night, and the next, we threw ourselves totally into the celebration, reminding each other that this was "the largest religious festival in the United States," and vowing that we would make a report of it at the next seminary luncheon. We had Hurricanes at Pat O'Brien's, ate oysters at Toujac's, and threw coins to the street performers. We waited for more than an hour at Preservation Hall to hear the jazz, but lost interest when it seemed like the line wasn't moving. I took a pamphlet every time a missionary approached us. I figured they were there for the religious festival, too, and that if they were going to have any pleasure in it at all, it would be from getting somebody to take their brochures. My friends just shook their heads at me.

And we went to most of the parades. We might have missed one or two somewhere, but you couldn't tell by looking at our piles of stash: beads, doubloons, and cups.

The morning of Fat Tuesday came and went before the Becket pilgrims woke up. For lunch, we had red beans and rice with big pieces of spicy andouille sausage, courtesy of our host. In the afternoon, feeling more recovered from the previous night, we began to plan our costumes. Smitty and Jenny were prepared, having brought with them the materials necessary to transform into a mule trader and his Indian squaw wife. Smitty had a long, straggly beard already, and he wore a big, ugly, felt cowboy hat, a well-worn leather vest, cowboy boots, and a necklace made of the horse teeth he'd gotten from a veterinarian he'd worked for in Texas. Jenny wore a leather top and skirt, with her dark, straight hair tied back under a leather headband. She even had a white feather sticking up in the back.

I had a red-and-white-striped, long-sleeved T-shirt from skits at summer camp, which I fancied made me look something like Marcel Marceau. I put on a pair of overalls I'd had for years, and tied knots at the corners of a blue bandanna and made it into what we'd called a "doo-rag" at camp, which fit on my head. To complete the look, I painted on a sad clown's face with a big blue tear coming out of one of my eyes. William and Pat had been extra devoted in their pilgrims' zeal the night before, and woke up with severe hangovers. Since they hadn't brought anything for a costume, anyway, they told us they'd see us later, if they could. We agreed to meet at the public bathrooms on Jackson Square that night at nine o'clock.

Smitty and Jenny and I hit the streets at about four that afternoon. Mardi Gras is not the best time to see New Orleans, but it's a great time to see the Greatest Show On Earth: people. The costumes, the faces, the drunks, the musicians, the jugglers, the beggars—all parts of a nonstop free carnival that was at the same time joyous and grotesque, beautiful and depraved.

Just before sundown, I parted ways with Smitty and Jenny, thinking they might like to have a little time alone. They were going to the parade route, to get even more beads and trinkets, but a melancholy mood had snatched me, and I felt the need for some privacy. I went to Jackson Square, the heart of the French Quarter, and was amazed to find it almost deserted. Most people were downtown to watch the parades. I sat under a streetlight, my back resting on the iron pole holding it up, and started to whistle. Whistling always connects me to Jake, and, feeling that bond, I was glad not to be completely alone after all.

I suppose my whistling matched the moment; I know I was trying to whistle "Just a Closer Walk with Thee," a staple of New Orleans jazz bands, but I think it must have come out sounding like the blues. I was surprised when an older couple threw me a quarter, thinking that I was a down-on-my-luck street performer. Some college girls walked by and, seeing my sad clown face, tried to make me smile. A few people gave me some bead necklaces they'd caught at one of the parades. One lady danced for a while, then walked on. I was having a great time, whistling and watching the people, especially once I realized that I was part of the show for them, as they were for me.

A young, clean-looking couple walked up to me and stopped. The young man said, "You know, I've been painting tears of sadness on my face lately." I recognized his words as a lure, but my lips were too tired to keep whistling, and I decided to bite.

"How come?" I asked.

In an answer designed to set the hook, he said, "Because of people like you who don't know the Lord Jesus Christ."

I took a deep breath to relax all the muscles that had tensed, and replied, "You're making a pretty big assumption there, aren't you, sport? You don't know me at all, who I am, what I do."

He looked down at me and continued, "Oh, I know who you are; I've been where you are before, friend."

My recently relaxed muscles went tense again; this time they were harder to ease. "Sit down if you've got something to say," I offered.

They sat on the sidewalk beside me, and we talked for over an hour. It was a fascinating conversation, especially after they adjusted to the fact that they were talking to someone who was not only not drunk or stoned but who also knew a little about the Bible. After they eased off trying to save me, I steered the conversation to my concerns about their methods. I told them I admired their commitment and didn't doubt their sincerity, but I thought the way they were going about it seemed to do more harm than good. I told them I questioned whether what they were doing was ministry, or just self-righteous self-congratulation. I told them I was concerned that they seemed to think the important part of what they were doing was what they were doing, rather than the effect it had on others; that I thought the goal of evangelism should be for the benefit of the people hearing the message, not so that the evangelist could be relieved of the obligation to evangelize.

The young man and I carried most of the talking. The girl fell into a pattern of latching on to something that was said and looking through her Bible until she found a verse that she thought applied to it. More times than not, her looking took a while, and by the time she read whatever she'd been looking for, we had moved on and the verse was no longer in context. She never once looked for a verse to support anything I was trying to say.

During one of her longer readings, I noticed a cute college girl looking at me. She saw that I had been caught by evangelists and, mimicking my clown face, pulled the corners of her mouth up with her fingers to make a smile. I gave her a sad sigh and shrugged my shoulders. She came over to give me a necklace; I took one from my neck and gave it to her. She kissed me on the cheek, despite the clown white, and then I couldn't help smiling. I wished her a happy Mardi Gras, and she walked away. The girl reading the Bible droned on, oblivious to everything but Scripture.

In a moment of revelation, I interrupted her. "Wait a minute! Wait a minute! Wasn't that ministry right there? Wasn't what just happened an expression of the love of God?"

Not understanding, the young man said, "There was no ministry there. Neither of you even mentioned Jesus."

"It might have been ministry," the young lady argued, "if that girl had seen that I'm holding the Holy Bible."

I ignored my muscles. "No, no! You missed it. That was an act of ministry right there—what she did, what I did. If all love comes from God, like it says somewhere in there, and that girl and I just exchanged some regular old human kindness to each other, isn't that spreading the love of God? Isn't that what you're supposed to be trying to do?"

I looked at the man and saw that he was considering what I'd said. The lady was too sure she was right to hear anything from me.

"There are different kinds of love," she began, but I interrupted, still watching the young man.

"Yeah, agape, eros, and all that. That girl tried to make me smile, just because she saw me sad. She gave me some beads for no reason but to make a complete stranger happy. I made her smile, too, and tried to help her feel a little better about herself. We ministered to each other and shared the love of God. Beads and smiles are cheap, but the meaning behind them can be pretty valuable. Tonight they are something more: odd sacraments of the love of God, outward and visible signs of inward and spiritual grace."

The young woman seemed confused but unconcerned. The young man, though, was thinking hard, which was encouraging, so I pressed on.

"You say you want others to feel the love of Jesus that you feel. And I say I want to help others be more aware of the love of God through Jesus that's all around us. Pretty much the same, right? What's the difference? Our methods."

The young man nodded; the girl was trying to find more ammunition in her Bible. I tapped her on the knee, and she looked up. I took off a bead necklace and offered it to her.

"I don't think you can actually spread love by planting guilt or fear," I concluded. "Maybe you ought to spread love by loving."

There was a long silence, and I looked at my watch to find that it was ten after nine. I told them I had to go meet some friends and invited them to come along. I was hoping that William and Pat would have recovered; I guess I wanted the evangelists to see that I had respectable-looking friends. But my more reputable friends had partied too hard the night before, so I introduced the evangelists to Smitty and Jenny, a mule trader and his Indian Squaw who were sitting next to the public bathrooms on Jackson Square.

Smitty thought we ought to wait a little longer for William and Pat, and I wanted to finish my conversation with the evangelists. The young woman left then, saying that she would pray for me. The way she said it, it sounded like a threat.

The young man asked me what I did for a living, and I told him I was a student. He asked me what I was studying, and I said I was in an Episcopal seminary.

"Oh," he mumbled, as if my words explained something. He told me he was a seminarian, too, at a Bible College in Ohio.

Once again, I told him he might need to take another look at his witnessing methods in light of their effects.

Jenny and Smitty noted that it was time to go. I held out my hand to the young man and told him my name.

As we shook, he offered, "My name's Mark."

"God bless you, Mark," I said.

"You, too, Buddy."

As we walked away, I began to whistle again, "Just a Closer Walk with Thee," this time with the jazz that it deserved. Smitty joined in, and Jenny twirled around, dancing and clapping her hands. An older man, more than a little drunk, heard us and reached out to us. Smitty shook his hand and wished him a happy Mardi Gras. I turned to see Mark watching us, and we both waved.

Ministry is a strange thing, I think.

The next morning, we went back to Grace Church for the Eucharist and Imposition of Ashes. During the corporate confession, we all confessed mightily, and in truth, I had a few things to confess—more than usual, anyway. Then we went up to the Communion rail for the priest to put ashes on our foreheads in the shape of a cross, as he spoke the Imposition of Ashes: "Remember that you are dust, and to dust you shall return." It's always a moving service, even more so for us that year, in stark contrast to the festivities of the last few days.

We thanked our hosts at their church, and hit the road again. On the way north and east, we didn't listen to any music at all—part of our Lenten observance. It was amazing how much longer the trip back was than the trip down had been.

When we got back to Becket, I found my middler project returned and graded. The professor I had asked to grade the paper gave me an "A" and attached a sheet of paper praising my work and commending my honest, no-nonsense approach. Dr. Sprague gave me a "D" and wrote in red on my cover sheet, "Insufficient, minimal work. I begin to wonder if you are truly called to the priesthood. Cute story, though."

William and Smitty were enraged for me. They wanted me to go to Sprague's office and demand satisfaction. They wanted me to go to the dean's office and register an official complaint. I told them I thought doing that would start a fight I could not finish. The grades didn't matter, I said. I told them I wanted them to leave it alone.

In truth, I didn't care that much about the grade. But to question my call to the ministry or to reduce the great, painful mystery of Paul's retardation to a "cute story" made me furious, and it hurt me deeply. The real truth was that I was too scared to do anything about it. I was afraid I'd get kicked out of seminary, that I'd never become a priest. I was afraid of disappointing my parents and Jake; I was afraid I was messing up something I thought God had set up for me.

February 24, 1980
Sunday

Dear Buddy,

I am glad you had you a good time down there in New Orleans.
You know I worry about you drinking too much.
That is all I mean to say about that.
I do not know what to tell you about Dr. Sprague.
It sound like your friend is right to say he is a bully.
But he is like Boss Wade.
He is a bully in the system that you are in.
It may be he could get you throwed out of seminary.
That is a pretty big stick to put in a bully's hands.
Is Dean a good man, or a friend of yours?
It may be that he could do something to help.
I expect he knows about this, as he is in charge of the place.
If you get the chance you might want to tell Dean and see can he help.
The glasses that that eye doctor sent off for has come in two or three days ago.
I am trying to get used to them.
It is much more clear to read or write. I am glad about that.
But some times I ain't sure where my feet is on the ground.
I take them glasses off to walk up or down steps.
They make my head hurt if I wear them too long.
Cornelius says I will get used to them if I will just keep them on.
In the prison library we got us a great big old book called a Concordance.
It is where you can look up a word in the Book if you can't remember where it is.
I expect you have them up there at seminary.
I looked for Lent, talking about a season before Easter, but I do not believe it is in there.
It may be that it is in that part you call the Apocrypha.
The Concordance does not cover them books.
But Lent ain't in the Bible as best as I can tell.
But it does make some sense, though.

I look out on the fields of the Farm, all dead and gray and brown.
It looks like the whole world is in Lent, waiting for Easter and springtime.
I am starting to feel like I am in Lent, too, ready to die so I can rise up with Jesus.
These damn glasses are making me dizzy now, even when I take them off.
Please forgive my handwriting.
I will try again next Sunday.

Your friend,
Jacob Jefferson

It scared me that Jake was talking about dying, and I wanted to cheer him up if I could. It occurred to me that he might want to look at some of the books I was using at seminary.

I went to the university bookstore and bought Jake a Revised Standard Version of the Bible. His Bible was the one he'd had since he was a child, old and fragile. While I was at it, I got him chewing gum and some expensive apple-flavored pipe tobacco. I couldn't find Prince Albert, and the other choices were at least that expensive and flavored with rum or amaretto or vanilla.

After I put the package down the mail chute that afternoon, it hit me that Jake was going to die. Not this week, maybe, or the next, but someday. And on that day, I would be left behind without Jake, the great friend of my life. I decided St. Thomas Aquinas was right in this case; losing him would be a privation of good.

21

Heights, Depths, Heights

My time to preach my second middler sermon at Morning Prayer came up five or six weeks after that. The Old Testament lesson was from Numbers 11, concerning Eldad and Medad. Chosen by Moses to be elders but not with the others when the Spirit of the Lord came, they prophesied anyway: "And a young man ran and told Moses, 'Eldad and Medad are prophesying in the camp.' And Joshua son of Nun, the assistant of Moses, one of his chosen men, said, 'My lord Moses, stop them!' But Moses said to him, 'Are you jealous for my sake? Would that all the LORD's people were prophets, and that the LORD would put his spirit on them!'"

I was flattered and humbled to realize that most of the seminary attended the service; we had a packed house. The chapel was most crowded if the sermon was expected to be exceptional, either positively or negatively. If it was assumed your sermon would be somewhere in the mediocre middle, a significant number of people skipped. Looking at the crowd, I hoped they were expecting a worthwhile sermon. When I saw the dean, he nodded to me; Dr. Sprague didn't make eye contact, busy scowling at nobody in particular.

When the time came for the sermon, I started by talking about Eldad and Medad, and about the young man who came and tattled on them. I told them I figured the young man was trying to protect Moses and perhaps trying to protect God. I offered that different people have different stories of how they are called to minister, and I marveled at Moses' graciousness in celebrating that God had called Eldad and Medad to prophesy, even though they were somewhat unlikely prophets.

I told them that several months before, a brave few pilgrims went down to New Orleans to represent Becket at "the largest religious festival in the United States," at Mardi Gras. I told them I thought we'd represented the school well, throwing ourselves fully into the celebration "at considerable risk to our sobriety." I said that other churches and seminaries were also represented, and that I hoped it would become an annual tradition for Becket to send a delegation.

I shared the story of the college girl giving me beads while the evangelist read from the Bible, my conversation with Mark, and Jenny dancing and Smitty taking the old drunk's hand. (I left out the part about why William and Pat weren't there.) In closing, I said this:

> That story isn't front-page material; there are no headlines in it. It's probably back in the classified pages somewhere. But I believe it's part of my calling, part of an ongoing series of events that form God's call to me. Mark and his partner helped me see myself as a minister, as a person who ministers through the living of my life, in a way I hadn't seen before. I believe God spoke to me that night, through unlikely sources. I hope He spoke to them through me, unlikely as I must have seemed to them.
>
> God speaks to us all in very different ways, because we hear Him in different ways. You and I are part of each other's stories now, part of each of us being called to serve God and His people.
>
> It may be that someone could question whether I am called to be a priest, because I don't speak or write in big fancy words, or because I'm not confrontational. There's nothing I can do about that. People may question your calling, for whatever reason. But God speaks to all of us, faculty and students, and through us, as unlikely as we all are, to share His love, to call each other into His service, to help us all find our ministries and support each other as brothers and sisters in Christ.
>
> "Would that all the LORD's people were prophets, and that the LORD would put his spirit on them!"

After I sat down, I looked up to see how the congregation was taking it. The dean was smiling; Dr. Sprague was gone. My friend Scott told me later that he saw Sprague leave; he was fuming, his face red as a beet. He knew I was talking to him at the end, defending myself in front of the seminary community, and he couldn't respond.

April 20, 1980
Sunday

Dear Buddy,

I thank you for the package.
You should not be spending your money on me.
But I am glad to have them things.
When you is in prison everything is just the same everyday, every week.
But them things you is sending me, they is new and different.
I tell you the truth I ain't real sure about that new Book.
It is like the Book I have but some of the words has been changed.
Some of it seems to make it more clear but some of it is like when you forget to put salt in the beans like something is just left out.
I am enjoying looking at it though.
I tried that apple tobacco.
It is sure different.
I believe I might keep it for special occasions and whatnot.
Please be careful with Dr. Sprague.
He is like a snake, best left alone.
I sure would not go messing with him unless I had to.
But he ain't got no call to question is you called to be a priest or not.
I would be a lot more likely to wonder about him.
I am glad you feel good about preaching.
That is a lot of the trick to it.
If you think you can do something you is a lot more likely to do it than if you think you can not.
I thank you for your concern about my health.
I am fine, just old.
I believe I must be 75 years old now.

My bones is getting tired.
I ain't in no hurry to die Buddy.
I am just ready for it when it comes.
I have lived a good life. I gone from the high places to the low places and back to the high places again.
I have done my best—at least some of the time—and I am ready to face my Maker.
When that day comes I will see my Joseph again and my father.
And I will meet our Lord face to face.
I will tell Him I am sorry for the wrong I done. I know as sure as I know I am sitting here that He will open up His arms and gather me in.
I believe He will tell me that my wrestling is over and that it is time for me to come on home.
I am pretty well used to these glasses now.
Cornelius says I am dizzy too much and keeps after me to go to the doctor for my pressure.
But I am getting used to that, too.
They are taking good care of me up in here.
They ain't no need for you to worry.

Your friend,
Jacob Jefferson

The rest of that semester went by with stacks and piles of reading and writing, but largely without incident. Dr. Sprague seemed to ease off a little, or at least we managed to stay away from each other.

I spent the summer on a beach in Texas, serving in a ministry that involved giving water, shade, and first aid to the hardest-partying group of people I've ever seen. When I went back to Becket for my senior year, Bill the Mercury Comet was covered with salt from the Gulf of Mexico. We welcomed the junior class, bright-eyed and scared. I had letters from William and Smitty, telling me about their new jobs and churches. My last year in seminary started with the realization that the time to be ordained and go to work was coming fast, and I was looking forward to it. And though I wouldn't have wanted any of the junior class to know, I was scared to death, too, just for a different reason.

Much of the fall semester was spent getting ready for the great bane of seminaries and seminarians: the G.O.E.'s. The General Ordination Examinations were a standardized set of tests and questions to determine that all seminarians in each of the eleven Episcopal seminaries were up to Theological, Pastoral, Ethical, Liturgical, Scriptural, and Church Historical snuff. We spent what seemed like an inordinate amount of time preparing to take these tests, worrying and agonizing and hoping that we'd do well. I usually tested fairly well, and I'd become confident in my ability to express myself; I didn't worry about it as much as I probably should have.

After Christmas break, the dean went to England for a sabbatical, and to my great consternation, Dr. Sprague was appointed acting dean. I waited for something dreadful to happen, but I think he was too busy deaning and preening to pay me much attention. I'm not proud to admit it, but I remember hoping he'd found a new target in the junior class.

The G.O.E.'s came in the middle of January, and I felt good about them. Some of the tests were objective, in the form of multiple-choice exams; the others were subjective, papers to be read by different priests all over the country. Somebody had encouraged me to relax, so I tried to have fun with it and hoped my reader would, too.

One of the questions asked what I would say if a young mother wanted to know how to explain baptism to her child. I wrote that I'd take the kid to watch *The Wizard of Oz.*

> At the end, when Dorothy and her friends come back to the Emerald City and are cowering before the huge fiery face of the Wizard of Oz, Toto the dog pulls away a curtain to reveal a man working some levers and dials. He says (with the voice of Oz!), "Pay no attention to the man behind the curtain!"
>
> This is, of course, the Wizard. The huge fiery face had been just a trick, and the Wizard of Oz was just a man. They're all very disappointed, and Dorothy says, "Oh! You're a very bad man!" to which the Wizard responds, "Oh, no, my dear. I'm a very good man. I'm just a very bad Wizard."
>
> And then, when he sees them face to face, and hears their needs and concerns, he is able to help them realize what they've had all

> along but couldn't recognize. The Wizard, just a man from Kansas, says to the Scarecrow, "Back where I come from we have universities, seats of great learning—where men go to become great thinkers. And when they come out, they think deep thoughts—and with no more brains than you have. But! They have one thing you haven't got! A diploma!"
>
> He gives the Scarecrow a diploma: a ThD, not a doctorate in Theology, but a Doctor of Thinkology. And right away the Scarecrow says, "The sum of the square roots of any two sides of an isosceles triangle is equal to the square root of the remaining side. Oh, joy! Rapture! I've got a brain!" He gives the Tin Woodsman a ticking heart pendant, and the Cowardly Lion a medal for bravery. If you watch the movie again, you realize that it was the Scarecrow who figured out how to get into the castle of the Wicked Witch. It was the Tin Man who was so upset when Dorothy fell asleep among the poppies that he almost rusted himself with tears. And it was the Cowardly Lion who led the way past the guards and over the walls to battle the Witch.
>
> Oz was not a Wizard, he didn't give any of them anything that they didn't already have, he didn't do anything magic—he just made the Scarecrow and the Tin Woodsman and the Cowardly Lion aware of what they already had but didn't recognize.
>
> When a child is baptized, it's not as if the priest makes that kid a child of God. The priest is not a Wizard, just a man or just a woman. In the water and the words we just realize it together, and allow it be more real.

I liked my answer: it was honest, engaging, and creative, and represented what I believe about sacramental theology. Weeks later, when I got my results, I realized that the priest who read it might not have liked it. It hit me right after I got my papers back, with that essay on top, bearing a big, circled, red "F" above the words, "Is this what they're teaching at Becket?"

And my whole world fell apart.

Out of the seven areas tested by the G.O.E.'s, I had passed only Old Testament. I was provisional in Church History and had failed the other five outright. Part of the problem was that my reader apparently hadn't cared for my light-hearted approach—his red marker heavily scarred my papers—but I had also not done well on the multiple-choice part.

In the last semester of my senior year, I had failed the majority of a test designed to protect the Church from seminarians who were poorly prepared or ill equipped to become priests. Dr. Sprague wasn't going to keep me out of the priesthood; it looked like I was going to keep myself out.

I stayed in my room the rest of the day and into the night. After he got back from the supper I skipped, Scott knocked on my door. When I didn't answer, he turned the doorknob, which I didn't usually lock, and came in.

"Buddy? Are you okay?"

I heard him as if he were at a great distance; it seemed like he was too far away to hear a response from me. Or maybe I just didn't have any desire to respond.

"Buddy?" He came over and shook my shoulder. I didn't want him to, but I couldn't stop him. "Buddy?"

I was sitting on my bed; he sat beside me. Later he told me he didn't know what to do or say, so he decided to talk to me as if nothing were wrong.

He had thought I'd be at supper, he said, and told me what he'd eaten. He told me about a seminarian getting into an altercation with one of the college students, something about one of them saving places in line. He thought the seminarian was just flexing his confrontation muscles. He told me that The Twins, two beautiful college students whom we'd often admired but never spoken to, had been at the next table, wearing tight jeans; he said they'd asked where I was. Even in the state I was in, that caught my attention, but I didn't believe it.

He talked about some papers he needed to write, and about his sermon for Morning Prayer coming up the following week. It all seemed like background music to me; I heard him talking but couldn't bring myself to pay much attention. Then he started talking about the G.O.E. results, and I could no longer maintain the distance I'd wanted.

"The hot dogs all passed with flying colors, of course. But most everybody else flunked at least one area. Some flunked two or three. I'll need to be retested in Liturgics and Church History myself."

We were both surprised to hear me say, "Retested?"

"Yeah," he replied. "I called my bishop this afternoon to tell him the results. He told me the Board of Examining Chaplains in my Diocese will have to sit down with me and make sure I know enough to get started as a priest. He said nobody knows all this stuff; the scholars only know their areas of expertise. He said to relax, that the Board of Examining Chaplains will be a lot easier than the G.O.E.'s. He called the G.O.E.'s God's Own Examinations!"

I sat quietly for a minute or two, trying to absorb his words. After spending most of the day convincing myself that I had no hope of ever being ordained, it took a while before I was ready to allow the possibility that I might get a second chance.

"Have you called your bishop?" Scott asked.

I shook my head.

"Are you going to call him?"

I shrugged.

Gingerly, he asked, "How did you do?"

I couldn't make myself answer; it would have made it too real. I nodded toward my desk, where I'd put the envelope with my papers and results. He found the envelope among the clutter of papers and mail, picked it up, looked through it briefly, and sat beside me again. After a few minutes, he said, "Buddy, we're going to work our way through this. If you're not supposed to be a priest, none of us are. We're going to work it out. First thing you've got to do is call your bishop. You've got his number, right; where's his number?"

The idea of calling the Bishop was a bucket of cold water hitting me in the face. I woke up from what seemed like an oddly unreal dream, absolutely determined that I was not going to call the Bishop. After a brief but intense discussion, Scott and I agreed that I would, but that it could wait until the next day. I'd come out of my funk, but I wasn't at all happy about it.

Scott got up and went to the door. He told me he had something to take care of, and he'd be right back. In about an hour, he came in with a clear plastic bag of lemons, a knife, and a saltshaker. He put them on my desk, right on top of the G.O.E. envelope, and left again, saying, "Stay right there."

Like I had someplace I might want to go.

In less than a minute he came back in with two unexpected and amazing sets: two bottles of José Cuervo tequila and The Twins.

"Buddy," he said, "I want you to meet Denise and Diane Bradway. I was talking to them at supper tonight, and they wanted to know where you were. I told them you could use a little cheering up, and here they are. Diane, Denise, this is Buddy Hinton, a senior seminarian from Mississippi."

By instinct, before I remembered how despondent I was, I stood up and told them I was glad to meet them. The Twins were beautiful and friendly, with sparkling brown eyes, dimpled smiles, short dark hair, and the aforementioned tight jeans. They both shook my hand, and then one of them asked if I had any music. She looked through my stack of albums and picked out the greatest hits of Lester Flatt and Earl Scruggs. I've always been a charmer.

Scott cut the lemons and taught us how to shoot tequila. By the time we figured out the proper order of things: lick the back of your hand, sprinkle salt into the wet spot, lick off the salt, drink a shot of tequila, and bite the lemon wedge, it didn't really matter all that much. You might not ever have the opportunity, so I'll go ahead and tell you: it's hard to maintain a despondent funk with Flatt and Scruggs playing bluegrass, tequila shots, and a pair of beautiful twins in tight jeans.

At some point, I came to the realization that things were not as bad as I had thought, and that it was good to be alive. When I told Scott my discovery, he poured us all a shot and held up his glass for a toast: "Friends, I have it on indisputable and impeccable authority: It's Good To Be Alive."

I suppose if this were a different sort of book, I could tell a steamy story about that night. Maybe you'll be disappointed that I don't. But the truth of it is that nothing scandalous happened. As boring as it is, Diane and Denise were respectable girls, and we were decent guys. We just drank, talked, listened to music, and laughed and laughed. It was precisely what I needed. By the time Scott walked The Twins back to their dorm, the tequila was gone, and so was my post-General Ordination Examination malaise.

I put the empty bottles on my shelf as a reminder, so I wouldn't forget again—It's Good To Be Alive.

The next morning I called the Bishop, as I'd promised Scott. He'd already gotten the results, from the seminary or G.O.E. Headquarters or somewhere, and was waiting for me to call. He told me that he was shocked and not at all pleased. He asked me to send my answers to the G.O.E. essay questions to his home address. After he read my papers, he would get back in touch with me. It was a short but agonizingly difficult conversation.

I put the essays in a new envelope, sealed it and addressed it, and started to take it to the post office. Then I reopened the envelope with my pocketknife and stuck in a note.

March 13, 1981
Friday

Dear Sir,

I'm very sorry that I failed the G.O.E.'s. I know this puts you and the Diocese in a bad spot. I flunked the multiple-choice part because I was overly confident that I knew the material and didn't study as much as I should have. Please be sure that I will study very hard if you schedule the Examining Chaplains to meet with me.

As for my essays, I'm hoping that I got a bad reader. I believe what I wrote. If these essays are as bad as the reader says they are, I probably should not be ordained.

Sincerely,
Buddy Hinton

Four long days later, the Bishop phoned and left a message for me to return his call. When I called him back, he was friendly and encouraging. He told me that he thought my essay answers were fine, that perhaps my reader had no sense of humor. He said he'd schedule the Board of Examining Chaplains for later in the spring, after Easter. He told me to study hard, and I assured him that I would.

A week or so later, I was at my desk, dutifully studying, when Scott stuck his head into my room, grinning like the Cheshire Cat. "Buddy," he said, "there's someone here to see you."

I grinned, too, thinking The Twins were coming back. I was just about to suggest that we try something other than tequila, which had left me with a headache and a Central American revolution in my intestinal tract.

But you could have knocked me down with a breath when he opened the door wide, and in walked Jake Jefferson.

22

Somethin' to Lean On

If Jake was correct in saying that religion is largely trying to explain what we cannot understand, then this had to be a religious moment for me. It's not every day when something happens that you know beyond any question to be thoroughly impossible. I felt like a kid who'd given up on Santa Claus being waked up on Christmas morning by the real Santa. I stared in dumb shock, trying to force it to make sense, without even a sliver of success.

"Hey, Buddy," Jake said. "It sure is good to see you, sure is."

My mouth must have been hanging open, but I still couldn't say anything. I did manage to stand up.

Jake chuckled to Scott. "Just look at the boy. All this education, and he still ain't got nothin' to say. C'mon over here and give an old man a hug, would you please?"

I stepped into his hug and melted into tears. He held me tight, putting one hand behind my head and guiding my face to his shoulder. I don't know how long I stood there and cried; when I looked up, Scott was gone.

When I was a kid, I'd get a scratch or a bump and bring it home for Mom to tend. Several times I remember coming into the house hurting but not crying until Mom saw the problem and cooed, "Oh, Buddy." Then I cried, when there was somebody there to love me through it. That's how it was that night with Jake. After I'd cried for all the twists and turns and ups and downs of the emotional roller coaster I'd been on, I started laughing in gratitude that he was really there, relishing the impossibility of it, taking in the joy of it until I wondered if I might be going insane. I didn't think I had, but it was as plausible an explanation for Jake's appearance as I could come up with right then.

After a while, he propped an oddly crooked walking cane I hadn't noticed against my desk and sat heavily on my bed. I sat at my desk and started to talk. I told him everything that was going on, and asked a hundred questions, not waiting for the answers before asking some more. How did he get out of prison, how did he get all the way to South Carolina, was he in trouble, how long could he stay, was he hungry? He smiled through the whole verbal barrage, reveling in the sound of my voice, and knowing that he'd answer all those questions and more when I ran out of steam.

After I ran out of questions, he took a deep breath and said, "They released me out of Parchman Prison a few days ago. I left out of there and stayed with Mabel and Cornelius for one night, gettin' myself ready to come on up here. Mabel told me I ought to call you up on her telephone, but I wanted to surprise you. I reckon I did, too."

His voice was a tonic for my soul, and I told him.

Tears filled his eyes. "I know. You are, too, you sure are." He looked at me, leaning from side to side as he sat on my bed, and beamed. "You a lot older than last time I saw you. More growed up. I always knowed you was goin' to be a fine man, now I see that you are."

"Jake, are you okay?"

"I'm fine, just fine. I'm back with my Buddy now."

"How did you get up here?"

"Cornelius took a day off from the kitchen, drove me up to Memphis, and put me on a Greyhound bus over here to Columbia. We rode all night. I tell you the truth, I slept through most of it, and I don't think I missed much. This is Cornelius's best Sunday church suit I'm wearin', see how his arms and legs are a little bit longer and whatnot."

For the first time I noticed his appearance. He was wearing a shiny black suit that bagged around his ankles and swallowed his hands. He was thinner than I remember, and much older. "You look great, Jake," I said.

He smiled a little smile, not accustomed to flattery of any sort, and a bit suspicious of it. "Yeah, well. I told ol' Cornelius any kind of clothes would be fine, just so long as it weren't prison issue. Mabel insisted I wear this suit, though, his best clothes. Cornelius said he didn't mind, and claims he can't go to church without this suit, which suits him fine. I told 'em I'd bring it back safe. I ain't aimin' to be the reason a man don't go to church."

Jake asked me to get his bag in from the hall. I thought he meant his suitcase, but it really was a bag—a laundry bag with "Parchman" stenciled on the outside. In the bag, I later learned, he had his Bible, a couple pairs of underwear, socks and T-shirts, all well-worn and bleached white, his toothbrush and razor, and a small cardboard box containing his framed picture of his son Joseph and a carefully folded handbill inviting people to "Come hear Little Jacob Jefferson, the Gospel of the Lord out of the Mouth of a Child." I put the bag by his feet, and he continued his travelogue.

"In Columbia I got on another bus on its way up to North Carolina or some place, and the driver let me out at a truck stop in Montclair. That ain't far from here, best as I can tell. I was goin' to call you on the telephone from there, and see could you come get me, but some boys heard me tellin' the lady that brung me a cup of coffee that I was tryin' to get to Becket College, and they come over and started up talkin' to me. I thought they was goin' to be rude to me, but they students here at the college. They said they didn't know you, but they knowed 'bout the seminary, and they give me a ride over here, and let me out right in front of this buildin'. I tell you the truth, walkin' up all them steps was the hardest part of the whole damn trip. I had to stop three or four times just to catch my breath, I sure did."

"Why didn't you tell me you were being released?"

"Well, hell, I didn't know it my own self 'til just 'fore it happened. They been talkin' 'bout it for weeks, but I'd only served 'bout seven and a half years of a twenty-year sentence, so it didn't seem too likely to me."

"Did they let you out for good behavior?"

"Well, yes sir, I reckon they did." There was an uncomfortable pause, and then he continued, "Buddy, I got somethin' I best go ahead and tell you. You just sit there and listen, all right?"

I nodded, my throat tightening with dread. I think I already knew what he was going to say, but as much as it hurt me, I had to let him say it.

"That doctor at the Parchman hospital did a whole long line of tests on me, pokin' at me everywhere he could and some places I thought he shouldn't. He took some blood and some piss and a fair portion of my dignity, listened to my heart beatin' and my breathin'. He took my blood pressure and give me all kinds of pills and whatnot. Then, 'bout two weeks ago, he told me that he was goin' to ask the warden and parole board and all them peoples could they just let me go. He said . . . he told me I ain't got all that long, and that I needed to 'put my 'fairs in order.'

"I told him I didn't have no 'fairs, but he told me he was goin' to talk to all them folks anyways. So I decided when I got out, I'd come up here and see what Becket was all 'bout. I just thought I'd come up here and see you."

"Jake, what's wrong with you?"

He smiled that incredible smile, his essential joy shining through all his pains and problems. "Nothin'. I'm just dyin', is all."

I guess I looked like I was about to start crying again; I know I felt like it. He leaned toward me and said, "Buddy, you remember that doe, long time ago, when you was a kid? She was dyin', she'd been shot, remember? That's the day I met you, Buddy, the day my faith started to heal. I just came along to help her die. They ain't nothin' wrong with dyin', it's just another part of livin'. It ain't my favorite part, but it's a part of livin' just the same. Sometimes all we can do is to help a body die."

"But what did the doctor say you have? Is it your heart?"

"He said I was like an old car that hadn't much been taken care of. My heart ain't doin' right, and I got too much pressure in my blood, and I got sources of the liver, or some such. He said I am in pretty bad shape."

"Cirrhosis? You have cirrhosis of the liver?"

"Yes sir, that might be the word he used, somethin' close to that, I believe so. He told me what all that meant, and that it come from all them years of drinkin' too much." Jake nodded at the two empty tequila bottles on my shelf to emphasize the word "drinking," sending his silent message loudly. "He told me they was so much wrong with me that if I was a horse, they'd just shoot me."

"The doctor said that?"

"Well, he laughed when I said it, and he didn't say it wasn't true. That's how it sounded to me, anyways."

"How long . . ."

"How long do I have? I don't rightly know, the doctor said he don't know. He said he just wanted to get me out of Parchman Prison so I could live in the time I had left. So I thought I'd come up here and see you for a few days, and then go back to the Restin' Place."

I could hear the capital letters in the way he said it. "Where?"

"Back to the graveyard by my place by the creek, Joseph's Restin' Place, and my daddy's Restin' Place. I'd like to die there if I could. I'll rest easy with them, sure will."

"But Jake—you can't just go off into the woods and die all by yourself!"

"I ain't goin' to be by myself, Buddy. I'm goin' home. I'm goin' to be with my daddy and my son, and then I'm goin' to be with my Lord."

"*No!*" We were both surprised by the vehemence in my voice. I continued, more in control, "No. I can't just let you die in the woods."

"Buddy, I am goin' to die, they ain't nothin' nobody can do 'bout that. The only question is when and where that's goin' to happen. I'd ruther it be down in my woods at the Restin' Place than in a prison or a hospital. I'd ruther be with Joseph and my daddy than amongst peoples I don't know. All them peoples dressed up in white with they rubber gloves and whatnot, they ain't goin' to stop me from dyin'; they's just goin' to drag it out some. We all got to die, all of us. Just let me pass more easy, Buddy."

I understood what he wanted, but it seemed like you couldn't just die like that, alone in the woods. I wasn't even sure it was legal. If I agreed to let him go, would I be consenting to his death? Would I be an accomplice to suicide? But it was his life; surely he didn't need permission from the government or the medical industry to die. What could happen? Could he get a ticket for unauthorized termination of life? Was it permissible to just dig a hole and bury him in it? I thought there must be something wrong with what he'd said, but at that moment I couldn't figure it what it was.

Jake went on. "But I do want to ask you somethin'. I've thought 'bout this a good bit, and I decided I'd like to ask you to do me a favor."

"What is it?"

"Would you preach my funeral, at the grave? I hear you're a fine preacher."

"Who's going to bury you, Jake? If you die all alone, I mean."

"Well sir, I thought 'bout that a good bit, and decided it don't really matter. If I'm just layin' there when you get there, I'd like you to dig me a hole next to the marker for my Joseph, but that ain't the important part. Only my body will be left, I'll be gone and on my way. What I want to know is, will you preach me a sermon? I believe I'd rest more easy if I knew I'd have some good words said over my grave."

Agreeing to preach his funeral felt like consenting to his death. But it didn't seem like I had much choice about either. "I will."

"You promise?"

"I promise."

"And do it right, now, like a funeral ought to be preached. It ought to be 'bout joy, and hope, and givin' thanks for a good life, not moanin' and cryin' and whatnot. Send me on my way happy, all right, Buddy? Send me on happy."

I thought about this, and after a minute I said, "All right. We'll talk about this more later. For right now, I need to figure out how we're going to do this. I need to find you a place to stay—we're not allowed to have overnight guests up on the third floor."

"Hell, Buddy, what are they goin' to do? Put me in prison, kill me? I'll sleep on the floor, right over there."

"No, you won't. You'll sleep in my bed, and I can get a couple of cushions from the TV room or somewhere."

Actually, I borrowed an inflatable camping mattress from a single middler named Danny. By the time I blew up the mattress and laid it out in a corner of my room, it was almost midnight. I had a hundred more questions to ask, but Jake was visibly tired, almost asleep on his feet. There would be time for questions in the morning.

The bathroom was down the hall. I wasn't actually trying to keep his visit a secret, but I figured I was in enough trouble without getting caught violating the seminary's overnight guest rule. It was designed to keep girls from spending the night with seminarians, as absurd as that was considering our total lack of appeal to the undergraduate girls, but there were a couple of residents up there who I was afraid would rat me out in a minute, if they thought it would earn them points with the faculty. I looked out into the hall, and the coast was clear.

Jake stumped down the hall to the bathroom, to get ready to go to bed. I was alarmed to see how much he was leaning on his cane. When he came out, I had a sense of how surreal it was to see an old black man walking down that hall in his white, prison-issue boxer shorts and T-shirt.

When he got back to the room he said, "You like my walkin' stick?"

"Yeah. Why is it all crooked like that?"

"It's made of bodark wood," he said, like that explained something.

I told him I'd never heard of it, and he told me it was also called Osage Orange. He said the wood was stronger than oak and tougher than hickory, that a walking stick made of bodark would outlast him and me both. When I asked him if his having a cane was connected to his liver condition, he said, "Hell, no. Boss Charlie made it for me at the shop 'cause I ain't been real steady on my feet. He said it was a goin' away gift. It's just my knees; it ain't my liver. I only carry it 'cause Miss Mabel said it makes me look 'stinguished. I don't really need it."

And with that, he lay down in my bed, and just as I was about to tell him again how glad I was to see him, I realized that he was already snoring.

The next morning I got up and went to Morning Prayer, and left lying Jake in my bed. Before heading to class, I went to the Bishops' Commons to get Jake a cup of coffee and a couple of doughnuts.

When I got back to the third floor, I found Jake sitting on my bed surrounded by Scott, Pat, and Danny. "Hey, Buddy!" Scott said. "Jake's telling us about his days as a tent preacher."

"Is that all right, Buddy?" Jake asked with a worried look. "I didn't ask none of these boys to come up in here. I don't want to get you in no trouble or whatnot."

"No, it's fine," I replied. "Hey listen, guys, I don't need to get in any deeper with the seminary, okay? So let's just keep it quiet that Jake is going to be staying with me for a few days. Can we do that?"

They all promised they would. They offered to help bring up food, and watch out for those we thought might make trouble. And I believe their hearts were in the right place. But it was such a juicy secret, and Jake was so much fun to listen to, that somebody told somebody, and somebody else told somebody else, and in a day or two the secret was public knowledge.

But to my surprise, nobody seemed to mind. Even Dr. Sprague didn't say anything about it. Several of the seminarians brought Jake some more comfortable clothing, khakis and sweaters and thick socks, although I must admit it was completely surreal to see my friend Jake in L.L. Bean hand-me-downs.

His third morning at Becket, I took Jake to Morning Prayer, which he loved. After the service, standing outside the chapel, he crowed, "All right now. Now I'm beginnin' to understand 'bout your church. It ain't just 'bout the preachin', is it?"

Scott and Danny, standing with us, laughed. I replied, "No, there's more to it than that. Liturgy and tradition, all that stuff."

"Scripture, tradition, and reason," Scott added, "the three-legged stool of Anglican Christianity."

"Three legs," Jake mused. "The Book, the tradition of the Church, and what you think today—three legs got to be more steady than just one or two, right?"

It struck me as odd to have taken for granted something that Jake had never known.

"Yes sir," I said.

He held up his cane for us to see, and said, "It's like this walkin' stick, just givin' you somethin' to lean on, helpin' you with your balance. I tell you, boys, I think it's wonderful."

"Well, some of it's wonderful," Scott agreed, "but some of it's just baloney."

Jake took a deep breath, stood back on his heels, and declared, "Well, I got to tell you: I like it, I sure do, baloney and all."

Danny had been a photographer in New Jersey before he came to seminary, and that morning he happened to have a camera with him for something he was doing for the university yearbook later. Jake was curious about it; he'd never seen a 35-millimeter camera, and this one had all sorts of bells and whistles. Danny asked Jake if he could take a picture of the two of us in front of the chapel, and Jake said he'd be proud to stand in a picture with me. I was surprised to realize I didn't have any pictures of Jake. We stood by the chapel door, grinning like fools, both of us proud to be with the other.

The next day, Jake and I went to Morning Prayer again, and I asked him if he'd like to come to the Morning Curriculum. He said he'd love to come, that he'd never been to a Curriculum before.

When we got to the senior classroom, I realized with dismay that the lecturer was Dr. Sprague. I guess, with Jake being there, and all my studying for the Examining Chaplains, I hadn't paid much attention to the Morning Curriculum schedule. I told Jake we should turn around and leave. The idea of Jake and Dr. Sprague in the same room wouldn't fit into my mind. But Jake said, "No, we's here now. Let's just stay back here in the back of the room. I'll keep quiet. Hell, it ain't nothin' but a Curriculum."

Dr. Sprague came in a few minutes late, as was his custom, wearing his proudly tattered black academic gown. He looked over his reading glasses and sneered, "Ah, Mr. Hinton. I see you've brought a guest. Would you like to introduce him to the class?"

I stood up and said, "This is my very good friend and mentor, the Reverend Jake Jefferson."

Everybody already knew who he was, of course; Becket's a small place with an active information underground. Jake stood, nodded to the class with a little wave, and sat back down.

But Dr. Sprague wasn't through with us. "Wouldn't you like to say a few words, Brother Jefferson?" he asked.

Jake looked at me for guidance. I didn't know whether to encourage him or tell him to run. Jake stood again and said, "Thank you, Dr. Sprague. I want to thank you all for welcomin' me amongst you. I been readin' in Buddy's letters 'bout Becket and whatnot for near three years now, and I sure am glad to come up in here and see it with my own eyes, I sure am."

Dr. Sprague clenched his jaw, and fairly mocked, "Oh, you're glad to be *amongst* us?"

Jake gave no indication that he knew he was being ridiculed. His smile was affable, innocent. "Yes sir, I sure am."

Dr. Sprague waited for the derisive laughter and was obviously surprised to hear none. Jake's essential integrity and honor shone like the sun coming up in the morning, making Sprague's sarcasm all the more dingy and offensive. I didn't know it at the time, but looking back on it, it was the shifting of the tides.

Dr. Sprague looked at me with steel in his eyes and snapped, "Please be seated, Mr. Jefferson. Today I will be addressing the archetypal categories of Dr. Carl Jung, most notably his work with the interplay between conscious and subconscious. I advise you all to take careful notes, as this is an integral part of your understanding of the thought patterns and emotional inventories of the poor unsuspecting parishioners upon whom we are about to release you. I assure you that they will assume a proper education is a critical prerequisite to their willingness to entrust you with their confidence. Wouldn't you agree, Mr. Jefferson?"

Jake stood with a soft groan and said, "I'm sure you are right, Dr. Sprague. I was listenin' to what you was sayin', and it sounded real good, but I tell you the truth, I ain't got no idea what you might be talkin' 'bout. But I 'magine you must be right."

Several members of the class laughed, but not at Jake. Having Jake there simply highlighted Dr. Sprague's absurd pomposity for all to see. Jake, seemingly unaware of his effect on the class, sat again, smiling his most guileless smile. Sprague's frustration might have been comical, if I hadn't been so filled with dread.

Dr. Sprague condescended, "What I said, my unschooled friend, is that you have to have a proper education to be an effective minister. Don't you think that's true?"

Jake hauled himself to his feet one more time. "Well, now," he began, "I don't rightly know nothin' 'bout that. You the teacher here, and what I think ain't really all that important." He moved as if he would sit back down, and I thought he was finished. I was just about to exhale a relieved breath when he continued, "But since you asked, though, I'll tell you. I think *you* need to have a good education to be a good minister. But I don't think *I* did."

Sprague stood as still as a fencepost, steaming with impotent rage. He must have been wondering what to say next, but Jake beat him to the punch.

"I'm sure all this baloney you been sayin' is mighty interestin' and all, but I don't see how it has much to do with the gospel."

By this point the whole class was laughing, everyone but Jake, Dr. Sprague, and me. I'd never seen Sprague so angry. I tugged on Jake's pants leg to get him to sit down, but he was enjoying the response of the class. And, I realized, he was daring Dr. Sprague to answer him, confronting him in his own way.

"Did you say 'baloney'?" Sprague snapped. "You think this is baloney, Mr. Jefferson?"

Jake grinned. "Well sir, Dr. Sprague, I s'pose much of it is, I sure do. What these peoples you teachin' really needs to know is 'bout lovin' the peoples in they churches, sittin' in they pain with 'em, givin' thanks for they joys with 'em. All this other psychology and whatnot is mostly just baloney, as far as I can tell, sure is."

When Dr. Sprague spoke again, his voice was pitched a note or two higher than usual, betraying a tremble that alarmed me all the more. "Are you telling this class, sir, that what I am teaching them is not what they need to know to be effective clergy? Are you telling us that we've wasted the last three years of our lives in irrelevant baloney?"

"Well sir, I don't know that I really wanted to say all that." There was another round of laughter from the class, and Dr. Sprague turned a shade of red darker. When Jake continued, he was dead serious. "All I know is what's important to me."

Again, Jake was starting to resume his seat, but Dr. Sprague, not willing to concede the last word, played his final and most desperate bluff: "Perhaps you think you could do better as a lecturer here."

Jake and I talked about this moment several times, and I'm still not sure why Jake did what he did. He said he thought it was an invitation to preach, and that he wouldn't be getting many more chances. But I wonder, too, if it was a chance for him to show Dr. Sprague up, and to show us all that education by itself is not enough.

He raised his head to look Dr. Sprague in the eye, and said, "Why, I thank you. It would be my honor."

You could have heard an ant sneeze in that classroom. Sprague cleared his throat, mustering what dignity he could, and said, "I'm not scheduled with this class again until next Tuesday, Mr. Jefferson. I trust that will give you ample time to get your lecture in order?"

Jake grinned and replied, "Yes sir. Hell, I been writin' this sermon my whole life!"

23

Words Are Powerful Things

The next few days were a busy, crazy, wonderful time. I prepared to be tested by the Board of Examining Chaplains, and Jake worked on his address to the seminary. He wrote a little, thought a little, and wrote a little more. When he asked me what I thought about this sentence or that paragraph, I tried to be as helpful as I could. We had several discussions about verb conjugations and acceptable grammar. I wanted him to talk the way he talked, but he wanted to "speak proper," the way a seminary lecture should sound.

At one point I was telling him how much I liked it, and I mentioned that we could make copies of it for my classmates. I thought I was encouraging him, but he worried that his handwriting would display his lack of education. I offered to type what he wrote, and that eased his anxiety, but it increased his concern about syntax, spelling, and sentence structure.

He worried that he would embarrass me, that his listeners would think him unintelligent, that he wouldn't be able to stand up for as long as it would take to deliver his address. He worked on it like a man with a mission, which I suppose he was, trying to distill the message of his entire life into a talk that wouldn't last longer than the congregation was willing to sit. When I told him he needed to relax, he said, "It's been a long time since I preached, Buddy, and I figure this will be my last sermon. I just want it to be a good one."

I suggested that he could include a collection of his sayings and bits of wisdom. He had a hard time believing that I quoted him from time to time, using things he'd written or said. I told him he had a real gift for saying things in a memorable way that people could understand. He balked at the idea, and said he couldn't remember much of what he'd said. I persisted, telling him that the students would like it if he could put some of his teachings into something like proverbs. He was exasperated with that notion, I remember, and finally exclaimed, "Hell, Buddy, I don't pay no attention to what I say: most of the time when I'm talkin', I ain't listenin.'"

It occurred to me that I had quite a few of these proverbs already written down, and I went to my closet and got out my shoebox holding his letters. We read them all, laughing at some and crying at others. I copied some of the things I thought seemed proverbial. Some of them reminded one of us of other things he'd said or thought important. We struggled to put them into some sort of logical order, and finally wrote them all out on three-by-five index cards and laid them on my bed to arrange them.

I'm reprinting Jake's lecture to the seminary here exactly as he wrote it—with some additions. He didn't always stick to what he'd written out and what I'd typed. Some of the improvised comments I remembered, and friends from seminary remembered others, so I think I present it here fairly close to the way he delivered it. When he strayed from his prepared remarks, I've used italics, beginning with his opening prayer. Some of the proverbs you've already read earlier in this book; a few of them reminded me of stories I needed to tell as part of our story. And some of them don't fit anywhere but here. Jake and I may have changed the grammar a little, but the wisdom is all his. And ours, if we let the words touch us.

After it was written, he read it over and over, silently and aloud. He told me he didn't want to trip over any of the words. I noted that he had it almost memorized, and he said he'd take the paper up there with him anyway, just in case. Then he read it again, and again.

Finally, the next Tuesday came, and we went to Morning Prayer. Almost everybody we saw clapped Jake on the shoulder and wished him luck. As we made our way to the senior classroom, Jake stopped and said, "Listen, Buddy, if you don't want me to do this, I don't have to. I ain't tryin' to make things no worse for you up in here."

"Just tell us the truth, Preacher Jake," I replied. Then we hugged and walked in together.

We were both surprised how crowded the senior classroom was. All of the seniors were there, and there were quite a few middlers and juniors, too. And neither of us had expected so many members of the faculty. It was standing room only; I stood in the back. Dr. Sprague was sitting off to the left, sort of by himself. He had a legal pad in front of him and a pen in his hand; too late, I saw that his plan was to take notes and dissect what Jake said, so he could mock him for the rest of my time at Becket. I hoped he wouldn't be rude to Jake, that he'd let him finish. It was Jake's *summa theologica*, and it ought to be preached.

Jake nodded once to Sprague. Sprague nodded back gravely, and made a gesture with his hand inviting Jake to the podium, a spider showing the fly where he could land.

Jake cleared his throat, put his glasses on, took them back off, took a little sip of water from the glass someone had provided, and cleared his throat again. Then he took a deep breath and began.

> *Dear Lord Jesus, have mercy. Help me say what you want me to say, and help your chilluns hear what you want them to hear. Amen.*
>
> Dr. Sprague, *professors of the faculty*, seminarians, brothers and sisters in Christ. I thank you for this chance, and I thank you for coming to hear what I have to say this morning. I suppose most of you are here for the sake of curiosity, not really expecting that I have anything much to say at all. I tell you the truth, you may be right. *This whole talk could be just more baloney, Dr. Sprague. These folks will tell us when I get done.*
>
> I am not a fancy man. I don't have any degrees, in theology or anything else. The truth is that I just barely know how to read. *I ain't never read nothin' much but the King James Bible and a commentary about the book of Genesis, but they's pretty good books.* So it may be that I don't have any business speaking to the students and faculty of your seminary of Becket University. It may be that I don't

rightly know how to say anything that you ought to hear. After all, I'm just an old black man from Beaumont, Mississippi.

But I do believe I have a claim on your time. It is not the claim of your curiosity, that's a claim you have made and will soon be relieved of. It is not the claim of Dr. Sprague's invitation to speak, that's no real claim at all, since it was an invitation given to show us all how "unschooled" I am. The claim I have is only this: the Lord Jesus had no more respect from the church authorities He spoke to than I have from some of you. After all, He was just the son of a Jewish carpenter from Nazareth in Galilee. *Galilee was the wrong side of the tracks back then.*

I have been a preacher for the better part of seventy years. I have never been a member of any church. I preached in a tent, mostly, going from town to town, never this far up north. For a few years I preached on the radio, too, on stations in Mississippi and Louisiana. For a long time I knew that preaching was what I was supposed to do. But I lost my wife to a banker, then I lost my son to a war, and then I lost my way. I struggled with pain and despair, and for a long time I just stopped preaching. *I just couldn't preach no more.* First I stopped believing, then I stopped hoping, then I stopped praying, and finally I stopped preaching. I figured God had given up on me, so I gave up on Him, too, and went off to live by myself.

And I would have stayed to myself, *hugging my pain to me tight like it was my treasure,* but God had not given up on me, and He sent somebody to find me. Buddy was just a little boy then, playing with sticks in the mud, but the love of God was shining so bright in this boy that I couldn't help but see it. When his friends called me names and threw things at me, he did not join them. When they disgraced the graves of my family, he told them to stop. In Buddy I saw something I had not seen since my daddy and my son died. I saw decency, respect, and hope. I saw the love of God.

So here I am, preachin' again. I 'spect this will be my last sermon. It ain't a sermon none of you 'spected to hear, I guess, but it's somethin' I needs to say, so I 'preciate you sittin' through it. Now I am ready to say what I have spent my whole life trying to understand, what I believe is most important that you have to teach and learn: the Gospel is about the love of God.

From the Gospel of John, chapter one, verse five: "And the light shineth in darkness; and the darkness comprehended it not." The writer, the apostle John, knew that there is darkness in the world, he never denied it. If there hadn't been, I believe Jesus would not have had to come. We spend a lot of our lives in darkness: in fear and in pain, without hope. But here is the Gospel; here is the Good News. "The light shineth in darkness; and the darkness comprehended it not." *You hear me now?* The darkness of the world, from outside us and from within us, will always be all around us. But the light shineth! *All the darkness of the world can't put out the light of Christ, it sure can't!* The light in our darkness is the life of Jesus, and the life He gives us, not just long time gone and far away; the light is here with us still, shining in our lives, in our stories, in the love of God that we give and receive among ourselves. That light, that precious light shines on, and shines most brightly in our darkest hours. *Not just in a book, not just in the church, not just when we're all fancied up and smellin' good—in my life, in your life, in what we's proud of and in what makes us ashamed. The light of Christ shines on, shines on in our darkness.* The love of God touched this old black man with the muddy hands of a little white boy, and that same love holds me up in front of you this morning.

I know you people are working hard, training people to be priests in the Episcopal Church, studying to become priests. I think that's a powerful, fine thing. I didn't ever have any kind of support from a denomination, nor even a congregation, and I think it would have been a good thing. Please don't think that I am saying what you're doing here is not important. I don't know why you all need to remember all the kings of Israel in order, and all that work on getting the hand motions in the services just right doesn't make much sense to me. But it doesn't bother me for you to study on that. Just so long as you don't forget what's important in all this: that the love of God comes to us from a lot of different directions. It comes from the Book, from the history and tradition of the Church, and we're grateful for that. *I never did know much about none of that, and I wish I had.* The love of God also comes from the people who sit in the pews and pay the bills; from folks you don't even know, old drunks at the county jail, people with no education at all, maybe even Doctors of Philosophy or Theology.

It may be that I don't really know much, and I may be proving that to you by standing up here like this. But I believe that if you want to, you can see the light of God in almost anybody. Maybe you could see the light of God in me, if you were looking. *It may be I could see it shine in you, through all your books and degrees. And if you could, and if I could, we might just see that you and I are brothers and sisters, all chillun of the same Father in heaven.*

Some of you will likely go on to be mighty preachers. Some of you won't ever do much good for anybody but yourselves. Some of you might become scholars of some sort or another, whatever good that may do. But none of you will be worth a damn if you forget how to love, if you let yourself pretend that ministry is about what you know, and not about the love of God.

For many years I caught fish in a bayou for a living. I ate what I caught or killed, and slept in a hut with a moss roof. I didn't read any of your fine fancy books, but I had a great long time to think. Now I have a chance to tell you some of the things I believe. *You don't have to take no notes, I'll give you mine if you want 'em. Just listen, though; you never can tell who might have somethin' to say worth listenin' to.*

Jake cleared his throat again, and adjusted his glasses. He looked up at me to get a sense of how he was doing. I saw Dr. Sprague follow his eyes, so that he was looking at me, too. I grinned and gave Jake a thumbs-up sign. Jake took another deep breath and continued with the collection of his proverbs.

When you can, choose what you say carefully, words are powerful things.
Most people are going to believe what they want to believe, most of the time.
Hope is more powerful than despair, but harder to hold on to.
Love is more powerful than hate, but hate is more appealing.
The best we can do is to be who God made us to be.
The best of what you and I have to offer is the Gospel, which is all about our hope in the love of God.
God loves you more than your mother does.

Being faithful is looking for the Truth, and the Light, wherever it shines.

A Christian has the Gospel to share, Good News for all of the children of God. *If you ain't joyful being a Christian, you ain't doing it right.*

The trick to living is not that you never mess up, but that after you do, you get up and start again.

We are all sinners, most of the time. *But that ain't all they is to us.*

We need to see ourselves as God sees us: as sinners He has forgiven.

It isn't enough for God or somebody else to forgive you; you have to forgive yourself. It is pure arrogance to hold on to something God has already let go of.

Shame will eat you up if you let it. It will suck all the joy out of your life if you are ashamed of yourself.

Some things will just have to be a mystery. I choose to leave them to God, and trust that He loves us.

Hell is when we get what we deserve; Heaven is when we receive what we've been given.

There is more to the world than I am able to know.

It is not an accident that God is invisible.

We have to have doubts so that we can have faith, and we have to have evil so that we can treasure good.

The opposite of faith is not doubt, but fear.

Faith is more powerful than fear, but fear is much easier to spread.

Fear is a powerful thing, but only when we let it run us.

There are only two kinds of people in the world, givers and takers.

The takers run the world, but the givers make life worth living.

It isn't hard to love people who love you, or who everybody else loves, too.

Once you are in a fight, all you can do is lose.

Addiction is a fearful thing. Alcohol will ruin your life if you give it a chance. Some people are addicted to money, and some are addicted to power and control.

We are not supposed to know everything about God. Some people think they know about God, and have Him under their control.

The Gospel is not about control, but about the love of God.

Everybody wants to believe they are better than somebody else. We get into real trouble when we give ourselves permission to hate some other person or group.

Don't ever let someone convince you that they are better than you.
Nobody's better than anybody else in God's way of thinking. *Ain't nobody no better'n you, and you ain't no better'n nobody else.*
The sins that are preached about the most are sins the preacher is not guilty of, nor tempted by.
No matter how long you work there, *or how many degrees you have,* it isn't your church.
If you pay too much attention to people telling you how wonderful you are, you will forget that it is God you is supposed to be pointing to, and not yourself.
No preacher worth his salt lets himself or herself be the star of the show.
We are all given a tiny spark of the Light of God to shine. We need to put all those sparks together, and share the Light.
Being faithful has more to do with asking questions than having answers.
Religion is largely trying to explain what we cannot understand.
The Bible is a collection of stories told to explain things that cannot be understood.
All healing comes from God, one way or another.
If you think you can do a thing, you are a lot more likely to do it than if you think you can not.
There are some messes that you did not make and cannot clean up.
Only a fool figures everybody else is just like him.
You cannot make somebody love you, or trust you, or respect you.
A few things that I know are good for the soul: to laugh with a close friend, some time to be quiet, baseball, honest music, the sky on a clear night, listening to the rain fall, a good strong cup of coffee, and drawing the right card to fill a straight.
If you can whistle, you don't have to talk all the time. *I believe some of y'all might need to learn to whistle.*
There isn't anything wrong with dying; it's just the last part of living before we graduate into a larger life. *We all got to die, all of us.*
Unconditional love is rare and wonderful in this life, but it is the substance of life with God in the next.
In the end, our stories are all we are, and all we have to give.
The Mysteries are ever before us.

Well, I reckon that's about all I know.

Now, in a few months, you seniors are going to be leaving this school, and taking your places in our Lord's Church. You are taking your spot in a long parade that has Jesus Himself at the head, followed by the Apostles and Saints, the Martyrs and all those people you read about in Church History, and hundreds and millions of people more like me, who had the love of God in their hearts and nothing but the hope of the Resurrection to bring them home.

Dr. Sprague invited me to tell you what I think is important for a minister to know. It may be that I've already said some of that. *I sure hope so, anyways.* The main thing I want you to know, the thing I am hoping you will hear and might even remember, is that the ministry of the church is about the love of God.

I believe you are just going to have to accept the fact that God loves you. Not just when you are good boys and girls, not because you are Episcopalians or because you goin' to be preachers, not because you deserve it, but because that's just how God is. God loves you because He is God, and He loves all his chillun, even the ones we don't like or agree with or look like.

You'll talk to people you would rather not be around, worry with people who don't like the hymns, and listen to people talk about things you're not interested in at all. You'll be asked to speak to groups of children who don't want to hear you, and old folks who can't. You'll have good sermons you're proud of, and others where you're still trying to figure out what you were trying to say after you said it.

If you do your job, you'll comfort some people and upset some others. If you do your job, you won't pay much attention to how much money people put in the plate. If you do your job, you'll sit with people in the smelliest times of their lives and wait for the right moment to tell them it stinks. If you do your job, you'll be asked to share the most joyful times in their lives, too.

But in all of it, the best and the worst and all that is between, your job is to share the love of God that brought you to this place, and sends you back out. *If you ain't doin' all that stuff in the love that God gives you to share, you just playin' like you's the Church, but you ain't really.*

I hope you know that a cowboy pushes the cattle where he wants them to go by scaring them, *hollerin' and makin' a lot of noise and whatnot,* and a shepherd leads the sheep by letting them trust him and leading them where they need to be. I hope you know that Jesus has called you to be shepherds, and not cowboys.

You take with you more than enough gifts to answer God's call. *Lord knows y'all are educated enough to bore peoples to death if you want to.* Preach to God's children—preach love, and hope in this life and for the next. Take care to listen to what you say to them, and to what they say to you. Proclaim the Gospel of Jesus Christ, and listen for the Good News in the mouths of those around you. Reach out to touch those in your care, and feel their support. Love them, and feel God's love for you in them.

And y'all don't take yourselfs so damn serious all the time. I tell you the truth, it wouldn't hurt none of y'all to laugh a little from time to time. If I ain't done nothin' in this sermon but give y'all somethin' to laugh at, I 'spect I done you a favor. If you can learn to laugh at yourselfs, you'll always have somethin' to laugh at, you sure will.

Dr. Sprague, I thank you for this opportunity. I hope I haven't wasted your time, or the time of your students. Thank you, and God bless you.

Jake collected his notes and began to make his way toward the door. Then the homiletics instructor stood up and started clapping. It seemed as if the rest of us were a bunch of firecrackers, just waiting for one of the others to pop before we went off, too. Once we started, though, there was a prolonged explosion of applause. Jake was walking toward the door, with people patting him on the back and thanking him for his words. He stopped at the door with tears in his eyes, humbled and honored. He faced the class and nodded his appreciation.

Dr. Sprague had taken his podium back and was trying to regain his class's attention. I think that had something to do with prolonging the applause we gave Jake. We were more than content to keep clapping so we could ignore Sprague. The rest of the faculty left at this point, not willing either to extend the ovation or to do anything to cut it short.

After some time, Dr. Sprague shouted, "Mr. Jefferson!" The class went quiet. Jake turned and faced him, his face a blank. "You still have over half an hour to lecture the class. Are you finished? Is that all?"

We all looked at Jake and waited.

He took a step forward and responded, "I just said what all I felt like I needed to say. Yes sir, I believe I said everything they needed to hear."

Sprague wasn't finished. "And so, for the rest of the hour I've given you for your lecture, what do you suggest these students do?"

Jake looked at his feet, weighing his response. He said, "Oh, I don't know. Maybe if they had a little extra time to read and write, they might could catch up on they homework and whatnot."

At that the class burst into applause again. Things were getting ugly.

Sprague sneered. "Oh no, my rustic friend. You still owe us thirty minutes." He seemed to think he had won a victory of some sort.

Jake smiled and waited for the room to fall quiet. Then he said, "No, sir. I have said everything I know to say."

"But there's still thirty minutes. I must insist that you either use the time I've given you, or apologize for wasting our time."

"It ain't your time. You only have the time God gives you."

"So that's it, then. You have nothing else."

Now those remaining in the room, just students, groaned their disagreement. A few were bold enough to grumble or murmur.

Jake had never been one to defend himself, but he seemed strangely angered now, his integrity being called into question. He stood up straight and said, "No sir. I'm not all educated like you are. I ain't nothin' but what you see. You asked me to speak to your class, and I did. If you want to pile more teachin' on them, they ain't nothin' I can do about that."

He started to sit down then, and I was thinking that it could have been much worse, when he added just one more thought: "But I do wonder: have you ever had a class stand up and clap like this when you was finished with all your talkin'?"

Dr. Sprague was incensed. "I will not be spoken to like that!" he screeched. "And especially not by someone like you! You will apologize to me."

Jake laughed at this. "No sir. I ain't goin' to apologize. You ain't got no power over me. Oh, I know you a big alligator in this swamp, and all these peoples, they's all under your power. But now you talkin' to somebody who ain't in your swamp. You got no power over me, and I can say what these peoples can't. I can say whatever I damn well please. You is a lot more educated than me, Dr. Sprague, but I think it may be you ain't really all that bright."

The classroom was as silent as a tomb. Jake had found the fire and thrown gasoline on it. Dr. Sprague was about to melt down. If it had been a cartoon, we could have seen the steam coming out of his ears. As it was, we knew it was there. With ice in his voice, he said, "*Mr. Hinton.*"

I suppose I should have expected something like this. "Yes sir?" I said.

"I will see you in the dean's office in five minutes."

"Yes sir."

And then Boss Sprague walked to the door. Nobody got in his way. Nobody said a word, until he was through the door and on the steps up to his office. Then the classroom exhaled as one, and an excited buzz began as the community digested what had happened.

I found Jake by the door, still being congratulated, and I said, "Good job, Jake. You did great." I leaned in a little closer. "I'm glad I got to hear you preach."

"I'll hear you preach every one of your sermons, boy," he said. "Yes sir, I'll be listenin', sure will."

24

The Acting Dean

I knocked on the door of the dean's office, and Dr. Sprague snarled, "Come in."

When I entered, I saw Dr. Sprague sitting at the dean's desk, with his back turned toward me.

I began, "Dr. Sprague, I—"

Without turning around, he struck out at me, his voice dripping with venomous derision. "You what? You apologize? You didn't mean for him to say all that?"

I was taken off guard; I hadn't known what to expect, but his reaction surprised me. "You invited him to speak this morning."

Now Dr. Sprague whirled around and faced me. No steam was visible, but the pressure of it was still there, and building. He was about to release it on me.

"Don't lie to me, Hinton. You and I both know that you wanted to disgrace me in front of the seminary, so you arranged for your backwoods preacher friend to come. You've had it in for me since the day you got here. You can't stand to be around someone more intelligent than you; don't think I don't see it."

I'd never seen a nervous breakdown, but I was starting to think this looked like a promising start on one. "Are you okay, Dr. Sprague?" I asked.

"Oh, sure," he ranted, "act as if you're concerned for me. We all know Buddy Hinton is some sort of modern-day cross between Tom Sawyer and Sir Galahad, right? Well, you're not fooling me, Hinton. I know who you are!"

It occurred to me right then that this was the third time somebody had told me they knew who I was, and that Brother Swayze and Mark the evangelist had been way off base. Suddenly I was surreally calm, as if this was happening to someone else. I asked, "Who am I, Dr. Sprague?"

"You're a fake! You're not so sweet and noble as they all think you are. I told you I would find the chink in your armor, and I have. You're jealous—jealous and petty. Just look at the trap you set for me! Using that poor old black man to do your dirty work for you. What's the matter, Hinton, afraid to take me on yourself?"

"I have been afraid of you, that much is true. You have power over me. But I'm not jealous of you, and I'm not a fake. Jake came here of his own free will, and he did and said as he pleased."

"No! You wrote that speech for him. It didn't even sound like him; that's not the way he talks! You put those words in his mouth."

"You're wrong, Dr. Sprague. You're wrong about Jake, and about me. You're the one who's jealous and petty. You're the one who's a fake. That's the way you are, so you think other people must be, too. 'Only a fool figures everybody else is just like him.'"

"See? That's what he said! They're your words, not his!"

"He's been telling me that for years. I was quoting him."

"No, no—no, you don't. You wrote that paper for him, every word of it. He couldn't have written it. He can hardly even speak intelligibly."

"He's not educated, but he's wise. 'You never can tell who might have something to say.'"

If Sprague was on the edge of having a nervous breakdown, I admit I was willing to give him a little nudge.

"*No!* It was you. You wrote that. He's just an actor reading your script. And those fools bought it. They think you got the best of me. But this isn't over yet."

"What Jake said in there is true. I have no idea why I disturb you so much, or why you have picked me to be your scapegoat. But you do have me in your power."

"Well, be that as it may. I will have an apology."

"I apologize."

"Oh, no, my conniving friend, it's not that easy. You will apologize for your friend, but not here, not now. Tomorrow, at the seminary luncheon, you will apologize to me and to the seminary. You will tell us how embarrassed you are by your friend's behavior, and you will promise to make him go back to wherever he came from. Do you understand that, Mr. Hinton?"

"I understand your demands. And if I don't do as you say?"

"Then I will feel it necessary, as acting dean, to have you dismissed from this school, for conduct unbecoming of a seminarian."

"You can't do that."

"Ah, but I can. And you know I will."

"Is that all, sir?"

"That's all. I'll look forward to seeing you tomorrow at the seminary luncheon."

I left the dean's office, wishing again that the dean was there. When I got up to my room, a small crowd had gathered. Jake was there, with Scott, Pat, Danny, a couple of other single students, and eight or ten of the married students who never came up to the third floor.

"Hi, y'all," I said.

"What did Sprague say?" asked Scott.

"He told me I needed to apologize to the seminary at lunch tomorrow."

The seminarians were indignant. All at the same time, they exploded, "Apologize for what?" "He's the one who ought to apologize!" "That son of a bitch!"

Jake waited for the initial uproar to subside, and advised, "Just apologize. It ain't nothin' but words. You don't owe me nothin'."

I almost laughed at the notion that I didn't owe Jake anything. I quoted him, "I can't apologize: 'Words are powerful things.'"

"If you don't apologize, what'll happen?" Scott wondered.

"Sprague says he'll dismiss me from the seminary. He's the acting dean."

Danny was quick to joke, "Yeah, he's acting like a dean, but he's not a very good actor."

We all looked at Jake, who repeated, "Just apologize. It won't hurt me none."

"I will not," I insisted.

There was a long moment, and then Scott asked, "What are you going to do?"

"I don't know."

"He's goin' to apologize!" Jake said. "If Boss Sprague wants an apology, he's goin' to get one. That's all they is to that, now."

I looked at Jake and murmured, "I don't know what I'm going to do." Then I looked at my friends. "But I'm not going to say that I'm ashamed of Jake."

After half an hour of energetic but pointless discussion, everybody but Jake and me left. Jake told me I was being mulish and pig-headed, and offered to apologize to the seminary for me. He told me he was sorry for messing everything up. But when he told me he was sorry he'd ever come up to Becket, I'd had enough.

"No sir. Jake, you're the best friend I've ever had. If this seminary or this Church can't hear the truth from a man like you, then I want no part of it. "

I lay on my inflatable mattress for a long time, pondering my options. Actually, I didn't have but two options, so I pondered each one thoroughly. Either I would apologize for Jake, and live with the shame of it for the rest of my life, or I wouldn't, and face the possibility of being expelled from seminary. After fifteen or twenty minutes, I heard Jake snoring. I sat up to watch his dear face in sleep, and listened to the steady rhythm of his breathing.

I skipped lunch and cut my afternoon classes, and took some time to think about what I ought to do. I had no doubts that Dr. Sprague would dismiss me from school if I didn't apologize. But how could I?

I thought about my life with Jake. I saw that doe again in my memory, and saw Jake speaking to her softly. I felt him wiping the tears off my face and looking at me as I threatened to hit him with a stick. I saw him fishing as the boys I grew up with found him at the creek. I saw the mud hit his back and heard the horrible, hurtful name they called him. I saw him against the Halloween moon, a smoking shotgun in his hand, and as he dished out a lumpy bowl of mysterious but delicious stew. I remembered him sitting on the fallen sweet gum, telling me the story of his life, proving the existence of God in leaves and squirrels, consoling me after my friend Andy's death, playing the harmonica, whistling. I saw the little glimpse of him at my confirmation, and remembered looking for him at my graduation. I felt again a sense of the excitement I felt every time I got a letter from him, once a week for almost eight years. My heart gave thanks again for his love, and for all the wisdom and insight he'd tried so hard to give me, my "inheritance."

It was largely because of Jake that I knew the path my life was supposed to take, and because of him that I'd had the nerve to pursue it by coming to seminary. Now I was being told I had to apologize for him, to tell the seminary that I was embarrassed by him, or I would be kicked out of school. I had to choose between Jake and the priesthood. It had been the direction of my life since the Bishop had preached at my confirmation, and it seemed to me like I would be throwing it away if I didn't apologize at the luncheon, if I was not willing to swallow my pride. Jake had already told me that I ought to apologize; in fact, I had already apologized to Boss Sprague in his office. It would be an unpleasant moment, and then it would be over. Everybody has to make compromises, everybody has to say or do things they don't believe; it's just part of life.

But it was a violation of my love for Jake to tell the seminary that I was embarrassed by what he'd said. To apologize for him to save my skin seemed like Peter denying that he'd known Jesus. It would be a lie, and I would be a fake, proving Dr. Sprague's charge. On the other hand, not apologizing seemed prideful, selfish, and wasteful. What would I do if I was kicked out of seminary? How would I make a living if I wasn't going to be a priest?

I tried to call my friend William in Virginia, but got no answer. So I made a collect call to Smitty's parish in Texas, and told him the whole thing. I told him that I'd known Jake since I was nine or ten, that Jake was like a second father to me. I told him about Jake coming to my confirmation, about the letters, and about Parchman. I told him that Jake was a huge part of who I was. I told him that Jake was dying, and about his visit to Becket. Then I told him about Jake's lecture to the senior class, and Dr. Sprague demanding an apology.

Smitty said he understood my dilemma, and that he'd call me right back. About an hour later, when the hall pay phone rang, I was surprised to hear William calling from Virginia. He said Smitty had called and told him all about it. They had discussed it at length, and decided that their advice, as odious as it would be, was that I would have to apologize. He told me I didn't really have a choice. "You can't just throw it all away, Buddy."

That night, I called the Bishop collect, at home. I apologized for bothering him at home, promised to pay him back for the call, and told him I had a problem. I told him everything, which took a while, but he listened patiently to the whole story. When I had the situation explained, he said, "Well. I don't think I've ever heard anything like this. Would it help if I called the dean?"

I told him that I'd forgotten to tell him the dean was in England for his sabbatical, and the Bishop asked me who was acting dean. When I hesitated, he said, "Sprague?"

"Yes sir."

He said (and this I know is a direct quote), "Damn."

We talked about my options, limited as they were, and he told me he couldn't tell me what to do. He told me he'd support me in whatever decision I made, and then said that with my G.O.E. results being what they were, getting dismissed from seminary could well be the end of my dream of becoming a priest.

"Damn," I said.

"Yeah," he said. "Damn."

I thanked him for his support and his honesty, and he asked me what I thought I would do.

"I don't know, Bishop. I . . . I just can't be dismissed from seminary. But I don't think I can deny Jake, either."

There was a long pause, and then he said, "I can't tell you which way you need to go, Buddy. I'll be there for you if I can do anything to help. You need to know that you'll have to live with whatever decision you make for the rest of your life."

"Yes sir."

The next morning, I skipped chapel and the Morning Curriculum.

The Wednesday luncheon started at noon. At ten after, I walked into the big dining room where the students and faculty had gathered. Most people were still eating; the weekly announcements had not yet started. I looked for Scott, intending to go and sit with him, but Dr. Sprague saw me first. He was on the far side of the room, and when he saw me, he grinned maliciously. He tapped his water glass to get everybody's attention. When he had it, he announced, "Ah, good. Mr. Hinton has decided to grace this community with his presence. Mr. Hinton, unless I am greatly mistaken, you have something you'd like to say to the seminary." He motioned with his hand that I should come up on the dais with him, but I stayed where I was.

"I do have something I'd like to say, thank you."

I felt everyone's eyes on me, and felt their support. Some of the juniors were trying to figure out what was going on, but everybody else knew, and assumed that I was going to have to apologize.

I cleared my throat. "Many of you know that Jake Jefferson, a dear friend of mine, has been visiting for the last week or so. About a week ago, he sat in on the senior Morning Curriculum and heard Dr. Sprague speak. When Dr. Sprague asked Jake how he'd liked what he'd said, Jake told him that a lot of it was baloney."

I heard a murmuring of comments and some laughter, and I held up my hand to quiet them before I continued. "Then Dr. Sprague offered Jake his next lecture time with us, which was yesterday, to share what he believes to be important for us to learn."

I paused to look at Dr. Sprague, who was sitting back in his chair with a little smile on his face, watching me like a cat watches a mouse that it's played with until the mouse has given up.

"Quite a few of you heard Jake's talk, I think. Please do me a favor and raise your hand if you heard Jake's lecture yesterday morning." Almost all of the seniors, most of the middlers, and half of the juniors lifted their hands, along with two-thirds of the faculty. Boss Sprague held up his own hand with a show of weary regret.

"Thank you," I continued. "Now leave your hand up if anything he said offended you." As one, all the hands went down—all but Sprague's. His eyes were narrow slits; he looked like he was grinding his teeth.

"Thank you again," I said. I had been talking slowly, deliberately, but now I needed to pick up the pace; I wasn't sure how long Sprague was going to let me speak.

"So far I've told you what most of you already knew. What you don't know is that after Jake's talk, Dr. Sprague made me come into the dean's office to see him. He demanded that I apologize to the seminary today at lunch, that I tell you that I was embarrassed by my friend Jake. He told me that if I did not, I would be dismissed from school."

There was a widespread intake of breath, and Dr. Sprague was standing now, beating his water glass with a spoon. But I was yelling, and the seminary was listening to me.

"But I am not a fake, Dr. Sprague, and I will not lie. I will *not* apologize for my friend Jake. I am *not* embarrassed by him. He is the best friend I've ever had, the best friend I ever *will* have. Jake did nothing but tell the truth in class yesterday. I'm here to follow the truth, and if the truth takes me away from here, then I'll follow it somewhere else."

There were cheers, and some applause, but it died down quickly as we all realized it was Sprague's turn. He took a sip of his water and said, "Are you quite finished, young man?"

"Yes sir, I believe I am."

Perhaps in more ways than one, I thought.

Then I turned around and walked out. Boss Sprague was shouting something at my back, but it didn't matter what Sprague said. I didn't need or want to listen to him say another word.

25

A Come-as-You-Are Celebration

I'd spent the morning packing, which is why I'd been late for lunch. Jake had put all his belongings in two boxes I'd gotten from the liquor store, and was waiting for me in the seminary chapel. It was time to go.

Bill the Mercury Comet sat in the parking lot of the Cranmer House, where the luncheon was. I was rolling before any of my friends even thought to catch up to me. I'd left them a note on the door to my room on the third floor, explaining why I had to do what I'd done. It was better for me if I could leave quickly, without any opportunity for arguments or good-byes.

I pulled up behind the chapel and went in to get Jake. He was sitting in the back, his eyes closed, his hands pressed together in front of his face like a child praying. When he heard me, he opened his eyes, and I saw that he'd been crying.

"You ready?" I asked.

"You did it?"

"Yes sir. It's time to go."

"You is some mule-headed fool, you know that?"

"So I have been told."

"Buddy, I could still—"

"No, Jake; it's done. I thank you, but it's time to go."

So we left. Jake got in the Comet with me, and when we got to University Drive, I took a left—away from Becket, away from Dr. Sprague, away from my friends and my dreams, away from the priesthood.

We rode for a long time in silence before Jake asked the obvious question: "Where we goin'?"

I answered, "Beaumont, I suppose."

"What you goin' to do, Buddy?"

"I'm going to help a friend pass more easy. And I guess I'll learn how to fish."

We rode for hours, through miles and miles of countryside and little southern towns, and finally pulled over when we saw a likely looking barbecue place. Over a delicious slice of lemon icebox pie, Jake asked if we could go through Riggsville on our way back to Beaumont. When I asked him why he wanted to go to Riggsville, he replied, "I made a promise I got to keep."

"How long will it take you to keep your promise?"

"'Bout a half a hour, I believe. Not much more than that, noways."

So we headed for the Mississippi Delta. The sun had set well before we came to Riggsville, and Jake told me we could stay with Cornelius and Mabel for the night. When I reminded him that he'd told me it would only take a half hour, he said, "You in a hurry, Buddy? You got someplace you need to be?"

When we got there, Cornelius was sitting in a rocking chair on the front porch of his home. The house was small but well cared for, with new white paint on the walls and flowers growing in pots on the front porch. Cornelius didn't know who we were, and was getting a little concerned about us until Jake opened the car door and got out.

Then Cornelius stood up and came down the steps, holding his arms wide open. "Preacher Jake! Good to see you, Jake, good to see you!"

They hugged, two old friends glad to see each other alive and well. Cornelius looked at me over Jake's shoulder and asked, "Is that who I think it is?"

Jake beamed. "I told you I'd bring him, and I did." To me, he said, "Buddy, I don't rightly know that you've ever met my friend Cornelius. Cornelius Jones, this is Buddy Hinton."

Cornelius shook my hand warmly. "I've heard a lot about you."

"It's nice to meet you, Mr. Jones," I replied. "I've heard a lot about you, too."

Cornelius invited us to come sit on the porch, and we did. I sat on the porch swing, and they sat in two of the chairs, leaving one for Miss Mabel when she got home. Cornelius had been smoking a pipe, and he offered some of his tobacco to Jake. Jake pulled his pipe out of his pocket, and they fiddled with that for a while. When the smoke of their pipes was drifting lazily in the still air, Cornelius said, "Mabel will be along after she finishes up at the Parsonage. She goin' to be real glad to see you, both of you."

"How she doin'?" Jake asked.

Cornelius rocked a little before answering. "Oh, fair, I s'pose. Fair to middlin'. Her knees is hurtin', and her back, too. But she's still as mean as ever, stubborn as a mule with a toothache. Just the other day she had me out plowin' our garden in the heat of the day. Said I had to hurry if I was goin' to be ready for plantin' on Good Friday when they's a plantin' moon. I told her, 'Hell, woman, we got a month and more 'til Good Friday.' But she didn't let it go. You know she's like a damn snappin' turtle—once they get aholt of somethin', they just ain't goin' to let go."

Jake smiled; apparently this was a well-traveled path for their conversation. "Not 'til it thunders."

Cornelius repeated, "Not 'til it thunders."

They laughed at what was apparently a familiar joke between them, and Jake said, "She's a fine woman, that Mabel. You some kind of lucky."

Cornelius smiled, and agreed, "Yeah, I knows it. I knows."

We sat for a while, and they smoked. Cornelius asked, "Buddy, you finished with your schoolin'?"

Jake had something to say, but I answered first. "Yes sir, I guess I am."

"So is you a preacher now?"

"Hell, he has been for years!" Jake replied.

And before I could say anything else, Cornelius said, "All right, then." It didn't seem like he was altogether pleased with my being a preacher, but like it was something that he would just have to accept. "All right," he said again. "Mabel will be glad to hear it." Then, looking at Jake, he said, "Yes sir, it's about to thunder up in here!"

I was completely lost. I didn't know whether we were talking about the weather, the priesthood, or snapping turtles. Cornelius must have seen me struggling; I thought he was going to help, but instead he said, "She'll be here directly. I cooks for near fourteen hundred mens up in there, and I still gets home before she does, cookin' for just them two."

Jake teased, "Well, you do have some mens helping you wash up out there at the Farm."

In a few minutes, Miss Mabel drove up in that same 1967 Chevrolet Impala we'd taken to the prison, and she parked behind my Comet in the driveway. She got out of the car talking, and it was a while before she stopped.

"Preacher Jake! Oh, praise God, it's good to see you! How you feelin', Preacher?

"Tolerable well, I s'pose, still up here on the sunny side of the grass."

"How long can y'all stay?"

I thought about saying "about a half an hour," but I really didn't have anywhere else to be, and I wasn't in a hurry to get there.

"Oh, I don't rightly know," Jake answered. "We's both free men here."

Out of prison, out of seminary—we *were* free men.

Miss Mabel asked Jake about his blood pressure, how his heart was holding up, had he been dizzy, and ten or twelve other questions. Then she asked me about seminary and wanted to know if I was through. I didn't want to tell her the story about Dr. Sprague and Jake's lecture to the seminary; it would have made Jake feel guilty, even though I'd been telling him all the way from South Carolina that it wasn't his fault. I also didn't want Miss Mabel to be disappointed in me. So I just said, "Yes ma'am," and let it go at that.

"So you's a preacher now?" she asked.

I didn't know what to say, but Jake answered for me. "I come to keep that promise I made you."

Miss Mabel looked over at her man Cornelius, who was leaned back with his eyes closed, and she eased back in her rocking chair, as if an old itch was being scratched. "All right, then," she said.

She got up then, and went inside. In a minute or two, I heard her talking on the phone; it sounded like she was inviting a bunch of people to come for lunch on Saturday. There was a great deal of conversation about who was bringing various dishes.

Jake and Cornelius talked about the prison, the kitchen, and the men who worked in there with them. It had only been a week or so, but they talked about everybody anyway; Jake was checking on his flock. Cornelius told Jake that Eugene was doing fine, and they shook their heads when he talked about Eddie.

I relaxed as I swayed in the swing. I listened to the crickets and frogs singing their courting songs, to the men talking, and to Miss Mabel inviting people to come over. I hadn't had much sleep the night before; I guess I fell asleep on the porch swing. The next thing I knew, Jake was shaking my shoulder and telling me it was time to go to bed.

Cornelius and Miss Mabel's son Abraham was off at school at Tulane University in New Orleans, and they put Jake and me in his room. He had posters of basketball players on all his walls, and a picture of Martin Luther King, Jr., above the words, "I Have A Dream."

Jake went right to sleep, lying on his back, but I couldn't seem to drift off. My mind swirled with images of Dr. Sprague and the Bishop and pieces of my dream lying shattered on the flat land of the Delta. Jake had said we were free men, and I couldn't get the idea to leave me alone. I was free from responsibilities and obligations, free from deadlines and examinations, free from needing to be at any place at any time. I had also been liberated from any purpose or meaning in my life. I was free like a domesticated animal released into the wild, and just as scared.

The next morning before the sun came up, Jake woke me to tell me breakfast was on the table. He told me that Mabel and Cornelius had to leave before long, and that I'd need to hurry to have breakfast with them.

So I got up, splashed the sleep out of my eyes, and joined them at their kitchen table for breakfast.

Miss Mabel said, "Good mornin', sleepy-head. You goin' to sleep the whole day away?"

Jake and Cornelius laughed; I tried, but I couldn't make it come out right.

Jake put a cup in front of me on the table and said, "This'll help. This right here is the best coffee in the whole world, it sure is."

It was scalding hot, but I blew on it for a minute and tasted it. It was strong and black, with a flavor I couldn't identify.

"A friend of ours grinds that up special for us," Miss Mabel told me. "It's got chicory in it. You like chicory, Buddy?"

"Yes ma'am," I replied. "I do now. It's very good."

Cornelius and Jake talked about going fishing that afternoon, and Miss Mabel leaned in close to me. "Buddy, I want you to know how much I appreciate you doin' this for us. It just means the world to me, and to Cornelius, too, just means the world to us."

Before I thought about it, I replied, "I'm glad to do it, Miss Mabel." But then I thought about it and asked her, "What is it you want me to do?"

The speed with which Miss Mabel downshifted from warm, friendly appreciation to out and out fiery righteous consternation was alarming. She stood up straight and snapped, "Preacher Jake. Did you tell Buddy what he's here to do?"

Cornelius stepped in and said in a conciliatory tone, "Well now, honey, it ain't like that now."

She ignored Cornelius, her eyes searing into Jake. Then, in a voice with shards of ice in it, she asked again, "Did you tell him or not?"

"Well, no," Jake admitted. "Not just yet."

She was indignant, and she turned her ire on Cornelius. "Well, I will be switched. You let me call all them folks and invite them over to see a weddin' and you ain't even asked the preacher?"

A wedding, like a snapping turtle, not 'til it thunders, you's a preacher now, I Have A Dream, lunch on Saturday . . . after I got all the pieces lined up, I could work the puzzle. Jake watched me figure it out, and when he saw me realize what was going on, he said with contrition, "Buddy, I should've asked you already. You is the promise I made. I brung you up here to marry Cornelius and Mabel."

If a snapping turtle bit you, according to country lore, it wouldn't let go until it thundered. Miss Mabel had been waiting for a long time to marry Cornelius, and she'd never let it go, like a snapping turtle waiting for thunder. Jake had apparently promised them some time back that I would do their wedding when I became a preacher, and Cornelius had agreed to it, in the same way people will agree to do something years from now, and then be surprised by it when the day to do it finally comes. That's why they were so interested to know if I was done with my schooling. That's why they were having so many people over for lunch on Saturday. It was Miss Mabel's dream. She and Cornelius were getting married, and I was performing the ceremony.

Well of course I knew I couldn't do it. I was about to tell them that I wasn't ordained, that I couldn't marry anyone, that it wouldn't be legal, that it wouldn't be ethical. But before I got all the words lined up in my head, I saw Miss Mabel looking at me, and remembered her saying just one minute before how much it would mean to her. They'd lived together for years, long enough to have a son off in college; surely the state recognized their common-law marriage. It wasn't as if I could get into any more trouble with the church. I'd never have to worry about that again.

So, feeling uncustomarily reckless, I said, "Miss Mabel, Mr. Cornelius, I'd be honored to perform your wedding ceremony."

You'd have done the same thing.

Cornelius and Miss Mabel breathed their relief, although it was clear that Miss Mabel wasn't quite through with Cornelius yet. While they went into the back of the house to get ready to go to work, and we could hear the muffled sounds of her straightening him out, Jake said, "Thank you, Buddy."

After a while, Cornelius and Miss Mabel came back into the kitchen and started talking about the menu for the reception, which sounded like it was going to be huge. Jake and I went out to sit on the porch and watch the sun coming up.

"Well, Preacher Jake, have you ever done a wedding?" I asked.

"No, Preacher Buddy, I can't say that I have."

"Neither have I."

"No, but we's 'bout to, we sure is."

"Jake, you know I can't really do a wedding."

He was indignant. "The Lord God Almighty authorized you His own self! He called you to be a preacher, what more say-so do you need? You been up there away at school for 'most three years and you still can't marry nobody? You been wastin' your time listenin' to a lot of baloney, that's what I say. But don't let it get out, we might get in trouble with some Boss Professor."

We laughed, and I asked, "Why aren't you doing the wedding?"

He shook his head and grinned. "I can't."

"Why not?"

"Well, for one thing, I ain't been asked, and for another, I am the best man!"

We laughed about that a long time. It felt like it had been a lifetime since I'd laughed so hard.

Miss Mabel and Cornelius went off to their jobs, and Jake told me he wanted to lie down for a while. He didn't want any of us to know, but I could tell he wasn't feeling well. His spirit was the same, his joyful soul, but his body was slowing down before my eyes. I thought I ought to be upset about that, but I wasn't. It was just getting to be time for him to die; he was reconciled to that, and I was getting there.

I thought about going to see Trey, but I didn't want to have to explain the whole thing. I wondered what was going on at Becket, whether my parents knew that I was no longer in seminary, or the Bishop. I thought that maybe Scott or someone from the seminary might have tried to call me in Beaumont, or ask my parents where I was. I wondered how I would ever be able to face my mom and dad and thought about how disappointed they would be. I realized how much I had wanted to make them proud of me, but now it was too late. I knew the Bishop would find out all too soon, one way or another.

After living for such a long time with my future laid out for me, it was odd to wonder what I would be doing a week from then, or a month, or a year. I wondered how long Jake would live, and what I would do when he died. I wondered if I would ever have a job, and what it would be. I wondered what my brother Lee was doing, and my sisters, Kathleen and Kelly. They were all married by then; every year at Thanksgiving, they brought more grandchildren to our parents' house. I wondered if I would ever settle down, get married, and have children. That morning, as I sat out on the porch swing, the future was ominously hidden from me. I'd wanted to be a priest since I was in the sixth grade. Right then, with no chance of being ordained, and no replacement plans immediately clear, my life didn't look too promising.

Then I wondered how I was going to do a wedding.

When Jake woke up, he found me sitting at the kitchen table with my Prayer Book opened to The Celebration and Blessing of a Marriage. I showed it to him and read a little. "Then the Celebrant, facing the people and the persons to be married, with the woman to the right and the man to the left, addresses the congregation and says 'Dearly beloved—'"

"What's a celebrant?" Jake asked.

"That's the priest. Or, in this case, me."

"All right now. So you just gets 'em all lined up right and say the words in this book right here. Ain't nothin' to it but to do it. Surely you already had enough learnin' to do that."

"Yeah, I suppose so."

He knew I was hurting inside, and he put his hand on the back of my neck. "You ain't a preacher 'cause the Bishop puts his hands on you. He ain't the damn Wizard of Oz, is he?"

I'd shown him my G.O.E. essay on the sacrament of baptism, and we'd talked a little about sacramental theology. I smiled wistfully, skimming over the service I knew I'd never get to perform, at least not legally.

"Buddy, he said, "you's a preacher 'cause God put the words in your mouth. You got the gift. Ain't no professor or bishop can take that away from you. Hell, we'll start our own damn church, call it the Church of Buddy."

I smiled at the absurdity of it, and Jake continued, calling in an imaginary crowd in a cadence well learned and practiced in years long since gone. "Come one, come all, to the First Church of Buddy. Welcome, welcome, one and all. Everybody's welcome up in here.

"If you's a *sinner*, this is the place for you. If you's a *saint*, this is your place just the same. If you's *rich*, c'mon in. If you's *poor*, c'mon in. If you's a *Christian*, you will find a home up in here. If you *ain't*, come and make yourself comfortable amongst us. If you been touched by *God*, come and tell us 'bout it. If you *need* His touch, come up in here and feel His love through us.

"Ain't nobody ain't welcome up in here, because the First Church of Buddy is a celebration of the Love of God *Almighty*, who made every one of us, and who loves us all. This Church ain't 'bout *fear*, nor *dread*, nor *guilt*. We ain't 'bout *condemnation*, nor *judgment*, nor *punishment!* Lord, no! This Church is talkin' 'bout the love of *God*. We talkin' 'bout the *Light* that shines in our darkness. We talkin' 'bout hope, not hope in our puny efforts, but our real hope in the love and mercy of God, who loves us no matter what we do. How 'bout it, Preacher Buddy?"

I said, "Amen," remembering to use a long "A." But Jake was having too much fun to let it go.

"Brothers and sisters, please welcome our chief pastor and preacher, the Reverend Doctor Buddy Hinton. All right, all right. Preacher Buddy, give us a few words." Then he spoke to the invisible crowd. "Y'all need to listen up, 'cause we got us a Preacher here, 'bout to take the pulpit now!"

I'd never played this game before and wasn't sure how to do it. I started, "Brothers and sisters," because it seemed like a preacherly thing to say, and was surprised to hear Jake continuing to talk. He said, almost to himself, "All right now. Preacher Buddy."

I continued, "Welcome to the First Church of Jake and Buddy, where you are *always* welcome."

Jake had closed his eyes now. ("Always welcome, yes Lord.")

It was like he was helping me preach. I went on, "Please come in and make yourself comfortable."

("All right, *preach* it.")

"If those shoes are hurtin' your feet, please feel free to take 'em off."

("Take 'em off, yes sir!")

"You don't need to wear your fancy ties in the presence of the Lord."

("You don't need 'em.")

"You don't need your expensive clothes."

("No, no.")

"You don't need to pretend to be somebody you're not."

("Look out now.")

"In this church, it's a Come-As-You-Are Celebration!"

("Praise God.")

"A celebration of the love of God!"

("There it is.")

This was no longer as silly as I'd thought it was going to be, but I kept on, getting into a rhythm. "And what are we celebrating, you might ask."

("What is it, Preacher?")

"In this dark and evil world, what have we got to celebrate?"

("What is they to celebrate?")

"Do you want to know?"

("Tell us, Preacher!")

"In the darkness, we celebrate that the Light of God still shines."

("Still shines!")

"In the face of evil, we celebrate that the Love of God is all around us."

("All around us!")

"We don't want anything from you!"

("Not a thing!")

"We make no claim on your soul."

("No, Lord, no.")

"All we ask is that you come and help us celebrate the love of God!"

("Help us celebrate!")

"We're not looking for your money!"

"Well, hold on there, Preacher Buddy. Don't never turn no money away."

Jake and I laughed until we cried. It was good for our souls.

26

Flyin' Over the Water

The wedding was scheduled for noon on Saturday. I told them I thought it would take about a half an hour.

On Thursday, Cornelius took off a little early from work, and took Jake and me fishing on a small lake a couple of miles away, on some land owned by Jack Crofton, an administrator at the prison. We sat on the bank and fished for an hour, even though there was a little aluminum boat under a tree. The fish didn't seem interested in our worms or crickets, so we kept our lines in the water and watched the clouds crawl across the spring sky. Jake leaned against a tree, put his hat down over his eyes, and fell asleep.

"You think we could use that boat?" I asked Cornelius.

"Mr. Crofton said I could," he answered, "but I never have."

We fished a little more, and I suggested, "I think we might catch more fish from the boat."

"That's what Mr. Crofton said, too."

Another minute dragged by, and I couldn't stand it anymore. "So do you want to use the boat?"

Cornelius looked at me like I was bothering him. "If I wanted to use that boat, I'd be in the damn thing."

I couldn't tell if he was angry or just playing with me, so I dropped the whole thing. We watched the corks float for a few minutes, and then he explained, "I ain't in the boat 'cause I ain't never learnt how to swim. I ain't about to get out there and sink."

I said, "That boat's not going to sink."

He grinned. "It ain't goin' to sink with me in it, that's for damn sure. I ain't gettin' in no damn boat."

"It looks like a pretty strong boat."

"I don't know nothin' 'bout no boats. I ain't never been in one."

"You've never been in a boat?"

"Hell, no. That's what I just said, ain't it?"

"Why not?"

"I done told you I can't swim."

"That water's not even over your head."

"Not when I'm sittin' here under this tree."

"No, I mean, if you were out in that boat, and it sank, you could just stand up. You wouldn't have to swim."

"Well, I already don't have to swim, if I just keep right on sittin' here."

I looked at him to make sure; he was definitely toying with me now. I looked at the lake, stood up, walked over to the boat, untied the rope, and turned the boat over. I pushed the nose out into the water a little, and then I came back to where Cornelius was sitting and took my line out of the water.

"Mr. Cornelius, would you stand up for a minute?"

"Why you want me to stand up?"

"I just want to show you something."

"What?"

"Would you just stand up?"

"What you goin' to show me?"

"That you don't have to swim if the boat sank."

"Why do I got to stand up for that?"

By this time we'd made so much noise that Jake was awake, watching us. He said, "You best just stand up, Cornelius. He ain't givin' in."

"He's 'bout as stubborn as you is, Preacher."

"I inherited it from him," I said.

Cornelius stood, and I took my cane pole and measured him against it. I marked the top of his head on the pole between my finger and thumb, and declared, "There. You're about that tall." I took a piece of string out of his fishing box and tied it around the pole at that spot. "If the water's no deeper than that, you don't have to swim, all right?"

"All right."

There wasn't a paddle, so I found a stick I could pole with in the shallow parts of the lake, got in the boat, and pushed off. I wasn't ten feet out from the bank before my feet started getting wet.

I made my way back, where both of the men were laughing at me with great energy. I pulled the boat out of the water, and Cornelius pointed out, "They ain't no plug in the back there."

The boat had a hole to drain water, and the plug was missing. "Why didn't you tell me?" I asked.

"I told you I didn't know nothin' 'bout no boats."

"You knew the plug was missing."

"Mr. Crofton said I'd have to stick somethin' up in there if I wanted to use it."

"Well, you could've told me that."

"Yeah, but I figured with you knowin' all 'bout boats and how deep lakes is and all, you'd know that your own self."

I dumped the water out of the boat and found another stick about the right size for a plug. I wrapped my bandanna around one end of it and jammed it in the hole as far as I could. I pushed off again, and looked back to see how the plug was doing. The water was leaking in slowly, but it looked like it would hold. When I got about ten feet out again, I put the cane pole down into the water to show that it was only about four feet deep.

Cornelius wasn't satisfied. "Go on out further."

So I went out another twenty feet. Still only about five feet.

But it still wasn't enough.

"Go on out."

I went into the middle of the lake. I stuck the cane pole down into the water and didn't find the bottom.

Chagrined, I started paddling with my stick, and when I was pulling the boat up onto the land, Cornelius said to me, "All right now!" Then he laughed and said to Jake, "Tellin' me that water ain't deep, and I wouldn't have to swim if the boat sank."

But Jake surprised Cornelius and me. "It does look restful out there on that boat."

"You want to come out in the boat?" I asked.

"Well, I don't know about that just now. I ain't never sat in no boat."

"Can you swim?"

"Why the hell would I know how to swim?"

I was surprised by the question. I figured everybody knew how to swim, that everybody took swimming lessons when they were kids. Then I thought about when I'd learned to swim, at the public pool in Vicksburg. In the early sixties, when I was taking swimming lessons, it was the all-white public pool. It seems incredibly dim-witted now, when I see it written down, but I don't think it had ever registered in me that "all-white" and "public" didn't make much sense together.

I remembered asking Harry at camp why the black campers didn't usually swim. Where would they have learned? And for the first time, I started to understand a little about being black. Not much, but I got a glimpse.

"I'm sorry," I said. "I really am."

"What're you sorry for?"

"I guess I'm a fool, thinking everybody's just like me. I just assumed everybody would know how to swim. All my life, I've had opportunities that y'all have never been allowed to have. I'm sorry for assuming, and I'm sorry that you never had the chance to learn to swim. Or get a good education. Or all of these other things I've taken for granted my whole life."

Jake was soothing. "Thank you, Buddy. But ain't none of that your fault. It ain't a mess you made, and it ain't your mess to clean up, you hear me?"

"Yes sir."

"Now you goin' to take me out in this boat, or not?"

Cornelius, silent through my awakening, warned, "Whoa, hold up here. Now Jake, you know this ain't a good idea. I don't think you ought to be doin' that. You can't swim. What if that boat tumps over?

What you goin' to do then? And you in poor health, you got to be careful 'bout that, too."

Jake smiled. "What you want me to do, Cornelius, wait 'til I get better? You think Buddy don't know how to keep the boat in the shallow water? It ain't 'bout swimmin', Cornelius, it's 'bout trustin' my Buddy." Then he turned to me and said, "All right, let's go."

I dumped all the water out of the boat and made sure my makeshift plug was still in there tightly. I left the front of the boat securely stuck in the mud and pushed the back end out a little into the water. "All right now, Jake," I said, "just step right here, and sit down on that front seat right there."

He was unsteady, but he got in and sat down. He put a hand on each side of the boat and asked, "Can I hold on like this?"

I told him he could, and stepped into the water. I pushed the boat around to get in the back, and the front went out into the water. Jake sat hunched over and still, facing me and holding on with all his might. Bless his heart, he was scared to death, but he was smiling the whole time. I got in as smoothly as I could, and pushed off with the pole. After a minute or two, Jake eased his grip on the sides of the boat and sat up straight. Then he grinned and let out a whoop.

"How you doin', Jake?" Cornelius yelled.

"All right, all right. I don't like it when the boat wobbles, though. Cornelius, it's like bein' a fish, or a bird, just flyin' over the water!" More quietly, he said to me, "It's like I done left my ol' body back there on the land."

Tears were running down my face. He was full of joy at this new experience, laughing like a child. What else had this old man never done? Had he ever ridden a ride at the fair? Would he like Chinese food, if I could convince him it wasn't cats and dogs? Would he enjoy seeing himself on videotape? There were so many things I'd taken for granted that he would never get to do.

"Jake, after the wedding, let's go to New Orleans."

"Well, all right, but you best get a new plug 'fore we do."

"What?"

"I said you best put a new plug in the back of this boat first."

"No, I mean, let's take the car to New Orleans."

"What for?"

"Just so you can see it."

"I don't have to see it, Buddy. They ain't nothin' in New Orleans for me. 'Sides, you seen it for me, and told me 'bout it."

"But don't you want to see it for yourself?"

"No, I . . . no." He looked thoughtful for a moment. "I ain't sure I got all that long, Buddy. It's gettin' harder to get out of bed every mornin', sure is. After the weddin', we best just go on down into my woods to the Restin' Place. We best get ready."

"But there's so much to see and do."

"Then you best see it and do it for me. You can tell me 'bout it later, all right, Buddy?"

I didn't say anything, and Jake repeated, "All right?"

My throat had tightened, and I still couldn't speak. So I nodded.

"Good," Jake said. "Now let's catch us some of them deep-water fish."

The fish weren't biting any better from the boat than they had from the land. So we drifted around the lake a while, "just drowndin' worms," Jake called it. At one point, I took my hook out of the water and leaned back to enjoy being out on the lake without having to watch the red and white bobber floating undisturbed. Jake asked me what I was doing, and I told him we weren't catching anything anyway. He said, "You ain't goin' to catch nothin' leavin' your bait in the boat, that's for sure."

Right before dark, the fish decided they couldn't resist us any longer. Cornelius and I both caught several passable bream—him on shore, and me still in the boat with Jake, who actually caught a nice-sized catfish.

By the time we were ready to leave, we had a respectable stringer of fish. Cornelius philosophized, "Best thing 'bout fishin' is that you can waste the whole afternoon and still have somethin' to show for it."

We took the fish back to the house, and about the time we were through cleaning them, Miss Mabel got home. She and Cornelius battered them in corn meal and cooked them, and we had fried fish for supper.

Jake took a bite of the catfish and told Miss Mabel, "That there's a deep-water catfish, that's why it tastes so good."

He winked at me as Cornelius grumbled.

We went back to Mr. Crofton's lake the next day, and Cornelius consented to go out in the boat—but only for a few minutes. Just as the sun was setting, we all caught some fish, whether we were on the land or in the boat, so I guess it didn't really matter after all. But it was an honor to show these two men a new experience.

Saturday morning came all too soon. Miss Mabel was up early, cleaning, polishing, arranging, and rearranging. When I got up, she pointed toward a spot under the trees in the backyard and told me I could set up the tables and chairs they'd borrowed from their church. The guests started arriving around 11:30, some of them bringing dishes that Miss Mabel put in the kitchen. Just before noon, the Swayzes came. Mrs. Swayze gave me a big hug, and so did Trey and Ann, even though she looked about ten months pregnant. The Reverend seemed distinctly uncomfortable with the whole thing, and shook my hand formally.

"So you're out of school now," he said, "and a minister."

"Yes sir, I guess I am."

And I guess I was. Right then, I was the chief pastor of the First Church of Jake and Buddy.

A little after noon, Jake called the congregation to gather in the backyard. He was dressed in an old blue suit that belonged to Cornelius, with the legs and sleeves rolled in a little.

He took on some of his tent preacher persona as he greeted the congregation. "Welcome, one and all. I am Jake Jefferson, the best man, and on the behalf of Cornelius and Mabel and they whole family, I welcome you all. I don't know most of y'all, and they's some of you that don't know nobody here but theyselves. We's goin' to have a reception here after the weddin' so y'all can all get to know ever'body. But first we is goin' to have us a weddin'!"

The crowd murmured their appreciation. But Jake couldn't resist a little joke: "Y'all listen for the thunder!"

All of Cornelius's friends laughed at that; the bride's side did not seem amused. Then Jake introduced me, saying, "The celebrant for the weddin' is Brother Buddy Hinton, a friend of ours."

He nodded to me, and I stepped in front of the crowd. I wondered if they were surprised that a young white man was doing the wedding, but I knew I'd have to leave that for Cornelius and Miss Mabel to explain.

The happy couple was standing on the back porch steps with their attendants, waiting for me to give them the signal. I nodded, and they began to walk through the crowd, which parted for them. Their sons, Benjamin and Abraham, came first, followed by Jake as best man. Then came Benjamin's wife Rosalee, Miss Mabel's sister Emma, and Mary Claire Swayze, the matron of honor. They all lined up just like we'd practiced the night before, and we were ready to start.

I had decided to use the wedding service in the Prayer Book and alter it here and there as needed. "Dearly beloved," I began, "we have come together in the presence of God to witness and bless the joining together of this man and this woman in Holy Matrimony."

As I looked at the bride and groom before me, it felt appropriate and right. He was dressed in a brand new blue and white seersucker suit, and he looked as proud as a man can be. She wore a beautiful white dress and a white hat with a little veil over her eyes. They were already married, legally as well as spiritually. Today was just a way to celebrate God's blessings.

But I knew there was more to my sense of rightness than their wardrobe or their relationship. It was right for *me* to be there, right for me to be a minister. As I read the prayers I'd practiced, I made a promise, to myself and my God, that I would find some way to do what I knew I was called to do.

At the appropriate time, I nodded to the best man, who read the Scripture passage from the Gospel of John from his King James Bible.

> And the third day there was a marriage in Cana of Galilee; and the mother of Jesus was there:
> And both Jesus was called, and his disciples, to the marriage.

> And when they wanted wine, the mother of Jesus saith unto him, They have no wine.
> Jesus saith unto her, Woman, what have I to do with thee? mine hour is not yet come.
> His mother saith unto the servants, Whatsoever he saith unto you, do it.
> And there were set there six waterpots of stone, after the manner of the purifying of the Jews, containing two or three firkins apiece.
> Jesus saith unto them, Fill the waterpots with water. And they filled them up to the brim.
> And he saith unto them, Draw out now, and bear unto the governor of the feast. And they bare it.
> When the ruler of the feast had tasted the water that was made wine, and knew not whence it was: (but the servants which drew the water knew;) the governor of the feast called the bridegroom,
> And saith unto him, Every man at the beginning doth set forth good wine; and when men have well drunk, then that which is worse: but thou hast kept the good wine until now.
> This beginning of miracles did Jesus in Cana of Galilee, and manifested forth his glory; and his disciples believed on him.

The next thing in the Prayer Book was the Homily, a short sermon. I could tell the people were starting to get hot and hungry, so I knew I wouldn't have to say much.

"Now it's time for a little sermon," I announced. "I think Miss Mabel and Mr. Cornelius invited me to do this wedding because they figured I'd keep it short." There was a little nervous laughter, and I looked out at the congregation and saw my dear friend Trey, expecting me to say something wonderful. He was standing next to his father, who expected me to say something scandalous. I was tempted to say something about Jesus turning the water into wine for the Reverend's benefit, but I saw Jake standing off to my left, and I let it go.

The homily went something like this: "Brothers and sisters in Christ, we're here to give thanks for the love of these two people, whom we all love and know to be generous, kind, godly people. It is nothing less than the love of God that Cornelius and Mabel share, the same love that created us, that brings us together today, and will carry us home when we . . ."

I couldn't say "die," not with Jake looking at me, only three feet away. I continued, ". . . when we pass from this life to the next."

I looked at Jake, who nodded his encouragement. "We come together to give thanks for their life together, for the gifts of their sons Benjamin and Abraham, for their family and friends, and, unless I am very much mistaken, to enjoy a great deal of very fine food!"

They all laughed then, even Reverend Swayze.

"Nobody came here today to hear me preach, so I won't. It will be enough, maybe more than enough, to remember that Jesus went to a wedding, and enjoyed the celebration of the love of His Father with His family and friends. We can do nothing better in this life than to celebrate the love of God.

"So I ask you to join in the celebration and blessing of a wedding, and to join in as the celebration continues, in the fine lunch waiting for us, and live in celebration throughout our lives and beyond."

Jake said, "Amen," with a long "A." Most everybody else did, too. Mrs. Swayze wiped the tears from her eyes, and Sister Emma blew her nose. Jake nodded, and we were ready to proceed.

The couple repeated their vows after me, and we asked God to bless the ring that Miss Mabel's mother had worn. It didn't fit her, but it was her wedding ring anyway, and God blessed it. Cornelius put it on her finger as far as it would go, and it was far enough.

At the end of the wedding, I said, "Mr. Jones, you may kiss your bride."

He clearly didn't know that was part of it, and was genuinely embarrassed to kiss her with all those people watching. "Do I have to?" he whispered to me.

I was about to tell him that he didn't have to, that it was just tradition, but before I could, Miss Mabel slapped him on his shoulder, "Yes, you have to!"

The congregation laughed, and he kissed her, right there in front of God and everybody. I laid my Prayer Book on the ground and started the applause.

Lunch was even more delicious than I thought it would be. We had ham, fried chicken, pork chops in gravy, roast beef, barbecued pork and chicken quarters; black-eyed peas, snap beans, corn on the cob, fried corn, sweet potato pie, coleslaw, mashed potatoes, rice and gravy, mustard greens, collard greens; rolls, biscuits, cornbread, homemade bread; pies, cakes, cookies, watermelon, and homemade ice cream. I ate until I was almost sick, and then I walked around a little and went back for more.

I talked with Trey and Ann for a long time. Their baby was due the next week, and they wanted to know if I would do the baptism. I asked Trey what his father would think about that, and he told me that was his father's problem, and that his mother was all for it. I told them the baptism wouldn't take place until the baby was three or four months old, and that we'd have to see.

"I thought you'd still be in school," Trey said. "Are you out early?"

"Yeah. They let me out early for good behavior."

"So where's your first church going to be?"

"Ah, we're not sure yet."

"Buddy, is everything okay?"

I wanted to tell him. He'd been a close and trusted friend for a long time, and he deserved to know the truth. But it was the wrong time, the wrong place. So I lied.

"Yeah, sure. Everything's fine. So, what are y'all going to name the kid?"

After a while, it was time for the bride and groom to leave. While he was waiting for Miss Mabel to change clothes, Cornelius took me aside.

"Buddy, I can't thank you enough for doin' this for us."

"You're very welcome."

"And I wanted to give you a little something."

I assumed he was talking about money, so I replied, "Oh, no, Mr. Cornelius. You don't need to do that. You take it and spend it on your honeymoon."

"What?" he said.

"You don't need to give me any money."

"I ain't goin' to."

"Oh. Well, what did you want to give me?"

Gesturing toward Jake to come with us, he took me out behind their little garden shed and pointed to a cardboard box. In the box were a mama dog and three puppies. The mama looked up at us and wagged her tail enthusiastically. She seemed to be a hound of some sort.

"That mama dog is Dulsey," Jake told me. Dulsey wagged her tail at the mention of her name. "She's 'bout as fine a coon-huntin' dog as you're likely to find anywheres in the state of Miss'ippi." You could see the pride in Cornelius's face. "All the guards out at Parchman Farm want one of Dulsey's puppies. They was real excited she was goin' to have this litter."

"So that's what me and Mabel want to give you for doin' our weddin'," Cornelius said. "One of Dulsey's puppies. They just been weaned this week. We's givin' you the pick of the litter."

I'd always wanted a dog, and Cornelius was obviously proud of this gift. So, even though it didn't seem like the most convenient time in my life to take responsibility for a puppy, I said, "Thank you, Mr. Cornelius. Thank you very much."

"Which one you goin' to take?" he asked.

I didn't know how to choose. They were all females, but one was a little smaller than the other two. The bigger pups were whining, but the small one was quiet. Jake reached in and picked her out, put her in my arms, and announced, "This here's your dog, right here."

"What you goin' to name her?" Cornelius asked.

This was all happening too fast for my mind to keep up. "I don't know," I said.

But Jake knew. "Jabbok."

Cornelius and I said, at the same time, "Jabbok?"

Jake smiled. "That's the dog's name. That's all they is to that."

And so it was.

27

Just Mutts

A few minutes later, we all gathered to throw rice on the newly married couple as they got into Mabel's '67 Chevy Impala. They were headed to Memphis for their honeymoon; they had a room at the Peabody Hotel. They both had to be back at work Tuesday morning, but they planned to enjoy their short trip.

Darkness began to fall before all the guests were gone. Jake had gone in to take a nap, and I helped Mrs. Swayze and a few of the women clean up.

I had no trouble getting to sleep that night.

Early the next morning, Jake and I put the puppy in the back of the Comet and headed south, down Highway 61. Around Leland, I asked Jake where he'd gotten the name "Jabbok." The word was vaguely familiar, but I couldn't quite place it.

"I thought you was learnin' 'bout the Book up there," Jake said.

I thought about my concordance, tucked away in a box in the trunk, and promised myself I'd look up "Jabbok." I figured I needed to know how my dog got her name.

Wanting to draw the subject away from my lack of biblical knowledge, I grumbled, "Like I really need a damn dog to take care of."

Jake was pacifying. "She's goin' to be a good dog. Her mama's a fine hound, best coon dog in the Delta, Cornelius says."

"Jake, she's just a mutt."

"Well hell, Buddy, we's all just mutts. That's why we got to take each other in."

The puppy was asleep in her cardboard box on the back seat. She really was a cute dog.

We drove down the Delta, mile after flat mile, past Arcola, Hollandale, Percy, Panther Burn, Nitta Yuma, Anguilla, and Rolling Fork, each little town looking about the same as the one before it. Finally, about mid-morning, we saw the hills. It was as if the Creator had used a huge rolling pin to flatten out the Delta, pushing all the hills down to Vicksburg in a pile. We drove through Vicksburg, past the National Military Park, and a few miles south to Beaumont.

I parked the Comet behind Mr. Howell's fish house, picked up the puppy, and followed Jake inside. Mr. Howell was still there, and was delighted to see Jake. They told a few stories on each other, and Jake asked him if he was still buying fish. Mr. Howell said he'd be glad to buy anything Jake could catch. I asked him if I could leave my car there behind the fish house for a few days. He looked at me like he thought that was more than a little strange, but he said he didn't mind.

My plan was that I'd get Jake all set up in his hut before I went to see my mom and dad. It had been over seven years since he'd been to his home by the creek, and almost three since I had. I figured we had several days of work to get it livable again. And, to be honest, I wasn't in any hurry to face my parents and have to explain the circumstances of my return to Beaumont. I would be grateful to leave the Comet behind Mr. Howell's fish house and keep it hidden.

I took Jake to a bait shop by the river, and he bought some supplies: a spool of fishing line, hooks, weights, and porcupine quill floats. I wanted to buy some cane poles and worms, but Jake assured me he knew where we could cut some canes and dig up some worms for free. He also bought three pounds of bologna, a wedge of yellow cheese, a big bottle of vegetable oil, a roll of nylon cord, cans of Vienna sausages and sardines, a box of crackers, a five-pound can of coffee, a box of shotgun shells, and some ice in a Styrofoam ice chest. I bought a large bag of Purina Puppy Chow.

I'd left Jabbok tied to a tree out by the car; by the time we got back, she'd nearly chewed through the rope. We drove back to Mr. Howell's fish house, where I stashed the car, and then I took Jake down into his woods.

He wanted to carry all our supplies, but I told him I'd carry just a few things and take him down to his hut. I could come back later for the rest of the stuff. I thought I'd have all I could handle just getting him and the puppy down the steep hills to his fishing place, where the creek was wide. I let Jabbok off the rope leash she'd nearly chewed through, and she followed happily, chasing after noises and splashing in the creek, but never getting out of our sight.

I had to keep telling Jake to slow down, to stop and rest. He was eager to get there, to get back to the Resting Place. It took us almost an hour, but we got there in one piece. It was a timeless place, nearly the same as it was that long-ago Halloween night when I was challenged to kick over one of the tombstones.

The place had not changed at all; it was me that had changed.

Jake checked the graves first, before anything else. They were undisturbed under the huge sweet gum, and he knelt there for several minutes, as still as one of the gravestones. Then he stood, slowly, painfully, and turned to face me with a big smile. "All right, Buddy, let's go to the house."

The hut had not fared so well. One of the main trees in the circle that formed the wall had died and fallen out away from it, tearing away the Quaker State sign. A sapling grew right in front of the fireplace.

"Well. All right," Jake said. "I s'pose we needed to make it a little bigger, anyways, since you and me is both goin' to be stayin' in there." He went into what was left of the hut and brought out an ax and a hand saw. He must've had them hidden in there somewhere; I hadn't seen them when I checked on the hut earlier.

"Buddy, see can you get some us firewood, please. Let's see if the fireplace will still draw the smoke out. If it don't, we'll have to build another'n, and might as well just build a new hut."

I broke some limbs off the fallen tree, and Jake started a fire. The smoke went up the chimney just fine.

Jake grinned. "All right now. Let's see can you use a saw. We need to get that fallen tree out of here. If you can saw it up in big chunks, we can saw the rest of it and split it up later. And we's goin' to need 'bout four poles tall as me. You can cut 'em out of a pine tree. That'll be straight wood, good for poles. They won't last as long as these cypress poles, but they ain't no cypress right around here, and we ain't goin' to be here long as all that, noways."

The saw was dull, but the wood of the fallen tree was easily cut, and the pine was soft. With a little sweat, a handful of blisters, and a stream of suggestions and advice from Jake, in less than two hours the dead tree was out of the way and we had four pine poles. Then he said, "I ain't got no shovel, so you is goin' to have to dig the holes out with that ax."

"How deep?"

"'Bout a foot or so."

"Tell me where you want them."

He marked the spots, measuring in his head. I dug the holes and set the poles down in them. "All right," he said approvingly. "Now you best get on up to your car and get all them supplies. I'll be workin' on the hut."

"Jake, I don't want you to do any heavy work, you understand?"

"Yes sir, Boss Buddy."

"I mean it."

"I know it, Buddy, and I 'preciate it. I ain't goin' to do nothin' you wouldn't let me do if you was here, I sure ain't. Now go on and go so you can help me when you get back. I mean to sleep in this hut tonight."

I told Jabbok to stay, and she wagged her tail merrily and came right after me. Jake told her she was mule-headed from birth, just like him and me. I had to laugh.

I got the rest of our supplies in one trip, slinging the fishing supplies in a plastic sack over my shoulder and carrying the ice chest in my hands. By the time I got back to the hut, Jake had packed the dirt around the poles and dragged the Quaker State sign over to form one of the walls, tying it to two of the poles with nylon cord.

"They's some big cane right over that ridge, or used to be," he said. "If you take the hand saw and cut me some of it, I can start workin' on these other two walls."

So Jabbok and I went and found the cane, and I cut about twenty stalks of it. I wrapped them together with Jabbok's leash and dragged them back to the hut.

Jake nodded at our success. "All right, then. Two or three more bundles like that and we'll be in business."

"How do we get some water to drink?" I wondered.

Jake smiled. "Get that blue bucket out of the hut, and take it down to the creek."

"We're going to drink water from the creek?"

"Well 'course we are. But first I'm goin' to boil it."

I took the blue bucket and brought it back full of water. Then I went to cut another batch of cane poles. Jabbok was tired of construction and had fallen asleep next to the fire.

When I got back, the blue bucket was still sitting where I'd left it. "Didn't you want me to get this water?" I asked.

"Yep, that was step one."

"What's step two?"

"Lettin' all the dirt and stuff settle to the bottom. Then I'll scoop out some from the top, careful so's I don't stir it all up, and put it in the pot to boil. Then it'll boil a while, then I'll let it cool, and put it in the white bucket. Then we can drink it."

"It's hard work just getting a drink of water down here."

"Yep. But it sure is good water when you worked at it that long, it sure is."

I went to get more cane, and brought it back. The second wall was starting to take shape. Jake told me to sit with him for a while, and he showed me how to use the top part of the cane, thinner and more pliable, to weave between the thicker bottom parts. With both of us working together, we finished that wall in short order. Jake took the water out of the pot and put it in the white bucket, and we started on the last wall. When we'd finished that one, the water was cool enough to drink. He was right; it tasted wonderful.

We tied the walls together with nylon cord and started working on the roof. When we were done, the new wing was finished. We celebrated with Vienna sausages and cool water. Jabbok enjoyed both, and so did Jake and I.

"Now, the new wing there is your room," Jake said. "I'll sleep in the old part, and we still got to fix the roof there."

I thought he would cut the sapling in front of the fireplace down, but he left it. "We can hang pots and whatnot on it, and it'll help hold up the roof." I tried to talk him out of it, telling him it was going to be in the way, but he disagreed. "It's the next crop of trees. One tree dies, and another comes in its place."

So we left it. We made a new roof out of cane, using the sapling as one of the supports. Jake told me we'd need to get some garbage bags next time we went up the hill if we wanted it to be waterproof.

That reminded me that I'd forgotten the Puppy Chow, and I went back up the hill to get it out of the car. Jabbok followed me, glad to be running around again. When I got there, Mr. Howell came out of the fish house; it was closing time.

"Hi, Mr. Howell," I said.

"Hey, Buddy. Listen, uh, is Jake all right? He don't look so good."

"Well, no. The doctor's told him he's pretty sick. His heart's bad, his liver's failing; there's nothing they can do, it's just a matter of time. He's come back here to die."

"Aw, dadgum it, I hate to hear it. Jake's a good man. I ain't sure why he robbed that bank, or why he done time at the Parchman Farm before that, but I know he's a good man. Why's he want to come back here?"

I told him about Jake's father and son in the graveyard down there, and briefly about why he'd gone to prison both times. He'd never heard any of it. "Well, I'll be durned," he exclaimed. "Listen, Buddy, if you fellas need anything, just let me know, all right?"

"Well, actually, could I get some garbage bags from you?"

"I don't sell no garbage bags. You'd have to go down to the—"

"Excuse me, Mr. Howell. I can't go to the store. I don't want to leave Jake down there alone just now. If you had a few garbage bags, maybe I could buy them from you."

So Mr. Howell sold me an almost-new roll of black garbage bags for five dollars. He told me they hadn't really cost him that much, but that the cash register was already closed and the deposit made up, so he couldn't give me any change. He said he didn't want me to think he was cheating me, but I told him I was glad to pay five bucks for the bags.

I assured him that it was okay, and went to get a box out of the trunk of the Comet. I'd bought two inflatable camping mattresses at the Wal-Mart in Clarksdale when we'd stopped for Jake to use the bathroom. I put the roll of garbage bags in the Wal-Mart bag with the mattresses and set off again down into the woods, with the bag of Puppy Chow over my shoulder, the Wal-Mart bag in the other hand, and Jabbok nipping at my heels.

Jake got me one of those lumpy bowls that had held my stew on Halloween when I was a kid, and I put some Puppy Chow in it. Jabbok wagged her little tail so hard I thought it was going to fly off. She ate the whole bowl, and stood by it waiting for a second helping. I gave her a little more, and she burped.

"She's goin' to fit in real good around here, she sure is," Jake observed.

We put black garbage bags over the entire roof, tying them down with the nylon cord. We finished just as the sun was setting, just in time. I looked at Jake, thinking he'd be proud of our accomplishment, but what I saw was an old man who'd worked too hard for too long.

"Jake, why don't you take a little nap?" I suggested. "Jabbok and I will go up and get your stuff from the car."

"No, they ain't no need to do that. I don't need none of that stuff, not really. I do believe I'll lay down just a little, though."

"Well, hold on a minute, I got something for you."

I took an inflatable camping mattress out of the Wal-Mart bag and showed it to him. I was ready for him to argue with me, but he just grinned. "Good. I was afraid I'd got spoilt sleepin' on a bed all that time. I ain't been lookin' forward to sleepin' on the ground again, I sure ain't."

I blew up his mattress and put it in the old part of the hut. He went in and lay down on it, and, judging by the time it took him to start snoring, went right to sleep.

I put a little more wood on the fire, just enough to keep it going, and walked over to the fallen sweet gum tree. Almost twenty years after it had been blown over, it was still strong and healthy. I sat in that same spot where Jake and I had sat so many times, and whistled for a while. It was good to be home, at the Resting Place.

28

The Resting Place

Jake slept for a couple of hours. When he got up, we made a supper of bologna, cheese, and some more of the best water I'd ever had. Once he went back to sleep, he slept through the night, snoring steadily. Jabbok and I climbed back up the hill before it got too dark, and got both of Jake's boxes out of the trunk. I put them in there with him and watched him sleeping for a minute. I thought about unpacking his boxes for him, but decided it would make too much noise. It would give him something to do the next day, and besides, it was his stuff, and I didn't feel right about going through it. I thought about going to get my stuff, too, but I figured it could wait until morning.

So I inflated my mattress and lay down. Jabbok snuggled up next to my leg and fell asleep. The last thing I remember is thinking how silly it was to be going to sleep before eight o'clock.

I woke up to the smell of coffee brewing, and another smell I couldn't place. The sun wasn't quite up, but Jake already had a fire going outside, with a coffee pot sitting in the coals next to the old black cast-iron skillet in which he was frying bologna. Jabbok was tugging at his pants leg, which she was delighted to release when she saw me up and about. When she wagged her tail, it moved her whole back end.

"Good morning," I said.

"Mornin', Buddy. How'd you sleep?"

"Fine, thanks. How'd you sleep?"

"Like a baby in his mama's arms. It's good to be back here, Buddy, it sure is; thank you for bringin' me."

"I'm glad to do it."

"I see you took some time to grease up my ol' fryin' pan, and I thank you for that, too. It worried me sometimes when I was up at the Parchman Farm, this ol' skillet rustin' away down here in the woods, just seemed wasteful, sure did. They's worth they weight in gold, but they take some lookin' after, too."

I didn't really know anything about skillets or cast iron, but I nodded to keep the conversation going.

Jake grinned and said, "Yes sir, a good skillet is like a good woman: worth they weight in gold, but they take some lookin' after, sure do."

I didn't know whether to nod or smile or try to enter into the comparison of two things I knew nothing about, so I was grateful when he changed the subject.

"You need to go see your mama and them, Buddy."

"I will."

"All right, then."

"But not today."

He seemed relieved, and to me that was confirmation that I needed to stay with him. "Well, whenever you needs to go, you just go, all right? I am goin' to be fine now, now I'm back here." He looked at me and smiled.

I smiled, too. "Yes sir, you're going to be fine."

He poured me some coffee in a lumpy clay cup and said that breakfast was almost ready. The coffee was hot and strong. Then he asked, "You 'bout ready to fish?"

"Yes sir, whenever you are."

We ate the fried bologna out of the frying pan and gave a little to Jabbok. Then Jake said, "All right now. You go and cut us six little cane poles, a little thicker than your thumb. If they's any that's yellow or dead, they'd be best. I'll stay here and clean up after breakfast."

I laughed and joked that there wasn't much to clean up. But he was serious when he said, "This skillet's 'bout as old as I am, and in a lot better shape. A good skillet's somethin' you got to take some care after—you remember that."

I went and cut the canes, and Jake got out the fishing tackle. We put the line on the poles and rigged them up with quills, weights, and hooks. Jake pointed to an old hickory tree. "Now you go on over there and push them leaves back with your foot. Them worms'll be right up under them leaves waitin' for you."

It sounded improbable to me, but I knew better than to question him. I pushed back the leaves, and four or five big nightcrawler worms started trying to wriggle their way back into the dirt. I picked them up and showed them to Jake. He pointed toward a tin can, and I put the worms in it.

"Now you just go get us some more worms," he directed. "They's only there in the early mornin', so you best hurry. Them fishes been waitin' a long time for me to get back up in here!"

I filled the tin can full of earthworms, some of them five inches long. Jake put a little dark, rich dirt on top of them, and we got the poles, his tackle box, and a five-gallon pickle bucket, and walked down to the creek.

The fishing place was the same as it had always been. It was no more than twenty feet wide, but I couldn't tell how deep it was. I asked Jake, and he said, "I don't rightly know how deep it is right there. But the biggest fish are down in there, 'specially when it gets hot."

We both fished three poles, sticking the ends in the mud. At first, we caught a little catfish every time we put a hook in the water, all of them too small to keep. Jake told me that Mr. Howell wouldn't buy a catfish much under a cubit long, and he looked at me to see if I knew what a cubit was.

I pointed to my elbow and then to the place where my thumb was attached to my hand. Jake nodded, glad to see I'd learned something about the Bible.

"All right, then."

After a while, after taking twenty or thirty little catfish off the hooks and tossing them back in, Jake had had enough. "Buddy, look here. We's catchin' these same little catfish over and over. Go back up to the hut, would you please, and get us that blue bucket. We need to get them out of here if we's ever goin' to catch they mamas and daddies."

So Jabbok and I went to get the blue bucket and brought it to where Jake was fishing. He was taking a small catfish off his hook when we walked up. He tossed it in the blue bucket and said, "Put us some water in there, all right?"

Once we caught about twenty small catfish and put them in the blue bucket, we stopped getting so many bites. Jake leaned back against a tree and said, "Tell me if I get a bite, now. I'm just goin' to rest these old eyes a minute."

I sat and watched the quills, all of them still. I started to whistle without realizing it, and wondered what the tune was. Then one of Jake's quills bobbed up and down, and finally went down to stay. "Jake, wake up!" I shouted. "You got a fish!"

He woke up with a start and grumbled, "I ain't asleep! Just restin' my eyes, is all." It took him a couple of seconds to figure out which of the three poles in front of him had a bite. Then he pulled up a big catfish, definitely longer than a cubit. "All right, now! That's what we been lookin' for, right here. This here is them little fishes' daddy, yes sir, this is they daddy."

I put some water in the pickle bucket, and he put the big fish in it. He beamed. "That's what we been waitin' for. Now let's see can we catch they granddaddy."

We fished most of the morning, and caught two more almost as big as that one. Around 10:30 or 11:00, he declared it a successful day of fishing. Jabbok had given up on us about an hour before that and was waiting for us when we got back to the hut.

"What you goin' to do with them little fishes in that blue bucket?" Jake asked.

I saw him watching me, waiting for me to answer, and I realized that he knew what to do with them; he just wanted to see what I would do. So I thought about it for a minute. We could put them back in the creek, but we'd be catching them again tomorrow. We could dump them out on the ground somewhere, but then they'd never grow up to be the next generation of fish, and besides, you'd smell them for miles. I answered, "I'll take them downstream and let them go."

"Downstream?"

"That way they won't be so likely to swim back up here for us to catch them again tomorrow."

"All right, then," Jake said with a smile. I'd passed that test. He made sure I remembered how to clean the big catfish, and then went in to take a nap. He told me I could take them up to Mr. Howell's fish house, and that I ought to get a couple of dollars for them.

Jabbok and I took the fish to Mr. Howell, who gave us a dollar for each of them. I took that money with some money I had left from seminary, got in the Comet, and went to a grocery store. I bought some salt, a red nylon collar for Jabbok, a deck of cards, a bag of macaroni noodles, and a can of Prince Albert pipe tobacco. I also got several rolls of toilet paper. I knew there must be some other things that we would need, but I couldn't think what they might be. Life was pretty simple down at the Resting Place.

When Jabbok and I got back, Jake wasn't at the hut. I went to check the graveyard, but he wasn't there, either. Getting alarmed, I yelled, "Jake! Jake!" Jabbok started to panic with me, thinking this was a fun new game, running around in circles and barking. I ran down to the fishing place, and there he was, watching two quills floating in the water.

"Didn't you hear me yelling for you?"

"Yep, sure did. I bet everybody on this end of the county heard you."

"Why didn't you answer?"

"I did. I yelled back, but you just kept a-yellin'."

"I didn't hear you yell."

"That's 'cause you was yellin'."

"What are you doing?"

"Just catchin' us some supper."

"Catfish?"

"Bream." He picked up a pole to show me he wasn't fishing as deep as we had for catfish, and he was using smaller hooks. "They's more bones in 'em, but I like 'em better. We just needs five or six good ones."

I looked in the bucket and saw that he already had three. I sat there with him for a while, and he caught four more before he could bring himself to stop. I took the pickle bucket back to the hut and cleaned the bream.

That afternoon, we played poker for macaroni on the ice chest. We both knew how to play some of the games, but for those we didn't, one of us taught the other: Acey Deucey, Low Chicago, Night Baseball, Follow the Queen, Hot Lunch at the Y, Mexican Sweat, and Push and Tiddle.

For supper, we had fried bream and cheese. We had to pick out a few tiny, clear bones, but it was wonderfully delicious.

And so it went, for almost two weeks, two magnificent weeks in the early spring. We got up every morning right after the sun came up and went to sleep just after it went down. We ate a lot of fish and bologna and cheese, but it was always appreciated. One night we ate a possum that Jake shot with his shotgun. It was terrible, greasy and rubbery; I couldn't even pretend to like it. It did make the fish the next night seem even better, though.

One afternoon I took Mr. Howell five good-sized catfish and two buffalo fish. He gave me ten dollars for the whole lot of them, and Jabbok and I took the Comet into Vicksburg to Kentucky Fried Chicken and got a bucket of the Colonel's Original Recipe. Jake fussed at me for wasting money, and then we enjoyed every finger lickin' morsel of it.

On the Thursday after I'd been there for four days, I knew I needed to go and see my mom and dad. I hadn't talked to them for over a week, and I didn't know what they might have heard. For all I knew, they'd called the police to send out a search party.

So, after I took the day's catch to the fish house, I took the Comet to the house on Ridge Road. I'd tried to leave Jabbok with Jake, but she'd pulled against her rope leash so hard I thought she'd choke herself. Jake told me if he let her go after I'd gone, she was just going to get lost trying to find me. So I took her with me.

Dad was at work, but Mom was home. I pulled into the driveway, and she came out the front door. She met me as I was getting out of the car, relief clear on her face, and gave me a big hug.

She asked, "Buddy, are you all right?"

"Yes ma'am, I'm fine."

"The seminary has called several times, wanting to know where you are. I told them we hadn't heard from you. The dean of the seminary called all the way from England, and left a number for you to call him over there. Are you in some kind of trouble? You're not hiding from the law, are you?"

"No ma'am, I'm fine, really."

"Where have you been?"

"I've been down in the woods, Mom. It's a real long story. I'd want to tell you, that's why I'm here. But if it's okay with you, I'd like to wait 'til Dad gets home so he can hear it, too."

She looked into the Comet and saw the puppy fogging up the back window with her breath. "Who's your friend?"

"Ah, that's Jabbok. She's sort of a wedding present."

"You got married?"

"No, I was . . . in a wedding."

"What kind of name is Jabbok?"

"I don't really know. I think it's in the Bible somewhere."

We went in, Mom called Dad, and Mom and I made a pot of coffee and a little awkward small talk. Jabbok fell asleep on the screened back porch. Dad came in and asked most of the same questions Mom already had, and I poured us all a cup of coffee before I started telling the story. I tried to leave some things out that I knew would disturb them more than I already had.

I started from the beginning, with the deer dying by the creek when I was a kid, and the Gray Man. I told them about the guys and me finding him fishing at the creek, and about camping out on Halloween. I told them I'd stayed the night in his hut and lied to them about it later. I figured I had to be protected by some sort of statute of limitations by now, but I have to admit I was gratified to hear Dad say how irresponsible that was on Lee's part, even all those years later.

I told them that Jake was the black man who'd come to church the day I was confirmed. Dad was glad to learn it; it solved a mystery in his mind. He said he'd always wondered who that man was, and assumed the people of the congregation had been so rude that he'd never come back. I told them about our friendship, and all the help Jake had given me, and all the letters he'd written. I told them that he'd gone back to prison, and why he'd done it, and that he'd been released early because he was dying.

I told them that Jake had come to Becket, and about Dr. Sprague inviting him to give a lecture, and his demand for an apology from me afterward. I told them that I hadn't done that, and how I'd left the seminary. I told them we'd stopped for a few days in Riggsville to go to a wedding of some friends of Jake's; I figured they didn't need to know I'd performed the service.

Mom asked me if I still thought I ought to become an Episcopal priest. "Do you still feel called?"

"Yes ma'am, I do. It doesn't look real good right now, but I'm not giving up. Right now, though, I need to be with Jake. I can't let him die down there all by himself. After . . . after he's gone, I'll call the Bishop and we'll see what we can do."

Mom started, "How long will . . ."

I couldn't bear the question. "I don't know. He's getting weaker, though."

"Buddy, I'm proud of you," Dad said.

Mom and I were both surprised. "For standing up to Sprague," Dad continued, "for sticking with your friend even though it cost you, for . . . becoming a man."

I started to say something but couldn't. I wanted to thank him for the affirmation, but there seemed to be something in my throat, something large and swelling. All my life my father had encouraged me primarily by pointing out where I could have done better. I should have been a better student (he was right about that); I could have been a better athlete (he was wrong there). He'd wanted me to choose a career that would bring financial security, and now it seemed the vocation that had called me to a life of what was likely to be difficult and under-compensated work was in real jeopardy. I had just confessed that I'd lied to them and probably broken a law to two. And now, in this moment, my rarely satisfied father was telling me that, at long last, he was proud of me. In this moment I saw both of us in a new light. "Thank you" would not have been nearly enough, even if I could have choked it out. I nodded, blinking back the tears.

"I'm proud of you, too, sweetheart," Mom agreed.

They asked me if I needed anything, and I told them about life at the Resting Place. Dad gave me a large flashlight, and Mom put together a box of canned food. I was especially glad to see some cans of stew and two cans of Spam. I didn't really know what Spam was, but it wasn't fish, and it had to be better than possum. As I went out to the car, Dad came with a shovel and said, "For when . . . for when you—"

"Thanks, Dad." I told them I'd see them when it was over, and promised I'd let them know if I needed anything. I drove away with a much lighter heart than I'd brought.

Jake and I fished the next day and on Saturday, but on Sunday we did just sat around and talked or played cards. We fried a can of Spam for lunch, and it was surprisingly tasty. Jake told me more about life at Parchman, and I told him more about life at Becket, but mostly we just enjoyed not having anything that we needed to do. In the afternoon, I tried to teach Jabbok how to sit, or stay, or something, but without any real success.

In the late afternoon, Jake said, "Buddy, I'm wonderin' if we could have us a mornin' prayin' service like they do up there at Becket."

"Sure, Jake. I'll have to go up and get my Prayer Book, though."

"That sure was a pretty thing, sure was, like God had swooped Hisself down amongst us. Could we do it right here, or do we have to be up in a church somewheres?"

"No, we can do it right here. We can have Morning Prayer tomorrow morning."

"Oh. I was hopin' we'd have us a service tonight, bein' Sunday and all."

"Well, we might want to have Evening Prayer, or Compline."

"What's Compline?" he asked.

"It's the last service of the evening, from back when the monks used to have five or six services every day. It's a beautiful service, one of my favorites. My friend Scott and I used to read Compline together."

"Do you have to do all the rest of 'em to get to that one?"

"No, you can just do that one, all by itself."

"All right. Let's look at that one, see can we have us some Compline."

So I went up to get a couple of Prayer Books, and we read Compline as the sun went down. My liturgics professor might have scolded me for reading Compline in the early evening fading light when the monks would have read Vespers, but I didn't see him anywhere around, and with the sun going down, our bedtime was getting close. Compline was originally bedtime prayers for the Benedictines.

We turned our Prayer Books to the right page, and I went through the service, telling him which parts I would read, and which parts he and I would read together. Where there was a place for a Scripture passage, I told him I wanted him to choose a passage and read it.

"Can it be from Genesis?" he asked.

"Sure, it can be from wherever you want."

"I just like Genesis the best, 'cause I know the most about it. I read that little book from the prison library on it, that commentary book."

When we were all ready, I started the service. "The Lord Almighty grant us a peaceful night and a perfect end."

We both said, "Amen." Ah-men.

We read Psalm 31 together, but I found a lump suddenly in my throat about halfway through verse 5: "Into your hands I commend my spirit, for you have redeemed me, O LORD, O God of truth."

I told Jake it was time for the reading, and he read from his old King James Bible, the book of Genesis, chapter twenty-eight.

> And Jacob went out from Beer-sheba, and went toward Haran.
> And he lighted upon a certain place, and tarried there all night, because the sun was set; and he took of the stones of that place, and put them for his pillows, and lay down in that place to sleep.

> And he dreamed, and behold a ladder set up on the earth, and the top of it reached to heaven: and behold the angels of God ascending and descending on it.
> And, behold, the LORD stood above it, and said, I am the LORD God of Abraham thy father, and the God of Isaac: the land whereon thou liest, to thee will I give it, and to thy seed;
> And thy seed shall be as the dust of the earth, and thou shalt spread abroad to the west, and to the east, and to the north, and to the south: and in thee and in thy seed shall all the families of the earth be blessed.
> And, behold, I am with thee, and will keep thee in all places whither thou goest, and will bring thee again into this land; for I will not leave thee, until I have done that which I have spoken to thee of.
> And Jacob awaked out of his sleep, and he said, Surely the LORD is in this place; and I knew it not.
> And he was afraid, and said, How dreadful is this place! this is none other but the house of God, and this is the gate of heaven.

Jake looked up from his Bible, and, glancing around us at the cathedral of trees overhead, repeated the patriarch's words for our homily: "This is none other but the house of God, and this is the gate of heaven."

We said the Lord's Prayer together, and then a couple more prayers. When we came to the *Nunc dimittis*, at the end of the service, I got choked up again and couldn't keep reading. But Jake read it in a strong, sure voice.

"Lord, you now have set your servant free to go in peace as you have promised; For these eyes of mine have seen the Savior, whom you have prepared for all the world to see: A Light to enlighten the nations, and the glory of your people Israel."

It was as if some committee somewhere had put this prayer in the new Prayer Book just for us. For the next four nights, we read Compline together. On the fifth night, he was gone.

We fished Monday, Tuesday, and Wednesday, but on Thursday Jake said he couldn't come. "I'm a little bit tired, Buddy. I best just stay where I am for right now."

I took him some coffee, but he didn't drink it. I fried him some bologna, but he couldn't eat it. In the afternoon, he looked like he was drifting away from me, as if he had one foot in another world.

"It's almost time now, Buddy," he said. "Almost time to go."

"Jake, are you hurting?"

"No, child, no. I feel so light, like I'm flyin' over the water, floatin' off up in the sky." He seemed to fall asleep with that pleasant idea sustaining a smile. Then, in a few minutes, he said, "Joseph?"

I didn't know what to say, so I didn't say anything.

"Joseph," he continued, "is that you?"

"Yes sir," I said.

"You a good boy, Joseph."

"You're a good father. And a fine preacher."

He smiled a little then, and fell asleep, his breathing ragged. In a couple of hours he woke and asked for some water. I brought it to him, and he drank a little. He said, "Buddy, they's somethin' I got to tell you, and I want you to listen to me, all right?"

"Yes sir." It was a holy time. I wanted to be there for him; I didn't want to cry.

"You know I been havin' a misunderstandin' with the Lord for a long while, but we's about to work it all out now. I'm about to leave my ol' body for real this time."

He looked away, and the tears flooded my eyes as I remembered him saying that when we fished in Mr. Crofton's boat. I blinked rapidly while he wasn't looking at me.

"Here's what I got to tell you. It's better to struggle honest than to settle for a lie. The mysteries is ever before us. That's my gift to you, Buddy. I give you the struggle of bein' a faithful man. I'm 'bout done with it now, so I best leave it to you. All right?"

"Yes sir." My throat was so full of emotion I could hardly talk. But I had to say this next, or I knew I'd always regret it. "I love you, Jake."

"I know it, Buddy, I know. I love you, too. I always will. I'll see you in the morning, all right?"

"Yes sir. I'll see you again." I couldn't tell if he was delirious, but I knew he was right—I'd see him again, after the long night of death, in the Resurrection Morning.

He fell into a deep sleep then, and didn't wake again. I watched him sleep through the night, and he was very peaceful. When the sun came up, he was still breathing. But his breath got more and more shallow as the morning dragged on, and he wasn't responding to me in any way. Just after noon, he shuddered, and all the air came out of him. His chest didn't rise to take another breath, and he was gone.

29

Depart, O Christian Soul

I thought I'd cry when the time came, but there was really no need. I knew I had a list of things to do, and that my time at the Resting Place was coming to an end, but I wasn't ready to move on yet. I went and sat on the fallen sweet gum and looked up into the branches of the trees all around. Spring had arrived while I wasn't watching, and the branches overhead were filled with birds and bugs bustling with the business of the season. A squirrel chattered and fussed with somebody I couldn't see, acting like there was something she wanted to protect; I wished I could tell her to relax.

It was a peaceful, holy death, as if Jake had just stepped out of his body and left it behind to go somewhere nearby. He'd done what he'd wanted to do: he'd come home to the Resting Place to die. He was with his father and his son now, and as sad as it was for me, I couldn't help but feel happy for him.

I leaned back against a strong green limb and felt a spot of sunlight reaching through the canopy of leaves to touch my face. I marveled that it could make its way through all the new leaves above, and realized it had come millions of miles through the darkness of space from the sun in a straight line right there to where I was sitting. I wondered how many people had died all over the world already that day, and how many had been born. Birth and death, light and dark, the significance of life and the relative frailty and unimportance of my own existence compared to the infinity and permanence of the universe filled my thoughts for a long while.

Jabbok woke from a little puppy nap, wagged her rear half, and yawned. She must've sensed that something had changed; she came over and sat quietly on the ground under my feet. We sat for a while, listening to the sounds of birds scratching in the fallen leaves for worms and seeds. I'd learned again that life is brief and precious, and I knew the world was a poorer place without Jake, but it was still wonderfully rich, and full of life, mine among others. It was getting close to time for me to get on with living, time to play the hand I'd been dealt.

Jabbok and I went to the Comet to get the shovel. I thought about going to see Mom and Dad, or calling them to let them know. But I couldn't leave Jake lying there, and besides, it seemed right for this to be a private time for solemn joy. I didn't want any sympathies and consolations just yet. There would be time for that later.

Jake had shown me where he wanted me to bury him: Joseph's marker was to the right of Jake's father, and Jake wanted to be buried to the right of Joseph. So I started digging, and cutting through the roots of the big sweet gum with his ax. I dug for at least an hour without making much headway because there were so many roots, but after I got about a foot and a half into the ground, it went more quickly.

Even so, after about four feet, I stopped. I'd planned to dig a grave six feet deep, mostly because that's what you always hear. But at four feet I'd come to a band of hard, dry clay, and I decided that was enough. Besides, if I'd dug much deeper than that, I was going to have trouble getting myself up out of the grave.

I went back to the hut and wrapped Jake in his blanket. I moved him off the inflatable camping mattress, let about half the air out of it, and folded it to put it in the bottom of the hole I'd dug. I suppose it was silly, but I couldn't imagine ever using that mattress again, and it made me feel better to think his body would lie on something soft. Then I went to the hut and picked him up. He'd never been a large man, but I was surprised that he was so much lighter than I thought he'd be; it was as if his soul had lent him some weight that was now gone. I carried him to the graveyard and lowered him down into his grave under the big sweet gum, putting his feet down first, and laying him out gently.

A few days before, I'd thought about wrapping him in garbage bags when the time came, but I remembered he'd told me one time that he didn't feel bad about using worms to fish with, because some day "them worms'll be feastin' on me." I let the worms have his blanket, too.

Throwing dirt on his feet and legs didn't bother me, but when I got to the point when it looked like the next shovel of dirt was going to cover his head, I had to stop and cry. It seemed so final; I would never hear his voice or see his smile again. I put all the dirt back in the hole, leaving a small mound over the grave.

I could have had the service and the sermon right then, I suppose, but I wanted to work on what I was going to say, and I wanted to leave right after the funeral. So I decided that the funeral would have to wait for the next day. It was odd to look at that little mound of dirt and think that Jake was under there, not breathing, not moving.

I'd memorized a prayer from the Prayer Book for this moment, and after fussing a while with the dirt to make it look right, I said it: "Depart, O Christian soul, out of this world; In the Name of God the Father Almighty who created you; In the Name of Jesus Christ who redeemed you; In the Name of the Holy Spirit who sanctifies you. May your rest be this day in peace, and your dwelling place in the Paradise of God."

I promised myself I'd get a grave marker when I could. I already knew what I would ask them to carve into the headstone:

The Rev. Jacob J. Jefferson
January 23, 1905–April 17, 1981
Evangelist, Elder, and Prophet
A Sinner, A Saint, and An Honest Man

I took four fishing poles and sawed them into pieces, then lashed them together with nylon cord to make a cross to put at his head. It seemed fitting, and I knew the cane would last for years, long enough for me to buy a marker.

The rest of the afternoon, I sat on the fallen sweet gum, whistling and thinking and working on the sermon for his funeral. I missed Jake, but I wasn't lonely. In truth, I felt him all around me, as I realized he must have felt his father and son. It was a communion of saints, and I wrapped myself in it like I would an old family quilt.

In the late afternoon, I caught a few bream for supper. After I ate the fish and carefully cleaned Jake's old iron skillet, I read Compline, with Jabbok's muzzle on my knee. I did reasonably well until I came to one of the prayers toward the end: "Keep watch, dear Lord, with those who work, or watch, or weep this night, and give your angels charge over those who sleep. Tend the sick, Lord Christ; give rest to the weary, bless the dying, soothe the suffering, pity the afflicted, shield the joyous; and all for your love's sake. Amen."

I worked on the sermon until well past dark, writing it out by the light of Dad's flashlight. I started to write down our story, the story of an old black preacher who'd lost his faith and a little white kid just discovering his. I sat on the fallen sweet gum and wrote until the full moon rose. When I went into the hut and lay down on my inflatable camping mattress, I had no trouble falling asleep.

The sun was already up when I woke with Jabbok curled up under my arm. My first thought was to make some coffee for Jake and me, until I remembered he was gone.

I went out and sat on the tree again for a long time, reading over my notes, trying to remember what I wanted to say.

I'd imagined I'd be talking to Jake in his grave, the way people in the movies talk to their buried loved ones. But the more I thought about it, the surer I was that I'd be talking not only to Jake, but also to his father Joe and his son Joseph, whose essence permeated the Resting Place. The truth of it was that I knew I would be addressing the entire Communion of Saints, all those who've gone before us and now await us in the nearer presence of God. I would be talking to my grandmother who'd died the year before, to my friend Andy Simmons, to Thomas Aquinas, and to all the saints famous and unknown who'd already welcomed Jake into the eternal realms of light.

But now, when the time for his funeral was upon me, it seemed like there ought to be somebody else there—somebody I could see.

I'd kept Jake a secret almost all my life, except for a few weeks at Becket, but now I felt like there ought to be someone there to give witness to his death, to celebrate his life with me.

I thought about it for a while, about who I would like to be there, but there were too many, and I didn't know how to choose between them. Finally it occurred to me that I ought to be wondering who Jake would like to be there, and the list narrowed to a fine point: Cornelius and Mabel Jones. Surely I could invite them to the funeral; surely they would want to be there. The idea appealed to me for a couple of reasons. First, I thought it would be wonderful for them and for me. They were good friends of his, and mine. They would want to know; even if they couldn't come to Jake's funeral, they ought to be given the option. And second, if I went to get them, it would give me some more time to get used to the idea that Jake was really gone before I had to preach his funeral sermon.

I've second-guessed that decision a hundred times over the years, but it's what I wound up doing. I believe I was mostly justifying the fact that I wasn't ready to do the funeral, and this seemed like a plausible, even noble delay. So Jabbok and I and took everything up the hill and put it in the Comet, still parked behind Mr. Howell's fish house, and headed north to Riggsville.

30

Have a Little Faith, Preacher

We drove up through Vicksburg and into the vast flatness of the Mississippi Delta. I turned on the radio, but it seemed like a lot of noise for what ought to be a quiet day, so I turned it back off. Jabbok slept most of the way.

By the time we got to Miss Mabel's house, it was about three in the afternoon, and no one was there. I thought about going to the Swayze home, but it didn't seem like a good day to risk crossing paths with the Reverend, so I decided to see if I could find Cornelius in the kitchen at Parchman instead. I was surprised that the guard at the gate remembered me until he told me he'd been at the wedding. He said I'd done a fine job. I thanked him and told him I needed to see Mr. Cornelius in the kitchen for a minute, and he told me to go on in. I parked under the huge oak tree and left Jabbok sleeping in the back seat with the windows down.

I knocked on the door of the kitchen, but there was no answer. The screen door was not latched and the door was not locked, so I went in to wait for Cornelius. I got some water to drink from the sink and was wondering if I could find anything to eat when I heard the screen door creak open behind me.

A huge man stepped into the kitchen, followed by a smaller, shifty-looking man who looked remarkably like a possum. They both wore the blue overalls and light blue work shirts issued to inmates. I recognized the large man as Eugene, Jake's "little brother." Some people are hard to forget.

The smaller man sneered to Eugene with obvious distaste, "This his little white boy?"

Eugene replied, "Yeah, that's his boy Buddy. I met him one time, in the kitchen with Preacher Jake. That's Buddy he always talkin' 'bout." Then he said to me with a meek innocence you couldn't expect, "He dead? Preacher Jake dead?"

"Yes, sir," I said.

The smaller man said, "Shut the door," and Eugene went and closed it. The man in charge looked at me like a wary buyer must look at a used car with a suspiciously low price on the windshield, trying to figure out what was wrong with me. I thought about running, but I didn't think I'd get far, certainly not all the way back to the guard at the gate. The door Eugene had just closed was the only way out, and the more I moved away from them, the more I would be trapped in a corner.

I didn't know what to do, but it seemed like it was time for me to do or say something. It seemed suddenly clear to me that I needed to be careful, or this could end very painfully. I decided I would try to be friendly, and held out my hand as I introduced myself.

"Hi. I'm Buddy Hinton."

The possum-man snickered. Something about him made me furious, just looking at him, and I realized that this must be Eddie. Jake had told me that Eddie was a sort of ringleader in the prison, an inmate Boss.

I'd never had the kind of reaction to a person that I had when I saw Eddie: I simply and purely loathed him. That was probably aided by the fact that Jake had warned me about him; Jake's concern that Eddie was waiting for me to come visit him in prison was the reason I'd never gone back to Parchman. There was something in his appearance, a smirk that seemed built into the lines of his face, that produced a visceral response from a place I didn't know was in me. He was slim to the point of being gaunt, probably a little over six feet tall, although he looked petite next to Eugene. His pencil-thin mustache was just a shadow above his lip, and his long hair was greasy and straight with an odd tint of red. I wondered if he'd colored his hair somehow.

It wasn't just the smirk that made him look like a possum; it was his eyes, too. They were never all the way open, but never still, either, as if he was always looking all around for something, for something he could eat, or something that might eat him. He had the look of a man who would do anything to get what he wanted. Every alarm in my head was going off, the hair on the back of my neck standing up.

Eddie was a rough man, and his language showed it. When I wrote out what I remembered him saying, I realized that although I'd love for my mom and dad to read this if it ever becomes a book, I sure wouldn't want them to read exactly what Eddie said. So let's just say he was crude and profane, and let it go at that. It was part of how he spoke, part of how he intimidated, but it doesn't have to be part of my writing, or your reading.

He didn't acknowledge that my hand was out for him to shake. He snapped, "I don't give a damn who you are. Some of my boys tol' me you was here. I thought we could have us a little chitchat."

"Who are you?" I asked.

"You know who I am." He was sure of his reputation, was used to it being part of his intimidation.

"No, I really don't," I lied.

Eugene said, "Why, this here's Eddie Walker."

I could tell that they both thought the name Eddie Walker was something I should think was important; I'm sure it was very important to the inmates there. I wanted to let him know it wasn't important to me, that he wasn't important outside the prison. I tried to look nonchalant. "I came to see Cornelius Jones. Do either of you know where he is, or when he'll be back?"

Eddie kept his eyes on me, but when he spoke, it was to Eugene. "Oh, yeah, he talks pretty, talks real good. What do you think we should do with him, Eugene?"

Eugene seemed to know more about what was going on than I did; he answered, "He ain't hurtin' us none, Eddie. Let's just talk to him, and let him go."

Eddie talked a little louder now, and a little faster. "Nah, I don't think so. Hell no. I bet he knows where the ol' fool's money is. And

I bet we can make him tell us. We might have to break a leg or two, but it sure would be a nice little handout when we gets out of this damn place."

"What money?" I said.

Eddie repeated in a crude imitation of me, "What money? Listen at him, lying to us. Hell, you can't trust nobody. Eugene, you know Preacher Jake left out of here to go see this fool; this here his boy. He knows where that damn money is."

I couldn't imagine Jake having any money. Surely, if he had any cash, he wouldn't be living down in the woods and catching fish for a living. "I don't know anything about any money," I said. "Jake certainly didn't have any that I know of."

Eddie's voice took on an alarmingly strident tone, like someone accustomed to being obeyed. "You a damn liar! You tell me where that money is. It ain't his, noways."

I stayed as calm as I could and repeated, "I don't know anything about any money."

Eddie said in a voice that chilled my heart, "They ain't nobody else in this buildin', ain't nobody near to help you, boy." He picked up a long kitchen knife and tested the edge of it with his thumb. It looked sharp. "By the time they find you, me and Eugene'll be long gone out of here. Nobody saw us come in or out, we was in our camp the whole time. I got boys who'll say so, too. Right, Eugene?"

"Eddie," Eugene said, "Preacher Jake's friend say he don't know nothin' 'bout no money. Maybe he don't. Maybe Archie was lyin'."

Archie? That was a name I'd heard a hundred times in Jake's story. Jake's treacherous wife Chantille had a brother named Archie. Could Eugene be talking about the same Archie who drove the truck and set up the tent, who planted the blind woman in Jake's congregation to be healed? I remembered Jake telling the story, how Archie had told him to have faith. He'd told it dozens of times, and it always had the same ending: "Yep, ol' Archie Preston tellin' me, 'Have a little faith, preacher.'"

"Archie Preston?" I guessed.

Eddie whirled around and asked, "How the hell you know Archie?"

"I don't. I just heard Jake talk about him, that's all. What did he tell you?"

Eugene started, "He tol' Eddie that Preacher Jake's hidin' a sack full of money he ain't never spunt. Archie told us—"

Eddie cut him off. "Hold up, Eugene. Let me do the talkin', okay?" Then he said to me, "Look, boy, we just want the ol' fool's money. We don't want no crap out of you. They ain't no reason for nobody to get hurt here today. Just tell us where the damn money is. I'll be gettin' out in 'bout a year and a half—early release for good behavior—be nice to have a little money to put in my pocket."

"Like I told you, I don't know anything about any money. How do y'all know Archie Preston?"

Eddie's mouth formed a smile, but his eyes remained menacing. "Archie and his lovely sister Chantille are relations of mine. He told me all about Preacher Jake Jefferson and his fake religion tent show. He said it was a great swindle, said they could really bring in the money. When I got out of prison, he said him and me was goin' to get us a tent and go around squeezin' peoples dry for Jesus! All tax-free, too, Archie said, 'cause all them fools give in cash. He said I could do all the talkin', that's what I'm good at. He'd already heard it all from Jake anyways, and he'd tell me what to say, all about that heavenly pie in the sky in the sweet by and by. He said that's all they want to hear, anyways. He said he knew what to say to bring in the sheep, and then we'd just watch the money come in."

I knew that my only hope was to stay calm and think clearly, but Eddie calling Jake's ministry a "fake religion tent show" made my blood run hot. It scared me that I had no more compassion for Eddie than I would for a snake or a kitchen roach. I don't think I'd ever really hated anyone with that sort of intensity, and I didn't like the sensation.

"Your cousin Archie might've been cheating people, but Jake was giving them hope," I insisted. "Some people are interested in more than just the money."

Eddie sniggered at the idea. "Yeah, fools like Preacher Jake. He walked away from a gold mine 'cause he figured out he'd been lyin' the whole damn time. What happened to his hope when he found cousin Chantille with a rich white man? What did he do then?"

"He left her."

"Is that what he told you? He hit that white man, like to kilt him. Then he went out and got drunk. He got good and drunk, and stayed drunk, too, 'til he got to Parchman Farm. And all that time he was takin' money from the people who come to hear the preachin.'"

Eugene showed no signs of having heard any of this before. "Is that true, Mr. Buddy?"

Eddie's smirk was menacing; I had to be careful. "It's true that Eddie's cousin Chantille cheated on Jake, and Jake hit the man. It's not true that he tried to kill him. He did drink a lot after that, and even more when his son Joseph died in the war. He never took any money from anybody."

"Don't be a damn fool, Eugene," Eddie said. "Ol' Preacher Jake was preachin' the love of God to the crowds, and then he took they money to buy whiskey after they left. Archie said they was a whole bag of money hidden somewheres, said ol' Jake wouldn't touch it, 'cause he was savin' it up for his boy."

He looked at me with the cruelty of a predator. It was a look of malice, savagery, and cold, unfeeling despair. It gave me a chill. St. Thomas Aquinas had allowed for the possibility of the personification of evil. It was an idea I'd rejected, but now, looking into the malevolence of Eddie's eyes, I wasn't so sure. It occurred to me that there was more at stake here than just my safety. My faith, Jake's faith, was on trial.

Eddie snarled, "Now the ol' fool's dead, his boy's dead, and cousin Archie's gone. I mean to have that money, you understand me?"

I didn't know how to respond. I didn't know how to deal with the pure hatred I felt for Eddie. I took a deep breath and was about to tell them again that I didn't know anything about any money, when I remembered something Jake had said when I was a kid.

I'd told him that some of the boys in my confirmation class had been mean to me, and he told me about alligators in the swamp, and the difference between the givers and the takers. He said that sometimes I would need to "put the love of God on 'em." I remembered him saying, "You just look in they eyes, and tell yourself that this mean alligator is a child of God just like you is." I wasn't going to out-hate Eddie, but maybe . . . if Jake and Jesus knew what they were talking about, maybe I could beat him with love. There was no way I could love Eddie with my love, so I'd have to try to love him with the love of God.

Eddie had me rattled, and I needed to regain my composure. I looked at him and said, with as much compassion and empathy as I could muster, "Eddie, I wish I knew where that money was, I really do. I'd be glad for you to have it. But he never said anything about it to me. I wish I could help you, but I just can't."

Eddie's smirk faltered, and then failed altogether. The malice in his eyes was replaced by suspicion. "You're lyin,'" he hissed.

My friend Trey the football coach would say that the momentum had changed, and that I needed to press my advantage. The idea of this snake spending Jake's money made me sick, but even worse was his threat of becoming a preacher to rake in the cash. He and I both knew that he couldn't bring in the money or the crowds as a preacher, but Eugene clearly believed he could. I decided that this would be a good time to call his bluff.

With a kindness I didn't feel, I said, "So, when you get out, why don't you and Archie start a tent ministry, like you planned?"

Eddie looked at me as if I were completely stupid. "Archie's dead."

"Dead?"

Eddie held his head back and laughed contemptuously. "Yeah, we had us a little fight in the mess hall some years back. Ol' cousin Archie was doin' a few years in here, and he had stole from me, stole a bottle of store-bought whiskey and two packs of cigarettes. I asked my friend Eugene to show him the error of his ways. I just wanted him roughed up a little, but Eugene here got a little carried away. Crushed his windpipe while he was tryin' to pick the boy up by the neck, ain't that right, Eugene?"

Eugene looked abashed. "I didn't mean to."

Jake had mentioned that fight in a letter, that they'd taken one of the inmates off to a hospital. I remembered it because he said that Eugene had been beaten by the guards and put in solitary, that Eugene was afraid of being in solitary. I wondered if Jake had ever known it was Archie, who'd caused him so much trouble; he never mentioned it again. He did say Eddie hadn't gotten into any trouble at all.

"Look," I said, "I'm just here to see Mr. Jones, to tell him that Jake died. I really don't know anything about any money. I never saw any bag of money."

"He's lyin', Eugene," Eddie said. "He just wants to keep all that money for hisself. I think maybe he'd be more likely to tell us the truth if you broke one of his arms."

I thought about running again, and I glanced around to see which way I could go. I thought, "Fake left, and run to the right—no, that never works."

Just then Eugene replied, "I don't want to hurt Preacher Jake's friend."

I can't tell you how happy I was to hear that.

"Eugene, he's got our money," Eddie argued.

Emboldened by Eugene's declaration, I broke in to say, "Hold on, now, wait a minute. I understand that Archie told you Jake had some money. I don't think that's true, but if it were, why would you say it's yours? Surely you're not telling me that Jake stole some money from you, are you?"

Eugene shook his massive head. "Naw. Preacher Jake never stole nothin'. It was—"

Eddie interrupted him again. "I thought you was gonna let me do the talkin'. That's what I'm good at, remember?"

Eddie pushed all my buttons; I wanted to hit him. I turned to Eugene and tried to use a soothing voice. "Eugene, you're a grown man. You can talk as much as you want. I'll listen."

Eddie was furious. "He ain't gotta talk to you!"

The surreal sense of serenity I'd felt in tense moments returned, and somehow I knew that I ought to appear to be relaxed while Eddie raged. I also realized that Eddie got incensed when I talked to Eugene and ignored him, and that was to my advantage, as frightening as it was. My best and only hope was for me to ignore Eddie and his knife and get Eugene on my side. "Eugene, he's right. You don't have to talk to me at all. But I'll listen to you if you want to talk."

Eugene was confused, and Eddie knew that his control was slipping. "Eugene," he pleaded, "he's got our money. Just break one of his arms, and he'll tell us where it is."

"I can't tell you where the money is, Eugene. I don't know anything about any money."

"He's lyin'!" Eddie screamed. "He's got our damn money!"

I was the embodiment of tranquility. "Eugene, I've never seen any money." Then, to impress the truth of it, I added, "By the love of God, I swear it."

But Eddie took us in a different direction. "The love of God?" He laughed derisively. "Aw, hell, he talks just like the ol' fool, Eugene. He just a young fool, is all he is. We ain't gotta listen to no damn young fool. He just gonna give you the same crap the ol' fool give you. Just look where it got him, Eugene, look where the love of God got Jake."

"We're all going to die, Eugene—you, me, Eddie—everybody dies. The trick is what we do with our lives, how well we live, how well we love, and how well we are loved."

"Don't listen to all this crap, Eugene! It's just more of the same stuff that ol' fool Jake got you all messed up with. You know it don't work. It ain't the love of God that's gonna get you nowheres. Them preachers just want our money, that's all. They just tryin' to keep peoples like us in line, doin' what they want us to do. We's just sheep to them, just sheep to herd around, push around."

"I'm not trying to push you around, Eugene. I'm just telling you the truth. You're a grown man. You're not somebody's dog, not somebody's mule. You make your own decisions. Who's telling you what to do here? Me, or Eddie? Who's telling you what to do?"

"You ain't gotta listen to him, Eugene. He just trying to confuse you." Eddie looked desperate to shift the subject back to ground that would be more profitable for him. "All this talk is just words 'bout somethin' we can't see. Preachers say they done seen God. They say Jesus tells 'em what to do. How come Jesus don't tell us what to do? How come we ain't never seen him? It's all a lie, you know it is, Eugene." He was soothing now. "You know it's all a lie."

Eugene was starting to listen to Eddie, hearing the familiar words that had kept him away from Jake. My surreal calm began to fray. It was time to take a chance.

"Eugene, why do you think Eddie is so afraid of God?"

"I ain't afraid of nothin'. They ain't nobody can—"

"Why won't he just consider that maybe there is a God? Why is it so important to Eddie that Jake is wrong? Did you ever wonder about that?"

Eugene answered, "No, I just figured—"

"You don't have to tell him nothin', Eugene!" Eddie snapped.

"What if Jake was right?" I continued. "What if faith is stronger than power? What if love is more powerful than hate? Why did you want to listen to Preacher Jake, Eugene? Why didn't Eddie want you to hear Jake talk?"

"I don't rightly know. Eddie says that—"

"Who would your mama say was right, Eugene?" I pressed. "Would she want you to go with Eddie, or with Jake?"

Eddie warned, "You ain't got no call to talk about a man's mama!"

I looked Eddie right in the eye, and, mustering all the courage and tranquillity I had left, I said, "I will say what I choose to say. I am not afraid of you. It may be that you can badger Eugene into beating me up, or even killing me. You might stab me with that knife. But I am not afraid."

While Eddie was trying to work his way through that, I turned back to Eugene. "Eugene, Jake told me you were a friend of his. He said you're a good, kind-hearted soul. He saw something in you that's good and true. I see it too, Eugene. But I don't think Eddie does. I don't think he wants to see anything in you that's good or gentle. He needs you to be hard and tough. You're just a dog for Eddie, just a mean dog for him to scare people with, a dog for him to kick around."

Eddie started to say something, but I didn't let him interrupt. "Why did you hurt Archie, Eugene? Were you mad at him? Had he stolen something from you?"

Eugene looked at Eddie before he spoke, obviously knowing that the honest answer wasn't what Eddie wanted to hear. "No sir. Archie never done me no harm. Eddie wanted me to hurt him—"

"Shut up!" Eddie was livid. "Why you talkin' to this fool? You don't owe him nothin', nothin' at all."

I knew I had scored a point, and kept at it, even though Eddie was moving toward me now, waving the knife so that I could see it. "I think Eddie's just using you, Eugene. You hurt Archie because Eddie wanted you to, and now you feel bad about it. You're the muscles he doesn't have. He wants to keep you angry and confused, so he can use you. Jake wanted you to be a man, Eugene. He treated you with respect, listened to what you had to say. You're just a mean dog for Eddie."

I stepped back, away from Eddie and the knife, until I was pressed against shelves of huge bags of corn meal and flour. Eddie raised the knife and pointed it at my neck, to remind me that he had the power here. I could see its sharp edge gleaming cruelly, and I vividly remembered the day I met Jake, how he'd used his knife to kill the doe that had been shot.

Eddie hissed, "Shut up, fool."

I looked into Eugene's eyes and whispered, "I'm not afraid, Eugene; I'm not afraid even to die. There are worse things that could happen to us than dying."

Eddie pressed the blade to my skin. I could feel my pulse against it. Eddie's voice was cold, heartless. "I said shut the hell up!"

I squeezed my eyes shut. I was too scared to think of anything else to say.

"I'm not afraid, Eugene. I'm not afraid to die."

I was scared to death.

I felt the knife at my throat, and then I felt a tug. I remember thinking I'd expected it to hurt more, and I assumed I was dead.

I opened my eyes to see Eugene standing over me, holding the knife, which he'd taken away from Eddie. Before I could take in what had happened, I heard the screen door slam; Eddie was gone. My hands went to my neck to check: it had been scratched in the struggle, but the wound wasn't serious. A murderer had saved my life, literally saved my neck.

"Thank you," I breathed. "Thank you."

"Yes sir," Eugene whispered. "You welcome."

"Where did Eddie go?" I asked.

"He just took off," Eugene said. "I guess he ain't sure about me right now."

"Are you going to be okay?"

"Yes sir. I s'pose so." There was a pause, and then he continued, "Can you and me talk for a minute, Preacher Buddy?"

My legs were sort of wobbly and weak right then, so I replied, "All right, let's sit down and talk." I sat on the big stainless steel table in the middle of the kitchen, and Eugene leaned against the counter opposite me.

I felt like a little boy next to Eugene. He looked down on me dolefully. "Preacher Jake passed?"

"Yes sir," I answered. "He died yesterday."

Eugene thought about that for a moment, and then said, "Preacher Jake was a good man."

I remembered the day I'd met Eugene in this same kitchen, and him asking me if I believed what Jake said. He said he believed Jake, but he believed Eddie, too.

"Yes sir," I said again. "He was a good man. Eugene, what do you think Jake was trying to tell you?"

"Well, I don't rightly know for sure. He talked 'bout love a lot."

"He sure did. What do you remember him saying about love?"

"Preacher Jake said that love is the best thing, better'n money, better'n havin' womens, better'n havin' mens do what you say."

"And what do you think?

"I don't guess I know. I guess it nice to be loved, for peoples to like you an' all. But Preacher Buddy, my life ain't never been that-a-way. Peoples is scared of me, always have been."

"And you don't like that." I sounded like my pastoral theology professor, role-playing Rogerian responses in pastoral theology class.

"No sir. I hates it."

"You'd rather people like you, want to be around you."

"Yes sir."

"Did Preacher Jake want to be around you?"

"Yes sir."

"Was he afraid of you?"

"No sir. I don't b'lieve he was."

"Why did he want to be around you?"

"I don't know."

"Why wasn't he afraid of you?"

"I don't know."

I said, "I know." Eugene's head had sunk down onto his chest, but at this he looked up. "I know why he liked being around you, and why he wasn't afraid. Jake believed in the love of God. That's why he wasn't afraid, because he knew the love of God would protect him. And that's why I wasn't afraid either," I lied, "not even with a knife at my neck. I knew the love of God would protect me, too."

Eugene was doubtful. "The love of God?"

I said, "Yes sir."

"I ain't never seen it," Eugene told me. "I ain't never seen Jesus. I ain't never heard no Jesus talkin' to me. If he up there, he ought to talk to all of us. I sure wish he'd say somethin' to me."

"I do, too, Eugene. I wish he'd say something to me, or show me a sign. Sometimes I wish he'd show everybody a sign, prove himself to us all. Then we'd just about have to believe in God, wouldn't we?"

Eugene nodded, and I continued, "But if we had to believe, we wouldn't really be believing. The only way to make somebody believe is to take away their choices, understand?"

He looked perplexed. I tried again. "If we all had to believe, not because we chose to but because we had to, it would be like making somebody love you. It would be like going to bed with a hooker. She'd do everything you paid her to do, but her heart wouldn't be in it. That's not the way it's supposed to be.

"We all have to choose how we want to live our lives, Eugene. You can live in love and hope, or you can live in hatred and fear. Do you want people to love you, or to be scared of you?"

Eugene whispered, "I wants peoples to love me."

"I know. That's the good Jake saw in you."

We sat there without a word for what seemed like a long time, until Eugene asked, "Preacher Buddy, what do the Lord Jesus want me to do?"

"I believe he wants us all to live in love, and in hope. He wants us to love each other as much as he loves us. You know he didn't make you to be somebody's dog."

Then Eugene leaned in toward me, like an oak tree suddenly flexible enough to bend over, and I appreciated again why people were always afraid of him. He whispered, "Preacher Buddy, why did the Lord make me like I is? Why ain't I smart, like you, or Eddie?"

It was the camper Paul's question: "Why did God have to make me a retard?" In the face of the real human pain wrapped up in this question, all the arguments of St. Thomas Aquinas seemed as straw to me. I could dazzle people with Aquinas's first four arguments, but I knew that the truth was in the fifth: this kind of stuff just sort of happens, for reasons we don't understand.

"I don't know," I admitted.

Eugene was disappointed—he really needed an answer to that question. I said quietly, "If I was making it up, I could make up an answer for you. I could just lie to you. You know I've got the smooth words to make it sound good. But I'm telling you the truth. I don't know everything there is to know about God, nobody does. All we have is what we believe. Preacher Jake said it's better to believe in love, and hope, and faith; Eddie thinks it's better to believe in making people do what he wants them to do because they're afraid. I believe Jake. So there's your choice, Eugene. This is like coming to a place where the road goes to the left or to the right, a place where you got to choose, one way or the other. Do you want to live believing in love and hope, or in fear and hate?"

Eugene sat, pondering.

I sat with him, quiet for a few minutes, and then I asked him, "Which way are you going, Eugene?"

He replied, "I don't rightly know. I don't know if all this talk about God is true or not. It's all terrible confusin' to me." Then he took a deep breath and said, "But I ain't goin' with Eddie no more." He looked at me, and I nodded my support. "I don't like myself when I's with Eddie," he whispered. "I don't want to be his dog." We thought about that for a moment, and Eugene added, "I think I might see can

I get into a different camp, away from Eddie. I don't want to fight no more."

I stood and held out my hand to Eugene. He took it as gently as he had the first time, in the kitchen years before, and looked down at me. I spoke with as clear a voice as I could muster. "Good luck to you, Mr. Jefferson. May God bless you and keep you safe."

He said, "Amen." And he handed me the knife. "Preacher Jake done good by you, he done hisself proud."

Then he turned and ducked his head to lumber through the door, taking care to close the screen door gently behind him.

31

Let Me Go, For the Day Is Breaking

A few minutes passed before I stood up to find a bathroom so I could check my throat and wash off the little bit of blood. I was standing by the big oak tree when Cornelius walked up to me, the concern obvious on his face.

"Is he . . . ." Cornelius couldn't make himself say it.

"Yes sir. He passed last night in his sleep."

"Where was he?"

"We were at the Resting Place. I buried him beside his father and his son."

A tear ran down Cornelius's face, and he wiped it off his chin. "Thank God. And thank you, Buddy." I couldn't think of anything to say, so he continued. "He sure loved you, Buddy. You was like a son to him, you know that?"

"Yes sir, I know it."

We stood for a moment, respecting each other's silence, until I remembered why I was there. "Mr. Cornelius, I was wondering if you and Miss Mabel could come to his funeral."

"You said you already buried him."

"Yes sir, but he asked me to preach for him at his graveside. I told him I'd give him a proper funeral, and I was wondering if y'all could come. You and Miss Mabel were about the best friends he ever had."

He said they would certainly come, and we stood in the shade of the big oak for a while. We talked about Jake, and I asked about their honeymoon trip to Memphis and all the places they'd been. I wanted to ask if it had thundered, but I wasn't sure if he would appreciate it, so I let it alone. He told me that both of them could come the next day, since the Swayzes would be going to the Country Club for Sunday lunch, and that's what we agreed to do. He invited me to come and stay at their house, but I told him that I wanted to get back to the Resting Place. It didn't seem right for Jake to be alone. I told him I'd meet them at ten the next morning in front of Mr. Howell's Fish House on Ridge Road, and I explained how to get there.

When Jabbok and I got back to Beaumont, I stopped by Mom and Dad's house to tell them that Jake had died and to invite them to the funeral. By the time the pup and I got back to the Resting Place, I was bone tired.

The next morning, I made coffee for our guests and tidied the place up some. I washed my face with some of the clean water, and heated a little to shave. I didn't have any shaving cream or a mirror, but I didn't have much of a beard, either. It just seemed respectful to be as clean as I could be for the funeral.

I picked the readings from Scripture I thought appropriate, and read over them in my Bible, a Revised Standard Version. Just before I went up the hill to meet Miss Mabel and Mr. Cornelius, I went to get Jake's King James Bible, which I wanted to use for the service. When I opened it, a piece of paper fell out, a note from Jake, in his handwriting. Some of it was faint, and some almost illegible.

April 9, 1981
Thursday

Dear Buddy,

If you is reading this, that means I am dead.

I hope you is all right.
Do not be sad for me Buddy.
I am fine now.
I am writing you this little short letter while you is at your mama's so I can tell you how I wants my funeral.
It may be that is prideful on my part to tell you how to do it. Here it is just the same.
Please read from Genesis, Chapter 32, verses 22 to 30.
That will make me a fine sermon and you will know how your dog got her name.
By now I expect you know I really like the story of Jacob in the book of Genesis.
You is Israel now. I pass my struggle on to you.
You will know what to say in the sermon.
You can read that passage from your Bible.
I think it makes a little better sense out of yours.
It is my best hope that you go back to seminary and become a priest like you ought to be.
Remember that I will be listening to every sermon you ever preach, so don't tell your peoples a bunch of stuff that sounds easy but you know ain't true.
I have a little money saved up I was going to give to Joseph but he died too early.
It ain't no big huge amount but it might help at the seminary.
The money is on the little girl's grave.
I hope it helps.
I was planning to give it to my son and now I reckon I have.
Jacob in the Bible had twelve sons as you might have learned.
Joseph was the oldest son of his favorite wife, two of his other sons was Judah and Benjamin, Joseph's younger brother.
So even though we ain't related by blood, Judah Bennie Hinton, I reckon you is pretty much my son all the same.
God gave me back my life through you.
Now you is here to celebrate as I go to my Restin Place, to be with my daddy and Joseph and Jesus.
When you get here I will be waiting for you.
I love you, Buddy.
I always will.

Your friend,
Jacob Jefferson

I leaned against the sapling that had grown up in front of the fireplace and cried all the tears I thought I didn't have left in me to cry.

After a while, I read the passage he wanted read in the King James Version, and then again in my Revised Standard Version.

I was in front of the Fish House at a quarter 'til ten, and Mr. Howell came out to visit. Every time I came up the hill, he asked me how Jake was doing, and this time I was dreading the question, until he asked it and I had an answer I really liked.

"How's Jake?"

"Much better."

When the congregation came together, there were seven of us: Miss Mabel and Mr. Cornelius, my mother and father, Mr. Howell, Jabbok, and me. It was an odd collision of worlds to see us all gathered in the Fish House parking lot. My concern that it would be awkward for my father to be there was completely needless: I felt a respect from my father that I hadn't felt before. He knew I'd made my way through a difficult time, and he was proud of me. Mom and Miss Mabel got along immediately, and were talking about their families as if they were old friends while the men all stood around clumsily searching for something to say.

We made an odd procession down the hill, with Jabbok leading the way. Mom stepped carefully until her panty hose had runs in both legs, and then we made better progress.

I showed everybody around the Resting Place. Each of them wanted to look into the hut, and marveled that Jake had lived there by himself for such a long time. Cornelius started telling Miss Mabel that he understood why Jake had wanted to go back to prison, but I stopped him and brought them all over to the graveyard. I pointed to his father's headstone, and Joseph's, and told them that's why Jake had lived here, to be closer to his father and son.

I got my Prayer Book and Bible, and Jake's Bible, and we were ready to start the funeral service beside Jake's grave.

I began, "I am Resurrection and I am Life, says the Lord. Whoever has faith in me shall have life, even though he die. And everyone who has life, and has committed himself to me in faith, shall not die for ever."

I read Genesis 32:22-30 from the Revised Standard Version of the Bible, just like Jake wanted.

> The same night Jacob got up and took his two wives, his two maids, and his eleven children, and crossed the ford of the Jabbok. He took them and sent them across the stream, and likewise everything that he had. Jacob was left alone; and a man wrestled with him until daybreak. When the man saw that he did not prevail against Jacob, he struck him on the hip socket; and Jacob's hip was put out of joint as he wrestled with him. Then he said, "Let me go, for the day is breaking." But Jacob said, "I will not let you go, unless you bless me." So he said to him, "What is your name?" And he said, "Jacob." Then the man said, "You shall no longer be called Jacob, but Israel, for you have striven with God and with humans, and have prevailed." Then Jacob asked him, "Please tell me your name." But he said, "Why is it that you ask my name?" And there he blessed him. So Jacob called the place Peniel, saying, "For I have seen God face to face, and yet my life is preserved."

Then it was time for the sermon. You may be relieved that I haven't included the whole thing here. As I mentioned at the beginning, the sermon became this book, so in a way you've been reading it all along. The parts of the sermon that are not telling the story of me and Jake, I put here, taken from my sermon notes.

> Dearly beloved, we gather here at this Resting Place to give thanks for the life, love, and ministry of Jacob Jefferson, and to entrust him into the loving embrace of our Lord.
>
> He asked me to read the passage from the Book of Genesis that tells the story of Jacob wrestling at the ford of the Jabbok. It is, I think, an intentionally mysterious story. With whom did Jacob wrestle? The writer of this passage wrote that "Jacob was left alone, and a man wrestled with him until the breaking of the day." He was alone, and he wrestled with a man? Was this a struggle within

himself? Or was there a man, or perhaps an angel? Or could it have been, as some have suggested, a divine Man? I don't know. Ah, praise God, I don't know.

When the wrestling match was over, Jacob said, "I have seen God face to face, and yet my life is preserved." When the match was over, his name was changed, from Jacob, which means Supplanter or Cheater, to Israel, which means One Who Struggles, One Who Wrestles. Jacob became Israel at the ford of the Jabbok, finding God and himself in the struggle.

Now our friend Jake has died, here at the Resting Place by the side of his creek, and passed on his struggle of being honest and faithful.

All his life, Jake wrestled with God, with people, with himself. There were times when that struggle got the better of him, but he kept fighting, against God at times, against the seduction of alcohol, against people who betrayed and used him, and against his own doubts and disappointments.

I was eight when I first saw Jake. It was 1964, in the simmering humid heat of a Mississippi summer . . . .

Here I told the saints visible and invisible the story of my life with Jake. Obviously, I was a considerably more succinct with them than I've been with you, but I figured they knew at least the significant parts of it anyway. When I came to the end of the story, after I talked about Jake's death, there was a long pause, and then I finished.

Now Jake is gone from this life into a better, fuller one, and we miss him. The great work of his life has been to shine the Light of God in dark places, to look into the Mysteries before us without settling on convenient but false explanations, to live and preach our hope in the love of God our Father. That struggle, that hope, that work I pledge myself to carry on. I undertake that work with his love and wisdom as my foundation and support, and with his joy, humility, and sense of humor as my example.

So we gather at this Resting Place to give thanks for the life, love, and ministry of Jacob Jefferson, who wrestled with God and with people, and prevailed. He was saint and sinner, son and father, teacher and friend. Today he takes his rightful place in the long parade of God's faithful servants through the ages. I name him a hero of the faith, and I release him into the loving arms of our Father.

"The Light shines in the darkness, and the darkness has not overcome it."

I closed with the last words he'd said to me, which I hadn't written on my notes, but which I could never forget.

"I love you, Jake. I always will. I'll see you in the Morning, all right?"

I read the rest of the funeral service, and did all right until I came to the blessing at the end, which I cried most of the way through. I wasn't really authorized by the Church to give a blessing anyway, so I suppose it worked out about right.

We stood for a time at the Resting Place, soaking in the tranquility of the place and the rightness of the moment. The birds flew from tree to tree; the squirrels chattered and chased each other; the bream and catfish waited for Jake and me to come drown worms for their lunch. Somewhere in the distance, a happy dog barked, maybe greeting her master, home from Sunday services. Life was going on, with or without my approval or recognition of it.

Then it was time to go. It was time to see if I could salvage my career in the ministry, time to get back to living my life.

When I got to the top of the hill, I looked back down, thinking I'd be saying good-bye, but it didn't feel that way at all. Jake wasn't in that grave. It was just his body down there. I knew he would be coming with me, and that I would see him again.

32

And When from Death I'm Free

Mom invited us all to come to their house for a big lunch: fried chicken, black-eyed peas, rice and gravy, and a chocolate pie for dessert. Miss Mabel helped in the kitchen, even though Mom kept insisting that she was a guest and didn't need to lift a finger. The three men realized they'd all been in the military at some point and compared stories.

After Dad asked the blessing, I noticed that the whites of the devilled eggs had snatches of different colors. It looked familiar, but I couldn't place it. After everyone had left, as I was helping Mom clear the table, I asked her why we'd had such a big meal. She looked at me with a funny smile, as if she couldn't believe I was missing something so obvious. Then she poured me a cup of coffee, put a chocolate bunny in front of me, and said, "Happy Easter!" The devilled eggs were made from the eggs Mom had been preparing the day before for the parish Easter Egg hunt.

It seemed like I'd been away from everything for months and months, but it had only been a little more than two weeks. Later, I figured out that I'd left Becket on April Fools' Day, appropriately enough, and preached the funeral sermon, even more appropriately, on April 19, Easter Sunday. Jake had died on Good Friday.

As we washed the dishes, Dad told me he was concerned that I must have broken some law in burying Jake without notifying the authorities. I told him I didn't think Jake's birth had ever been registered with the state, so I thought his death wouldn't need to be, either. He looked dubious, but I assured him that all Jake's family was gone, and none of his acquaintances were in a position to call the police on the case, since all his friends other than me and Miss Mabel and Cornelius were serving time.

Mom told me the dean had called from England again. He said it was critical that I return his call. She told me the seminary had also called two or three times, as had the Bishop. She insisted that I needed to call them all back, and I promised her I would. But it was Easter Day, and they would have to wait.

Mr. Howell left after lunch, and while Mom and Miss Mabel were fussing in the kitchen, I lay down on the couch to take a little nap, and I didn't wake up until after my parents had gone to bed. Mom left me a note saying that Miss Mabel and Cornelius had gone back to Riggsville, and inviting me to make a roast beef sandwich. I sat at the kitchen table for a long time, thinking about the next step and trying to figure out how I could get back into seminary. At some point, I thought I'd ask Jake what he thought about something, and I realized all of a sudden that the days of asking Jake were gone. The struggle was mine alone now. As happy as I was for him, it was a sad and lonely moment for me. There would be many more moments like it; I miss him still.

The next morning, I called the dean of the seminary in England. It took some doing, but Dad and I figured out that when it's nine in the morning in Mississippi, it's either three or four in the afternoon in England. A secretary of some sort answered the phone and said that she could take a message. About an hour later, the dean called me back.

Talking on the phone was difficult because of the time delay. Finally, he told me to be quiet and let him do the talking. He told me he'd heard the entire story, from Dr. Sprague, from other members of the faculty, and from several of the students. He told me that Sprague did not have the authority to dismiss a student from the school, that even he, the real dean, would have to go through channels. He had put Sprague on a leave of absence, to get some counseling at a center in Arizona. He told me he'd talked to my bishop, that I would need to call him, and, assuming the bishop agreed, that I should get back to seminary as soon as I could.

He figured I'd only missed about a week of class, since we didn't typically do much classroom work during Holy Week. He said that for me to make amends, and to satisfy his own personal curiosity, I would need to write out the story of my relationship with Jake, and how I'd gotten into the situation with Jake and Dr. Sprague. When I asked him how many pages it had to be, and did I need footnotes or a bibliography, he laughed and told me to "just tell the damn story."

I called the Bishop at home, as he was taking the day after Easter off. He was understandably not so affable about the whole thing. He'd been worried sick, he said, but now that he knew I was all right, he was just angry. I told him that I was sorry to cause him such concern, and I shared the whole story. Well, almost the whole story; I told him everything I'd told my mom and dad, anyway. He said that this was not acceptable behavior for a priest in the Episcopal Church, and I assured him that I would be on the straight and narrow from now on. He warned me that I would have to do very, very well with the Board of Examining Chaplains.

It wasn't until I was packing up to go back to Becket and saw Jake's last note to me that I remembered the money. "The money is in a bag on the little girl's grave."

I went back to the graveyard and looked around until I saw the headstone for Annie Washington. I'd seen it that Halloween night long ago, and remembered being struck by the fact that she died when she was only six. Jake and I had talked about it when I was younger; I remember he seemed as disturbed by the death of a child as I'd been. Her grave was covered with a carpet of thick green moss, and I could tell where it had been broken apart and put back together near the marker. Sure enough, buried not two inches under the moss was a black plastic garbage bag. In it was a paper grocery bag containing a thick wad of bills. I replaced the moss and went to sit on the fallen sweet gum. I counted out the money: $17,840.

Eight hundred and ninety-two twenty-dollar bills.

All this time, Jake had had thousands of dollars hidden away from the world, hidden from himself.

I went and sat by Jake's grave, thinking I would talk to him. But I'd already said everything I wanted to say, so I just sat for a while and enjoyed the peace.

The next morning, I got up before the sun, and put all my stuff and Jabbok into the Comet, heading for Becket. It takes about ten hours without stopping, more if you have a puppy that might pee on the floorboards if you don't stop every half hour or so, so I had plenty of time to think. On the way, I decided that the notes from my funeral sermon would become the basis for my paper for the dean. A few miles later, it also occurred to me that a day might come for that paper to become a worthwhile book. Now, as I write this, I can only hope it has.

A month or so after coming back to Becket, at the Wednesday Eucharist some members of the junior class handed out a sheet of paper with the texts for several "new" hymns. The Episcopal Church was in the process of revising our hymnal, and we were trying out some hymns that hadn't been in the old one. I didn't realize until my eyes filled with tears that one of them was the same tune I'd heard Jake whistling so often. It was the mournful, triumphant tune that I'd associated with Jake for almost twenty years, and now we were trying it out for the first time. I sat in my pew and cried so hard that I couldn't see the words swimming on the paper. I put my head on the back of the pew in front of me and sobbed, and my friends left me to my grief.

It wasn't a new song, just new to the Episcopal Church. The tune is WONDROUS LOVE, from *The Southern Harmony*, 1835, and the text is an American folk hymn.

> What wondrous love is this, O my soul, O my soul!
> What wondrous love is this, O my soul!
> What wondrous love is this that caused the Lord of bliss
> To lay aside his crown for my soul, for my soul,
> To lay aside his crown for my soul.

To God and to the Lamb, I will sing, I will sing,
To God and to the Lamb, I will sing.
To God and to the Lamb who is the great I AM,
While millions join the theme, I will sing, I will sing
While millions join the theme I will sing.

And when from death I'm free, I'll sing on, I'll sing on,
And when from death I'm free, I'll sing on.
And when from death I'm free, I'll sing and joyful be,
And through eternity I'll sing on, I'll sing on,
And through eternity I'll sing on.

Postlude

It's been more than ten years now since Jake died. I'm an Episcopal priest, serving a little congregation in a small town in Mississippi.

Miss Mabel and Cornelius came to my ordination in the same church where I'd been baptized and confirmed, and they sat in the front pew with my parents. I offered to marry them again so it would be more legal, but Miss Mabel said they were as married as they were ever going to be. I didn't even try to explain it to Brother Swayze, who sat harrumphing next to my dear friend Trey, and Mrs. Swayze already understood. Miss Mabel and Cornelius were understandably lost through much of the service, but they sang with gusto when we came to "What Wondrous Love Is This," a new hymn they'd known all their lives. They looked like they'd found some familiar ground to stand on.

The picture of Jake with me outside the chapel at Becket, which Danny took before Jake's address to the seminary, hangs on my office wall. I have my arm around his shoulders, and we're both grinning from ear to ear. It's how he wants to be remembered; I'm sure of it. From time to time, someone will ask me who that man in the picture is. I tell the members of the parish I serve that the man with the wonderful, warm smile is my dear friend Jake, the Jake I mention in my sermons from time to time.

His bodark walking stick is propped in the corner of my office, waiting for the day when I need something to lean on. His old iron skillet is in my kitchen; some Saturday mornings when I have time, I fry some bologna to get the day off to a good start. Actually, it's the cleaning and oiling of the skillet that means something to me, more than the fried bologna.

Not a day goes by that I don't remember Jake's smile, or hear a faint echo of his mournful whistle, or recall something he said. I'm grateful for the things I see in myself that remind me of him: a sense of joy and humor, an appreciation of the love of God as the primary message of the gospel, a willingness to say that I don't know, or that I could be wrong. Most of all, I thank God that I had a friend like Jake, who passed on to me the struggle of being a faithful person.

Sometimes now, not often enough, I take the time to look up into the night sky. It takes no effort at all to close my eyes and see Jake on that Halloween night long ago, looking up at the moon sailing through the clouds after the rain had passed, and to hear him saying, as his father had said to him and I will say to my son one day, "The mysteries is ever before us."

Made in the USA
Charleston, SC
20 April 2015